W9-APL-923

"Don't be daft, girl,

I can't take three females off across the ocean to the wilderness..."

"Why not? Better the wilderness and freedom than forced marriages to men old enough to be our fathers."

"You're gently bred," he said. "You aren't used to the rigors of the American winters—"

"I'm young, and healthy, and strong," Christina countered.

"And you've never done a lick of work in your life."

"I'm intelligent enough to learn anything any other female has learned, and desperate enough to accept a few risks. Take us, Vilas—take us with you. Arrange passage for us, sign us on as indentured servants."

His response was more feeble. "Servants are indentured for years. Three to five years, anyway."

"So by the time I'm nineteen or twenty-one, I'll be free of the indenture. And in that length of time, perhaps..."

She hesitated, tears misting her eyes. She wanted to say, "Perhaps you will realize I am a desirable woman and love me as I love you," but she could not. Instead, she added, "Perhaps I will have found a suitable husband, a man of my own choice."

WILLO DAVIS ROBERTS
To Share a Dream

W🌐RLDWIDE

TORONTO • NEW YORK • LONDON • PARIS
AMSTERDAM • STOCKHOLM • HAMBURG
ATHENS • MILAN • TOKYO • SYDNEY

First published November 1986

ISBN 0-373-97028-5

Copyright © 1986 by Willo Davis Roberts. All rights reserved.
Philippine copyright 1986. Australian copyright 1986.
Except for use in any review, the reproduction or utilization of
this work in whole or in part in any form by any electronic,
mechanical or other means, now known or hereafter invented,
including xerography, photocopying and recording, or in any
information storage or retrieval system, is forbidden without
the permission of the publisher, Worldwide Library,
225 Duncan Mill Road, Don Mills, Ontario, Canada M3B 3K9.

All the characters in this book have no existence outside the
imagination of the author and have no relation whatsoever to
anyone bearing the same name or names. They are not even
distantly inspired by any individual known or unknown to the
author, and all incidents are pure invention.

The Worldwide design trademarks, consisting of a globe surrounded
by a square, and the word WORLDWIDE in which the letter "O" is
represented by a depiction of a globe, are trademarks of
Worldwide Library.

Printed in Canada

To Emilie Jacobson

Chapter 1

As CASTLES GO, Kenwood was a small one. Yet it seemed impressive enough to Christina's eyes, dominating the rugged beauty of the Cornish coast as it had for nearly four hundred years.

There were no other buildings in sight, the village being hidden beyond the low hills to the north; Kenwood Castle rose starkly against the skyline, its outer walls of great blocks of granite concealing all that was within except for the four towers. From one of those flew a scarlet pennant, announcing to any traveler who might approach that the earl of Kenwood was in residence.

Christina had strolled along the well-worn path at the top of the bluff, thinking her own thoughts as she was wont to do, and her expression as she turned back toward home was troubled.

She had just turned sixteen in this early summer of 1691; she was no longer a child, but a woman, she thought, for all the good it was doing her.

The wind swept in off the sea, blowing her hair around her face in a cloud of pale red-gold, so that she put up both hands to hold it back. Far below, in the cove with its narrow strand of beach, a dark figure moved, and Christina's mouth unconsciously tightened.

Roxanne. As Christina watched, unnoticed from the cove, her half sister headed for the precipitous trail that would bring her eventually to the path on which Christina stood. No, she decided, she had no wish to encounter Roxanne, who had now paused to examine something the surf had washed in. Perhaps if she hurried she could reach the castle before Roxanne gained the top of the bluff.

Christina walked with the lithe stride of one used to the fields and moors. The hours that she spent in the open, away from the castle, were the most precious to her of any part of her day.

She loved this place where she had lived all her sixteen years. She thought it must surely be the most beautiful spot in England. When she had once carelessly expressed this to her sister Megan in Roxanne's hearing—odd, how she always thought of Megan as her sister, when she, too, was a half sister—Roxanne had laughed in a condescending way.

"How would you know? You've never been anywhere else!"

This was true. Yet her father had spoken of distant places, London even, and described them for her. All fell short, in her imagination, of Cornwall. She knew that the earl left home only when necessity demanded that he travel, and that when he returned he always settled into his chair before the massive fireplace in the main hall with a sigh of relief.

"Ah! Christina, bring me a drink, by God, to celebrate being home! Roxanne, fetch my slippers, get rid of these boots! Megan, love, see if there's a bite to eat for an old man without waiting for supper, eh?"

He had been heard to say, cheerfully and without rancor, that the things he missed most when he must be away were his horses, his dogs, his children and his wife, in that order.

Jacobina, his third and present spouse, always seemed to take this in good humor, though Christina had detected a glint of something other than amusement in Jacobina's cool blue eyes.

Well, he was home now these past five days, and for the last three of them the earl of Kenwood had not risen from his bed. The servants were beginning to comment guardedly upon his condition, for it seemed no food or drink stayed on his stomach, and his sheets must be changed as if he were an infant.

"It will pass, no doubt," Jacobina had said, smoothing back a tendril of blond hair that escaped from her coronet of braids. "Let's try some ox marrow soup and see if he'll take that nourishment."

The soup had come up, as everything else had. When Christina had peeked into his chamber earlier in the day, her father was not vomiting but lay wan and spent, while Sadie bathed his forehead and closed eyelids. No words were exchanged between maid and mistress, but Christina had not missed the anxious expression on Sadie's face. Clearly the earl was not improving.

Jacobina had decreed that it would be best if she did not attend her husband. There was, after all, the possibility that whatever ailed the earl could bring down others. Sadie was a servant, and therefore expendable. Jacobina was the mother of the heir and would not risk carrying any malady to her son.

It was true that there was gray at the earl's temples and that he referred to himself as "an old man," but until now Christina had never thought of her father as aged. Seeing him this morning had made her sharply conscious of his mortality.

And her own, she reflected now, walking briskly along the path. Not that she felt her own end was imminent, but what would her future be if her father died?

She was under no illusions as to how her step mother felt about the three of them, Christina, Roxanne and Megan. She veiled her hostility behind heavy lashes and sweet words, at least when the earl was present, but her only genuine concern was for her son, Thomas. And, of course, for herself. Oh, yes, definitely for herself.

If it was my husband who lay suffering, Christina thought, I would be at his side to comfort him.

If it was Vilas.

As always when she thought of her cousin, her pulses quickened. She had, she supposed, been in love with Vilas since they both were children. He had never given any indication that he thought of her in a romantic way. When she was ten and he fourteen, she had announced that she would marry him one day, and Vilas had laughed and reached out to tousle her bright hair, not taking her seriously.

Everyone else had laughed, too, and Christina had not brought up the subject again. But the intent, the hope, was still there.

She wished that Vilas would come to visit, as he sometimes did, riding across the hills on that magnificent black stallion to appear at the supper table without warning. She wanted to talk to him about her father and what might happen when the time came that the earl died, though she earnestly prayed that that time was not yet.

So strong was her need to see her cousin that Christina swung sharply about, the wind whipping her skirts as well as her hair, to stare northward from whence he would come.

For a moment shock immobilized her and then disappointment replaced anticipation. It was not Vilas, tall and muscular and fair, with a gaudy scarlet cloak flying behind him, but a heavier figure, and dark. Though he was too far distant to make out his face as yet, she recognized the horse.

Lord Windom. Again, without conscious thought, Christina's mouth tightened. He came often, these days. He purported to be the earl's friend as well as neighbor, but his visits had not slackened while the earl was away. Indeed, it seemed to her that Lord Windom came overmuch these days, when he might better have been tending to business at home.

"Oh, drat!"

Christina *thought* the expression was *oh, drat*. It didn't pay to enquire too closely into Roxanne's expletives. They were no more than might be expected from a girl of her background of course, though after three years of living in civilized surroundings at Kenwood one might have expected some improvement in speech and manners.

Pausing to watch the approach of Lord Windom had been a mistake, for now Roxanne had intercepted her path. The possibility did flicker through Christina's mind that, perhaps for the first time, she and her half sister shared a common opinion, for Roxanne looked no more welcoming toward the visitor than she did herself.

Whatever else she thought about the younger girl, Christina was honest enough to admit that Roxanne was stunning. Her black hair was wild and windblown, yet this could not detract from the perfect oval face, the lively green eyes, the mouth as full and pouting as if her lips had just been stung by a bee. Now anger marred the lovely features.

"It's Windom again," Roxanne said, and even her voice had a husky, musical quality. For her beach-combing efforts she wore an old dress that had once been Christina's, but her bosom was more full than Christina's had been at fifteen, and the material was strained to the utmost.

Since the remark only stated the obvious, Christina made no reply and would have gone on if Roxanne hadn't unexpectedly pursued a conversation.

"Have you seen Himself today?"

This was the way she had always referred to the earl. Even after her mother died and she'd been brought to the castle from that hovel she and Leonie had shared, Roxanne had never addressed the earl as "father," the way the others did. It was always "Himself," unless she spoke to him directly, in which case it was, "my lord," although there was something in her tone that made it sound less respectful than when others used the same mode of address. The earl had only shrugged when Jacobina suggested once that the girl was in need of correction.

"She'll learn," he'd said, and that had been three years ago. Whatever Roxanne had learned, it had not been translated into better manners.

Christina cleared her throat. "Yes. I looked in on Father a few hours ago. He was asleep."

Roxanne fell into step with her on the path. "I, too. He looks fit to die."

Although she'd considered the same thing only minutes earlier, Christina protested. "He's been very ill. Anyone would look terrible after such an illness."

"You think he's getting better, then?" It was a challenge, flung at her as if daring Christina to make such a statement.

Innate honesty compelled Christina's reply. "No. No, I don't. I think he grows weaker with each passing day."

Roxanne gave a snort that appeared to be satisfaction, though whether over Christina's agreement with her own opinion or personal gratification over the situation was unclear. Christina had no idea how Roxanne really felt about the earl.

"Father's in no condition to receive a visitor," Christina said, almost to herself, as she watched Lord Windom galloping toward the main gate. The drawbridge was down—indeed, she had never seen it otherwise—and horse and rider clattered across it with a great racket, vanishing from sight.

Roxanne made the snorting noise again. "Unlikely that it's Himself Windom comes to see, anyway. More like it's Lady Jacobina."

Although her own mind had run in a similar vein, Christina felt mild shock at hearing the idea voiced this way. "Why would he?"

Roxanne had a robust laugh. "Why would he, indeed? She's a bitch, and another man's wife, but I suppose a man looks at things differently. She *is* beautiful. I wonder if he's taken her to bed yet, or if they're waiting for Himself to die first."

Christina drew in a harsh, painful breath. "That's a terrible thing to say!"

Roxanne only shrugged. "If you think that's not on his mind, you haven't paid attention to the way he looks at her. If Himself dies, why, what would be more advantageous than to add this estate to his own? A rich and beautiful wife, a sickly heir to additional lands, what more could a man want?"

The casual reference to her father's demise was more than Christina could take. She quickened her pace, leaving Roxanne moving more slowly behind her on the path. She crossed the drawbridge in time to see the servants taking Windom's horse and opening the wide double doors that permitted entry to the great hall.

She would not follow his footsteps and risk encountering the man she so intensely disliked and distrusted. Christina moved instead across the courtyard to a smaller door that opened onto a narrow passageway. She didn't want to meet anyone at the moment, not even Megan.

ROXANNE WAS NO MORE ENAMORED of Lord Windom than Christina, but she wasn't intimidated by him, either. She entered the great hall to see him mounting the broad stone stairway; the sunlight touched him through the stained-glass window halfway up, at the landing, making his white shirt take on for a moment the glow of rubies, emeralds and sapphires.

Just as she'd suspected, Roxanne reflected. He would be going up to Lady Jacobina's private sitting room, no doubt to ask politely—in front of the maid—about Himself. And then, when the maid had been sent for tea, or brandy, or whatever his lordship desired, would Jacobina and Windom embrace? Kiss, or fall upon the Lady Jacobina's pink brocaded bed for a more thorough romp?

No, probably not, Roxanne decided reluctantly. Not upon the bed, not yet. There was still a chance, however slight, that Himself would recover and that a loyal servant might carry tales to him if he did. Lady Jacobina would not be stupid enough to jeopardize her present exalted status, not when she'd only to wait for Himself to expire in order to do whatever she liked without hazard. From the look of him, it might not be long.

Roxanne waited until Windom had disappeared from view before climbing the stairs herself. She had no wish to encounter the hulking nobleman with the hot dark eyes, the too-full lips, the hairy arms and hands. He'd never touched her, scarcely noticed or spoken to her, yet Roxanne knew with an instinct born within her the kind of man he was. One to stay away from.

Her own quarters in the castle were in another wing from those of Himself and Lady Jacobina and the Heir. Ever since she'd learned to read and write—Himself had been adamant about that and made it clear that he would overcome her resistance through force, if necessary—she had thought of Thomas as the Heir, in capital letters.

Thomas, at the age of four, was the terror of Kenwood. Roxanne was probably the only individual who had ever boxed his ears or swatted him across the behind, as he so richly deserved. And since the time the little brat had run squalling to his mother about such an episode, and Lady Jacobina had actually smacked her face, Roxanne had reluctantly joined the others, family and servants, in refraining from touching him.

Her boots scuffed along the stone floor of the corridor, slowing as she heard voices coming through an open doorway. Megan's room. Of all the inhabitants of the castle, Megan was her favorite.

Roxanne paused. Megan was on the floor, setting up toy soldiers for the child crouched beside her. Roxanne studied them, this half sister and half brother, not making her presence known.

Megan seemed younger than the twelve years, which should have made her nearly a woman grown. She was slender and had a delicately pretty face. Her pale hair had none of Jacobina's brassy gold, yet held a beauty of its own, falling long and straight down her back or, as now, dropping forward to touch the floor as she positioned another soldier. Unexpectedly dark lashes concealed her gray-green eyes, the eyes that always looked kindly upon everyone. Including the Heir. Anybody would know by looking at her, even before she spoke, that Megan was of a gentle and sweet-tempered nature.

The Heir was on his knees, absorbed in the toys, his pale face for once gleeful rather than petulant. His lackluster light brown hair stood in spikes on his small head, as if he'd run his fingers through it recently. His twisted foot was not apparent at the moment. Suddenly he lifted a hand and swept through the line of soldiers, sending them flying in every direction.

"I've killed them all!" he cried.

Megan sat back on her heels and surveyed the chaos. "No Tommy, we were going to put them *all* up, remember? Come on, help set them up again."

"You do it," Thomas said. There was a note of authority in his young voice suggesting that he was accustomed to giving orders.

Megan's voice was patient as she began to reassemble the toy soldiers. "All right, I'll set them up one more time. But if you knock them over again, before they're all arranged, you'll have to do it by yourself next time. I mean it, so be prepared."

Obediently the little boy sat back, allowing Megan to do the work. Roxanne shook her head and moved on along the passageway. Trust Megan to accomplish what the rest of them could not. If it were up to *her*, she'd throttle the little beast, and his beautiful mother with him.

She let herself into her bed chamber. It contained a canopied bed, a dressing table with a precious mirror, two brocaded chairs and rugs to warm the cold floors. There was no fire in the fireplace today, since in early June it was considered to be unnecessary to have heat for anything but cooking.

It was a large and luxurious room, as fine as those of Christina and Megan, and she had slept there for three years, almost. Yet there was no sense of belonging, of coming home, when she closed this door behind her.

When she thought of home Roxanne had to stifle a wave of homesickness, even after all this time. She missed her mother, who though perhaps having none of the elegance of Lady Jacobina had been a warm, exciting, beautiful woman. Their cottage had consisted of a single room, smaller than this one, in which they had cooked and slept and entertained. If she closed her eyes she could almost convince herself that she stood there again, aware of the low, smoke-darkened beams overhead, the smell of the hearth fire and roasting rabbit, the strings of herbs and roots hanging from the walls, Leonie humming as she pummeled the bread that would be eaten thickly spread with honey.

She hadn't known how to read then, nor to write, and had not worn fancy clothes—even this castoff of Christina's was finer than what she'd been used to—and the table had been set with chipped crockery rather than fine china and silver, but she'd been happy there.

Roxanne walked to the embrasure from which a single window looked out over the sea that she loved. It was not at the ocean she looked, however.

The walls were so thick that on each side of the window there was room for a seat some four feet long. These were padded with velvet-covered cushions so that one could sit in comfort in this area that was like a small room. From under one of the cushions Roxanne removed a thin, leather-bound volume.

She would not admit it to anyone, certainly not to the earl of Kenwood, who had insisted she be taught to read, but she had become as hungry for the written page as for the fish and fowl and bread put daily upon her plate. One by one she had been hiding within her clothes books from the study downstairs to be carried away and read in private. Even those that she did not understand fascinated her, the way the words were printed upon the pages so that one man's wisdom might be passed along to another, perhaps a hundred years later.

Roxanne sprawled along the cushions, unaware of the picture her clear skin and dark hair made against the scarlet velvet, and opened the book.

Reading was the one thing in which she found joy in this place. Within moments she was totally absorbed, forgetting all else but the enchantment to be found in the book.

Chapter 2

CHRISTINA HAD, of long habit, lived in a world of daydreams. Many of them were of her cousin Vilas: romantic dreams in which the two of them roamed the fields and the shore together, as they had done in childhood. Only now they were not engrossed in whatever the sea had washed up or the baby rabbit Vilas had caught in his snare—and, at her plea, turned loose again—or in a race across the grassy bluff, which Vilas always won, though sometimes not by much.

Now the daydreams had taken on a different nature, not unlike the disturbing dreams that came at night, the ones that filled her body with mingled delight and shame, wherein Vilas did not only kiss her upon the forehead but also upon the mouth, and his hands roamed in stirring caresses such as she had never known in actuality.

She was thinking of Vilas now as she moved silently along the stone passageway. He had not visited Kenwood for nearly a month, and she longed for his company, his laughter. There had been no laughter since the earl had taken to his bed.

It had, for a time, appeared that Vilas would fall heir to Kenwood castle and the surrounding estate, for the earl's wives could not produce a living male child. Although the earl held no animosity toward the younger man, Vilas was, after all, no more than a rather distant cousin; his lordship had truly reached a point of desperation by the time Jacobina gave birth to Thomas. The fact that the child was imperfect and sickly came as a severe blow, but it seemed now that Thomas might survive to manhood, and even a son with a crippled foot was better than no son at all.

Had Vilas remained the heir, he would eventually have come here to make his home at Kenwood, and that was what Christina would have desired above all things. Now this would never be, not unless something happened to Thomas before he reached maturity.

The boy continued to be sickly, though Christina, who was never ill, privately thought that if his mother had allowed him to run out-of-doors in the sunshine and fresh air he would have been much sturdier and healthier. Her own appetite always increased when she'd been active outside, and Thomas was a picky child at table. It was no wonder he was frail and pallid. He was protected from every danger, however slight it might be, and did nothing to build up muscle or strength. Vilas, who had always run wildly free, courting danger wherever he could find it, was the most magnificent specimen of manhood in Christina's experience. His muscles rippled and swelled with exertion, and his strength was phenomenal. He would never have developed those muscles if he'd stayed at his mother's knee.

Christina had never cared for her stepmother—Jacobina made it clear from the start that she had little interest in the earl's daughters by two previous wives and a mistress—but she had genuinely looked forward to the birth of a younger brother.

Megan's imperfection might have cost her life in infancy, had it not been for Christina, but no such danger threatened Thomas. A twisted foot would not keep him from inheriting, and that was the main thing. And Jacobina was fiercely protective, although there was none who wished him ill.

At least, Christina thought now, coming out of another reverie about Vilas, nobody would if he were not such an obnoxious brat. For her own part, she simply avoided him. This was seldom difficult, since he spent much of his time with his mother or in his own quarters. Even a small castle allowed for many detours around anyone she did not want to encounter, and the less she saw of Thomas, the better. Unlike Roxanne, she had never struck the boy, but the temptation could be strong.

"You ask me, he's on his deathbed," the voice came clearly from the kitchen she was passing. "Though you wouldn't think it, the way her ladyship treats him. He needs more than ox marrow soup, yet she's not even sent for anyone to bleed him."

Christina stopped, one hand outstretched to touch the cold wall as if to keep her upright, heart suddenly beating with uncomfortable force. They could only be speaking of her father.

On his deathbed? Dear God, no! she protested wordlessly. Coming so close on the heels of Roxanne's opinion, from servants whose own best interests would be served by the earl's long life, the words were chillingly convincing evidence when added to her own observation.

"I've been here nigh on to thirty years," another voice—the cook's—interjected. "And I got no place else to go, 'cept to my sister's in the village, her in that little rat hole of a cottage scarce big enough to take in another. Yet I doubt I'll last long here when his lordship goes. *That* one I can't stand, and that's a fact. Does she come into my kitchen with her fancy airs, insulting a woman as has been cooking all her life, and her knowing nothing of the matter, 'tis likely I'll be out of a position."

Another voice chimed in as Christina stood, out of sight through the open doorway. Elspeth, who had been serving the earl of Kenwood and his family for nearly as long as the cook. "Aye, her ladyship will run us all off and bring in servants from Broadmoor, no doubt. I've already talked to my daughter about a pallet in her kitchen when the time comes. Once his lordship is gone, she'll show her tongue and her claws with a vengeance, I'll wager."

Christina drew a painful breath. Broadmoor was the adjoining estate, the ancestral home of Lord Windom, who was even now presumably above stairs with Jacobina.

Tears stung her eyes. The servants were always the first to know what was going on, and Jacobina treated them as if they were wooden posts, without eyes or ears. It was clear that whatever she and Windom did together had not passed unnoticed by the staff of Kenwood; certainly they spoke openly between them of these things.

If only she herself had someone to talk to! For a few moments Christina didn't hear the gossiping in the kitchen, swept as she was by a wave of longing for Vilas, for his comforting presence and reassuring good sense.

There was no one at Kenwood in whom she could confide her fears. She and Roxanne treated each other much the same way as Jacobina did the servants, exchanging words only when they were essential and then with no warmth. Under other circumstance she might have approached her father with her problems, but he was past helping anyone, it seemed, most of all himself.

There was always Megan, who seemed more her child than 'her sister, but Megan was only twelve. She was such a gentle, shy little thing, as easily frightened as the baby rabbits caught in the snares. When alarmed, Megan would stand poised as if for flight, pulses beating visibly at her temples; a hand would be pressed to that other pulsation at the base of her throat where the disfiguring mark was covered by the high-necked gown she invariably wore. Christina would not inflict upon the younger girl any of her own apprehension, at least not until there was no choice. She couldn't bear the thought of those soft gray-green eyes fixed upon her like those of a wounded dove, waiting to be put out of her misery.

If only Vilas would come!

Once more the words from the kitchen penetrated her mind with chilling impact.

"I tell you it's true," Sadie said, her young voice vehement. "She brings him the draught, and after it he's always worse. He'll have calmed down, sunk almost into a stupor, and she brings him the watered wine, and it begins all over again—the convulsions, the vomiting. Ask Daisy, she spent the past two nights with him after I'd gone to bed, and she'll tell you the same thing."

Christina had already taken a step, not wanting to hear any more, but the maid's tone was convincing, though her meaning was almost beyond belief. Christina remained frozen in position.

Almost, but not quite.

For the matter of seconds there was silence in the room beyond the open doorway, broken only by the crackle from the hearth and the heavy *thwack*, *thwack* as someone chopped vegetables on the block.

It was Elspeth who broke the silence. "You'd best watch your tongue, girl, if you don't want it cut out. If she's poisoning him, she'll not stop at dispatching you, as well."

"I'll not touch a morsel or a drop," Sadie said emphatically, "that's not shared by the entire household. There, is that ready to go? I'd best get back with it, for all the good it's going to do. He'll simply throw it up again."

Christina waited for no more. It wouldn't do to be caught listening here in the passageway. She slipped soundlessly past the doorway and was out of sight before the servant emerged with the earl's tray.

Was it true? Was Jacobina giving her father something to make sure he didn't recover from his illness?

What in God's name could she do about it? Jacobina was his wife, privileged to bring him food or drink, to order anyone else out of the earl's room; no one would question her, no matter what she did.

Her boots made scuffing sounds on the stone stairway as Christina raced upward. She would write a letter to Vilas, she decided, and send it by the earliest messenger. Perhaps Vilas could think of something to do before it was too late.

There were voices in Megan's room, both recognizable. Her sister and Thomas.

"Christina, come and share our tea!" Megan called out, and the older girl paused. "We've cakes today, as well as bread and butter."

Christina hesitated, propelled by the urgency of communicating with her cousin, yet hating to disappoint Megan. She could seldom deny her little sister anything, even something as routine as sharing tea.

Thomas was already at the tray, stuffing one of the small cakes into his mouth with both hands, until Megan remonstrated quietly. "One bite at a time, Thomas, remember? Here, let Christina have one before you've eaten them all."

Christina sank onto a low stool, reaching instead for the bread. For a moment nausea washed through her as she remembered Sadie's words about eating or drinking anything not shared by the entire household. And then common sense took over. There was no reason why Jacobina should wish to poison *them*, and certainly not her son.

"The last cake is mine," Thomas said brazenly, staring her straight in the eye.

"You've already had three," Megan protested, but Christina shook her head.

"One's enough for me. I'll have another slice of bread, though. I get hungry, being in the outside air. You do so much with Thomas, it's a wonder you don't get him out on the beach. It would do him a world of good."

Thomas spoke through a mouthful of cake. "I don't like to go to the beach. It smells of fish and seaweed, and it's cold and wet."

Before Christina could refute this dreary picture, Megan sighed. "Lady Jacobina fears he'll get a chill. I've orders not to take him beyond the courtyard. Here, would you like a sip of wine?"

Again the memory flashed vividly through her mind, of the draught that Jacobina administered to the earl; again Christina set the fear aside. As long as they ate and drank with Thomas, she could be assured of doing so in perfect safety.

God in heaven, she thought, was she accepting it as true? That her stepmother sought to hasten her husband's end with poison?

She *was* hungry; not even her thoughts were enough to depress her appetite. As she ate, Christina observed the younger members of the family, and she felt a surge of renewed affection for Megan. Megan, who would have been allowed to die had it not been for herself.

Ursula, the second wife of the earl of Kenwood, had been a lovely but fragile woman, unsuited to childbearing. Christina remembered her as an older version of the girl before her now, with soft fair hair and greenish-gray eyes, gentle and soft-spoken. She had allowed herself to be persuaded that the curse cast upon her husband by the gypsy Leonie was no more than an outpouring of vituperation by a woman scorned. Until two sons were born, eleven months apart, only to die within hours of their appearance into the world.

No one could blame Ursula for being apprehensive at the termination of her third pregnancy. Even Christina, only four years old at the time, understood that there was something amiss, that her ladyship wept and was not comforted by the earl's assurances that a gypsy's curse was superstitious nonsense and could not affect his progeny. There were too many others who thought otherwise.

Christina, drawn by Ursula's cries, had come to hover outside the door of the room where her stepmother struggled to bring forth another babe. No one paid any attention to her. The memories were somewhat dimmed, now, but she'd gone over them often enough to keep them reasonably accurate in her recollections.

It was Elspeth and Cook who attended the birthing, and to their credit they'd kept the secret to this day, as far as Christina knew. The way that servants gossiped, that in itself was close to a miracle, though perhaps the cook and the maid themselves were less to be credited than the threat his lordship had made to them after he'd seen the infant.

Ursula had taken one look at the product of her mating with his lordship and commenced to set up an unrestrained keening. Christina had a misty recollection of her father's face, twisted in some emotion she had not been able to identify, swearing both serving women to silence.

"If word of this gets beyond this room," he'd said in a tone to shred the meat off their bones, "I'll have you hanged. Literally, legally, on whatever pretext it takes. Do you understand what I say?"

The women had both nodded, speechless with fright. Elspeth held a mug for the mistress to sip, and at last Ursula had ceased her moaning and lay limp upon the pillows.

To this day Christina had never heard a whisper of scandal.

She had not understood the meaning of the hubbub and had crept closer through the shadows to peer into the cradle where the baby had been placed. Lady Ursula lay spent, sunk into torpid slumber; there was no one to deny Christina the right to look at this new sister.

She didn't remember the little brothers who had died; this was the first infant of her memory, except for those of servants, and she leaned against the cradle, peering down at the impossibly tiny face.

The baby had been loosely wrapped, and its red face screwed into an unhappy grimace as it emitted faint protesting sounds. Christina poked tentatively at the face and was amazed by the warm softness of the small cheek.

Behind her, unaware of her, her father continued to speak harshly. "If I ever hear the slightest rumor, I'll know where it came from," he said, and a moment later the door closed behind him.

The cook and the maid had conferred in low tones. "A bloody shame, it is," the cook murmured. "Poor little tyke. Bad enough she's a female, but a blemish like that—ah, better she dies like the other ones!"

The child beside the cradle had no idea what a blemish was. She did comprehend some of the words, the ones about the baby dying.

Why? Why should this tiny sister be better off dying?

Christina prodded further and the wrapping slid aside, revealing the spreading reddish-purple stain on neck and chest.

She stared at it, fascinated, then tugged at her own frock to see if there was anything comparable on her own breast. There was not.

Was that it? This colored mark, did that make it better for the baby to die?

She didn't know. Nobody told her anything. Yet in the following days she came back time after time—they were paying attention to her now and shooed her out if they saw her—to look at the infant in the cradle.

"She don't want to nurse it," somebody said once, sourly, as the baby cried and jerked its arms around when it was freed of its wrappings.

"Maybe it's best that way," someone else replied.

Once Christina tried to ask the earl about it, but her father was drinking heavily and only shook his head. "Don't bother me, child," he said, and sank back into despair and apathy.

There was in the castle at that time a scullery maid who had given birth to a child out of wedlock; she kept it on a pallet in the kitchen, and Christina had observed with interest when Midge opened her bodice and fed the child.

It was to Midge that Christina brought her little sister, who, since she was not expected to survive, had not yet been given a name. The baby was tiny, yet still a handful for a four-year-old. The wrappings trailed on the floor, and the infant whimpered as Christina handed her over.

"She's hungry. Feed her, too."

Midge cast a startled glance at cook and Elspeth, busy with their kitchen chores. "God in heaven, ain't her ladyship nursing the babe? And there's no wet nurse for her?"

Probably the other two women had exchanged guarded glances, though Christina hadn't noticed that. She had pressed forward, insistent, hearing Elspeth say, "Go ahead, feed the poor mite. Her ladyship hasn't much milk yet."

"After four days?" Midge asked, but she willingly bared a breast and held the infant to it. "Ah, she knows how to suck, at any rate! What a greedy little begger she is!"

There had been a consultation between the servants, and Elspeth was chosen to speak to his lordship. She had been nervous and diffident, putting it to him that if his wife could not feed the child, Midge would be willing to do so.

In truth the earl did not care one way or the other. In spite of his hopes, he still did not have a son, and even this second legitimate daughter was so blemished that he feared for all his family should the witch hunters learn of the dreadful mark. Damn the gypsy, anyway, he'd ought to have throttled her, as he'd more than once considered doing.

"Do as you like," he said carelessly, and from that time on Megan was not taken to her ladyship for nursing, but instead lay in a cradle near Midge's child, in the kitchen, guarded by Elspeth from close examination by anyone else.

Christina heard the muttering as they all agreed it was not right, and she spent a good deal of her own time around the kitchen, leaning over the beds where the babies slept, watching as they were changed and fed.

When Lady Ursula recovered her strength—as much as she was ever to do—she recovered as well some of her interest in her child, for she was at heart a decent woman. She gave her a name and the infant was christened; as she grew, Megan was a pretty, biddable little girl, and no trouble to have around, except that only Elspeth, among the servants, was allowed to see her in the bath or to dress her. Her disfiguring birthmark remained a secret.

She was more Christina's baby than anyone else's, however. Christina held her hand as Megan took her first tottering steps. Christina comforted her in the midst of night terrors. Christina read to her and protected her from any who would have been unkind. When Lady Ursula died in a final futile attempt at producing an heir, it was to Christina that Megan turned for the love that she both needed and was so willing to give to any who would accept it.

Megan looked up at her now, smiling, amused over something Thomas had said. Christina smiled back, not having heard what it was, wiping her fingers free of crumbs.

"I have a letter to write," she said, rising. "Thank you for tea. Behave yourself, Thomas; if you spill things deliberately that way, not even Megan will put up with you."

Thomas made a face at her, trailing a sleeve in the puddle of wine on the low table. He was disappointed when neither of the girls commented again on his actions, for Megan had risen to step into the passageway after Christina.

"Have you seen Father today? Do you know how he does?"

"Very poorly, I'm afraid," Christina said soberly, the memory of the conversation she'd overheard earlier stabbing at her with the sharpness of a roasting skewer.

Megan sighed and brushed back a strand of long pale hair. "Poor Father. I wonder if he would like to see Thomas?"

"I don't want to go see him," Thomas said loudly, behind them. "He's sick, and Mama says I must not go near him for fear I'll get sick, too. I don't want to be sick."

"It should be safe to stand in the doorway," Megan said in her gentle voice. "So that he will know we're there. What do you think, Christina?"

If he was being poisoned, as Sadie thought, his illness could hardly be contagious. Christina moistened her lips and replied evenly, "I think he'd like to know we're all anxious about him. Just don't disturb him if he's resting."

She went on toward her own room, while Thomas began to whine in protest. Trust Megan, though, to bring him around. The smile that began at that conviction faded, however, almost at once.

She must think what to say that would bring Vilas quickly; she prayed all the while that he'd be able to prevent whatever seemed about to happen with the earl. God knew she was helpless on her own.

She opened the door and let herself into the room where she'd slept all her life and wondered in despair what would happen to her, to them all, if her father died.

Chapter 3

MEGAN KNEW that she was virtually the only one, aside from his mother, who held young Thomas in genuine affection. Though chagrined that the boy had a deformed foot, the earl was pleased that he finally had an heir. He did not, however, enjoy his son's company, and had recently begun to make noises that were to Jacobina quite distressing.

"The boy's old enough to be riding a horse," his lordship had asserted. "Why, even my daughters had been set in the saddle by his age. We'll commence riding lessons as soon as the weather takes a turn for the better."

Jacobina fixed him with a smile and a steely eye. "Have you considered, milord, that if he takes a tumble your heir might break his neck?"

He stared at her, vexed. "Well, dammit, woman! Would you have a son so mollycoddled he can't straddle a horse? What sort of man will he be?"

His wife's answer was smooth. "He'll be alive, rather than dead like the rest of your sons." Before he could respond to that, other than to turn a mottled red and white, she added, "He's only four, after all. There's plenty of time to learn to ride when he's older and stronger. As long as the rain continues, any outdoor activity is out of the question, at any rate. You know how sensitive his lungs are to cold and damp."

Jacobina, having an excellent sense of timing, had then swept out of the room before her lord could marshall further argument.

Privately, Megan thought her father was right in that Thomas should learn to ride. The child was, however, terrified of the great beasts in the stables, and she understood that, too. He had looked at her with wide, frightened eyes. "They won't make me do it if Mama says no, will they?" he asked.

"Every man learns to ride," Megan reassured him. "And they won't let anything happen to you. At first, perhaps, Father will take you up before him on his own horse."

This had the opposite effect from what she'd intended, for the earl rode a magnificent stallion with a temperament not unlike his own. Thomas pictured himself being thrown off and trampled by those vicious hooves.

"I won't," he said in his childish treble, "I won't ride his horse."

"Perhaps a pony, then," Megan suggested. "We'll ask Father if you can have a pony, and get used to it when it's a baby. Then you won't be afraid of it, and eventually you can ride it."

The earl had promised to consider the matter, but nothing happened regarding a pony before he was taken ill. Megan had wondered if she should speak to the head groom about the matter herself.

It was time now to take the little boy back to his own quarters, where he would rest so that he might be in a good humor when the family sat together for supper. The earl did not believe in children being settled in a distant part of the castle with a maid or a governess for the evening meal; he believed in having them, well behaved and silent, at the table. How else could they learn what would be expected of them as adults?

They walked along the passageway where the winter chill still lingered in the stone walls. Thomas had put his small hand into hers, for he trusted Megan; it was warm and pliant there, and she felt a rush of affection for the boy. As she had been Christina's child, so Thomas was her own. The child that she would never have delivered from her own body.

Megan had been aware, for as long as she could remember, that the purple blotch that marred her otherwise white skin was a punishment for the sins of her father, but had no idea what those sins had been. Long before she was born, a gypsy named Leonie had spat a curse at the earl, condemning his offspring to death and deformity. Megan knew she would have died shortly after birth had it not been for Christina's intervention. She did not hate her poor mama for having had such a difficult time in coming to love her, for Mama had been perfect and Megan was not.

She told herself that she had adjusted to and accepted her lot in life. No man would ever look upon her with favor, not once he'd seen the blemish. Mama had said it, sadly, and Elspeth too, with pity. There would be no husband such as Christina and even Roxanne could expect to find, not for Megan. She would, if she were lucky, remain at Kenwood as a maiden aunt, perhaps, allowed to tend and love other people's children.

Thomas's hand was sticky, and she wondered if she'd ought to go back and clean it before they entered Lady Jacobina's chambers. Her ladyship had an aversion to stickiness. But they were already nearly there, and the distance was considerable, to retrace their steps. Megan decided to request a basin of water once they'd reached their destination.

The door was, as usual, closed. She knocked lightly and opened the door, drawing Thomas with her into the spacious room.

To her surprise, the chamber was empty. And then she heard voices in the adjoining room, a man's and a woman's.

"Would you have me sound Beaker out about it? No doubt I'll meet him at the Stag and Hen on the way home, and quaff an ale or two with him." The voice was that of Lord Windom, which brought Megan to a halt. She did not really care for the man; he had a way of looking at any female as if his gaze were capable of stripping off her garments, to reveal the blemishes. On the rare occasions when she met him face-to-face, her hands rose of their own volition to her throat, as if to screen what he might detect there.

"Why not?" Lady Jacobina said, in that high, light voice she affected when she was on her best behavior. "And see about Hunnicutt, too, while you're at it. He's had his eye on Christina for ages, but my lord and master won't hear of any such alliance. There, thank you, milord, I do believe you've repaired it."

A moment later the pair of them emerged from the bed chamber, Lady Jacobina affixing a pendant on a long chain around her neck.

"Mama, I had cakes for tea," Thomas said eagerly, and before Megan could pull him back, he'd wrapped his arms around her, leaving a smear on her apricot-colored gown.

Jacobina stared down at it, loosening the child's hold. "Megan, please see to it that his hands are washed. And that he has a change of shirt. What's that all over it, wine?"

"I spilled it," Thomas said, exuberance fading.

"So I see. Where are your manners, child? You haven't greeted Lord Windom."

Thomas stared sullenly at the big, darkly bearded man. "Good afternoon, milord," he said, sounding sulky.

Windom ignored him. "I'll be going, then milady. I'm sorry to hear that your husband continues to be indisposed. I'll be riding this way again on Thursday week; I'll look in with hopes of better news."

"Yes, by then surely the news will be better," Jacobina said smoothly. "I'll walk you to the door, milord."

They stood talking in lowered voices for a few moments while Megan cleaned up her small charge. Her mind wasn't on Thomas, however, but on the conversation that had not been intended for her ears.

Beaker and Hunnicutt. Megan knew who they were, men from the village, not of noble birth but of moderate means. Beaker was the owner of a fine ship that carried merchandise across the ocean to the New World, including goods belonging to the earl of Kenwood. He was a rotund, jolly sort of man, though there was something about his eyes that made Megan wary of him when they chanced to meet.

Hunnicutt was a comfortably situated merchant, at some forty years of age a lean, straight figure with a clever mind and restrained speech, at least in the presence of the gentry.

Meagan's thoughts swirled around, sorting out what she'd heard. Was Lady Jacobina considering Hunnicutt and Beaker as potential suitors for Christina and Roxanne?

Instinct told her that neither of her half sisters would welcome any such liaisons. Heaven knew who might attract Roxanne, but it would not be either of the men Jacobina had mentioned. And Christina, for all that she thought it a secret, was in love with Vilas.

Megan was half in love with Vilas herself. Of course he treated her as he might a little sister, and she had schooled herself to acceptance as fact that no man would ever love her as a woman. She didn't think Vilas would believe her marked as a witch even if he knew about the terrible blemish, but she would not willingly put the matter to a test.

It was only Christina she trusted implicitly, though she was beginning to put some tentative trust in Roxanne, as well. Roxanne didn't know about the birthmark, and her mother had been stoned to death as a witch, but Roxanne was kind to her. Megan absorbed kindness as a sponge soaked up seawater.

Though she did not fully grasp all the ramifications of the conversation she had overheard, it left her uneasy. The earl, in the careless way he had with dogs and children, more or less protected his daughters from his present wife. He would not, Megan hoped, allow Lady Jacobina to marry anyone off against their will.

Yet if her father was as ill as it appeared he was, then what? Lady Jacobina would have little or no consideration for the wishes of the stepdaughters who were, at best, only nuisances in her life.

She would, Megan decided, tell Christina what she'd overheard.

On the following day Lady Jacobina sent for a physician.

"I fear," she said, a frown marring her pretty brow, "that milord is more ill than we've believed. This morning he could not keep down even a swallow of broth, and he continues to be wracked by convulsions. 'Tis perhaps time he was bled and physicked."

"About time," Elspeth muttered under her breath as she passed behind Christina's chair, which was far enough from Lady Jacobina's at table so that there was no danger of the mistress hearing them.

Christina's throat closed so that she could eat no more of the food before her. Across the broad table, Roxanne, too, lost interest in the soup that had just been served and put down a crusty chunk of bread.

"Perhaps," Jacobina said, her own appetite seemingly unaffected, "his lordship would benefit from a visit from each of his children. In case the physician is unsuccessful in restoring milord to good health. I've decided to allow Thomas to stand in the doorway of his chamber; it won't do to draw too close to the bed."

Christina saw Roxanne's normally vivid color fade and felt that she, too, had grown pale. Certainly she felt cold and sick at the pit of her stomach. She dared not look at Megan, two places down at her left. Did Megan understand what was happening?

It was not until the plates—mostly untouched except for that of Lady Jacobina—had been carried off and chairs were scraped back on the stone floor as the company dispersed, that the three half sisters found themselves alone in a corner of the great hall.

Christina wished that the fire had been lit in the huge fireplace; she would have welcomed its warmth and comfort. Megan looked to her with frightened eyes and spoke softly so that her words should not carry to the servants still removing bowls and platters from the table.

"Father's dying," Megan said. "Isn't he?"

"If he's not," Roxanne said, and there was a harshness in her tone reminiscent of the earl, "he will be, by the time he's been bled and physicked. Ma used to say there was no faster way to dispatch a dying man than calling on the services of a physician."

Christina fought the emotion that clogged her throat. "I'm amazed she thinks we should visit him. She's discouraged it until now."

Roxanne had an answer for that, too. "No doubt she thinks it's too late for him to say anything to us, or we to him, that could threaten her own position. It's safe, now, because neither we nor he can do anything." Her lovely face flushed in anger, and Christina was forced to conclude that Roxanne *did* have concern for the man who had sired her. "What a bitch that woman is! I wish Ma was still alive; she'd know how to deal with her ladyship!" She turned on her heel and left, half running up the broad stairway.

Megan's greenish eyes swam with unshed tears. "I've tried to find a moment alone to speak with you, Christina. When I took Thomas back to his mama yesterday afternoon, Lord Windom was there in her chamber. I overhead them speaking of Mr. Beaker and Mr. Hunnicutt in a way that made me most uneasy."

Christina, drawn out of her concern for her father, felt the concern shift toward herself. "What way was that?"

Megan repeated what she had heard, and saw Christina's mouth go flat, though it trembled slightly.

"Do you think they meant the men as possible suitors for you and Roxanne?"

"I'd never have either of them," Christina said tightly, "nor would Roxanne, I suspect. Dear God, what are we going to do? Oh, if only Vilas would come!"

"We could send for him," Megan suggested, brightening.

"I've already done so, but that's no guarantee he'll come. I didn't know of these latest developments, and he may be from home. He spoke of going to London, and he may have done so and not yet returned. Megan, if you hear any more of this nature, tell me at once."

"Yes," Megan agreed. The two were interrupted by a howl from the stairs. "Oh, dear, Thomas has hurt himself! I must go."

Christina heard the boy's caterwauling and Megan's comforting words without either registering in her consciousness. She would write these additional details to her cousin and make her plea for help even stronger.

The apparent proposal to sound out Beaker and Hunnicutt, when combined with what she'd already been aware of, had appalling connotations.

Roxanne was a fighter. She'd never allow anyone to marry her off against her will; Christina guessed that the other girl was quite capable of plunging a knife blade into the breast of any man who might have forced himself upon her, legal marriage or no. There had even been times when Christina wondered if Roxanne did not carry a strong enough strain of the gypsy blood to have some mysterious powers of her own, though there was no overt evidence of that. It was simply that Roxanne *acted* as if she knew things that others did not.

While she—she would never have the courage to protect herself in such a way. No, more likely the blade would plunge into her own breast, though that, too, was unlikely.

She moved swiftly up the stairs, wording the letter in her mind so that it would carry sufficient persuasion to bring Vilas at once.

But already, she feared, it was too late for her father. She must now put her mind to saving herself and her sister.

Sisters, she amended, unaware that she had just crossed an invisible line by adding Roxanne to her own side in this struggle.

Chapter 4

ROXANNE STOOD IN THE DEEP EMBRASURE for a long time before Sadie, the maid, left his lordship's chamber. Her legs became cramped, and she was aware of the chill that seeped out of the stone on all sides of her.

There was no reason, of course, why she could not have gone openly to view the earl as he lay on his deathbed. Lady Jacobina had given permission, almost issued an order, to his children in that regard. Yet Roxanne could not bring herself to do so; she did not want to see her father in the presence of anyone else, knowing as she did that a maid would carry a report to the others below stairs. And whatever that reaction was—she was not sure, herself, what it would be—there was bound to be critical comment.

She knew the servants did not like her. In her fairer moments Roxanne could admit that part of that dislike was her own fault, for the way she'd acted, like a young savage, when the earl of Kenwood had brought her here, kicking and scratching and in an anguished state over her mother's death.

A greater part of the animosity the staff felt for her, however, arose from things over which she had no control. She might be the daughter of Himself, but not a legitimate one. And her mother had been a gypsy, whose curse on this household had, many believed, caused deaths and malformed infants.

A scalding wave of grief arose within her, and Roxanne could not have said whether it was for her mother, dead these three years, or for the father she had never wanted to claim, or for herself. Perhaps it was for all three of them, the one in the grave, the second well on his way there, and she— Where was she heading, once Himself was dead?

Down the passageway she heard the scuff of Sadie's slippers, and sank backward into the shadows until the girl had passed by with her tray.

It would take Sadie five minutes to reach the kitchen, another five to return, plus whatever time she needed for what she did there. Knowing Sadie, she'd gossip a bit and perhaps find a morsel to eat before returning to the sickroom. It was unlikely anyone else would come while she was gone, so Roxanne should be able to visit, unbeknownst to anyone else.

Her own feet were virtually silent. Roxanne moved to the doorway, hesitating there before she approached the bed.

A single candle burned, throwing the earl's face into sharp highlight and shadow. It was a stranger's face, chiseled in planes of suffering and starvation, much thinner than when she had last seen it.

She thought of herself as looking like her mother, the gypsy woman Leonie, and did not see that any of the strength and character of this man was duplicated in herself.

With a quick glance to assure that no one moved in the corridor, Roxanne entered the sickroom and drew near the comatose form on the bed.

Her heart was pounding with fear. No one had yet contracted whatever ailed him, though Sadie had been at his side daily from the time he'd taken to his bed. Still, there was always the chance that his illness *could* be communicated to someone else.

His breathing was shallow, so shallow that for a moment or two she thought he'd already expired. The one hand she could see lay flaccidly at his side, the strong fingers relaxed, the veins standing out on the back of it. Odd, she'd never noticed before that his hand looked old, like those of her grandmother who had died a year before Leonie's death at the hands of the villagers.

Roxanne stared into the rugged face, at the silver-streaked hair—surely it had not been so strongly streaked before?—at the prominent nose, the chin that remained firm even in his present state, at the lids that covered his once-rapacious eyes, convinced for a moment that they would open and he would stare at her and speak in that voice she'd always thought so harsh.

Nothing happened, however. Roxanne became aware of the sour odor in the room, the sickroom smells that turned her stomach.

She spun abruptly and plunged into the passageway, gasping, sucking in air to replace that in the room of death. She had no doubt at all that Himself was dying. No matter what the physician did when he arrived, there would be no saving this man.

She hurried away, not toward her own quarters in the other wing, but to a back stairway that led to the lower courtyard. She needed fresh air, and privacy, in equal measure.

She stumbled on the stairs and nearly fell, righted herself, and reached the door at the bottom. There was no one about in the courtyard, though voices could be heard in the stable, across the way.

Roxanne turned in the opposite direction, feeling the cool night air sweep across her heated face, clearing her head and her lungs.

The sobs that tore through her chest were for herself, she decided, for what would become of her now? She had not wanted to come here, indeed had fought to the best of her twelve-year-old ability to avoid it, and she had no love for the inhabitants of Kenwood, except perhaps for Megan. Lady Jacobina would soon rid herself of an embarrassing illegitimate stepdaughter, either throwing her out on her own, or marrying her off to some inferior villager.

Better she should take matters into her own hands, snatch the initiative away from the woman she knew to be her enemy.

But where was she to go? What was she to do?

A wave of bitterness swelled her breast. If Himself had left her alone, she'd have learned something useful, such as how to serve meat and ale in the Stag and Hen, or the Seaman's Inn down on the shore. As it was, she'd learned nothing of value while at Kenwood. Reading and writing, what were they worth in a society that did not share this ability? Knowing how to read was only one more thing that set her apart from those who might otherwise have been her equals.

Of course there had been suspicion in the village of the gypsy's daughter, though none had accused her. Whether or not that was due to the earl's admission that she was his issue was something she could only guess at.

Longing overwhelmed her, for the full bosom and firm arms of Leonie to comfort her, for the cluttered, smoky cottage where she'd grown up, for the nameless cat that had been killed along with her mother when the stoning took place.

She didn't know how long she cried. When the storm of tears was over, Roxanne blew her nose and considered her future. At fifteen she was a woman grown. She could marry—she was under no misapprehensions about her looks and knew that beauty would easily win her a husband, though her illusions did not extend to belief in living happily ever after—or she could find a way to support herself. Perhaps there was not so much to being a tavern maid, and that certainly could lead eventually to an attachment to some man that might prove mutually advantageous.

All she knew for certain was that she would not remain to allow Lady Jacobina to decide her future. She would keep that right for herself.

Roxanne turned and made her way back inside.

IT SEEMED TO CHRISTINA that the castle itself held its breath as they waited for the physician to emerge from the earl's bed chamber. Voices were hushed, tasks undone, footsteps muffled.

She had seldom felt more alone. Thomas had the sniffles and was confined to his room; Megan was with him, inventing games that could be played amidst the bedcovers, making up tales to entertain him.

There was no sign of Roxanne, and Christina would not have approached her or confided in her even if the younger girl had been present. It was not until the family gathered for supper that the household heard the physician's report.

Amesbury was a portly gentleman with wine stains on his front; the fringe of graying hair around his bald pate was frizzy and seemed to Christina a macabre sort of halo as he took his place at table, beside Lady Jacobina.

Only after he'd drained his wineglass, had it refilled and sipped again were his listeners given the benefit of his professional opinion.

He wiped his mouth on the back of one fleshy hand and sighed. "Ah, milady, your wine cellars do you credit! Yes, girl, just a bit more," he said to the serving girl who hovered at his elbow.

His smile reflected his gratitude for the wine, then sobered as he glanced the length of the table. "I fear not even an excellent wine will help his lordship, though you can of course attempt to get some into him."

Lady Jacobina nodded her smoothly coiffed blond head. She wore deep blue tonight, which set off her eyes, and not even her worst enemy could have denied her beauty.

"How did you find my lord, sir?"

"Gravely ill, milady. Gravely ill. I have bled him copiously, which may give him some relief. If it does not, on the morrow I'll try a physic. Oftentimes once the bowels are purged, and the body rid of its poisons, recovery can take place. Be assured, milady, that I'll stay in attendance as long as I'm needed." He was perhaps unaware of the look on his face as he took in the hearty fare being brought to the table in bowls and platters, the odors drifting toward him in a way that made his nose twitch. "I shall do my best for his lordship, I assure you."

Odd, Christina thought through the smothering fear, that he should choose the word *poison*. Would he be able to tell, if the wine that Jacobina administered daily contained anything designed to shorten her husband's life? But no, how could he?

She glanced across the board at Roxanne and found the girl's face inscrutable. Had it not been for the fact that Roxanne also seemed to have lost her appetite, Christina would have thought her indifferent to the earl's fate, for the girl had an ability to conceal her thoughts that Christina envied.

The meal was interminable, until, at the midpoint when it had become increasingly awkward to pretend to eat, there was a sudden gust of cool air and a familiar figure strode into their midst.

Reactions were varied.

Lady Jacobina, had anyone been observing her, would have been noted to be unable to prevent an involuntary tightening of her beautifully shaped mouth and a spark of anger in her eyes.

Christina's heart leaped with joy; she had pushed back her chair and risen automatically at the sight of her beloved Vilas. He could not yet have received her second missive, unless he'd met the courier on the road, so he didn't know the extent of the difficulties; would he give her away, letting everyone know she'd begged him to come, and why?

Vilas lifted a hand in greeting. "I've ridden all day, and I'm famished. Can you serve another, milady?"

His thick fair hair was windblown, his cheeks ruddy beneath the tan. Correctly, he had addressed his hostess first, but he scarcely waited for Jacobina's murmured assent before he took a seat next to Roxanne and accepted the glass of wine that was immediately proffered.

"I see the physician is here. Is his lordship worse, then?"

Amesbury nodded heavily, not speaking until he'd torn the flesh from a goose leg and washed it down with wine. "De Clement, is it not?"

"Aye. Vilas de Clement. Your memory serves you well, sir. How goes it with my cousin?"

Amesbury shook his head. "Not well, though I've taken appropriate steps and put the leeches to him. Time will tell."

Vilas paid no obvious attention to Christina, other than to smile at her across the table. She exhaled a soft sigh of relief that he did not expose her.

Vilas ate as heartily as the physician, though being more restrained in his consumption of the wine. When the meal was concluded, he put his request to Lady Jacobina.

"Is there any objection to my looking in on his lordship?" he asked.

Nothing but ordinary courtesy showed now on the lovely face. "None whatever, Vilas. By all means. Elspeth, see that our cousin has a candle to light his way."

Christina's heart raced. She did not want it to be obvious that she consulted with Vilas, but she must speak with him as quickly as possible. When he went up the stairs carrying the candelabrum, she held back until he'd disappeared and the rest of the company had scattered. Then she moved as swiftly as she could without attracting attention, heading toward her father's chamber.

The door stood open and Vilas held the candles aloft, staring impassively at the man on the bed, turning at the sound of her footsteps.

"From the look of him, the leeches are too late to help. He scarcely breathes."

Sudden tears made her eyes sting. "Yes. Vilas, did you get my second note?"

"Second? No, I received one. I thought perhaps my level-headed cousin had unaccountably become hysterical, like an ordinary female, but I see that's not the case." His mouth, wide and expressive, softened perceptibly. "I wish I knew something to do about it, Chris, but what is there? I'm sorry. Truly sorry."

"Vilas, there's more than I told you at first. I heard the servants talking. Sadie's been spending most of her time here with Father, and she says that Lady Jacobina gives him a draught of wine and water every day, and that each time he's drunk a little he becomes worse. Sadie thinks she's poisoning him."

She was breathless and her fears had deepened. The accusation came out so baldly, so impossible; what if he didn't believe her?

Something shifted in his face, or was it only that he moved the candelabrum so that the light struck him from a different angle?

"Poison?" he echoed quietly.

"And Megan heard her talking to Lord Windom—he's here ever so frequently these days, both when Father was away and since he's been ill—regarding Beaker and Hunnicutt, in the village."

That didn't alter his expression, so Christina floundered on, feeling incoherent and desperate in her need to reach him. "She said Hunnicutt's had his eye on me, but Father would never consider such a union. Only Lord Windom was going to sound him out—it could only have been about arranging a marriage, Vilas! I'd rather die than marry someone like that, someone I didn't love!"

Loveless arranged marriages were the rule rather than the exception among the gentry, but Vilas didn't remind her of that.

"And Beaker? Isn't he the shipowner?"

"Yes. Beaker, perhaps, is intended for Roxanne."

Unexpectedly, humor touched his face. "Poor fellow, if she's not similarly inclined. She'll cut out his gizzard and feed it to the pigs." The amusement faded. "Chris, are you sure there isn't a lot of imagination at work here? I know that Lady Jacobina was never overly enamored of his lordship, but it's hard to believe her capable of his murder.''

Christina swallowed. She hadn't said that word, not even to herself. "All I know is what I've overheard. And I'm so afraid!''

To her greater distress, the tears spilled over; she put up both hands as if to hold them back, as useful a move as employing a sieve to catch tea.

Immediately Vilas set down the candelabrum and reached for her, wrapping strong arms about her, heedless of the way she was wetting his shirtfront.

"Christina, don't! I know you love your father—I loved mine, as well—but every man dies eventually, and the rest of us go on until our own time. He's had a reasonably long life, and a good one; he can have no regrets, other than leaving his children behind, and all you have to worry about is servants' gossip and something overheard by a child who may well have misinterpreted the whole matter.''

His words did nothing to assuage her grief and apprehension, but her body responded to the arms about her. How often she'd dreamed of being held this way, to be nestled against the lean, powerful length of him. She clung to him and allowed herself to let him stroke her hair, pat her shoulder.

"You'll stay, won't you?" she asked at last, lifting a tear-streaked face to his. "Until we know—what's going to happen? To help us, if Lady Jacobina does intend to arrange some horrid marriages for us?''

"Yes, of course. I have a month yet, and a good deal can be decided in a month.''

Something inside her, some warning, set off an alarm. "A month? Before what?''

He picked up the lighted candles again and with the other arm encircled her shoulders, steering her through the doorway. "Before I sail. Be of good heart, Chris, I may not be the heir apparent any more, but I've some influence, I think. We'll work together on this.''

She refused to take another step until she understood what he was saying. "Sail. Where are you going to sail to?''

"The New World. I've been thinking of it for months and have signed on with a vessel leaving in just over four weeks.''

His grin flashed, the grin that usually reduced her to jelly but now held no charm for her whatever. "After all, what is there in England for me? I've no inheritance to speak of, and there are fortunes to be won in the New World, adventures to be had. Come on, dry your tears, put a good face on the matter, and give me time to see what I can find out. His lordship isn't quite gone yet, and his constitution has always been a strong one. He may still fool everyone, and recover."

In a state of shock, Christina allowed herself to be propelled along the passageway, supported by his arm.

The arm he was going to take away to the New World.

Swamped in despair, she scarcely heard his voice, could not remember afterward what he'd said.

It was not until she'd retired for the night, feeling weepy and exhausted, that the idea finally came to her, the idea that could save not only herself but Megan and, perhaps, Roxanne, if she cared to be included.

She would persuade Vilas to take the three of them with him, to the New World.

Chapter 5

THE DREAMS CAME, the strange, erotic dreams that stirred both shame and delight. Christina woke with a not unwelcome heat flooding her body, regretful that the memories of that sleeping experience were so vague, that she could not quite remember what it was that she and Vilas did together in her nighttime imaginings. Kisses, yes, there had been kisses, warm and gentle, and her cousin's hands upon her—but exactly where and how he had caressed her was not entirely clear. She strained to remember, and could not; the memory was fading quickly, leaving only tantalizing sensations.

She lay for a moment in the comfort of her bed. Vilas. Vilas was not only in her dreams, he was here, at Kenwood Castle. She would see him today, and perhaps they would walk along the cliffs above the ocean and talk together.

Today, she thought, he might realize that she was a woman now, no longer a childish cousin.

She was smiling as she threw back the covers and dressed quickly in the chill morning air. Not one of her everyday dresses, yet not one of her best, either—it would not do to arouse Lady Jacobina's curiosity about the reason for finery—ah, this would do! She selected a gown in a rich, soft green wool and that set off her eyes and her red-gold hair, a dress that had long ago belonged to her mother. In those days it had probably been worn to social gatherings—a musical evening, perhaps, for the Lady Elinor had delighted in music, Christina had been told—but the gown was now worn enough to be acceptable for less exalted occasions.

She felt a moment of nostalgic longing, that she might have known the woman in the portrait—once hung in the great hall, now relegated by Lady Jacobina to the library, which held no interest for the present mistress of the castle—the Lady Elinor who had been her mother.

There were women among the villagers who lived to see their children grow up. The gentry, it seemed, were less hardy. So many of them died in childbirth. A pity that Lady Jacobina had proved the exception.

Struggling with the fastenings on the dress, Christina felt a moment of guilt at the thought, then quickly banished it. It was true. Either of the earl's previous wives would have been preferable to the present one; she could not believe that Elinor or Ursula would have resorted to poison to rid themselves of an irascible husband. Probably not even the gypsy, Leonie, would have turned poisoner, although Christina was not absolutely certain on that score.

Leonie might have needed only another of her curses to do the job, if she desired it done, which could have been accomplished from the comparative haven of her own cottage. Only, of course, in the end the hut had provided no such safety. Perhaps there was no safety, anywhere, for anyone. Certainly not for herself, not if what she suspected was true.

Her room was cold; the sunlight did not yet penetrate the narrow windows. Christina took up a thick wool shawl to wrap around her shoulders, then paused to adjust it so that while it gave her warmth it did not disguise her bosom. Not while Vilas was at Kenwood. A bosom was one sign of maturity, and while her own had not the overblown contours of Roxanne's, Christina was justifiably proud of her figure.

She moved quickly along the stone corridor. It was early; the Lady Jacobina would not rise for hours yet, and probably neither of her half sisters was awake, either. Christina was usually astir long before anyone else. Except, perhaps, for Vilas. He, too, often rose with the sun.

Her heartbeat quickened, just thinking of him. Her cheeks felt hot, as she recalled those half-lost dreams. Did he ever dream such things, too? Had he ever dreamed of *her*?

Before she sought out Vilas, however, she must look in upon her father. She must be assured that he had survived the night.

Her footsteps slowed as she approached the door of the earl's chamber. Sadie dozed in the chair beside the bed, rousing guiltily when Christina paused in the doorway.

"I was just restin' me eyes," the servant said, starting forward. "He's had a quiet night, he has."

Too quiet, Christina thought, nearing the bed. The earl might have been carved of wax, so still he was. His breathing scarcely lifted the covers over him.

She stared down into the familiar face. Her father had been good to her, in his own fashion. Given a long life, he would have seen to her comfortable future, would have arranged a marriage with some suitable member of the gentry.

Not with Vilas, though, she thought sadly. No, though he got on well enough with the young cousin who had once been the heir presumptive, the earl had dismissed Vilas de Clement as a young fool, given too much to gaming and whoring to be worthy of filling the earl's own shoes.

Yet the earl himself had taken pleasure in relating his own exploits of youth. His lusty appetites for wine, women and sport were legendary.

Christina stared down at him now, unable to control the tremor that ran through her. There was no doubt that he was dying, and with him died her own future, unless she could persuade her cousin to her scheme for escaping.

Did Sadie guess some of her thoughts? The servant girl hugged her arms across her chest. "He's had a good life," she said.

"And now it's nearly over," Christina said softly. "You've seen people die before, Sadie. He is dying, isn't he?"

"Seems as like," Sadie agreed. "Though he rested quietly enough through the night and so far into this day."

"Has Lady Jacobina been in to see him?"

"This morning?" Sadie's plain face reflected shock. "'Twill be hours afore she's up and about."

"She hasn't administered anything to him, to eat or drink?"

"Not since the physician came. That one has bled him twice already. It made his lordship more quiet, so maybe that's a good sign."

For a moment the two girls locked gazes. They were nearly of an age, one gently born, the other set to running errands in the Kenwood kitchens at the age of four; their lives had crossed and recrossed, but there was a vast difference between them which both recognized and accepted.

"Do you really think the leeches ever help anyone to recover?" Christina asked.

Sadie swallowed, hesitating. "Not as I ever saw, milady. But there's those as says it helps, in some cases."

It would not help in this one. Neither of them spoke the words, yet each knew the truth was clear to the other. Christina stretched out a hand to touch the one outside the coverlet, the one thickly corded and veined, the hand that had held reins and weapons and dogs and children—yes, and women, too. The hand was cool, yet a pulse still beat visibly in the wrist.

"Father?" She bent over the bed, beseeching him. "Father, can you hear me?"

There was no response. No help here for anyone, not even for himself.

"You must be hungry, if you've been here all night," Christina said. "Go down and get something to eat, and sit before the fire, Sadie. I'll stay a bit."

"Oh, thank you, milady. I won't be long," the servant girl promised eagerly.

When she had gone Christina continued to touch her father's wrist. He was not dead yet, perhaps there was still some flicker of life there that could be encouraged. Perhaps if he knew what was happening—

Her voice was very soft, close to his ear as she dragged the chair closer to the bed and sank onto the edge of it. "Father, you can't give up. We need you, Megan and...and Roxanne...and I. Even Thomas needs you. There is much amiss at Kenwood; the castle cries out for your strong hand—"

There was no sign he heard, and there was no strength in the hand. Christina leaned her head against the earl's shoulder and allowed the tears to come.

When the spasm of weeping had passed, her resolution was stronger than it had been before. She must persuade Vilas to take them with him to the New World. When Sadie returned she would go at once in search of him.

VILAS DE CLEMENT, however, had already left the castle to ride into the village. He wore the scarlet cloak, not for the warmth of it but because he liked the way the wind blew it out behind him, liked knowing the picture he made astride the great roan stallion.

He was halfway there when he spied the slim figure ahead of him, dark hair billowing about her shoulders, striding freely along. She paused and turned at the sound of his horse, then went on, not looking up at him until he reined in beside her.

"Well, if it isn't the fair Roxanne, running away from the look of it. If you were going to take only a dress or two, why not something better than the rag you're wearing, or is there a velvet one in the bundle?"

Her green eyes were cool. "A rag suits a gypsy's get, don't you think?"

"Oh, so now you're your mother's child, not the earl's. Well, close as he is to dying, I suppose one's as good to descend from as the other, though I wouldn't put too much emphasis on being half gypsy if I were you. Where you heading?"

Roxanne gave him a sardonic smile. "To London, to visit the queen, of course. With all my jewels and finery I should impress her enough to take me on as a lady-in-waiting, don't you think?"

He had the thought that she was pretty enough to take the queen's fancy—or the king's, for that matter. And bright, too. He'd thought her a hellcat when the earl had brought her home, screaming and scratching and spouting every profanity her twelve-year-old tongue could bring forth. Even then there had been the promise of beauty beneath the dirt. Now the faded brown dress could not hide the perfection of the body it covered, and the face—the face was devil or angel, he couldn't say which.

"Well, I'm not going all the way to London," he said, "but I'll give you a lift as far as the village." He reached down a hand, which Roxanne ignored. "If you're holding out for a coach and four, girl, it'll be a long wait. Unless Lord Windom comes riding out with his new coach. I understand it's being repainted, and he'll want to show it off."

"Lord Windom!" There was contempt in the tone as well as the way the girl spat into the grass. "I wouldn't be fool enough to accept a favor of *that* one!"

He still leaned forward with hand extended toward her. "You're as intelligent as you are beautiful, then. Intelligent enough to save yourself another three miles of walking, I should think. Come on up before me, and you'll reach the village in no time.''

Roxanne considered, then took his hand and allowed herself to be hauled up in front him. One arm encircled her waist to steady her, and she felt a trickle of excitement run through her. Christina was besotted with him, she knew that for all that the other girl thought it was a secret, and Megan gave him calflike glances as well, but Vilas de Clement was no wealthy lord. Not unless the Heir failed to survive childhood and Lady Jacobina was unable to produce another son.

Still, Vilas was a man, money or no. A young and virile man. And Roxanne, too, had her nocturnal dreams, though as yet the man in them remained faceless. Vilas was handsome, he was amusing, and he was cleaner than most—three years earlier the latter would never have occured to her. Besides that, she'd love to see Christina's face if they came riding into the courtyard together.

That wouldn't happen, of course. She wasn't going back to Kenwood. Still, why wear out her shoe leather unnecessarily? Why not ride?

Vilas kicked the horse's flanks, and they sped across the moors. He was showing off, and she knew it, but it was fun, anyway.

He slowed his mount at the top of the hill overlooking the village. It huddled along the shore on a small cove, a cluster of houses and shops, the buildings scoured clean by the wind off the sea.

She had been there often enough as a young child, before the villagers had turned on her mother; not so often since she'd gone to live at Kenwood. Nothing had changed that she could see.

"You want to ride in with me or would you prefer to arrive on your own?"

"I'd best arrive on my own," Roxanne decided, and again felt that anticipatory warmth surge through her as his powerful arm lowered her to the ground.

Vilas didn't ride on, however. "What is it you're thinking, girl? To find employment, now that the earl is nearing the end? You don't care to remain at Kenwood?"

She regarded him with derision. "For what? To fall into Lady Jacobina's pit? She's only beginning to dig it, but it will be there. She hates me almost as much as I hate her; she'll see me buried, one way or another, as soon as she's put Himself under the ground. I'm better off returning to my own."

"To your own," Vilas echoed softly. "But are they your own? You've been gone for a time, and they may remember your origins with less than enthusiasm, Roxanne. Well, I wish you luck. And if you don't find it, I'll be heading back again midmorning."

He lifted a hand in farewell and was off, riding breakneck down the slope, a dashing figure with that scarlet cloak billowing behind him.

Roxanne followed more slowly, disturbed by his words. It was true the very villagers she was about to approach had stoned her mother to death in a frenzy of fear against the suspicion of witchcraft. Yet she was not her mother; she was the earl's illegitimate daughter—though there was little shame in that, in a village half populated by bastards, she thought—and she knew she was attractive, healthy and sturdy.

That the attractiveness would weigh against her was something she did not consider.

Early as it was, the village was astir. The fishermen had gone out, but a few men worked on their boats on the strand; others mended nets, and still more tended the drying haddock.

As Roxanne started along the main street, her heart began to pound. Was Vilas right? Would she meet with hostility because of who she was?

The Stag and Hen was open and doing a moderate business. All heads turned her way as Roxanne stepped over the threshold, and for a moment conversation ceased. Then the hum of subdued voices resumed.

Color high, she threaded her way between the tables to the proprietor. Rupert Hailey was a man addicted to his own food and drink, from the look of him. He was fatter than she remembered, from the few occasions when he had visited Leonie in the cottage at the edge of the wood.

She saw that he recognized her. A grin spread across his round face. "Yes, miss, what can I be doing for ye?"

Not *milady*, she noted. Well, that was all the better, wasn't it? Who was going to give employment to a member of the gentry? She had lived at the castle for three years, but that didn't make *her* gentry, and she'd always known it wouldn't.

"I'm looking for work," she said, keeping her voice low, unwilling to have the men around her hear the words.

"Work, is it?" The grin broadened. "And what can ye do, now?"

"Serve meals and ale," she said boldly. "Sweep up, wash mugs, whatever there is to do in a place like this."

"And ye've experience at that?" The new voice was sharp, as sharp as the face that appeared from the lean-to at the back of the place. The woman had a nose that a man could shave with, Roxanne thought.

Without waiting for a reply, the woman reached out and snatched Roxanne's wrist, turning her palm upward. "With this ye're going to carry slops and scour pots?" Her own hand was rough and strong, so strong that Roxanne could not pull free. "Ye've not worked in a kitchen before, and there's plenty who have, should we be in need of help. We ain't. Be off with ye, and don't be taking the bread out of the mouth of someone what needs the wages!"

"I need the wages," Roxanne said. Her tone was low but firm. "My hands were tough enough once; they will be again."

"Not in our establishment, they won't." The woman cast an angry glance at her husband, who was shrugging in disappointment. "Get ye out of here, girl, before I set the dogs on ye!"

For a moment Roxanne wanted to put her hands around the scrawny neck and throttle the woman. Holding her head high, cheeks flaming, she said in a voice clearly audible throughout the room, "Thank you so much for your consideration, ma'am."

The woman snorted and turned on her husband. "Ye got nothing to do but stare, ye great dolt? I asked for the new barrel of ale an age ago, and I ain't got it yet!"

Roxanne was shaking as she emerged in the sunlit street. They knew who she was, every bloody one of them knew who she was, and she hadn't missed the ripple of laughter that followed her exit. Damn them all to hell, she thought in fury. Why didn't she have as much right as the next one to earn her bread and board?

There were two more similar establishments, the Red Cock and the Seaman's Inn. It was a good thing, she thought bitterly half an hour later, that she hadn't expected much; she certainly hadn't been disappointed, then.

The old hag who ran the Red Cock had a crossed eye and thick lips; she had fixed her good eye on Roxanne's face and spat on the floor, missing Roxanne's toes by an inch. "The only way ye'll find a position in this place, me dear," she said in what appeared to be an attempt at humor, "is on yer back with yer heels in the air! Won't nobody look at that face and them hands and think yer good for aught else!"

The man who ran the Seaman's Inn put it more subtly, but just as unmistakably. Grosver's wife was a well-known slut who tolerated the innkeeper's lecherous behavior and was unlikely to overrule his decision, but his leering suggestion left Roxanne humiliated and furious.

"It'll be a cold day in hell that I give over to the likes of an invitation like that one," she told him. And then, so angry that she was unable to stop further words, she added, "I shouldn't wonder but what the devil himself will consign this place to the flames, just so you'll feel at home!"

The sly smile vanished. "Get out of here, you strumpet! No better than yer mother, I'll wager, and look out ye don't meet the same bad end!"

Eyes stinging, Roxanne came out for the final time into the sunlight. There was nowhere else to try, not in her home village. She could go up the coast, try another town, she supposed. But already she was hungry, she knew that by night she would be cold, as well, and she hadn't a farthing to her name.

The earl had done her no favor by taking her to Kenwood, she thought in overwhelming resentment. Now she was neither fish nor fowl; she belonged nowhere. She was qualified for nothing.

Well, she wasn't ready to crawl into bed with a slug like Grosver. She might use a man for her own purposes someday, but she'd be damned if any man would use *her*.

When Vilas rode up the hill in his gaudy cloak half an hour later, she rose from the rock where she'd been sitting beside the path. There was no sign of tears, and her head had a jaunty tilt to it.

"It seems I'm needing the ride back," she said, and Vilas thought with admiration that she sounded born to the purple, as regal as the Lady Jacobina herself.

He pulled her up before him, drawing the cloak around her as best he could, for she felt cold. "I take it no one was in need of anyone with your expertise."

Roxanne twisted within the curve of his arm to look up into his teasing countenance, her head brushing his chin. "I must look further afield," she admitted.

He chuckled. His hand rested just below her breast, and he resisted the impulse to cup its softness. If he correctly judged her mood, he thought in amusement, she would probably throw him off his own horse.

"Hang on," he told her, and urged the stallion to a gallop, back toward Kenwood Castle.

Chapter 6

CHRISTINA SAW HER COUSIN and her half sister ride into the courtyard, watched as Roxanne slid off, skirts swirling to show an immodest amount of leg, assisted by Vilas's strong right arm.

She had once or twice ridden before him on that great stallion, and the recollection gave rise to a twist of jealousy. Not that she thought it meant anything other than that Vilas had saved Roxanne a walk from wherever she was, for he would have done the same for any maid walking his own direction. But she envied the inevitable closeness, the solidity of his arm around the waist, his broad chest to be leaned into, the purely pleasurable sensations of touching and being touched.

Certainly, when Christina ran lightly down the stone steps and into the courtyard, there was no indication that the excursion had been enjoyable for either of them. Roxanne met her gaze in stony silence, passing by to enter the castle. And Vilas was sober as he handed his mount over to a groom and turned to greet her.

As usual when she was with Vilas, Christina felt slightly breathless. "Have you learned anything yet?"

He forced a smile—perhaps for the benefit of any watchers—but his words were grim and held low, so that only she could hear.

"Enough to know the village—probably the entire county—expects to hear momentarily of the earl's demise. Word of his condition has spread. There's much speculation as to how long her ladyship will remain a widow."

"She dishonors my father while he yet lives," Christina said, not trying to conceal her hatred of her stepmother. "And she'll have no concern for any of us, except Thomas, once he's gone."

"She's thinking about your interests, it seems. I spoke to Master Hunnicutt, in a casual way, of course, over a mug of ale. My guess is that you're right about Windom having spoken to him at Lady Jacobina's request. There was something about him, the way he licked his lips when he asked about you, the gleam in his eye... Yes, he's only waiting for the earl to succumb, and he'll be up here sniffing around your skirts, and with her ladyship's full approval."

Christina blanched, but before she could speak Vilas went on. "Our little shipowner, Master Beaker, only dropped in for a bite of mutton pie while I was exchanging pleasantries with Master Hunnicutt. He, too, seemed in unusually bright spirits. I can't imagine that he'd think Roxanne would have him, voluntarily, but since she's been refused employment by every establishment, he may think she can be forced."

For the first time his smile became natural. "I've a notion he's wrong; that one has claws and teeth. He might get more than he bargains for. But it's clear they're all waiting eagerly to see what happens over the next few days."

Christina couldn't contain her anger. "My father has been a good man, and they've benefited from his generosity, every one of them! And yet no one cares that he's dying! That the wretched woman he took to wife is poisoning him!"

"They don't know about that, except, perhaps, for Windom. It wouldn't surprise me if he assisted her in finding the proper method of getting rid of the old man. The others are only thinking of themselves, Chris; it's the way of mankind. They were loyal to your father, but now his time has passed they will switch their loyalty immediately to whoever succeeds him, even such a little dolt as Thomas, because it's in their own interest to do so. If Lady Jacobina weds Lord Windom, you can be sure that however much they dislike him privately, they'll give him public support because it will cost them dearly if they don't."

"Is there nothing to be done about my father, then? No way to stop what's happening to him?"

"I don't see what, or how. I looked in on him, too, and spoke to Sadie; her ladyship hasn't been nearer him than the doorway since old Amesbury arrived. I don't think she's giving him anything now, and Sadie says she always took away the glass he drank from, so there's no way of testing whatever it was in the wine or the broth. He's in bad shape, Chris, and being purged and bled won't help him regain the strength he's lost."

"Vilas, we can't stay here and allow what she's planned to happen to us! I'd rather die than marry Master Hunnicutt, with his fishy eyes and his cold hands and—" She choked, reaching for him, and felt a rush of joy when he took her hands in his own warm ones. "We have to get away! We have to be planning, now, because judging by the way Father looks today we don't have long! She won't waste any time in being rid of us, even Megan...."

Vilas ran a hand through his fair hair, his blue eyes bleak. "My mother might take in you and Megan; I doubt she'd tolerate Roxanne—"

"No. No, Vilas, that's not the way to do it. She wouldn't settle for that even if your mother were willing, and you know she hasn't the means to feed extra mouths. There'll be no financial help from Lady Jacobina, and your mother lives too nearby. We need to escape entirely from her ladyship—"

"If I had the money I'd send you all to London," Vilas said. He had a wide, sensitive mouth, and Christina felt an urge to touch it, to ease the pain she saw there, even at the cost of her own. "Or to anywhere away from here. Yet there is no money, not enough to set up another household—it's one of the reasons I've decided to seek my fortune elsewhere, in the New World...."

It was the opening she had been waiting for. Christina's face took on a radiant glow; her green eyes sparkled. "Yes! Yes, I've heard there are many opportunities there, for women as well as men! They need colonists, and many worthy citizens have made their homes there. We could, too, all of us..."

Her words faltered as she saw the change in his expression. "What are you talking about?" he asked.

"Take us with you, Vilas," she pleaded. "Take us to the New World, too!"

"Chris! Don't be daft, girl, I can't take three females off across the ocean to the wilderness."

"Why not? Better the wilderness and freedom than forced marriages to men old enough to be our fathers, men we loathe and despise...."

Bewildered and appalled by this turn of events, Vilas released her hands and stepped back from her. "You're mad! I'm working my way over on a ship, and if I like the sea I'll scarce touch land once I get there, except to load and unload cargo! I can't be responsible for three females."

"Then we'll be responsible for ourselves. Only get us on that ship, too! Take us anywhere, as long as it's away from here!"

"Chris, use your head. I can't, I can't even pay my own passage; that's why I'm working for it! How could I come up with enough to transport three more of you? And what would happen to you once you got there? It's true the colonists are more men than women, and perhaps many of them are seeking wives, but you'd have no guarantee that the men you'd have to settle for would be any improvement over Beaker and Hunnicutt. We'll be arriving in the Massachusetts Bay Colony in the fall, and I've heard the winters are bitter cold and difficult. You can't land on a foreign shore without money, without the proper clothes and supplies, even if we could get around the cost of the passage!"

Desperate, Christina sought a solution. She had to leave Kenwood at once, she *had* to, or face a lifetime of misery and bitterness. No peril in the New World compared in her mind to the certainty of a living hell here in Cornwall, if left to Lady Jacobina's mercies.

And the answer came, as if divinely inspired. She had heard talk, last spring, when a peasant tenant had drawn Lord Windom's wrath by sailing for that same distant land, in a similar move to escape poverty and subjugation to his betters.

"We will sign on as indentured servants," Christina said. "They have need of them, I'm told. The ship's owners will carry us there and receive pay from those who need our services in the New World."

For a moment Vilas looked stunned, and then he began to laugh. "Services! For the love of God, girl, what services? Roxanne was unable to find a position scrubbing pots or serving ale here in our own village! And she the daughter of a gypsy who once did those very things. Look at you! Who is going to hire you to empty their slops and make their beds and scrub their floors? You wouldn't know where to begin to do any of those things."

Her cheeks flamed, and her voice grew sharp with the need to make him understand. "All the people who do those things had to learn, didn't they? Do you think me so stupid as to be incapable of learning? Roxanne couldn't find employment, no doubt, because of who she is, of who her mother was, not because she's sickly or too stupid to learn to work! The villagers haven't forgotten Leonie the gypsy, whose curses led them to stone her to death, and they're afraid of her daughter, I'll wager! Besides that, what wife wants her husband to be tempted by someone of Roxanne's looks?"

"The wives in the New World will have the same qualms," Vilas assured her. "And not only about Roxanne. You're a beauty in your own right, and even small Megan is beginning to have a womanly look about her; there are men who will be drawn to that angelic little face, and any wife will know it."

"Then what do you suggest?" Christina demanded, her hands curling into fists to keep herself from striking out at him. "That we simply pretend we don't know her ladyship has killed our father, that we go as lambs to slaughter with the men she has chosen for us, knowing we will live out our lives in misery?"

Her passion reached him. He stared at her uncertainly, at last acknowledging that her plea had some justice to it. "You're gently bred," he said at last. "You aren't used to the rigors of the New World's winters...."

"I'm young and healthy and strong," Christina countered.

"And you've never done a lick of work in your life."

"I'm intelligent enough to learn anything any other female has learned and desperate enough to accept a few risks. Take us, Vilas, take us with you. Arrange passage for us, sign us on as indentured servants...."

His response was feeble. "Servants are indentured for years. Three to five years, anyway."

"So by the time I'm nineteen, or twenty-one, I'll be free of the indenture. In the meantime I won't have to worry about not having a place to sleep, or food to eat; whoever buys my papers will see to that, won't he? And in that length of time perhaps..."

She hesitated, tears misting her eyes. She wanted to say, "Perhaps you will realize I am a desirable woman and love me as I love you," but she could not. Instead she added, "Perhaps I will have found a suitable husband, a man of my own choice."

"You don't fully realize what you're asking," Vilas said, but defeat was already there in his voice, whether he knew it or not.

"I do," Christina assured him. "Only make the plans, book the passage for us. We will not hold you responsible for us after that, I swear on my father's grave."

For long seconds he looked at her, and then he sighed. "All right," he conceded. "Let me see what I can do. I can't promise anything yet, I don't know about this business of indenturing servants. But I'll ask."

"Good." She breathed the word on a sigh of relief. "And God bless you, Vilas."

She scarcely took in the mingled doubt and dismay he felt at having been coerced into agreement with her. She reached for his hand, squeezed it and turned abruptly away, thoughts churning. Now she had to talk to her half sisters so they could formulate their own plans.

Any future, no matter how uncertain or dangerous, seemed better than what awaited her here, at Lady Jacobina's direction. And she would be going to the New World, where Vilas would also be.

THE EARL OF KENWOOD continued to breath. He was twice more bled and purged; he offered no resistance to this treatment, and in only a day's time it seemed that the flesh wasted from his face and the hands that lay still beside him.

Amesbury shook his head dolefully. "I've done all I can for him, milady. But I must be honest with you. His lordship's prospects are grave."

Jacobina held her head high; a ray of sunlight that made its way through one of the high windows touched her brassy hair and alas, unbeknownst to her, illuminated the faint lines around her eyes and mouth. "We can only be brave about what we must face, then," she said soberly. "My son is young to lose his father, but I will see that he is brought up as his lordship would wish his heir to be."

Roxanne, watching from her place farther down the table, ground her teeth in vexation. Hypocrite, she thought, and wished for some way to repay this woman for the evil she did.

Roxanne could not bear to look at her stepmother and let her gaze drift over the rest of the company, despising most of them, including herself. She had been so certain she could find a position to support herself; instead she had been humiliated and shamed.

There were two guests at table for the midday meal, in addition to the physician who tore the flesh from a goose leg with yellowed teeth and forgot to maintain his sorrowful demeanor at the sight of a suet pudding. "Ah!" He flicked a bit of skin off his doublet, leaving a greasy stain. "What a pity we cannot get some of this good food into his lordship! You set a worthy table, milady. Master Beaker, you'll want some of the pudding?"

Master Beaker accepted with a broad smile. "Indeed. Indeed." He helped himself to a generous serving as Elspeth held the platter for him.

Pig, Roxanne thought. That's what he reminded her of, a hog ready for market. Round face, small porcine eyes, a mouth that was always smiling yet too loose-lipped to be anything but disgusting. And Lady Jacobina thought to marry her off to *him*?

Her eyes caught his inadvertently, causing his smile to broaden, and Roxanne looked hastily away. Never. If he ever tried to take her to bed, she'd butcher him for the swine that he was, legally married or not.

Lord Windom. Handsome, in his own way, she supposed, but he made no effort to conceal the sort of man he was. His dark eyes were fastened hungrily on Lady Jacobina, as if he would take her here on the table, amidst the trenchers and goose bones. Earlier in the meal, those predatory eyes had raked across Roxanne, and she had been chilled by what she saw—or thought she saw—in their depths. There was no doubt he wanted Jacobina, but he would never be satisfied with one woman. If he ever came here to live—Kenwood was a finer residence than his own—no female would be safe from him, not even old Elspeth with her scrawny limbs and withered face.

Megan. Megan's face was pale; she ate with little appetite, her attention on her plate as if she shut out all that went on around her, except for Thomas. It had become Megan's task to see to Thomas at table, to keep him quiet. He was even more pallid than Megan and as picky as usual. Quietly the girl coaxed him to try this and that, tempting him with morsels from her own plate.

Master Hunnicutt. Roxanne hadn't missed the significance of his presence, the same as that of Beaker. If what Megan surmised was true, it was Beaker for herself, Hunnicutt for Christina, and whatever her ladyship had said to them in the privacy of her sitting room, it had given them reason to smile and enjoy the following meal. What would Christina do if she were handed over to Hunnicutt? No doubt she would quell her revulsion and tamely submit, Roxanne thought derisively. No knives for Christina, no courage in that whey-faced female to defend her virtue and her honor.

And then Roxanne looked across the table at the older girl, and her conviction faded somewhat. Christina, too, concentrated on her plate, but she ate with better appetite than usual. And there was color in her face, more than the customary glow accounted for by her brisk walking along the cliffs. Glow, yes, that was the word. Even as Roxanne observed, the corners of Christina's mouth quirked upward, ever so slightly.

What was going on? What had transpired to raise Christina's spirits at a time when all seemed gloom and doom?

Christina's lashes suddenly lifted, and the green eyes—eyes very like her own—stared into Roxanne's. For a moment it seemed that she would speak, for her lips parted, and then the shared glance was broken, as Christina applied herself to a tough slice of mutton and daintily licked the juice off her fingers.

Roxanne's perceptions abruptly sharpened. Yes, something there. Vilas, maybe? She turned her head to see him, but if there had been something exciting between them, some illicit liaison, Vilas gave no such evidence.

As a matter of fact, Vilas was downright glum. He didn't join in the conversation, as was his wont, and though he ate heartily enough, it was easy to see that his mind was elsewhere.

Intriguing. Roxanne refilled her own plate from the trencher set before her and tried to figure it out.

"Will you put the leeches to him again today?" Lady Jacobina asked, and Roxanne was jerked out of her reverie. Surely the woman wasn't serious!

Amesbury drained his wineglass before replying. "No, no, not until tomorrow. Master Hunnicutt has asked me to look in upon his old mother while I'm in these parts, and I'll ride back with him this afternoon. Don't fear that I will neglect my patient here, however; with any luck I'll return in time for supper." He belched.

"I have every faith in you," her ladyship proclaimed.

For a matter of seconds Roxanne sought Christina again, and she realized that for all their differences, they had one thing in common: their hatred, and their fear, of Lady Jacobina.

When the meal concluded, and the men were milling around making desultory conversation about hunting and how much they regretted the fact that the earl could not exercise his dogs or his horses, Roxanne was even further intrigued by the stepsister who had for the most part ignored her for the past three years.

As Christina passed by, without appearing to pay her any attention, she said under her breath, "Meet me in Megan's room in half an hour. It's important."

Roxanne stared after her, then caught herself before anyone else should notice. She snapped her fingers at one of the great hounds snuffling hopefully under the table. "Come along, Gustav, let's get some exercise."

Christina was climbing the stairs; Megan was wiping some of the mess from Thomas's chin and nobody was paying any attention to any of them. Even Vilas had a moody, glazed appearance as he passed her on the way outside.

Well, whatever was on Christina's mind, she'd be there to hear it, Roxanne decided.

Chapter 7

CHRISTINA HAD NOT BEEN SURE that Roxanne would be there; she had decided that if the other girl didn't come, she could simply shift for herself in the nearing crisis. And then, ashamed, she had amended that decision: she would explain all to Megan, and let *her* relay the rest to Roxanne. Not even a dog deserved to be abandoned to Lady Jacobina.

Roxanne arrived, however, a scant two minutes after Christina had silently made her way through the corridors and let herself into her younger sister's chamber. Megan sat stitching upon something—a shirt for Thomas, it appeared—and waited patiently for the news, whatever it was to be. Only the flutter of the pulses in her temples revealed her inner agitation.

For a wonder Roxanne didn't knock, but opened the door without warning, closing it silently behind her. Her appraisal took in Megan at her sewing and Christina standing in the embrasure gazing out over the moors. Roxanne looked regretfully at the empty hearth, rubbed her hands together as if to warm them and waited.

Christina felt the trickle of excitement in her veins, but it was not quite enough to subdue the fear that had been there first. She spoke quietly, so that if any had noticed the unprecedented assembly of the three girls and listened at the door, it would be impossible for them to hear. For the most part she thought the servants would show loyalty to the earl's daughters rather than to Lady Jacobina, at least as long as the earl lived, but only to a point; and it was quite possible that one or two of them might already be in her ladyship's favor and special service as spies.

She addressed Roxanne directly. "You know my—our—father is dying."

Roxanne made a rude noise. "A blind and deaf imbecile could tell that."

Christina suppressed her annoyance at the response; this was too important to allow pettiness to endanger the plan. "You're also aware, then, that it's likely our lady stepmother has given him something to hasten the end? And that once it comes, her plans for all of us will surely be unwelcome?"

Roxanne glanced briefly at Megan, still making her tiny stitches. "She told me what she'd overheard between herself and Lord Windom. And I'm not so stupid I failed to see how they devoured us with their eyes today at table, Beaker and Hunnicutt."

"There's no need to go into that, then. But before I say another word—" Christina paused in unconsciously dramatic fashion "—I must swear you both to secrecy."

Predictably, Roxanne frowned. "Why?"

"Because I don't care to entrust my own future safety to someone who may blab in the wrong place," Christina snapped. It was difficult for her to deal with this changeling who had in some ways usurped her own place with the earl. "Do you swear?"

"I swear," Megan said softly.

Roxanne's hesitation was brief. Her curiosity was great, her own fears loomed larger by the moment, and besides, she would make her own judgment about the need for secrecy, if it came to that. "Very well," she said, shrugging.

"We cannot stay at Kenwood once Father is gone; we all know that." Christina's voice and face were earnest. "I had hoped that appealing to Vilas might help us solve the problem of where to go, what to do. And then he told me he is sailing for the New World within the month."

That announcement had the desired effect. Megan's mouth sagged open in dismay, and Roxanne's frown deepened. "He's said naught of it."

"He said it me," Christina assured her. "Ask him if you like. Vilas is not one of those excluded from my plan. In fact he's at the very heart of it."

"His mother . . ." Megan began doubtfully.

"No. I've a better idea than that. I've asked him to take us with him to the New World."

Roxanne's stunningly beautiful face registered incredulity. "And he's agreed?"

"Yes. At least, he's inquiring into the possibility of passage. He says he cannot take responsibility for us beyond that, and I've promised we will not hold him to more, if he will only get us on the ship."

"And what is he—or we—planning to use for money?" Roxanne asked.

A faint color touched Christina's cheeks. "This is the part in which you'll have to agree—or keep silent so that Megan and I can go on as planned. We can probably pay our passage by signing on as indentured servants in the colonies; there is much need of such servants."

"Servants." Megan murmured the word, undismayed. "Yes, I suppose that is possible. I'd rather be a servant in any household rather than risk . . ." Her voice trailed off, the thought incomplete.

"Servants," Roxanne echoed, in a totally different tone. "Well, they won't have me in the local village, but I expect it might be different in the New World. I haven't forgotten all I knew before I came here to the castle." Her gaze became speculative. "What sort of work did *you* expect to be able to perform?"

Christina's flush deepened, though her words were steady enough. "I'm aware that I've hardly been trained for domestic service. However, I'm young and healthy, and I can learn. I intend to ask Cook and Elspeth to instruct me at once in household matters. That should excite no suspicion; after all, it's only to be expected that I will eventually marry and have my own household to supervise. It cannot be so very difficult to learn to cook a meal or sweep a floor."

"Your sewing is very fine," Megan put in. "And you read nicely. Perhaps there might be a need for such abilities."

"When do we go?" Roxanne asked.

"You're agreed, then?" Christina pressed. "Both of you?"

"Yes," Roxanne said without hesitation, and Megan nodded, though more slowly.

"What about Thomas?" she asked.

"Thomas?" For a moment Christina was blank. "Why, he'll stay here with his mother, of course. She won't harm the Heir; he's her own guarantee of a comfortable future."

Megan had put aside her sewing. "That's the only reason she cares for him, though. She gives him no affection; indeed, she can scarcely bear to have him touch her unless I've scrubbed him first and then stay at hand to remove him when she tires of him. If I leave him he'll have no one who cares about him for himself, poor lamb."

"Wretched little monster, more like," Roxanne commented. "And what will staying behind accomplish for you, outside of being married off to some fat, ill-smelling villager, the same as Christina and me?"

She didn't miss the quickly exchanged glance between the other two girls.

"No, I don't think she'll force Megan into a marriage," Christina said. "She knows how good she is with Thomas; she depends on her." Lady Jacobina was not, as far as she knew, aware of Megan's affliction, the birthmark that had been concealed all these years. "It's to her own selfish good that she wouldn't treat her the same as you and I, though I'd hate to see you stay behind and chance it, Megan."

And Megan, her fingers worrying the shirt on her lap, seemed to be thinking it over.

Something there that I don't know about, Roxanne thought, but what on earth could it be? Why should Megan be immune from a forced marriage? Her age was no detriment; she was nearly thirteen, and many maids were wed by then.

"I'll have to tell Vilas how many go," Christina said. "All of us, all three? Megan?"

The younger girl moistened her lips. "It's true *she* has every reason to protect Thomas. But if she married Lord Windom, how safe will he be? There's no advantage to *him* in raising a sickly, spoilt child."

Shocked, for she had not considered this, Christina gaped. "You think he'd harm Thomas?"

Roxanne gave a short, humorless laugh. "For gain that one would throttle his mother. A stepson would be of no consequence. Accidents are easily arranged—a fall while walking a parapet, a tumble under the hooves of a horse while learning to ride, drowning in the surf... There are a thousand ways to get rid of one small boy." She saw Megan's distress, and firmed her voice. "What good could you do if you stayed here? You couldn't protect either Thomas or yourself against Lord Windom. Come with us, Megan.''

After a moment, tears shimmering in her gray-green eyes, Megan nodded. ''Yes,'' she said, ''I'll go, too.''

As PROMISED, the physician returned in time for the evening meal. The critical assessment among the staff was that he would keep his lordship alive as long as possible simply to give himself access to the earl's table and his wine cellar.

Amesbury was bubbling with gossip as they took their places and the trenchers were carried in, piled high with grouse and venison and boiled haddock. ''Master Hunnicutt's mother has much pain in her joints, and her tongue is a cutting blade—they say she was that way even before she suffered the joint pain— but an extra ration of wine each day should soothe her disposition somewhat. Or perhaps not—sometimes it works the other way.'' He laughed immoderately, the only one who did, except for Lady Jacobina's cool smile. ''Whilst I was there I delivered a baby for one of his maidservants, lanced a boil on the behind of the first footman and applied a poultice to an ugly suppurating wound in the hand of a stableboy; fell onto a pitchfork, poor lad. I wouldn't be surprised if he loses the hand. Ah, that looks tasty indeed, milady.''

He speared a goodly slice of venison, considered, and helped himself to a second. ''I'll look in on his lordship after supper; how is he holding up?''

''There is no change,'' Lady Jacobina said calmly. ''He seems too far sunk in stupor to administer anything by mouth; he did not swallow when we tried to give him a spoonful of broth, and there seemed little benefit in letting it run out upon the bedclothes.''

''Ah, yes. One can do little under those circumstances,'' the doctor agreed, shaking his head. He slid a few boiled vegetables onto his plate, the juice dripping onto the table. ''Perhaps I won't wait until morning to bleed him again, after all, since his case is critical. I will consider it.'' He commenced to eat.

Christina found it difficult to swallow. She made a pretense of chewing, wondering if she would choke in an attempt to get it down. How she hated them both, the physician and her stepmother! If only both of them could be gotten away from the earl, was there a chance the poor man could yet survive? But there was no way to do that, none whatever.

She glanced at Vilas and saw nothing in his face; it was as expressionless as Roxanne's. She hoped she was as well able to school her own, to hide her feelings from Lady Jacobina's icy blue eyes.

"Ah, there was a bit of excitement in the village just as I was starting for home," Amesbury said, making a valiant effort to maintain the conversation no one else cared to join. "Perhaps you saw the smoke?"

Vilas stirred slightly. "Smoke? What burned, sir?"

"The Seaman's Inn, to the ground. Fortunately all hands escaped, though with little more than their lives. Mistress Grosver had been in the process of changing her gown after some oaf had spilled his ale all over the old one, and she was forced to run into the street in her petticoats when the place went up in flames. Total loss, I should think. Nothing but charred timbers and the chimney to show where the inn stood."

Christina was aware of sudden tension in the girl across the table from her. Roxanne was staring at the physician, breathing suspended.

Roxanne, who never spoke at table, breathed a husky question. "How did the fire start?"

"I didn't hear. Someone's carelessness, I suppose. That's how fires usually get out of control. Boisterous crowd there when I stopped in earlier—thirsty after my ride, you know. Things get out of hand when ignorant men have too much to drink." He took a long swallow of his ale.

"Too bad," Vilas observed. He was looking at Roxanne, not at the doctor, and Christina was further puzzled. What could either of them possibly have had to do with a fire in the village?

The moment passed, the meal was endured. Amesbury climbed the stairs to check on his patient. Christina managed to maneuver close enough to her cousin to speak softly to him without being overheard.

"We're all going. The three of us."

Vilas gave her a less than enthusiastic look. "I'll do what I can," he said, but she wasn't dampened by his manner.

Vilas was going to the New World, and she would go too. For the moment it was the best she could hope for.

Chapter 8

NO ONE WOULD HAVE KNOWN the sisters were conspirators. They stayed away from one another, and there were no meaningful glances at table.

Megan tended her small charge, rebuked him when he kicked her in the shins, then burst into tears.

Thomas stared at her in alarm. When she doubled over on her stool, face buried in her hands, he pried her hands apart and burrowed into her lap.

"I didn't mean to hurt you, Megan," he said. "I'm sorry."

It was the first time in memory that anyone had heard the Heir apologize. Megan wiped her face on her apron, struggling for calm. "I've tried so hard to teach you," she said. "People won't like you if you are unpleasant to them, Thomas."

"I don't care about that," he said, withdrawing from her touch, uncertain. "It doesn't matter if they like me or not, if I am to be the earl."

"Oh, but it does. Life would be ever so much nicer for you if people liked you," Megan assured him.

"Mama likes me, sometimes," Thomas stated. "And Papa. And you."

Just when she'd thought her grief under control, Megan's eyes brimmed again. "But Papa is very ill, he's dying. He won't be here to protect you against those who dislike you, Thomas. It would be better if you tried to be nicer."

"I'll still have you," Thomas asserted. "Mama says I'm a cripple and needn't ride a horse or learn to fight. So it won't matter if I'm nice or not."

Megan stared at the small pale face. "But what if the time comes when...when I cannot be with you?"

"You shall be." For all his pallid frailty, there was an autocratic streak in the boy. "I shall tell Mama to make you stay here with me forever and ever. You shall set up my soldiers and tell me stories and share my tea and cakes, for as long as I like."

He stared at her, daring her to defy this statement, and Megan produced a watery smile. "Very well, milord," she said meekly, and Thomas laughed.

But as he sat amidst the toy soldiers, arranging his battles, speaking sharply to her when she did not place the armies precisely according to his wishes, Megan ached inside.

It wasn't his fault that he was so spoiled, so unlikable. She was quite possibly the only person in the entire world who had ever loved him completely, or ever would. And she was leaving him behind, to a woman like Lady Jacobina, perhaps to the care of Lord Windom, as well. Once she set foot on that ship for the New World, she would never see Thomas again. She might never know what happened to him.

And he, poor, bewildered, abandoned child, who would he turn to? Who would soothe his hurts, kiss him when he needed it, try to correct him in his wild ways?

After she had taken him to his mama, Megan sat for a long time staring sightlessly out across the hills, letting the tears come as they would. Anyone seeing her reddened eyes would assume her sorrow was for her father, or even for herself.

Was it wrong of her to plan to leave? With the disfiguring purple stain hidden beneath her clothes she seemed, outwardly, the same as anyone else. Yet she knew that for her there was no happiness to be found such as even a tavern keeper's daughter might expect, with a husband and children of her own. If the earl lived, if she could have stayed on here in safety, she would have been content to do the best she could for Thomas.

She could still tell Christina that she would remain. She could take her chances with her ladyship and Lord Windom.

But Roxanne's words haunted her. "Accidents are easily arranged and you couldn't protect either yourself or Thomas against Lord Windom."

It was true. She would have to go with her sisters. Megan leaned her head against her updrawn knees and wept.

IN THE MORNING, the earl was dead.

Sadie, who had sat through the night beside him, nearly

suffered a fatal attack of her own when she discovered this, for she had fallen asleep, and woke to find him stone-cold.

She could not face her ladyship; she went, instead, to fetch the physician. He was roused from his sleep in an ill-humor, but came immediately when he understood the situation.

"He's dead, all right. Well, well, that time comes to us all, sooner or later," he said philosophically. He drew the cover up over the once-proud face. "At least the poor man is out of his misery, eh? I'll see Lady Jacobina when she awakens—tell her maidservant to call me at once—and in the meantime, since I'm up and dressed, tell Cook I'd like a bite to eat as quickly as possible."

Sadie was only too happy to flee the sickroom. She met Christina in the corridor and immediately burst into tears.

Christina stopped. "Is it . . . my father?"

"He's gone, milady. In his sleep—peaceful, like."

Peaceful, Christina thought. When he had suffered vomiting and diarrhea and convulsions, when he had sipped at the deadly poisoning his smiling wife had held to his lips, when he had endured the leeches and the purging and fallen at last into a comatose state. Had it been peaceful, then, for him?

She bit her lip, and Sadie rushed past her for the stairs.

Should she go and see him, one last time, in private? He would be laid out in the great hall, and his tenants and the shopkeepers and villagers would come to view the remains, but that would not be the same. Christina hesitated, then turned resolutely away. No, she had said her farewells to her father. Now it was time to protect the living.

She sped through the passageway toward the room where Vilas stayed when he was at Kenwood. She burst into the room without knocking.

Vilas turned toward the door, staring at her with surprise and annoyance. "For the love of God, protect me from eager cousins," he said. "I might well have been in my smallclothes, or in nothing at all."

"Father's dead," she said.

His expression changed. He crossed quickly to her, still fastening his garments, and when Christina reached out for him, he put his arms around her. "I'm sorry, Chris. Oh, Lord, I hope he went peacefully."

"In his sleep, Sadie said. Vilas, there's no time to lose. Once he's buried she won't delay. I pray God she'll give us that much time, at least, but I wouldn't put it past her to be rid of us yet today or to make the arrangements for it, anyway."

"She'll observe the proprieties," Vilas said, setting her aside so that he could put on his boots. "She wants to be well-thought-of in her own circles. My guess is she'll be off for a visit to London before she takes Lord Windom; God knows she's been whining about not being allowed to go for months past."

"Maybe so, but I'll wager she'll dispose of the three of us before then. Vilas, there's no time to waste. We must have passage on that ship, and at once!"

He pulled on the second boot and stamped his foot down into it. "The damned ship doesn't even sail for nearly a month! I told you that when I said I was going to the New World!"

Christina was white to the lips. "But we don't have a month! I'm sure we don't! There must be other ships, something... Vilas, we are not safe here now!"

"I know. I know, Chris. Look, I'll do what I can. I'll ride off this morning, as if I didn't know about his lordship, if nobody intercepts me to tell me before I can get my horse. It's early yet, the stablehands may not even be up and about. I'll do what I can. In the meantime, lie low. Don't cross her ladyship, stay in your room, prostrate with grief, anything. Just don't draw her attention or her wrath. Don't do anything to make her notice you or think about you. I'll be back as soon as I've been able to arrange something."

She wanted to cling to him, to draw courage from his embrace, but he was already moving toward the door. When Christina followed she caught only a glimpse of his scarlet cloak as he disappeared down the nearest stairway.

THE NEWS SPREAD like melting honey on hot bread. The jaunty pennant that had announced to any passerby that the earl was in residence came down. In its place flew the symbol of death.

Lady Jacobina was sober, dry-eyed and calm. She ordered the bathing of her husband and sent for those who would prepare his bier and others who would build his coffin. She selected the garments in which the earl of Kenwood would be interred. Pages were sent out with messages to neighboring gentry, including Lord Windom, who came with gratifying alacrity to support the beautiful widow.

"No need for a potion to calm that one down," Amesbury observed to the first of those who arrived to view the remains and partake of the bounteous table that would be set very shortly. "She's a brave lady, she is." And all those within hearing murmured their acceptance of the words.

Christina tried to obey Vilas's admonition not to draw attention to herself. She broke the news to Megan herself, feeling it kinder than to allow some servant to do it; for a few moments they embraced and their tears mingled.

"We really have to go now, don't we?" Megan asked, choking.

"Yes."

"When?"

"As soon as Vilas can make the arrangements. Pack your things, Megan, and be ready. I suppose we cannot carry overmuch, but take practical garments, warm ones. I've heard the New World has bitter winters."

When she left her sister, Christina climbed to the parapets to watch for Vilas's return, and though the June sun was warm, she had never felt colder in her life.

ROXANNE HEARD THE NEWS from Elspeth when she entered the kitchen for a morsel to eat before she went down to the beach for the solitude she craved. She had more on her mind than the earl's death; she had seen Vilas ride away and hoped he went to find solution to their problems. Her own, she reflected as she bit into the heel of bread she carried with her down the rocky path, seemed to be multiplying.

A pity the Grosvers hadn't burned up with their Seaman's Inn, she thought. Although there were others, customers, who had heard her angry, incautious words, too.

If there were those who had heard them and blamed her for the fire, Vilas would know of it when he returned. She would intercept him and find out.

She had not seen her mother stoned to death. She had only been told, after the fact, when the earl had come on his great horse and announced that he was taking her to live at the castle. Yet in her imagination, Roxanne knew the scene well.

Leonie, walking proud and straight and beautiful with her black hair flying wildly about her face, carrying the basket of mushrooms and herbs to sell in the village. And the first stone, taking her unaware, between her shoulder blades. Leonie would have spun, angry, perhaps shouting invective at the one who had hurled the stone, and then a second one would have struck her in the forehead, so that the blood trickled down into the dark gypsy eyes.

In Roxanne's nightmares the attack went on and on. Stone after stone, until Leonie fell to her knees, until her voice was silenced, until her blood soaked the earth around her.

Roxanne's mouth grew dry, thinking about it now. Would they stone her, too, for uttering a malediction against the inn and its owners? A curse that had come to pass within hours?

She didn't know herself if she had believed her mother was a witch. She didn't know if her own angry words carried any special power. But witch or no, if the villagers believed, they might come after her, as they had waited for Leonie.

The sea lapped placidly at her feet as she strode along the sand, and suddenly Roxanne lifted her face to the sky and shouted into its brilliance, "Damn them all to hellfire forever for their sins and their ignorance! Let them rot in their own offal if they seek to harm me or turn me away!"

A rock tumbled down the bluff, and she spun, heart in her throat. It was only Vilas, that crimson cloak billowing around him in the wind that everlastingly blew from off the sea.

"Your tongue's caused enough trouble for a day or two," he called down to her. "Try keeping it silent for a bit, and you may get out of here in one piece."

She stared up at him, once more composed, at least outwardly. "I don't take your meaning."

"You take it, all right," Vilas contradicted. "You told old Grosver and his missus you called upon the devil to consign their establishment to the devil and his flames, and there are those in the village today who are remembering your ancestry."

Roxanne laughed. "If I were really a witch, I'd have burned it down around their ears, taking their stinking carcasses with it. They both escaped, I heard."

"Escaped, and they're stirring up the old stories. Be warned, Roxanne. If they come for you, her ladyship won't protect you, you can bet on that. Even Beaker, much as he wants you in his bed, won't go against a crowd maddened for blood. Stay quiet, stay out of sight. For once in your life, be prudent."

The smile was still on her face, though a trifle fixed. She would have liked to dismiss his warning with scorn, but she could not, quite. The words came unbidden to her lips. "Have you arranged us passage, away from here?"

"I have. In three days' time. On one of Beaker's own ships. How's that for a laugh?" But Vilas wasn't laughing. "So fasten your lip, girl, play out your mourning like a dutiful daughter and be prepared to leave when I give the word."

He wheeled his mount and rode away, out of sight as soon as he left the brink of the cliffs.

Roxanne chewed the remainder of her bread thoughtfully. Three days. And on Beaker's ship. He would suffer apoplexy when he learned of it, she thought hopefully.

And then she added, aloud, to herself and the sea, "And may he not learn of it until after we've sailed."

Three days. They seemed an eternity.

Chapter 9

CHRISTINA FELT as if she groped through a nightmare, from which she had no hope of awakening.

The waxen figure on the bier in the great hall was no one she had ever known. She found it difficult to believe that the dead man had ever lived and breathed. It was possible to walk past him without thinking, without feeling, though she avoided the hall as much as possible, for it was full of people most of the time.

Megan went about her customary activities with Thomas; where Roxanne was, Christina had no idea, and did not care. It was a different matter with Vilas.

She longed to be near him, to learn the details of the upcoming voyage, to talk with him freely as they had done as children. Yet Vilas joined those who came to pay their last respects; he spoke to all, from the meanest tenant farmer to the gentry who came from miles around.

She could not approach Vilas under the eyes of all those observers, and particularly not before Lady Jacobina, who presided regally from her chair at the end of the hall. It was positioned so that the afternoon sunlight would reach her, lighting her head with the brassy coronet of braids. She wore black, but even that somber fabric only served to set off her blond beauty. Her slender fingers were heavy with gold and silver rings; when she moved her hands, the light caught the flashing brilliance of precious stones, as well.

Christina did not appear at the long table set up for the refreshments offered to the mourners; she did not want her stepmother to notice her even there, to remember what she had in mind for this unloved daughter, perhaps to take immediate steps toward arranging her future. Several times Christina went hungry for hours until it was possible to slip into the kitchen and fill a plate to be eaten above stairs, rather than risk that ill-advised attention.

That it would be easy for Jacobina to discuss plans for her stepdaughters was plain to see. Master Beaker was there, for once suppressing the jolly image he usually presented, and several times Christina, watching from the gallery above, saw him in private conversation with the new widow.

Hunnicutt, too, was there. His cold gaze roamed the great hall, and Christina drew back, fearing that he would see her, though what he might do in that event was unclear. She told herself that there was no reason for anyone to suspect the earl's daughters of plotting to escape whatever fate held for them here, yet she was terrified that somehow a clue might be dropped, the conspiracy intercepted and thwarted.

The only bright spot in her life at the moment was Vilas, and he did not come near her, nor was he ever to be found when she attempted to seek him out.

The hours passed with interminable slowness. Christina had packed and repacked the trunk she would carry with her to the ship, changing her mind half a dozen times about the most practical garments to take. She had consulted, briefly, with Megan, and was satisfied that the younger girl was ready. Roxanne was left to her own devices.

Megan had confided the latest of Roxanne's perfidies, as they seemed to Christina. Her foolishness could cost them all dearly if the villagers chose to act before their ship sailed, the others as well as the half-gypsy waif. How could the girl have been so stupid as to utter what had sounded like a curse upon the tavern owner?

"They speak of it in the kitchens," Megan murmured, intent upon finishing the shirt for Thomas before she had to leave it behind. "They say—" she hesitated, moistening her pale lips "—they say she is a witch."

"Perhaps she is," Christina said crossly. "The inn *did* burn to the ground within hours of her careless speech."

Megan looked up beseechingly. "Do you think they will harm her?"

"Who knows what the ignorant savages will do? And to us, too, if we're with her when they come? After what happened to her mother, you'd think she'd have a modicum of common sense, but no, she throws fuel on the fires by bringing down curses on their heads."

"She thought someone would give her employment," Megan said in her soft, even voice. "And they all turned her away, and harshly. She was desperate, as much so as we are."

Christina sighed. "I know. I know. I only pray that whatever action the villagers decide to take, they will delay it until we are gone from this place."

Megan still neglected her sewing. "Will they say that I, too, am a witch, because of... of this?" She lifted her fingertips to touch her gown where it covered the birthmark.

"No, no, of course not. No one will ever see it. You're always careful to keep it covered."

"But if someone should learn of it? Megan persisted.

"They won't," Christina assured her, needing the confidence herself. "Only remain ready, so that when Vilas calls us, we can leave without delay."

Three days, Vilas had said. They were the longest three days in her life, she thought. Two gone, and one more to endure. Perhaps she would go to bed early, in the hope that sleeping would make the hours pass more quickly.

And then she came awake in the darkness, bathed in cold perspiration, knowing there was someone in the room with her.

"Who's there?" Her whisper was intended to challenge and instead quavered uncertainly.

"It's me," Vilas said, sounding brusque. "It's time to go. Get dressed, wear something dark that won't show up if there's anyone watching. I'll be back for you in a few minutes."

She sat up, holding the quilt against her breast for another moment of comforting warmth. "But we've another day to wait!"

"Not now, we haven't," Vilas said grimly. "Master Grosver has drunk enough to move against the one he thinks responsible for the burning of his establishment, and he has enough other fools with him to create trouble if there isn't a sensible man in the bunch. More than likely they'll be here within the hour; I rode like a demon to get here ahead of them. Luckily they don't have enough horses to go around, and that will slow them down. Where's your bundle?"

"Bundle?" His words had brought her out of bed, impressed by the urgency of the situation. "My trunk is packed. It's there, by the door."

"Trunk?" he echoed incredulously. "God's blood, girl, how do you expect me to transport a trunk all that way?"

"I can't go without clothes, can I?" She was shivering, groping for the garments she had laid out the night before, feeling strange to be momentarily naked in the same room with him, even though it was too dark to see. "You said the winters would be cold, that we'd need warm clothes."

He swore under his breath, damning females and their pea-sized brains, cursing Roxanne for having precipitated an additional crisis when they already had all they could reasonably be expected to handle. "You'll need blankets, they don't furnish any on board."

He jerked the covers off the bed, accidentally coming in contact with her naked hip with one arm; Christina felt a jolt of lightning through her body, then tugged at her garments, pulling them on any which way.

"I need the clothes, Vilas," she begged, though it was not clothes she was thinking of.

His blasphemy was low but vehement. "Where is the blasted thing? Christ, it weighs as much as a horse! You can't be serious about taking this much!"

"There's no time to repack now," Christina almost wailed. "You said we had to hurry!"

"All right, open the damned door, then, and pray to God I don't fall down the stairs with it and break my bloody neck!"

"Shall I call Megan and Roxanne?"

"I've already wakened them. Wait here until I come for you," he said, with an anger that bordered on brutality. He was, Christina reflected, hearing his not-quite-silent progress away from her door, more closely related to her father than she had previously realized.

She was tempted to go to Megan's room and wait there, but Vilas's temper held her where she was.

It seemed an age before she heard him returning. Several times she had crossed the dark chamber to peer out toward the path to the village. Would Grosver and his followers come with torches, or would the approach be more stealthy, through the blackness? What would they do when they got there? Surely they weren't contemplating storming the castle and demanding that the witch be handed over to them? What would Lady Jacobina do if that happened?

When she whispered the question, Vilas practically spat a reply. "The bitch will probably hand her over to them—what better way to be rid of the stupid wench? Come on, we're going down the outside stairway to the stable courtyard. Don't make any more noise than you have to."

He reached for her hand, and though she sensed the anger and perhaps even the fear within him, she drew comfort from his strength and the warmth of him.

The others were already there, waiting. There was no moon, no illumination of any sort; had it not been for the breathing of the horses, Christina could not have told the courtyard was not empty as it should have been in the middle of the night.

"If it weren't for those damned trunks," Vilas said softly, "we could get by without taking half of his lordship's stables with us. As it is, I'll have to get them back here before dawn, get them rubbed down and cooled off, so nobody will realize how you left. I have one more day to put in an appearance and pretend to innocence, and by God, I'd better get away with it, after all I'm going through to save your skins."

Christina thought it prudent to remain silent. She was hoisted up on the horse, which skittered a little until Vilas spoke to it in a more soothing tone than he'd used on any of the females in his care. It seemed that she was not the only one accompanied by a trunk, but how could they go off across the sea to a cold and foreign land without clothes? Men had so little understanding of such matters.

She was more used to walking than riding, but she had to admit they made better time on horseback. Once they were out of the keep, onto the soft earth instead of stone paving, the sounds of the horses' hooves were less alarming, though there was still the soft jingle of harness and the creak of the ropes that held the trunks in place on the led animals.

No one spoke. The sea in its assault on the cliffs would cover small noises, giving them some protection if anyone else was abroad. It was warmer here, even with the breeze off the water, than it had been within Kenwood's walls, yet Christina could not relax.

If Grosver attacked Roxanne, would he punish her companions, as well? Even if he didn't, they would be exposed: their trunks and their midnight flight would be revealed, and they would be dragged back to Kenwood in disgrace.

For a moment she wanted to strike out at the other girl with hostile words; Roxanne imperiled them all, even Vilas. Lady Jacobina would not take kindly to his part in the plot against her.

"Halt!"

The command brought her heart into her throat, and Vilas's knee brushed her own as his mount was reined in.

"Listen," he said unnecessarily.

The voices were faint, but they were there, in the distance. Between them and the village. Megan made a small, frightened sound.

"Quiet," Vilas said. "They may pass without hearing us."

Roxanne spoke for the first time. "If I judge our position right, there's a path down to the beach only a short distance ahead of us. They'd be less likely to hear the horses if we were on the strand."

"We'll break our necks trying to ride down that path in the dark," Christina protested in a whisper.

"Dismount and lead them on foot," Vilas decided at once. "We can go the rest of the way on the beach, can't we? And so avoid taking shod horses through the middle of the village?"

"Aye, there's only one place we'll have to wade through the water, and even at high tide it's easy enough on horseback," Roxanne asserted.

Already the voices were frighteningly nearer. Vilas dismounted, reaching up first to assist Christina, who was closest to him. For a heart-stopping instant she felt the lean length of his body against her own, and then he was turning away toward one of the others, leaving her on her own.

She moved forward cautiously, for the path was precarious even in daylight, leading the horse. Please, God, let them remain protected from the villagers who sought a witch.

The realization came with crushing force as she felt sand, rather than rock, beneath her feet, wiping away the relief she might otherwise have felt on having safely descended the bluff.

If the girls were attacked, exposed, she herself might be thought a witch. No one else knew of the mole under her left breast, but there were those who felt such an imperfection was a mark of a witch, the means by which she would suckle a familiar.

No one had seen the mark, and when Christina herself had discovered it a year or two earlier, she had been dismayed by it. But gradually, over a period of time, she had almost forgotten it was there. Until tonight.

Someone jostled her in the blackness, and then a familiar arm came around her waist, steadying her. "Stop a moment," Vilas said, and she stood within that encircling arm, feeling his breath warm upon her temple, aware of her own increased heartbeat.

Above them, at the top of bluff, the villagers marched past, while the small band waited beside the sea, silent, inwardly praying or cursing, each in his own way.

Chapter 10

THE OARS CREAKED and the waves slapped against the bow of the dinghy; for the first time Christina began to comprehend the magnitude of their undertaking, as they moved toward the barely visible hulk of the ship at anchor a short distance away.

Beneath them the sea rose and fell, rose and fell. Only a fathom or two deep here, she thought, but once they sailed the ship would be out of sight of land for weeks, and around and below it the waters many times the present depth.

A sprinkling of stars made the darkness less absolute. The men strained at the oars against the incoming tide, silent now. Their cursing had far surpassed Vilas's when they lifted the trunks onto the sand. "We'll have to come back for those," one of the men said, faceless in the night. "The damned boat'll swamp if we try to carry the baggage and the women, too."

"We wasn't figurin' on makin' two trips," the other man added, and there was a pregnant silence until Vilas said, "All right. I'll pay for the second trip, as well."

Beside her Megan was shivering, though it was not cold. Christina put her arm around her sister and they huddled together, fully aware now of having broken their ties at home, of being adrift on a perilous journey that would take them away from England forever.

The ship loomed above them at last, and there were grunts of satisfaction from the seamen. "Up ye go, one at a time," one of them ordered gruffly. "The ladder's right there; put yer hands on the rungs, then yer feet and up ye go."

It sounded easy, but a rope ladder was a far cry from a wooden one. Christina went first, heart hammering; the rope was wet and slippery beneath her feet and she could only find the higher rungs by feel with fingers gone suddenly numb.

And then she was at the top, glad for the covering darkness that made her awkwardness less apparent as she went over the rail and half fell onto the wooden deck.

Megan came next, then Roxanne, and finally Vilas.

"There's no need, mate, we'll see 'em safely stowed away," said the gruff one.

"I'll see them settled myself," Vilas stated in a tone that brooked no argument. "I'll pay you when you land me back on shore, to get the baggage. And mind you no word of their being on board gets out before you sail, or I'll have your bloody necks."

"We told ye, ye pays for silence, ye gets silence. Come on, this way."

Even at anchor, the ship was a living thing, Christina thought, allowing herself to be guided along the deck. Its movements were barely perceptible here, yet it shifted and groaned around them.

A light showed briefly when a hatch cover was raised; she blinked and was grateful for the lantern as she climbed down a wooden ladder this time. She was tired, very tired, though every sense was wide awake.

"Here it is. Snug and comfy, like," the gruff one said. In the glow of the lantern she could see him, bearded, stocky, dark. He exuded the aroma of rum. "Be another passenger, time we leave, but ye can spread out until then."

Spread out? Christina wondered in distress. There were to be four people in this cramped space, for possibly as long as two months? She had never been in a room this small in her life— a pantry at Kenwood was far larger—and there was but one tiny window—porthole?—to provide fresh air.

Her eyes caught Megan's and saw the same uncertainty mirrored there, but Roxanne threw the bundle she carried onto one of the lower bunks with a sign of satisfaction. "I'll take this one," she said.

Vilas spoke to the man who had accompanied them. "I'll meet you back on the rail in a few minutes, Hildorn."

The dark man had been staring admiringly at Roxanne. He licked his lips and withdrew with obvious reluctance. "Whatever ye say, sir."

"It's so . . . tiny," Christina said, sounding breathless.

"You see why I didn't think you should bring the trunks," Vilas said. "You'll have to climb over them every time you move." He threw the quilts he carried onto the other lower bunk. "Some advice, cousins. Stay off the deck until the ship is under way. There are those on shore who have been known to use spy glasses. Your hair, especially, Chris, would be a dead giveaway. The seamen are a rough lot, and you'll need to keep your wits about you if you mingle with them. This would have worked out a good deal better if we'd all sailed on the same ship, because then I could have given you some protection; as it is, you'll have to manage the best you can, and I hope you don't wind up wishing you'd stayed at home and married the merchants Lady Jacobina picked out for you."

Christina felt a wave of icy shock. "You mean you . . . won't be on the ship with us?"

He gazed at her in exasperation, reaching up to hang the lantern on a beam overhead. "I've passage on the *Rachael Dorne* in twenty days' time. If I were to suddenly announce a change of plans, it would arouse suspicion about you. I have to return to the castle, pretend I wasn't up all night shepherding you three around and that I know nothing of your stealthy flight. If they're wise to you before this old tub sails, they may pull you off from it. It wouldn't surprise me if Lady Jacobina expects other benefits than simply getting rid of you from Masters Hunnicutt and Beaker."

Christina felt faint. "I thought surely we'd be travelling together. Does this mean . . . we won't see you again?"

"Not before you sail, certainly. The *Rachael Dorne* is a much faster ship than the *Edwin J. Beaker*; we'll probably reach the New World before you do, or shortly thereafter. There aren't so many people in Boston Town that I won't be able to seek you out, so don't worry about that. Don't trifle with the sailors—" this last was addressed sternly to Roxanne "—not if you wish to retain your virginity for the duration of the voyage. The best thing would be for the three of you to remain together at all times. I've done all I can. Godspeed, and good luck!"

He lifted a hand in farewell, and Christina reached out to grasp it, seeing the circle of paler skin on his ring finger. "Your father's signet—"

"How do you think I paid for this? I hadn't enough cash to bribe a parson to let me into a church."

"But ... we're to sign on as indentured servants. Our masters will pay the passages."

"They won't pay the bribes for getting you on board a day before the ship sails and keeping still about it. I have to go. I'll see you in the New World."

Stricken, trembling, Christina sank onto the bunk where he'd dropped her bedclothes.

This hadn't worked out the way she'd planned at all. And mostly because of Roxanne's inability to think before she spoke. She glared at the other girl, but Roxanne did not notice. She was busy spreading quilts on the narrow berth.

"We might as well sleep what's left of the night," she said, and proceeded to crawl in and stretch out. "Are you going to put out the lantern or must we sleep with it shining into our eyes?"

The words she wanted to say made her tongue tingle, but Christina held them back. "If I blow it out, there's no way to light it again."

"Who cares? When we wake up, it will be dawn," Roxanne pointed out, and closed her eyes.

Christina stared down at her, wanting to slap her. Then she looked at Megan and brought herself under better control. "Do you want to take the upper bunk, and I'll take the lower one?"

She waited until her sister had climbed to the bunk overhead, then put out the lantern and took her own place. The bed was hard, the ticking too sparse, and she felt as if she were in a coffin, for it was surrounded on all sides except the one that opened onto the narrow aisle.

She wondered bleakly if she would be able to retain her sanity in these cramped quarters, especially with a stranger yet to come occupying space in it. It was done, however; there was no turning back. She fell at last into a troubled sleep.

THE MAN NAMED HILDORN came in the morning, first with their trunks, which took virtually all available space, and then with their breakfast.

"Some kind of hue and cry ashore," he commented, his keen dark gaze raking their faces. "Somebody missing from the castle over the way." He grinned, showing bad teeth. "We sail on the evening tide. Our other passenger will be aboard by then. Enjoy yer breakfast."

They stared at the unappetizing food, which was poorly prepared and of inferior quality. Only Roxanne ate it all. "Half-cooked and half-warm," she observed with relative cheerfulness. "Evens out, doesn't it?"

"If it's this poor in port, what will it be like after weeks at sea?" Christina wondered dismally.

"Probably worse," Roxanne told her. "Better get used to it, or you'll starve before this is over." In actuality she hadn't liked it any better than Christina did, but she'd be damned if she'd be a whiner like *that* one, she told herself.

They had all used the slop bucket stowed under one of the bunks, and the pervading odor began to turn Christina's stomach, though it was certainly familiar enough. "Can we open that window for some fresh air?"

"I think it's called a porthole," Roxanne said, pushing against the small frame. "And yes, there it goes. I wonder if we dump our own slops through it, or if someone comes to empty it?"

Megan, her fingers for once idle, set aside her wooden bowl. "What are we going to do to occupy the time, before we sail?"

"The same things we'll be doing for the entire voyage," Roxanne suggested. "I'm going to read." She opened her trunk, awkwardly because there was so little maneuvering space and extracted a book, clearly one of several.

"No wonder Vilas complained of its weight," Megan said. "I wish I'd thought of books. Read aloud to us, Roxanne."

Somewhat to Christina's surprise, Roxanne did. She had a pleasant voice, husky and melodious, and she read amazingly well for someone who had never so much as seen the printed word, except on the signs of public houses in the village, until three years earlier. The book was poetry, and after a time they all were caught up in it and took turns reading aloud after Roxanne's voice wore out.

Even with the book, the time passed slowly. The midday meal was an improvement over the morning one, a thick fish chowder with chunks of bread; they ate more heartily and lay back on their bunks, wishing they dared go on deck for a breath of air.

"Tell us a story, Chris," Megan suggested. "The kind you and Vilas used to tell me, when I was very little, where we each made up a part of it."

Christina glanced at Roxanne, feeling self-conscious, but they must, after all, pass the hours in some fashion. "Well, all right. Once upon a time there was a princess—no, three princesses—who lived in a castle. Their father grew ill and died, and their wicked stepmother decided to rid herself of them by marrying them off to three oafs who herded sheep. They would have to go and live in hovels built into the hillsides."

Christina wound out the tale, roughly paralleling their own situation. It seemed silly, but Megan had begun to smile. Then abruptly Christina threw a challenging look at Roxanne. "Your turn," she said.

If she had expected to catch Roxanne at a loss, she was to be disappointed. Neither of the others had any idea that Roxanne had such a vivid imagination. Within moments she had them both laughing at the humorous turn of events with the princesses, all of whom developed into spirited and daring young ladies, who dealt with the shepherds by introducing them to the pleasures of love in exchange for an improvement in living conditions, all while having outlandish and hilarious adventures. Roxanne brought the story to the last line before she turned it over to Megan.

The younger girl's eyes were bright. "And they all lived happily ever after!" she crowed in triumph. "Oh, Roxanne, is that really what it's like, falling in love, being loved by a man?"

Roxanne shrugged. "How would I know? But it's the way I want it to be. When the right man comes on the scene, I'll know it at once. And I'll enjoy learning all about the loving part." She looked boldly at Christina, as if expecting to be rebuked in this.

Christina, however, had known for years who she loved. She had not expected to be allowed to marry Vilas, even if her father had been the one to arrange a marriage, but she had hoped that at least she would have a season in London and an opportunity to meet other young men, one of whom might take her fancy.

One could not have grown up in a closed community such as Kenwood, listening to gossiping, giggling servants, inadvertently coming upon maids and stablehands tumbling in the hay or on the meadows, and remain totally ignorant of the interaction between the sexes. Though Christina's observations of the marriage bed were less than titillating—the earl's wives had not seemed to her enchanted with their marital duties, unless they kept it a secret, behind closed doors—but the servants all enjoyed a lusty, robust attitude towards matings, legal or otherwise, so there must be something to it.

Besides that, the recent stirrings in her own body promised delights she could only imagine, and those dreams, which she never quite remembered clearly enough, had whetted her appetite to know more.

She had made no response to Roxanne's thrust, and the younger girl felt the need to prod further. "Of course," she said, "I may not wait for the man I can marry to taste of this love business. Any attractive man should prove interesting...."

She paused to see how this was being taken, then added in a deceptively lazy way, "Like our cousin Vilas, for instance. He has a magnificent body; I saw it once, when he was bathing in the sea."

Megan's eyes grew round. "Naked?" she asked.

"Of course, naked. How else would he bathe, or would I know what his body was like? Magnificent," Roxanne repeated, watching Christina closely.

Christina went first pale, then rosy. The idea of Vilas and Roxanne lying together nearly asphyxiated her, but she knew she was being goaded. She clamped her teeth together to keep from speaking.

"The kitchen wenches all speculate about him," Roxanne added. "Sadie saw him once, too; she was carrying water and didn't know he'd already undressed to wash after a long ride. You ought to have heard her, describing the form of him, to Elspeth and Cook."

Megan sighed. "Vilas *is* handsome. I can't imagine him or any man making love to me, though. Since it will never happen—" she paused, biting her lip "—I suppose it's best I not even think about it."

"Why not? You'll be thirteen before we reach the New World," Roxanne pointed out. "If not Vilas, there will be someone else."

Again she intercepted that look between the other two girls. She was reclining on the bunk; now she raised herself on one elbow and scrutinized them more closely. "What is it? What secret do you keep?"

Megan moistened her lips, but before she could speak, Christina did so, and firmly.

"It is nothing. Only she is an innocent child. Let's try another story. You begin this one, Megan."

Roxanne did not press the matter, but she continued to speculate. There was something, some matter of importance here, that she did not understand. Ah, well, she would, she told herself. Before the voyage was over, there would be no secrets.

She gave herself up to planning her part of the story Megan had begun.

Chapter 11

UNTIL THE VERY MOMENT that she heard the anchor chains being raised, Christina hoped that Vilas would return to see them off.

Their single porthole was on the wrong side of the ship to give them a view of the shore. There was no way to know if he watched from there or if he remained at Kenwood putting on a front of innocence, perhaps throwing off pursuit.

How had Lady Jacobina taken their defection? Gone into a rage, hurled objects at whatever servant had the misfortune to be within range, cursed and sworn vengeance? Or had she simply been glad to be rid of them? Except for Megan, of course. She would miss Megan sorely; there was no servant at the castle who would relish the task of rearing young Thomas, and if the boy's mother had to endure his presence more than a few minutes a day, she would undoubtedly grow even more bad tempered than she already was.

Their cabin mate arrived, breathless, hauling various bundles, as the chains began to rattle, signifying that the voyage was under way.

"That bunk's still empty," Roxanne said, indicating the one over her head.

The woman was in her thirties, perhaps, and of wiry build, though with a bosom straining at the seams of her simple brown kersey gown. Plain, yet pleasant of face, she nodded. "Aye. Let me catch me breath from climbing that horrible ladder, and I'll heave me things up there. Ain't much place to put anything, is there?"

She had a right, Christina realized suddenly, to resent the amount of space occupied by their trunks, for they took more than their share. The woman said nothing in this regard, however.

"I'm Daisy Meeks," she announced. "Bound for Boston, to meet me husband, Oliver. He's a freeholder," this last was said with pride, "and he's going to have a house waiting for me, does this wretched excuse for a ship ever get that far."

She did not seriously seem intimidated by the prospects, however, and by stepping onto Roxanne's bunk managed to hoist herself to the only area where she could sit down. "Ah! 'Tain't Buckingham Palace, but it'll do, I reckon."

The woman looked down at Christina, who felt compelled to introduce herself and then the others. Daisy Meeks's ordinary face took on animation.

"Them three from the castle? The ones the county's been looking for, this past twenty-four hours? Imagine! And here ye are, all safe and snug!"

"They are looking for us, then?" Megan asked timidly.

"Looking for ye! My good Lord, I should guess! They thinks ye got away in a coach, though, they ain't looking for ye to be on a ship! Fancy coach, they say, belonging to that Lord Windom—just nicely painted in scarlet and gold, I seen it meself a few days ago—and the trail led out plain enough from the castle, but it was pitched into a ditch with a broken wheel some distance to the east, on the road to London. Found enough belongings left in it to convince 'em it was the three of ye, all right, so they're looking on down the road. Clever of ye, I'd say."

"Clever of Vilas," Christina mused. "I wonder how he managed all that, before daylight, and with a crowd milling around last night, too."

"Oh, the crowd wasn't milling for long. Her ladyship sent 'em packing in short order, threatened to set the dogs on 'em," Daisy reported. "Something about a witch. Ain't no witches here, is there?"

"No, that must be someone else," Roxanne said smoothly, before Christina's expression could change to anything readable. "We're taking turns reading. I hope that won't bother you."

"I can't read, so I can't take a turn, but I won't mind listening," Daisy assured them. "My Oliver, now, he learned to read and write. He's been indentured to a minister who taught him. I took his letters to the parson in the village to tell me what they said. Mayhap when I get there Oliver can teach me, as well, if I'm not too old to learn.''

"Nobody's ever too old to learn to read," Christina assured her. "If this voyage is as dull as it seems likely to be, we might pass the time teaching you, if Roxanne will share her books.''

"Hah! Won't that surprise Oliver, if I show up knowing my letters! Well, I'd be grateful, that I would.''

It was Megan who made the countersuggestion. "I wouldn't be surprised but what you could teach us something, as well, Mistress Meeks.''

"Oh, call me Daisy. Everybody I ever worked for just called me Daisy. What on earth could I ever teach the likes of ye three?''

"Have you worked as a maid? Or a cook?''

"Aye, if it's work around a household, I've done it," Daisy admitted, punching a bundle into a semblance of a pillow.

"Well, we haven't," Megan admitted. "And we go to be servants in the New World. It might be that you could give us some advice about household matters, so that someone will be willing to take us on.''

The bargain was struck, though Daisy seemed torn between admiration and amusement at the idea of three young ladies of quality scrubbing floors and carrying slops. She didn't ask why they preferred that to living at Kenwood; no doubt tales of Jacobina had reached the village, and for all her lack of education, Daisy was no fool.

"The ship's moving," Roxanne said, and for a moment they were all silent, awed by what they had undertaken.

LADY JACOBINA DID NOT RISE until nearly noon, so it was not until then that she learned of the defection of her stepdaughters.

The matter came to attention when young Thomas began shrieking in rage and knocking over every loose object in his chamber as Mathilde was arranging her ladyship's hair.

Jacobina frowned. "Whatever is that fearful racket?''

Mathilde's fingers trembled as she secured the last braid into place. "Master Thomas, I think, milady.''

"Well, tell Megan to put an end to that caterwauling at once. I have a delicate head this morning." In truth, she had drunk too much wine the previous night to celebrate having safely planted his lordship in the family burial plot, a celebration she had shared with Lord Windom in a most enjoyable way.

"Aye, milady," Mathilde agreed, and scurried off. Shortly thereafter, because the door to Jacobina's chamber had been left open, her ladyship heard, even more clearly, another scream of pure rage and one final crash. A moment later Mathilde was back, pale to the lips.

"Well? What's going on?"

"He...Master Thomas is...put out, milady, because no one has brought him anything to eat."

"Did you tell Megan to see that he's fed at once?"

Mathilde moistened her lips. "No, milady. She...she's not there. He hasn't seen her so far today."

The frown came easily to Jacobina's face; in fact, she had frowned so often that some of the lines were becoming permanent, though she had not yet realized this. "What do you mean he hasn't seen her today? Where is she?"

"I couldn't say, milady." Mathilde hesitated, then added, "She hasn't eaten yet, either, milady. None of them has."

"None of them?" It must be the wine she'd drunk; none of this made sense. "None of whom?"

"Lady Christina and—" the staff had never found a comfortable mode of address for the earl's illegitimate daughter "—the other one, the gypsy."

The pain in her head increased as Jacobina attempted to sort this out. "They're all still in bed? All three of them? And Thomas has not been fed?"

"So it seems, milady." The tremor was in more than Mathilde's fingers now; she would bear the initial brunt of her ladyship's wrath, for all that she was not the cause of it.

Jacobina rose swiftly, then slowed as her speed sent another jolt of pain through her head. She pushed past her maid, heading for Thomas's quarters, where she found her son, looking singularly unattractive even for him, sitting in the middle of the bed, not dressed, sniveling and whining.

"Stop that at once," Jacobina ordered. "Why are you still in bed?"

Aggrievedly, Thomas wiped his nose on the sleeve of his nightshirt. "Because nobody came to dress me. Nobody brought my breakfast." Outrage was etched on the small pale face. "I have been all alone!"

Within half an hour Lady Jacobina knew the dreadful truth. Megan was gone. Christina was gone. Even the sly and insolent Roxanne had vanished.

The servants, shaking in their boots, denied any knowledge of this state of affairs. Vilas, roused from an apparent drunken stupor—certainly he reeked of the earl's best brandy—stared at her bleary-eyed. "Gone?" he echoed stupidly. "Not together, surely. They don't even like each other!" He staggered slightly and clutched his head, wincing. "My God, you don't suppose that rabble last night somehow made off with the three...?"

"The rabble were never within the walls," Jacobina stated with conviction. "When threatened with boiling oil, they retreated in short order." The fact that there had been no boiling oil available seemed not to have occurred to them. "Where are they? You've always been in their confidence! Where did they go?"

Vilas sank onto the edge of his rumpled bed and rested his head in his hands. "Excuse me, milady. Would you mind not speaking in quite such a...shrill voice?"

Behind her, having followed in his nightclothes, Thomas commenced to wail. "I want Megan to bring me something to eat!"

Lady Jacobina snapped. "Shut up!" she screamed at her son, for the horrible truth was now clear: she was left with this miserable child and no Megan to do the dirty work.

Vilas moaned audibly. "I think I'm going to be sick."

Jacobina heard the sounds of his retching as she moved back along the corridor, determined to get to the bottom of this affair with or without the cooperation of Vilas de Clement.

That, however, was not easily accomplished.

The servants professed to know nothing of the matter. No one had seen the girls, no one had heard anything unusual during the night. No food was missing from the larders, so far as could be determined, though with the number of guests in the castle over the past few days this was difficult to determine with certainty.

There were no horses gone from the stables. It was not until Lord Windom, in a state of frenzied fury, arrived in midafternoon with the report of his stolen and damaged coach, that the story seemed to clear.

Yet though a few personal items identified as belonging to the girls remained in the coach, there was no sign of the trio themselves.

"They can't have vanished into thin air!" Jacobina said, by this time sufficiently aware of the effect on her head of shrieking, so that she remembered to control her voice. "Where did they go?" She had bought favors of Hunnicutt and Beaker, with the promise to them of rich rewards, and how was she to fulfill those obligations now? And how was she to manage with a brat who had not yet, in nearly four hours, ceased to call for his precious Megan?

Lord Windom cared little about three insignificant females. He was incensed about his coach and the fact that one of his horses had been injured, and another had not yet been recovered. Vilas, emerging from his chamber looking wan and hollow-eyed, offered the suggestion that after the coach was wrecked, the stranded travelers might have gotten a ride in some farmer's wagon.

Jacobina swore to search them out and checked her jewelry to make certain none of it was missing. It didn't make sense. Where could they go? How could they support themselves?

The only thing that was certain was that all three of her stepdaughters had disappeared.

THE *EDWIN J. BEAKER* was a sturdy, ungainly vessel, built to carry cargo, not for comfort. The crew's quarters, they were assured, were even more cramped than their own. All were served the same fare at table, a selection that grew more monotonous as they increased their distance from England.

Once they were out of sight of land, their decision was unanimous: despite their cousin's warning, they would remain in their cabin only when darkness or the weather so decreed.

The sea air was clean and sweet; the patched sails billowed above them driving them ever farther from Cornwall, ever closer to the New World. For the first week the sun lifted their spirits, and they took to spreading a quilt on deck to take advantage of it, sitting in a small group as they talked or read or gave Daisy Meeks her reading lessons.

Daisy repaid their efforts by relaying what information she had about their destination, as learned from her husband. "Likes it there, he does," she asserted. "Them Puritans have strict notions about behavior, and the penalties be severe for them as ain't careful about observin' the laws, but there's all kind of work for a man as wants it, and money to be made. Their religious convictions don't keep the Puritans from business, no sir."

Oliver had not written in any detail about the country itself, nor the town of Boston, other than to say it suited him. It was the opportunity there for an ordinary man to own a house and a plot of ground, to provide for his family that intrigued him.

"He says a man can go out in the woods and shoot a deer for his own pot, and no one's to say he's poaching from the gentry," Daisy related with obvious pleasure. "Don't matter what he hunts, rabbits or deer or whatever; they don't belong to nobody else. Imagine, having a whole deer for meat! And fish, he says there's fish to be had on the docks for a pittance, or a man can go catch his own if he's a small boat." She wrinkled her brow in an effort to remember the term. "Shallops, they call 'em. Everybody has boats, he says."

Megan regarded the older woman solemnly. "Does he say anything about being an indentured servant? We hardly know what to expect."

"Well, as I told ye, he was indentured to a minister. Strict fellow, rather full of himself, but fair-minded for the most part. Oliver lived well enough, ate at the same table as the family. Not like the gentry in England." Remembering, then, that the girls came from this privileged class, Daisy flushed. "Well, Oliver did his job, and they provided him with whatever he needed. Same food as theirselves, a pallet in the corner of the kitchen—warmer there than the bedroom where the master slept, he said—and clothes and shoes when his wore out. Two years he lived there, and then he'd earned out his indenture. I reckon it will be the same for the three of ye." She hesitated, then added in a burst of candor, "Better'n working for one of the great houses here. The reason my man left Cornwall, ye see, was that they'd likely have hanged him here, for no fault o' his own. He was tending sheep, and a pack of dogs set on 'em, ran four of 'em over the cliffs into the sea. Wasn't nothing Oliver could've done to prevent it, him with but one dog and his own two legs, but he was responsible, ye see. The sheep was lost, and the master was fit to be tied. The way he was ragin' on, Oliver thought it best to get beyond his reach, and there was a ship leavin' that very night.... Like to killed us both, partin' that way, but better the colonies than the gibbet."

Megan regarded her thoughtfully. This woman, so plain, so poor, loved a man wholeheartedly, and he obviously loved her, as well, or he wouldn't have sent for her to join him in the New World. She felt a pang of sorrow, that she could never hope for the same. A man might find her fair of face, though compared to either Roxanne or Christina she was quite ordinary in looks, but when he knew about the imperfection, the purple stain on her throat and breast, that would be an end to it. It had been made clear to her from infancy that her disfigurement was not only ugly but dangerous, in the waves of witch-hunting that swept over the countryside periodically. She remembered how Roxanne's mother had been stoned for a witch, and she shuddered.

Daisy saw and nodded in mistaken understanding. "That wind's got a rare bite to it, ain't it?"

There were four other passengers, two married couples. The Reverend and Mrs. Tallworth were in their sixties, plainly dressed, reserved in manner. They tended to keep to themselves, though they too, spent as much time on deck as possible. The other couple were the Dellinghams, some twenty years younger, and more inclined to be sociable, though Mistress Dellingham suffered from seasickness.

This was a malady much to be feared. Megan had felt a touch of queasiness their first day out, but Daisy Meeks rose to the occasion. "My Oliver says ginger tea's the thing, very strong and not too sweet. Let me get some hot water and we'll all have a cup, and you'll see. It'll take the sickness away."

And so it proved, though Christina thought being in the fresh air rather than remaining in the cabin helped as much as anything.

Captain Stratton was a burly, uneducated man, who ran his crew with an iron hand. The seamen might look at these unattached females, but none was overbold about approaching them, not with Stratton clomping about the deck on his wooden leg. They joked, however, that he could not approach without being heard.

Megan had stared at the wooden leg. "What happened to his real one?" she wanted to know.

Hildorn, a grin parting his dark beard, was happy to tell her. "Pirates," he said.

She echoed the word in a hushed voice. "Pirates?"

"Aye. The *Edwin J. Beaker* was boarded by pirates, and a battle ensued. One of the devils nearly cut the captain's leg off, and later the ship's surgeon had to amputate it at the knee."

"Pirates," Roxanne mused when the sailor had moved on. "Now that would be exciting, wouldn't it?"

"I shouldn't think this ship would attract pirates," Christina said uneasily.

"Why not?" Roxanne demanded. "We carry supplies for the colonists, don't we? If pirates were to take them, they could sell them to the same people and keep the profits."

"But don't pirates attack mainly vessels known to be carrying precious jewels and gold?" Megan wanted to know.

"Food and guns and ammunition are valuable in the Bay Colony, I should think," Daisy offered. "They're trying to get started farming there, but the wild Indians keep 'em hemmed in, and much of the land is too rocky to work without a fair bit of preparation. I shouldn't wonder if the *Edwin J. Beaker* wouldn't draw a pirate; it's too slow to escape and would be easy pickings, seems like."

Yet they didn't seriously consider such a complication in their lives. The ship plowed through the Atlantic, leaving first England and then Ireland, far behind. Except for the tedium of day after day with nothing to see beyond sky and endless gray swells, the journey was uneventful. And the sisters dreamed their dreams of their lives to come in the New World.

Chapter 12

THE VOYAGE SEEMED ENDLESS.

Except for the cramped quarters and the poor quality of the food, they suffered little actual discomfort, as long as the weather held. Three weeks out of England, however, when the skies turned sullen and the wind blew so that the *Edwin J. Beaker* struggled to the crest of every swell, then wallowed into the trough in a sickening plunge, not even Daisy's ginger tea could keep their stomachs intact.

Staying on deck was impossible. Even the sailors risked being carried overboard as they went about their duties. With four women vomiting into the bucket at all too regular intervals, the cabin became a place of disgusting odors, and they could not air the place out because to open the porthole was to invite an unwelcome cold shower.

For four days the *Edwin J. Beaker* pitched and tossed, and the landlubbers lay spent in their bunks. There were no stories, no readings, no conversation, only moans and whimpers, interspersed by the occasional frantic scramblings to reach the slop bucket.

On the fifth day they woke to clearing skies and calmer seas. The passengers emerged on deck, feeble and tallow-faced, sucking in clean air in appreciative gulps. Their appetites quickly returned, and by the following day someone joked and everyone laughed.

The worst was over.

There was no way of judging how far they had come. The winds had taken them somewhat off course, though Captain Stratton assured them this had now been corrected. He expressed doubts that the storm had cost them more than a day or two.

Long before there was any possibility of seeing land the travelers took to standing at the rail, staring westward, speculating on each cloud that hung on the horizon, hoping against hope that it was the shore of the Massachusetts Bay Colony.

Every passenger was on deck enjoying the sunshine one late afternoon when a shout went up from the crow's nest.

For a moment expectant faces were lifted toward the seaman high above them in the rigging, and then the call came again. "Sail, ho!"

Sail, not land. Still, it was a variation in their monotonous routine, and all attention turned to the north, in the direction where the seaman held his glass.

"Captain, sir!"

Stratton strode across the deck, his wooden leg thumping. "Can ye make 'er out, Whitten?"

"Not quite yet, sir," the sailor said, but there was something in his voice that sent a ripple of uneasiness through the watchers. "But I think . . . maybe ye'd best take a look, sir."

A profane response reminded the seaman of the captain's inability to climb the rigging with a peg leg. "You, Hildorn," he snarled, "have a look, if yer not blind, too!"

Hildorn accepted the glass and was off like a monkey to the crow's nest. He steadied the telescope, and long minutes passed before he made his report.

"She's English, sir!"

A collective sigh of relief ran through the assembled company. Within a short time everyone could see the dark speck on the horizon; the two seamen remained aloft, however, and within moments more it was possible for the naked eye to make out the vessel rapidly approaching.

Even Christina, knowing little of ships, could see that this one was nothing like the old tub in which they had sailed. A schooner with three tall masts and hundreds of yards of billowing canvas, she seemed to fly over the waves at a speed far greater than their own, with the grace of a soaring gull.

There was no reason to think that Vilas could be aboard this approaching ship, yet her heartbeat quickened. If he had left England in such a craft as this, it might possibly have caught up with them as they neared the New World; there would be no comparison between the two vessels when it came to speed.

The schooner was heading straight for them, and it was possible now to make out the figurehead on the prow, a brightly painted lady with an impressive bosom even as seen from a distance.

Aboard the other ship, the watchers heard shouted commands. The canvas was altered, the speed reduced. Christina, hoping in spite of all logic, scanned the faces of the men lining the rails, searching for a familiar fair head and perhaps the scarlet cloak. Christina felt Megan's hand creep into her own as they stared across the expanse of water that narrowed perceptibly; the ship swung around, exposing the crew more fully now, and a few yards away Captain Stratton loosed an oath that was surely more than bad temper.

"Damned pirate!" His color was alarmingly mottled, pale and splotchy red, and his big rough hands had knotted into fists. "It's O'Neal, damn his bloody eyes!" He bellowed an order, and his crew sprang into action, putting on sail. Even to the uninitiated, it was clear that he meant to attempt to flee.

Christina heard Mistress Tallworth cry out in alarm, and "God save us!" her husband muttered. The Dellinghams clung together, speechless with terror.

"Pirates?" Daisy Meeks echoed, a hand clutching at her throat, mouth going slack.

"The one who cost Captain Stratton his leg?" Megan whispered, all color washing out of her face.

Roxanne faced the oncoming vessel, green eyes sparkling, dark hair blowing in the wind, full lips parted...but not in fear, Christina saw. In anticipation. Roxanne was almost smiling, watching the striking figure who stood at least half a head above his crew members. His stance alone would have conveyed the fact that he was the one in command.

The passengers on the *Edwin J. Beaker* could see the faces clearly now, across the slate-colored water. Male faces, grinning, tanned. One of them wore a black patch to cover an empty eye socket, which certainly did give him a piratical air, but the thing that held the watchers in the grip of fear was the way the ship's guns were trained upon the wallowing *Edwin J. Beaker*.

There was a puff of smoke as a warning shot was fired in their direction, the sound leaving their ears ringing painfully.

Christina swallowed hard. Surely they had not escaped from the Lady Jacobina and her plans to marry them off to tradesmen only to be ravaged by pirates!

Beside her, Roxanne examined the newcomers with parted lips and rapid breathing. For there was something about the tall man—O'Neal?—that made the blood rush in her veins.

Not only was he tall, he was powerfully and trimly built; his black hair was ruffled by the breeze, and even though he was still yards away, she knew that his eyes would be dark, as well, and that he was the most incredibly handsome man she had ever encountered.

"Ahoy, *Edwin J. Beaker*! Heave-to!" The call came across the water in a confident shout, for what choice did they have?

O'Neal shouted another order, and a longboat was lowered. Captain Stratton, after the cannon ball had crossed over his stern and dropped harmlessly into the sea, countermanded his own orders, his face choleric. The *Edwin J. Beaker* rolled sluggishly; it was clear to one and all that there was no way it could outrun the other ship.

Half a dozen men scrambled down the ladder to the longboat, followed by the man who was obviously their captain. In silence, the passengers and crew of the merchantman watched as the rowers brought the longboat alongside.

"Lower a ladder, Captain," O'Neal commanded, and though it seemed to Christina that Stratton might drop dead of apoplexy, he gave an angry gesture indicating that the order be obeyed.

The pirate captain, if such he was, was the first over their rail, moving with a lithe grace that sent strange sensations through the watching Roxanne, sensations so exciting that she had trouble with her breathing.

He turned his head, eyes seeking out their captain, and she saw the scar on his right cheek. A knife, or perhaps a sword, had left its mark forever. Yet what might have seemed a disfigurement did not, somehow, diminish his attractiveness.

"Captain Stratton, good day, sir," the newcomer said, and his voice, too, was distinctive, deeply timbred, brashly confident, perhaps mocking. Roxanne was awash with emotion as she had never been before.

Stratton's color was so poor that it would not have been sur-
prising if he'd suddenly clutched his throat and fallen senseless. He choked on his own words.

"This vessel sails under English papers and flag, you ruf-
fian!"

"As does the *Revenge*," O'Neal said easily. "By writ of their
majesties, William and Mary." He stood as a man does who is
used to a pitching deck beneath him: comfortably balanced,
agile and surefooted. His smile showed flashing teeth and,
perhaps, a touch of malice.

Observing, as yet unobserved herself, Roxanne was aware of
quickened pulses, rapid breathing. God in heaven, but he was
magnificent!

Stratton did not share her admiration. He glared into the
younger man's dark countenance and spoke with a snarl.
"You've no rights aboard this ship, sir! You're nothing more
than a pirate!"

"A privateer, sir. There's a difference."

"A privateer doesn't prey on the ships of his own country!"
Stratton spluttered.

The amusement faded on O'Neal's face; his dark eyes narrowed, and his lips thinned perceptibly. "A privateer may, at
his discretion, use the authority granted to him to right his own
wrongs, as well as those against the Crown, Captain. I suggest
that we retire to your cabin for a drink and a talk, unless you
want our business to be shared with your passengers and your
crew."

He waved a negligent hand toward the girls standing a few
yards away. And then, as if really seeing them for the first time,
he stared for long seconds at the three sisters, his gaze settling
finally upon Roxanne with her windblown black hair and the
figure not entirely concealed in her voluminous garments.

For the space of half a minute his eyes locked with hers. She
felt singed, as if actual sparks had jumped between them.

"I'll have no drink with you," Stratton rasped, breaking the
spell.

"Then I'll have a jot of rum by myself," the privateer stated,
and headed for the cabin, leaving the master of the merchantman to follow or not, as he chose.

To Roxanne's disappointment, O'Neal did not glance at her as he passed; she would have been astonished to know how much he saw without appearing to: the lovely face, the blowing dusky hair, the darkly lashed green eyes, the creamy skin and the fullness of the breasts beneath the fabric of her gown were all indelibly imprinted in his mind.

Several of O'Neal's subordinates had followed him aboard the *Edwin J. Beaker* and stood alertly at the rail awaiting their captain's return. Stratton had followed after his uninvited guest, leaving his passengers uncertainly facing the sailors from the *Revenge*. The mere name of the privateer ship was enough to send chills through them.

Megan moved her hand slightly in Christina's grip. "Are they pirates?" she murmured.

"I don't know," Christina replied, also in low tones. The sailors were regarding them with the normal, healthy interest of young men too long at sea and deprived of female company. "Don't look at them, don't encourage them." She hesitated, then added, "She flies the British flag, and he claimed to be a privateer commissioned by the king and queen. If this is some private quarrel between himself and our captain, there's no reason to think he means any harm to the passengers."

A little of Megan's fear seemed to abate, and Christina prayed that she was right about O'Neal's intentions. Curiosity pricked at her; *was* the privateer the one who had fought Stratton and necessitated the amputation of his leg? Yet it was O'Neal who had indicated that he had a wrong to be redressed, and that Stratton was his enemy.

Beside her, Roxanne asked in a conversational tone, "Do you think they'll rape us?"

Megan jerked in alarm, which Christina immediately sought to assuage. "Of course not!"

Roxanne grinned. "If they do, I hope it's the captain who chooses me." But she was looking at the sailors, who grinned back even though they could not have heard her words.

Christina wanted to smack her. "You're frightening Megan," she said, biting off the words. "There's no reason to think they'll do anything to us. You heard them; this is some personal matter between their captain and ours. They're privateers, not pirates."

To the disappointment of the sailors, Roxanne drew her cloak around her, covering her throat and bosom. "I'm not sure the difference is great enough to matter," she observed. "Who is this O'Neal? Did you ever hear of him?"

Christina shook her head. "No. I think it was a mistake to stay here on deck. We should have locked ourselves in our cabin the minute they fired that cannon."

Roxanne laughed. "So we could be blown to bits without seeing it coming? I'd rather know what's happening."

Christina sent an uneasy glance toward the armed sailors at the rail. "I don't expect to be blown to bits. They only fired a warning shot, and Captain Stratton isn't prepared to fight with them. They may simply take what they want from the stores we carry, though it sounded as if there is something personal between this O'Neal and our captain. Or perhaps it's Master Beaker he has the quarrel with. No, I'm only saying that we shouldn't do anything to draw their attention. Let them take what they want and leave us alone."

"That youngest one is rather dashing, don't you think?" Roxanne openly stared at the sailor with the eye patch.

Anger stirred within her as Christina struggled to control her tone. "It's not only yourself you endanger, but Megan and me, as well," she said in a low voice. "Don't flaunt yourself with these men, Roxanne. It's a dangerous game."

An answering anger sparked in Roxanne's eyes. "Don't tell me what to do. What makes you an authority on men? Or privateers?"

Color touched Christina's cheeks. "I don't pretend to be an authority on either. But this O'Neal frightens me, and we have Megan as well as ourselves to consider. Why provoke them? Why take unnecessary risks?"

"We took a considerable risk just getting on this old tub," Roxanne said coolly. Her smoldering gaze drifted to the *Revenge*. "Now *there's* a ship. I'll wager she can go like the very wind!"

"That she can, mistress. Would you care to come aboard for a demonstration?"

O'Neal had appeared suddenly behind them, grinning. The scar gave a malevolent look to the otherwise handsome face, and he exuded the aroma of rum. He had paused and waited with one raised eyebrow for Roxanne's reply.

There was no sign on her face of her inner agitation. She smiled slowly. "A tempting invitation, Captain O'Neal, but one I must decline, I suppose. We are...expected, in the Massachusetts Bay Colony."

"A pity. Well, we put in at Boston often enough. Perhaps there will be another opportunity." Whatever he might be now, O'Neal had been reared a gentleman, for he bowed. "Your servant, mistress."

He stepped past her to gesture to his men. "Come along, there's a trunk to transfer to the *Revenge*. Be quick about it."

The seamen moved with alacrity toward Captain Stratton's cabin, bringing forth a small trunk that was heavy enough so that it took two of them to get it over the side. After a moment there was a thud, as if the burden had slipped and fallen the last few feet into the longboat, followed by a series of oaths.

O'Neal bent over the rail and added his own profanity, castigating his men for their clumsiness. Then he swung a long leg up and over, onto the rope ladder, pausing just before his head disappeared from view to give them a final smile.

"Captain Shea O'Neal of the *Revenge*, at your service, ladies," he said, and then dropped out of sight.

Christina let out a small breath of relief. He was gone. That was the end of him, praise be to God. She hugged Megan reassuringly.

The other passengers were near to collapsing in the release of tension. Reverend Tallworth was patting his wife's hand, for the woman was close to fainting. Daisy Meeks let out a long breath. "For a few minutes there I wondered if I'd got this close to my Oliver only to die before setting foot in the New World. My heart nearly tore my chest apart; I think I'll go down and rest for a bit."

"We'll come with you," Christina said, guiding her younger sister in Daisy's wake.

Roxanne, however, lingered where she stood until the privateer had rescaled the side of his own ship, the trunk had been wrestled up to the deck of the *Revenge* and orders shouted for hoisting sail.

She saw, before O'Neal vanished from sight, that the man made an impudent salute in her direction, though she could not be certain it was intended for her alone.

Arrogant devil, she thought. It would not be the last time she saw him; she was sure of that much. The trickle of excitement within her threatened to become a flood.

Chapter 13

THAT CAPTAIN STRATTON was in an ill humor for the rest of the voyage was unmistakable. When he spoke at all, his surliness made crew and passengers alike shy away from him. Not even the first mate knew what had been in the chest removed from the captain's cabin, and speculation was rife: it was said to have held gold, coins, valuables of some sort, and no one knew whether the treasures belonged to Master Beaker or to Stratton, but either way, the captain had cause to fear for his future.

Christina and the others, however, gave more thought to their own futures. They were rapidly approaching the end of their journey, and they had no way of knowing what awaited them in the Massachusetts Bay Colony.

"We'll all be able to stay together, won't we?" Megan asked softly, and Christina could only murmur that she hoped so. It would be a large household that would need three bound servants at one time, she feared.

Roxanne let her imagination soar and described notions so absurd even Christina had to laugh at them.

"It will be the wealthy who will take us on," Roxanne insisted. "So it's not unlikely we'll have rich suitors. We are, after all, very attractive, and there's a shortage of females in the New World."

"Because so many of the original settlers have died," Christina reminded her. "The winters there are cruel, 'tis said."

Roxanne gave her a level look. "You might have thought of that before you sent us off halfway round the world."

"The choice was your own," Christina told her, annoyed. "You could have stayed with Lady Jacobina and Lord Windom, who undoubtedly has wed her by this time."

"And have to dodge him in the passageways?" Roxanne asked derisively. "I know his sort. Enough of them came to visit Ma." She was at once sorry she'd added the last; she had seldom talked about her life before Himself brought her to Kenwood Castle. But no one probed further on that subject. "No, I was ready to come. I didn't belong at Kenwood anyway. I've a notion this New World will suit me fine, so long as I find a comfortable niche there, which I've every intention of doing. Ah, dear God, I'll be glad to stand again on firm land that doesn't pitch me off my feet!" She put out a hand to steady herself as the ship rose and then fell beneath her.

Daisy, wedged into her bunk with her bundles and blankets, injected an observation. "My Oliver says the females don't stay single for long. A widow—or a widower—is encouraged to re-marry as soon as possible. It's a man's duty to support a family, a woman's duty to raise one. If a female hasn't a man to support her, the community must do it. At least it's not like at home, where a woman on her own might starve for all the gentry care." And then, remembering to whom she spoke, she flushed. "These Puritans look after their own."

Megan stirred uneasily. "Only we aren't Puritans. They fled England to escape religious persecution, but from what Mrs. Tallworth has said it sounds as if they set standards difficult for others to meet. And they have little tolerence for those who do not believe as they do."

"They make the laws," Daisy agreed, "and inflict them on others, Puritan or not. Yet my Oliver says there's more freedom in Boston than he ever had in Cornwall. And yer all beautiful young ladies; ye'll have no trouble finding mates once yer indentures are up. It may be," she added in a burst of enthusiasm, "that there'll be suitors willing and able to buy up yer indentures in order to marry, so that ye needn't work them out after all."

But, Christina thought, the one she wanted was Vilas, and he was penniless. He'd be in no position to buy her free of indenture even if he took the notion.

Roxanne twisted a dark curl around her finger. "I should think privateers would be as wealthy as anyone."

Christina regarded her doubtfully. "Would that satisfy you? To live on wealth stolen from someone else?"

Roxanne shrugged. "Why not? French ships, Dutch or Spanish ships, they're fair game, aren't they? Queen Mary and

King William have issued papers that make it all legal and re-spectable.''

Megan's voice was very quiet. "That O'Neal flew the flag of England, yet he took something from another English ship. How can that be legal and respectable?''

"He had some personal quarrel with our jolly captain,'' Roxanne said, dismissing that consideration. "Or maybe with Master Beaker, whom I'd have been forced to wed if I'd stayed in Cornwall. More power to O'Neal if he's righted a wrong there.''

They came, of course, to no conclusions. None on the ship, except for the crew, had ever been to the New World. Daisy's Oliver had written, though briefly, and she put her own inter-pretation on his words. None of them knew what they came to in this distant land.

And then, when the crew were convinced that they were within a day or two of land, the weather took a turn for the worse.

They woke in the morning to pitching seas. The temperature had dropped sharply, so that they bundled up in their warmest garments. Rain sluiced across the portholes and the heaving bow, keeping them below decks where even Roxanne's outra-geous romantic tales failed to keep them entertained. Daisy made it to the galley for hot water for ginger tea, and they sipped at it, hoping to ward off yet a final attack of seasick-ness.

The winds rose to gale force. Christina shivered, thinking of the men who must brave the rigging to change the set of the sails, and there were times when the *Edwin J. Beaker* heeled over so far that they clung together in terror, holding their breaths until the vessel was able to right itself, convinced that at any moment they might find themselves actually sinking.

All day the storm continued. Late in the afternoon they were trying to take their minds off their discomfort by listening to a poem Roxanne had composed. It was a romantic epic, about a fair maiden rescued from bandits in a forest, and since she re-cited it in an impromptu fashion and rhymed it carelessly, they were forced into occasional laughter.

"And then the handsome knight pressed her to his bosom and kissed her gently on her parted lips," Roxanne related, "and he said—"

Suddenly the ship shuddered along its entire length, and there was, somewhere above them, a sharp cracking sound.

Roxanne fell silent, eyes raised toward the sounds of running feet and shouted oaths.

Megan, also looking upward, drew in a deep breath. "It sounded as if—as if something came apart!"

"Aye," Daisy agreed, "that's what it sounded like. God in heaven, what'll become of us if we've been thrown onto the rocks!"

"It would have sounded differently if we'd hit rocks," Christina declared, though her heart was pounding with dread. "Perhaps someone should go up and see what it is. If . . . if the ship is sinking, we don't want to be trapped here."

"If we hit rocks, we must be near to shore," Megan murmured.

"Only can't none of us swim," Daisy pointed out. She was pale, but reasonably composed under the circumstances. "There's some islands off the coast, I understand. Maybe we ran aground on one o' 'em."

"We're not aground," Roxanne disagreed. "We're still wallowing badly. It must be something else. I'll go and see."

She scrambled off her bunk and out the door, but the sounds of her feet on the ladder were drowned out by the bellowed orders of the captain, which they could not quite make out from their cabin below decks. The message was clear, however; some catastrophe had struck, and the crew were attempting to cope with it.

They waited in silence. Christina closed her eyes and prayed. Not death by drowning, she begged. Not when they were so close to the end of their voyage, not without ever seeing Vilas again. She opened her eyes and looked at Megan, white to the lips, perhaps doing her own praying. If Megan died it would be Christina's fault for bringing her here halfway round the world. Megan would have been safer at Kenwood than on this miserable old ship. As long as she made herself useful to Lady Jacobina, Megan would not have been harmed.

"It's the mizzen mast," Roxanne reported a moment later. She had obviously gone on deck, for her hair was windblown and wet, and her gown clung damply to her shoulders and bosom. "It cracked and came down, and there's canvas all over the deck. Captain Stratton is near to apoplexy again."

"What will happen now?" Megan wondered, her lips moving as if they were made of wood. "Can we make it to land?"

"There's land in sight, though Hildorn says it's not the mainland, but a rocky island. They're making for it as best they can." The ship rolled, and Roxanne clutched at a bulkhead to keep from being thrown off her feet. "I think we'd best gather our belongings, though God knows if we'll be able to get anything off with us."

Moving about was difficult, for the ship shuddered and pitched, a wounded creature at the mercy of the winds and the towering seas. Christina's fingers were numb, like her mind, as she secured her bundles as best she could. Would they be able to bring the ship in to shore, or would it have to be abandoned, and their baggage with it? There were two longboats, but she wasn't sure that passengers and crew could all be accommodated at once.

The sailor sent for them appeared almost too quickly. He, too, was frightened, and this increased their own apprehension.

"Ye'll have to leave all that," the boy said, gesturing at the trunks and bundles. "Cap'n says come at once."

The next half hour, or however long it was—it seemed eons—passed in a blur. Christina remembered the chill of the rain on her face, the strength of the wind tugging at her cloak and hair, and the churning at the pit of her stomach when she made the mistake of glancing down into the slate-colored sea before she began her climb down the rope ladder. She remembered the insecurity of the ladder, which swayed and bumped against the hull of the ship; the rapidity with which her fingers turned to ice so that it was difficult to hold on; and the frailty of the longboat once she'd reached it, where a seaman grasped her under the arms to lower her into its bow. One of his hands was bloody, and it smeared on her cloak, but within moments the rain or the splashing saltwater had washed the stain away.

She looked up and saw Megan descending, reaching out to hug her close when her younger sister stumbled past the assisting sailor, felt the tremor and was not sure whether it was Megan or herself who shook in cold and terror.

Roxanne came down the side of the ship, her full skirts billowing out to expose ankles and calves in their dark stockings. For once even she was pale, though there was naught of panic in her actions. She crawled forward and knelt at Christina's feet, reaching out to wrap an arm around Megan. "Don't worry," she said through chattering teeth, "we'll make it to the island, and someone is sure to rescue us from there. We're within a few miles of Boston Harbor, and the ships go past all the time."

The *Edwin J. Beaker* rolled above them, so that for a moment it seemed their longboat would be crushed, and Daisy fell the last few yards, landing in an undignified heap. Wincing, she eased into a reasonably decorous position and waited for the others.

It wasn't until the oarsmen were pulling toward the lowlying island that Christina realized Captain Stratton was not among those in either boat. She stared backward through the rain, seeing that the vessel wallowed helplessly without so much of its sail. Would Stratton stay with his ship, even if it went down?

She turned away, looking toward their immediate destination, and was somewhat reassured. The island seemed large enough to offer them safety, and they were headed for a small beach where it should be easy to land.

The longboat nudged the shore, driven by the sea so that it skewed sideways before the seamen leaped out and threw their backs into running their craft well up onto shore. The passengers were unceremoniously hauled out onto firm wet sand.

Megan turned at once to look at the floundering ship they had abandoned. "Will the captain go down with it?"

"Any luck and it won't go down," Hildorn speculated. "Does he leave it, his cargo will be fair pickings for anybody else as wants it and can take it." Astonishingly, he chuckled. "Was I Cap'n Stratton, I might choose to go down with the bloody ship rather than face Master Beaker after him lettin' Shea O'Neal make off with the strongbox."

"He hadn't much choice," Megan observed, wrapping her wet cloak more tightly around her, ignoring the rain that had soaked her hair and was trickling in around her neck.

"No, he'd not," Hildorn admitted, turning away, "but try explaining that to Master Beaker."

There were others besides the captain still on board. Through the driving rain, they could see the men scurrying about, attempting to get the fallen canvas out of the way and to bring the vessel around into the wind, so that it might have some chance of avoiding destruction.

"The trees there'll offer some shelter," one of the seamen told them, and the passengers obediently turned away from the sight of the crippled ship and climbed the bank. There they huddled together, and where only moments before they had feared for their lives, they now began to consider the inconvenience of losing all their earthly possessions.

Roxanne listened to the Tallworths' complaints and then began to laugh, earning a sour look from the minister's wife. "Ah, how quickly the fear passes, once there's solid land under our feet. I'd give more for a warm fire in a humble cottage right now, and a bowl of steaming soup, than for anything I left on that tub. Come on, let's sit down, close together, and see if we can warm each other."

It was not working very well, because they were all drenched to the skin, but at least now the trembling was from the chill, not from terror. And only a few minutes later they forgot their discomfort.

"Praise God! We're rescued!" Master Dellingham cried out, and ran down the bank, waving his hat wildly. "It's a ship, a ship to save us!"

The others stood up and joined him, oblivious now of the rain on their bared heads, instantly warmed by excitement.

And then Roxanne gave a gurgle of something that sounded so much like amusement that Christina's attention was drawn away from the three-masted schooner that had appeared out of the storm, heading toward Boston Harbor.

"What is it?"

Roxanne's cheeks were rosy with the cold, her green eyes bright with elation. Even with her wet hair plastered darkly to her head, she had seldom been more beautiful. "It's him," she said. "It's Shea O'Neal, and the *Revenge*!"

And so it was. The small crowd on the beach fell silent as the schooner edged closer to them, closer to the disabled *Edwin J. Beaker*.

The faces of the watchers were, for the most part, stricken. Only Roxanne's lips were touched with the hint of a smile; only her blood surged with excited anticipation rather than uncertainty and dread.

Within minutes she would see Shea O'Neal again. Never in her life had she wanted anything more than what was about to happen.

She forgot she was cold and wet and hungry.

Roxanne waited on the narrow strip of sand for her destiny.

Chapter 14

CAPTAIN STRATTON REFUSED AID from the privateer, bellowing his hatred and his fury from the deck of the *Edwin J. Beaker* in a voice that carried across the water to those stranded ashore.

His passengers, cold and wet and hungry, were not as standoffish, though there was apprehension among them. O'Neal had, after all, removed something of value from their own ship more in the manner of a pirate than that of a privateer commissioned by their own king and queen.

However, their discomfort and their fear of the unknown on this uninhabited island overcame their aversion for O'Neal. He offered assistance, and they accepted.

The storm was dying down by the time they once more took to the rope ladder—climbing this time rather than descending—and though the wind still drove the rain through their garments to the skin, it was no longer of gale force sufficient to snap masts.

Roxanne was the first passenger to step onto the deck of the *Revenge*. A sailor who was surprisingly cheerful considering his soaking state met her with a grin. "This way, mistress, and we'll have you warm and dry in no time," he offered.

Roxanne hesitated. O'Neal himself was nowhere in evidence at the moment. "My sisters will be along in a minute," she said. "I can wait for them."

"They're at the other end of the longboat," the sailor pointed out. "They'll be last aboard. No need to catch your death here waiting; they'll be along directly."

Her decision was quickly reached, for the water made icy trickles down her neck and into the hollow between her breasts. "Very well," she said, and followed him below decks.

It was immediately apparent that the cabin to which she was conducted could belong to no one but the captain. As on any vessel, his quarters were compact, but this cabin was nowhere near as crowded as the one she had shared with three others on the *Edwin J. Beaker*. It boasted more comforts, too, in a longer bunk—no doubt especially built to accommodate O'Neal's six-foot frame—crimson hangings and a writing table secured by bolts to the floor. There were a few books in a niche beside the bed, and an object that she recognized at once: the trunk that had been taken from Captain Stratton.

Suspicion shot through her, and Roxanne hesitated in the doorway. "Surely there is somewhere more appropriate than Captain O'Neal's quarters for us to go," she suggested, though that trickle of excitement within was building rapidly to a torrent.

"Cap'n thought this'd be most comfortable," the seaman said. Was there a glint of amusement—or something else—in his dark eyes? "No privacy in the crew's quarters, ma'am. There's some female trappings in that trunk over there, so you should be able to find something dry. I'll be back directly with the others, ma'am."

There was some logic in what he said, and the cabin was warm and dry. Roxanne stepped across the threshold and allowed the door to be closed behind her, though after a few seconds she tested it to be sure she had not been locked in.

Unfortunately there seemed no way to secure the door from the inside, either, but she didn't dwell on that. She crossed to the trunk the sailor had indicated and felt a surge of pleasure.

Where had a pirate—no, a privateer—come by such things as these? No matter, whether he'd stolen them or not, it was providential they were at hand. God knew she wanted nothing more than to divest herself of the soaking garments she wore, and these would make it possible.

She selected a gown of jade velvet, similar to one she had admired at home on Lady Jacobina, and a moment of pawing through the trunk's contents provided undergarments, as well. The gown gave off a faint fragrance as well as dust that made her sneeze; that was of little importance.

A lantern, lighted against the early evening dimness, hung from a hook in the ceiling, making patterns of light and shadow that moved with the rise and fall of the ship. Roxanne stripped off her sodden garments and dropped them in a heap, then quickly rubbed herself as dry as she could on a towel and pulled on the undergarments.

She was reaching for the gown when the door swung inward and Shea O'Neal stood framed in the opening.

All her senses quickened. The swinging lantern cast his face into first relief and then shadow; the scar on his cheek alternately appeared and vanished, but the smile on his rather thin lips remained constant.

"Well," he observed, stepping inside and reclosing the door, "it seems I should have knocked."

"Since you expected I'd be changing my clothes," Roxanne retorted, sounding cool in spite of the heat that raced through her, "it would have seemed the gentlemanly thing to do." Her half-exposed bosom rose and fell more rapidly under the borrowed chemise, which was a bit tight and did little to conceal anything, but she was determined not to allow him to intimidate her.

O'Neal laughed. "Not many give me credit for being a gentleman, though in truth I was reared that way. The younger son of a baron, actually, and though there was no money or property to come in my direction, the breeding is there. If that matters to you," he added deliberately, his dark eyes holding her green ones.

"Why should it matter to me?" Roxanne countered. She picked up the jade velvet gown and shook the remaining dust from it, prepared to pull it over her head.

O'Neal held his place near the door, which in this tiny cabin was not more than two arms' length from her. His voice, however, stirring prickles along her spine, made her feel as if he touched her.

"Do you really need to put that on just yet? You are...quite beautiful, the way you are."

The prickles spread along her bared arms, and her nipples grew taut, as if with cold, but it was not cold she felt. No doubt he could see them, beneath the thin cambric of the camisole, damn him. Could he also discern the other response to his proximity, the unfamiliar, frightening yet tantalizing sensation in the most private part of her body?

"The one thing lacking in life aboard ship," O'Neal said slowly, softly, "is the lack of opportunity to engage in...social contact... with young ladies. This would seem a perfect chance to... remedy that."

"I'm not accustomed to socializing in my undergarments," Roxanne informed him, though the truth was that she was unaccustomed to socializing at all. Certainly she'd never met anyone before remotely like Shea O'Neal. She made a movement as if to pull the gown over her head, but he put out a hand and took a step forward, stopping her.

His hand was cool and rather rough skinned, yet no touch of velvet could have sent such waves of pleasure through her. It was, however, mixed with other sensations as well, and though she felt dizzy and almost drunk—the way she'd felt when she'd tried out Himself's brandy, unbeknownst to anyone—she retained her wits.

There was no brutal force exerted as he held her upper arm. None was needed to make his point. His face was closer, now, the dark eyes rapacious—at least in her own mind—the mouth smiling, the scar both repelling and fascinating at this range. And the hand on her arm grew warmer and sent out tremors through her entire body.

Roxanne stared into his eyes and willed her words to be calmer; instinct told her that this man would be more excited, and more demanding, if she showed fear. "Do you intend, sir, to rape me?"

"Rape?" He echoed the word incredulously, the dark brows rising. "Nay, mistress, you do me injustice. I've no need to rape. There are plenty of females willing to share my bed; I merely invite you to let me teach you something of the art of love, for I judge you to be a novice in that area."

He saw the anger jump in her eyes and shook his head, chuckling. "Please, do not take offence! Every maiden, even one as lovely as yourself, must be an innocent until she is awakened to the pleasures of the flesh." He grew serious. "I can think of nothing that would give me greater joy—and, I hope, you would share it—than to teach you what every woman, even the Puritans, would know. And you, I judge, are no Puritan."

Her blood was thundering in her ears; had he spoken any more softly she could not have made out the words for the pounding of it. "I'm no Puritan, but I do not give myself to any man who asks," she told him.

"Of course not. But I am not 'any man,' am I? I have just rescued you from a cold, wet and hungry night on that miserable little island. There are many women who would express their gratitude...." He ran his hand up her arm to her shoulder, and Roxanne was unable to suppress a shudder of reaction.

Yet she retained some semblance of sanity, while her reply came in a gasp. "I do indeed thank you, Captain, though another ship would undoubtedly have passed by and rescued us tomorrow. I am relieved not to have spent the night on the island, but not so much so that I am willing to surrender my virtue as an expression of my gratitude." She hesitated, then blurted ingenuously, "If you relieve me of that, you do so by force, sir!"

For a moment she thought he would accept that challenge, and then humor glinted in his dark eyes. "Oh, no. I've yet to become so desperate for female companionship that I resort to that, mistress. Yet I feel I should leave you with at least a hint of what you might enjoy, before you rejoin the others."

His hands tightened on her shoulders—burning her skin—and he bent to brush her lips with his own. Roxanne swayed, for all her imaginings caught off guard; this was so much more powerful than she could have expected, and it would have been easy to give in to him, to allow him to carry her backward to that bunk behind her....

For brief seconds the pressure of his lips increased, and she felt the heat of his probing tongue. And then he released her, saying with a casual air that made her want to strike him, "Come, get dressed, and I'll show you where your sisters are. I've given orders that a meal be prepared. You must understand that we've been at sea for a month, so the fare is not what I could offer you after a visit to port for supplies."

To add to her chagrin and humiliation, he took the jade gown and lifted it over her head, helping her to adjust it, his hand brushing her breasts as nonchalantly as if he did this every day. "There! Very pretty, mistress! You must keep the gown; it could never adorn anyone else as perfectly as it does you.

Drape your wet things over the table and the chair to dry, and we'll go."

She was hardly able to stand. She felt fury at him, and a disappointment stronger than her relief. He had bested her at what was, essentially, her own game, and she resented it.

Their next encounter, Roxanne told herself, would be different. She didn't know how, but she knew there would be another encounter, and that there would be a time when she would make Shea O'Neal crawl for her favors.

She allowed him to escort her out of the cabin, and she was nearly composed, at least on the surface, when they joined the others.

Chapter 15

CHRISTINA HAD BEEN used to walking the moors even in inclement weather, but somehow the chill and the wet seemed worse now. There was no warm fire, no dry clothes, to go home to. There was only a crowded cabin where they had been ushered for shelter from the storm, heavy with the smells of wet wool and the distressed murmurings of those who, now that staying alive seemed assured, worried about what had happened to their belongings and how dangerous this O'Neal fellow was.

Megan's teeth were chattering. "They said they would feed us," she said. "I wish they might also find us some dry clothes." She looked up into the grinning face of one of the seamen, who was clearly enjoying the diversion of having rescued a group that included pretty young females. "Sir, what will happen to our own ship?"

The grin widened. "With any luck, milady, it'll wind up on the bottom of the sea and its captain with it."

Megan regarding him with a sad dignity. "Everything we own is on that ship, sir," she reminded him. "We have not even a change of garments, and we're soaked to the skin. Is there no chance our trunks can be saved?"

Gallantry overcame his levity. "I don't know, milady. I'll speak to the cap'n about it. It could be that old Stratton would let us transfer it; the sea's calming down enough so it might be managed, though I doubt Cap'n O'Neal will want to dally here for long. We're on our way into Boston Harbor with a load of goods for sale, and we've been at sea long enough to be low on grog and fresh supplies. We hope to be celebrating in some Boston tavern by the morrow, and this is no place to be when the tide would carry us in. In the meantime, though, you'll feel better for some hot food, such as it is; it'll be ready shortly."

Christina's green eyes scanned the company in the crowded salon, or whatever it was. There was no comparable quarters on the *Edwin J. Beaker*, and though it was not exactly luxurious or spacious, she was grateful to be there. "Where's Roxanne? She came aboard ahead of us, didn't she?"

"Yes, she was the first one up the ladder," Megan agreed. Her pale lips had a bluish tinge. "I don't see her, either."

"The brunette lady?" the sailor asked. "I believe she's been taken to Cap'n O'Neal's cabin."

Alarm sent Christina's voice upward. "Whatever for? If he harms our sister—"

The sailor waggled a protesting hand. "Never fear, milady! Cap'n O'Neal is always the perfect gentleman! She was taken there for her own comfort, I'm sure. She'll be appearing directly, once the meal is served."

Christina stared at the youth, for he could be no older than herself. He didn't sound like an uneducated seaman, no more than Shea O'Neal had done. "Excuse me, but you sound recently come from one of the great houses of England, not a pirate seaman."

His grin flashed again. "Not a pirate, milady. But a seaman, indeed. 'Tis one of the choices a younger son has, when he doesn't fancy the church or the regimentation of the army for the rest of his life."

The fact that he was obviously from her own class gave Christina courage. "Pray tell us, why our sister should have been singled out for attention from your captain, if his intentions are honorable. Why is she, any more than the rest of us, in need of the comfort of his cabin?"

He shrugged. "I don't ask questions of Cap'n O'Neal, milady, only obey his orders. 'Tis true, though, that I've never seen any female come to harm at his hands, and I've shipped on with him near a year gone. Don't worry. Ah, there comes your food. It'll warm you. Go and eat, and you'll feel better, and when the opportunity arises I'll ask the cap'n about your baggage on board the old *Beaker*."

He turned to go, and Christina stopped him with an urgent question, one that had been burning in her since he'd announced that he was, indeed, of the gentry.

"Have you knowledge of a . . . a kinsman of ours, a Vilas de Clement? He comes from Cornwall, and intended to sign on a ship in return for his passage to the New World. . . ."

The youth shook his head. "Sorry, milady. I never heard of him." He moved away, not looking back, and Christina felt as if the cold lump in her stomach grew even heavier and colder.

"He's right about the food. It's steaming, so at least it's warm," Megan observed. "Let's eat, and pray that Captain O'Neal will rescue our trunks."

The meal was nothing elaborate—hard biscuits and some sort of porridgelike stuff, which they learned was made of ground corn, a product of the New World. It was unfamiliar, yet had a pleasant taste and texture. With the others, the girls ate hungrily, and it did make them feel better.

They had returned their bowls for second helpings by the time Roxanne appeared, and then the wretched girl drew all eyes. Christina didn't blame her for having changed into dry clothes if they were made available, but why in heaven's name didn't the chit have sense enough to cover that jade velvet gown with her old cloak or something else that would have been less flamboyant? Even if Shea O'Neal hadn't entered the cabin directly behind her, it would have been clear where the gown had come from. Christina felt her cheeks go hot.

Roxanne displayed no embarrassment whatever, though her color, too, was high. She crossed directly to them, accepted a bowl of the steaming mush with a smile of thanks and took her seat at the bolted-down table opposite Megan. "I hope it's filling. I'm starved."

Megan, staring at the gown, forgot to eat. "Where did that come from?"

"From some unfortunate victim of Captain O'Neal's, I suppose." Roxanne spooned mush and swallowed it. "It was in a trunk he'd apparently taken some time back; it's dusty, but warm and dry."

"How nice for you," Christina said in a level voice, "that he cared to provide it."

Roxanne looked startled, then laughed. Several of the men nearby turned to stare at her; Mistress Tallworth stared, too, her lips pursed with disapproval.

"Are you suggesting that I had to pay for it in some way?" Roxanne asked, for once having the wit to keep her tone down so that it didn't carry to the entire company. "I assure you, I did not. My virtue is intact."

The smile she gave Christina was infuriating, for it conveyed humor and contempt—both at Christina's expense. Christina hated herself for sounding so stiff, but she was unable to restrain a reply. "Your virtue or lack of it is of very little interest, except as if reflects on Megan and me."

Roxanne chose not to answer that, concentrating instead on cleaning out her bowl. Megan, distressed, looked from one sister to the other. The color had come back into her face, however, and her teeth no longer chattered. "I hope they'll get our clothes. I fear going into indenture in the fall of the year without adequate garments to get through the winter, especially if it's as cold as we've heard."

Shea O'Neal had been speaking to one of the mates. Now he sauntered toward their table, moving so gracefully that even Christina would have had to admit to admiration. It wasn't hard to see why Roxanne was attracted to him. Yet it seemed plain to Christina that the man was a rogue, and dangerous.

"Captain," Roxanne said, turning her head when the man would have passed them by, "is it possible for you to retrieve our trunks? Our own belongings?"

O'Neal paused, lifting one foot to balance himself with it placed on the end of a bench. He was so close to Roxanne that his boot touched her skirt. "From my old friend Captain Stratton? I doubt he'd let my men aboard even to save his own worthless life. He's unwilling to accept assistance—at least from the *Revenge*—to draw his ship into the harbor. It will limp in on the tide; he's lost a mast, but the vessel itself is as seaworthy as it ever was. Which isn't saying much, admittedly, but there's no reason to think he'll fail to bring your belongings to port. In the meantime, ladies, there are some things in my cabin—any of my men will direct you there—that will allow you to get dry. Excuse me, we're about to get under way; I want to stand well clear of the island in case the storm is not entirely over, though I think by the time we make land tomorrow we may see sunshine again."

Roxanne did not join them when, after the meal, all the women were allowed to search for something wearable in O'Neal's trunk. Poor Mrs. Dellingham was too stout to fit into any of the garments; she had to settle for wrapping herself in a voluminous dark cloak without being able to shed her own soggy garments.

Christina turned from the trunk with a deep blue woolen gown that looked as if it might do for herself, to see Megan holding a gown against her chest, her eyes wide with concern.

Christina knew at once the reason for her younger sister's discomfiture. The other women were simply shedding wet gowns and undergarments as quickly as possible, the need for warmth overcoming the modesty they might otherwise have displayed.

Megan had never revealed her disfiguring birthmark to a stranger; she knew it could well be dangerous to do so. It had been awkward, sharing a cabin with Roxanne and Daisy as well as Christina, to dress and undress without letting them see the birthmark. Megan knew they'd considered her odd, to claim such privacy, and Roxanne, at least, was impatient with this undue modesty. Yet she could not trust anyone with her secret, not when exposure might raise suspicions about witchcraft.

If only Roxanne were here, Christina thought impatiently, she could divert the attention of the others, or help shield Megan from their view as she changed. Although she might not have done it without explanations, for Roxanne was as ignorant as these relative strangers of the imperfections that might be misinterpreted as signs of the devil.

"Perhaps I'd better just . . . wrap up in a dry cloak," Megan suggested softly.

Christina put a hand over the younger girl's and found it icy. "No. You'll catch your death staying wet. Here, I'll help you. Turn away, and I'll hold my cloak around you."

Megan moved quickly, her pale skin showing goose bumps as she peeled off several layers of sodden wool and cambric. Before she had exchanged them for the dry things, her teeth were chattering again.

It was with profound relief that Christina helped with the buttons; only when she turned away from Megan, who struggled now with her tangled hair, she found Mrs. Tallworth watching them with curiosity. For a moment her heart lurched; had the woman observed anything out of the ordinary? Christina spoke quickly—too quickly?—in an attempt to put down any suspicion.

"My sister takes a chill very easily," she said. "I hope she won't be ill from all that exposure."

The minister's wife made a grunting sound. "We'll be lucky we don't all take ill after what we've been through this day."

Megan added her bit, sounding more normal than Christina had to her own ears. "But we're alive, which we might not have been. What if that mast had snapped while we were still far out at sea? We could have been driven aground in some remote place where no one would have come along to rescue us. Oh, it does feel better already, just to be dry!"

The moment passed, and Christina did not think Megan's birthmark had been seen. It was, she thought, no more than foolishness to attach too much importance to the mark; no one could be sweeter or kinder or less dangerous to anyone than Megan, yet there were many who would view her with alarm if they knew about the stains.

They might even, she thought uneasily, condemn *her* for the tiny mole beneath one breast, but the mole was much more readily concealed than Megan's birthmark.

The villagers had stoned Roxanne's mother to death for a witch, she recalled, but reports had it that no marks of any suspicious nature had been discovered when the body was prepared for burial.

"What are we to do with these?" Daisy wondered aloud, lifting her cast-off garments. "I doubt Captain O'Neal wants female petticoats and stockings draped all over his cabin until they dry."

None of them had been aware of the door opening until Roxanne spoke. "On the contrary," she said, closing the door behind her, swaying a little with the motion of the ship, "Captain O'Neal has given over his cabin to us until he can deliver us into Boston in the morning. There isn't bed space for us all, but there are extra blankets in that chest over there, I'm told, and we can at least have privacy and floor space for ourselves."

The two older women were allotted the bunk, which they took with no thanks to the younger ones; the other four wrapped up in blankets on the deck, and while it was not totally comfortable, it was certainly better than curling up on the sand on the island, with the rain sifting down on them through the trees.

Christina lay for some time after the sounds around her indicated that everyone else was asleep. Tomorrow they would be in Boston. Tomorrow they would presumably meet their new master, to whom they would be indentured for a period of three years.

Apprehension caused a worse chill than the wind and the rain had done. It had been her idea to come here, and though she had no regrets at leaving Kenwood Castle and Cornwall, it was impossible not to be concerned about what would happen now. Three years stretched ahead, seeming far longer now than it had when she'd been eager to escape her stepmother's scheming plans for the future. She prayed she'd done the right thing by bringing Megan and Roxanne here, though it appeared Roxanne could shift for herself if need be. Christina hadn't missed the air about the girl, nor that of the pirate O'Neal—he *was* a pirate if he preyed on his own country's ships, no matter what excuses he made—when they had entered the salon together. Probably nothing untoward had occurred, no real impropriety—for one thing, there hadn't been much time—but Christina had the distinct impression that Roxanne was a plum, ripe for the plucking, and that she'd little enough sense to resist being plucked by a rogue, be he sufficiently handsome.

No, she wouldn't waste time worrying about Roxanne. She'd included her in the plan to flee from Kenwood because it was the only decent thing to do; Roxanne would have been as much at Lady Jacobina's mercies as she and Megan. But Roxanne could look out for herself if she chose. It was Megan Christina must protect and see to.

If only Vilas would find them as soon as he, too, arrived in the New World, she thought, squirming in an attempt to find a more comfortable position on the wooden planking. She could endure anything, even three years of scrubbing pots in someone else's kitchen, if she knew that Vilas would be waiting for her at the end of that time. If he was allowed to visit her occasionally, so that she had something to look forward to. If he professed to care for her, as she cared for him.

Christina sighed deeply. How different things might be if Vilas had sailed on the *Edwin J. Beaker*, too.

Yet he must be nearing Boston by this time. She had no doubt that he would seek her out when he arrived. He might even find a way to buy out her indenture, and Megan's, and when he was ready to settle down . . .

She smiled to herself in the darkness, listening to Mrs. Dellingham snore a few feet away. She was as bad as Roxanne with imaginings.

But she was young and healthy and optimistic, despite the uncertainty she faced.

Seeing Vilas in memory, she continued to smile as she fell asleep.

Chapter 16

OVERNIGHT, the storm dissipated.

They sailed into Boston Harbor in bright sunshine, the *Revenge*'s unwitting passengers lining the rail to catch that first glimpse of their new home.

Megan's color was high, and there was eagerness in her voice. "It's beautiful! All those marvelous leaves—what kind of trees are they, I wonder?"

"Maples, oaks and birches, for the most part, if you're talking about the ones with the scarlet and gold leaves," a masculine voice said behind them. "It's the prettiest time of the year here."

Shea O'Neal was so tall he towered over the others, and he walked with the grace of some wild, feline creature, swiftly and silently; no one had heard him coming. Only Roxanne smiled at him, though there was no open hostility; he had, after all, saved them from an extremely uncomfortable and frightening night.

Christina stared across the bay toward the welcoming land, at the confluence of the Charles and the Mystick rivers as they joined the sea. It was very different from Cornwall, which had a misty green beauty she had always loved; instead of softly undulating, mostly treeless hills, the landscape here seemed more sharply defined, with granite outcroppings and less precipitous cliffs and far more vegetation; the autumn color surpassed anything she had ever imagined.

Somehow, the land gave her courage. They had safely traversed the savage sea, leaving the dangers of Kenwood behind them, and now everything about this new world beckoned. They were still far enough out so that she could not make out detail about the city of Boston, but it was clearly not the primitive village she had half expected to find. There were hundreds of houses, far more than in the only villages she had ever seen at home, and many of them were substantially constructed with brick and stone, as well as of wood. Far from being thrown into a backward society, she guessed with rising excitement that they had come to live in a place that had much more to offer than had their surroundings at home, for there were church spires and public buildings, as well as dwelling places. The harbor was full of small boats, and there were half a dozen ships also, while on the docks swarms of men loaded or unloaded cargoes.

There was no sign of the *Edwin J. Beaker*, however.

"Captain O'Neal," Christina said, sounding a bit breathless, "can you tell us the fate of our baggage?" And then, realizing how selfish that had sounded, she amended, "And our ship, of course, and Captain Stratton and his crew."

"She survived the last of the storm, at least. The old tub was wallowing in our wake at dawn," O'Neal said cheerfully. "I've no doubt your trunks will follow you onto the docks within an hour or two. If not—" and he grinned, so that Christina thought he would be extremely handsome had it not been for the scar "—the tide will wash the old *Beaker* back out to sea until the next high tide."

Roxanne spoke up, the lilt in her voice revealing her own intoxication over this new land. Or was it, Christina wondered, this pirate captain rather than Boston that brought the sparkle to her eyes and the smile so readily to her lips?

"We are to be signed out as indentured servants, and until Captain Stratton comes ashore, we don't know where to go or what to do. He's to make arrangements with prospective employers to repay our passage money."

"A pity the old hulk didn't go down entirely rather than just losing a mast," O'Neal observed in a manner suggesting that he meant it. "And Captain Stratton with it. You'd then be free to make your own ways."

"You've some long-standing feud with Stratton," Roxanne stated, inviting him to expand on it.

O'Neal only nodded. "You'll have to excuse me, ladies, or these lads of mine will send us flying into a wharf. Until Stratton shows up, consider yourselves my guests."

He was gone, shouting orders, and the men in the rigging scurried about taking in sail.

"So we still don't know what the feud is about," Roxanne commented wryly. "Well, at least we aren't to be dumped onto the wharf to shift for ourselves." She leaned both elbows on the rail, peering landward. "I hadn't expected a real city. It's like London, almost."

"You've never been to London," Christina objected at the same time that Daisy Meeks spoke up.

"Oh, my, no! *I've* been to London, and it wasn't nothing like this! London's much bigger, ye can walk for hours and never get from one side of it to the other, and it's dirty—not much in the way of pretty trees, except in a few parks, and so many people. This is nicer, far nicer. I don't suppose my Oliver has guessed when our ship will arrive, and he won't be expecting me on no privateer, but wouldn't it be lovely if he met me on the dock?"

It would, indeed, be lovely to be met, Christina thought. The land was welcoming; she'd yet to know about the people. She'd heard enough about the Puritans to be uncertain of the reception they would give to a trio from one of England's great houses. The three of them had discussed this matter at length during the voyage and had thought it might be best to be vague about their origins, but Daisy, when they finally consulted her, had a different opinion.

"There's no way ye're going to make anyone think ye came from some cottage in a Cornwall village," she said positively. "Not the way ye look or dress or speak. Ye might as well be honest about yerselves."

Roxanne's response had been blunt. "Will anyone want us as servants, indentured or not, then? They won't expect us to know anything worthwhile, which for the most part is the truth."

Daisy laughed in wry amusement. "The truth is, if ye'll excuse me saying it, that whether ye admit to ignorance or not, ye're bound to display it when the time comes. On the other hand, ye're all pleasant to look upon, ye're young and healthy and strong, and no doubt they'd rather tell ye how to carry slops than to do it themselves."

If only she knew what it would be best to say to anyone who sought indentured servants, Christina thought, straining to see the town that was quickly growing more visible. It was a busy place, none of the slow stolid pace of her home village about it. The buildings she could now make out clearly were sturdy and well designed, and if this Boston was less impressive than London, why it was less intimidating, as well.

The *Revenge* dropped anchor a few hundred yards from the wharves; a boat was lowered to take Daisy and the Tallworths and the Dellinghams ashore. Daisy hesitated, then gave each of the trio a quick hug before going over the side.

"God bless ye," she said, and was gone.

The two older couples contented themselves with brief nods before their departure. The girls were left standing on the deck, emotions washing over them with the impressions of this new place.

Soon, Christina thought, giving her imagination free rein. Soon they would know the turn that their lives would now take, and she wasn't sure whether she was more eager or more fearful for it to begin.

HALF AN HOUR after the first boat had taken passengers ashore, with the *Edwin J. Beaker* not yet in sight, O'Neal appeared at the rail, ready to go ashore.

Christina spoke impulsively, without consulting her sisters. "Might we go ashore, too, sir? We've been too long aboard ship; we yearn for solid ground beneath our feet."

"Yes, let us go," Roxanne agreed at once, and Megan nodded eagerly.

"Why not?" O'Neal gestured with one hand. "Come along, it's a fine day to get a close look at Boston Town."

And so they descended into the longboat, smelling the land smells of woodsmoke and tar, hearing the voices of men at work; Megan reached out a hand to Christina and then to Roxanne, and the three of them sat, clasping hands, until it was time to scramble up the ladder—a wooden one, this time, that didn't sway beneath them—onto the wharf.

"I've business to attend to. I'll be gone an hour or more, at least," O'Neal told them. He was decked out in a courtly, flamboyant style, at odds with the sober garb of the men working the docks, topped off with a cape that put Vilas's scarlet one in the shade, for in addition to being of crimson velvet it was lined with the rich dark pelts of native beaver. "My men will be over there—" he waved a hand toward the shops that faced the wharves "—making up for weeks of deprivation, and I don't recommend that you seek them out there. Return here to the longboat when you're ready to go back to the *Revenge*. No one will bother you."

They stood for a moment, watching him go, a peacock among sparrows, Christina thought. And with all the arrogant confidence of a lion amidst sheep.

Megan looked around, anticipation making her seem to glow. "Where shall we go?"

"Anywhere that's dry land," Roxanne said. "I've had enough of the heaving deck of a ship to last me a day or so. We seem to be attracting some attention."

While it was true that the men industriously moving cargo looked at them, there was nothing intimidating in their glances. Megan drew her cloak around her throat, though the sun was warm on their faces. "I don't think we're dressed the way Puritan women dress."

"True," Roxanne said, tossing her dark head so that her hair swung magnificently around her shoulders. "Yet we've put back on our own clothes, still damp as they are—and I've no taste for Puritan styles even if we had any such. So drab and plain they are! Come on, let's walk over that way. There seems to be an open place where we can stretch our legs and enjoy this sunshine."

There was, indeed, great enjoyment in the warmth of the sun and their surroundings. They walked at a leisurely pace, with Roxanne at least taking pleasure as well in the glances of those they passed. There were shops—those nearest the waterfront being mostly chandlers and cooperages and others dealing in the needs of seafarers—and eating places from which the aromas set their mouths watering. "Meat," Megan said wistfully. "Fresh, roasted meat. I do hope we'll be taken on by someone who sets a good table."

Christina slowed as they passed a shop with a tiny window offering a single display, a silver tea set, that was as fine as anything Kenwood could boast. This New World clearly offered more than wild Indians and austerity. "Anyone who can pay for indentured servants will surely be able to provide for

them," she said. "It occurs to me, that though we've discussed all sorts of possibilities, we haven't made an important
decision."

"Oh, what's that?" Roxanne held up a hand to brush back
a blowing strand of hair, aware of the scrutiny from across the
cobbled street of a pair of gawking youths.

"Captain Stratton said we'd have some say about who takes
us on. I mean, all he's interested in is getting his passage money.
If more than one master offers for us, we may be the ones to
choose. So we should know, beforehand, if we intend to stay
together. In the same household, if that's possible."

"Oh, yes," Megan said at once, but Roxanne had come
abreast of a window that sent back her own face in reflection;
she was too gratified by even this limited view to concentrate on
what Christina had said.

"Well?" Christina prodded, and Roxanne reluctantly resumed her steps beside the others.

"Well, what?"

"Well, Megan and I want to remain together if we can. Do
you care to remain with us, or do you want to go off on your
own?"

Roxanne considered. "It depends-on what offers, doesn't it?
Who knows, it might be to our advantage to split up. And it
would take a wealthy household in this place, judging by the
size of their houses, to take on all three of us. I see no need to
decide now."

Christina made an exasperated sound, but pursued the matter no further. Boston Town was too interesting to allow Roxanne's contrariness to spoil their first view of it.

Their stroll brought them at last to a large, open area, a
common where cattle and sheep grazed; a band of small boys
ran whooping across the grass until they were admonished by
a soberly dressed man of middle years.

The man gave them a startled glance before he went on his
way across the common, a glance that made Christina distinctly nervous.

"We're going to have to do something about our clothes,"
she said. "Everyone's looking at us as if we were sideshow
freaks."

"What do you suggest?" Roxanne asked reasonably. "We have no money and only the kind of clothes we wore at home. I don't care if people look at me."

Christina suppressed a surge of annoyance. *That* was clear enough. "A prospective employer might not want bound servants who draw too much attention. And we must find placement before Captain Stratton sails; he'll want his passage money."

Roxanne avoided stepping in a splatter of cow dung and turned back the way they had come. "That won't be in a hurry. He'll have to replace a mast, which I doubt can be done overnight. I'm beginning to feel very hungry. I don't suppose you have any money to buy a bun or something?"

"Where would I get any coins?" Christina asked. She, too, was hungry. "No doubt if we return to the *Revenge*, your Captain O'Neal will see we're fed."

The last was meant as a gibe; Roxanne only laughed. She didn't at all object to the reference to *her* captain. The way he had smiled at her while they were rowed from the ship to the wharf had sent tingling excitement through her, though she had for the most part kept her lashes modestly lowered so as not to seem too bold.

Except for the sidelong glances conveying so clearly that their appearance set them apart from the local population, their return walk was uneventful until they had nearly regained the waterfront. And then, ahead of them in the narrow street, some sort of confrontation broke out.

Several women in dark gowns with white collars and their heads concealed under demure caps were gathered around a fifth female figure; their raised voices reached the approaching girls.

Suddenly the odd figure pushed through between two of the others and ran toward the trio of newcomers, who came to an abrupt halt. The distraught woman who fled had a look of panic that was impossible to misinterpret.

Christina stepped to one side of the street, drawing Megan with her, but Roxanne remained directly in the path of the stranger and her pursuers.

"Spawn of the devil!" one of the latter screeched, and stooped to pick up a stone. The girls watched, stunned, as the stone was flung, taking the unfortunate victim in the back and nearly knocking her off her feet.

Christina sucked in a horrified breath, then held it when she saw Roxanne's face.

"She's naught but a witch!" another woman shrieked, and a second stone was thrown, and then another. Not a dozen yards from the watching girls, the victim went down.

Christina knew instinctively that Roxanne saw the poor woman as her mother, stoned to death by hostile villagers. Yet it would not do to become embroiled in someone else's problems, not under their present circumstances, she thought in a panic. They could easily jeopardize their own lives.

"Roxanne! No!" she cried, but it was too late. Roxanne had scooped up a few stones of her own, and she stepped boldly forward until she faced the assaulters, the victim at her feet.

Christina knew she had only seconds to decide her course of action, and that whatever it was might be crucial not only to the woman curled in a fetal position on the cobblestones but to the three of them, as well.

Chapter 17

"STOP!" Christina released Megan's hand and stepped forward, shoulder to shoulder with Roxanne. "Whatever this woman has done, this is surely a matter for the authorities, not for fellow citizens to handle!"

Roxanne was poised to throw, and Christina touched her other arm, fearing that if another rock were pitched—particularly against the majority of four angry females who faced them—there would be genuine bloodshed with themselves outnumbered in the middle of it.

Roxanne's arm was rigid, the muscles tensed, but she withheld the rock as the women stared at them, both astonished and furious at this interference.

"Is this uncivilized behavior the way things are handled in the New World?" Christina demanded, and prayed that none of the others would throw their stones, either. They would undoubtedly be aimed at herself and Roxanne rather than at their original victim, and she cringed at the thought of such impact even as she hoped she would have the courage to hold her ground. "For shame!"

The male voice from behind her at first sent her heart hammering in increased fear, and then her bones seemed to melt as if to water in the aftermath of tension.

"The young woman is right," the man said. "It is not your place to punish a transgressor, whatever her sins. That is a matter for the magistrate and the council to decide. Be gone! Be about your business!"

He had come out of one of the shops, and Christina, drawing in a painful breath, dared to look at him.

He was an old man, seventy or more, but he carried his big, rawboned body erectly, and there was nothing frail about him. Blue eyes blazed beneath thickly tufted white brows; a shock of equally snowy hair protruded from beneath the hat that seemed customary for these Puritans.

The women had frozen in place, lowering their stones but not otherwise moving, until the newcomer bellowed in a voice that made Christina jump again.

"Be gone, I said! Be about your business!" And then, to the woman crouching on her hands and knees, "And you, as well, before I inquire further into what you've been up to, to bring this retribution upon yourself! Go home and think upon your sins, and plead for Divine forgiveness!"

The woman raised her head. She was perhaps forty, with an ordinary face that was neither pretty nor notably plain, but somewhere in between. Her lips stretched in a nervous smile, marred by crooked teeth with one incisor missing. "Yes, sir!" she agreed at once, scrambling to her feet. "Yes, indeed, thank you, sir!"

She paused to look at Roxanne and Christina, the former still clutching the rock she had intended to throw in the woman's defense. "And to you, too, young mistresses! My thanks!"

She hurried away, disappearing around a corner, while the man who had stepped into the fracas touched the broad brim of his hat in salutation and left the girls standing there in the middle of the street.

Christina let out a sigh of relief. Her legs were trembling. "I thought maybe they were going to stone all of us."

Roxanne regarded her with a curious expression. "I didn't expect you to step in."

"I didn't expect to, either. It just seemed...the only thing to do, if you weren't going to get hurt, as well as the woman they were chasing." Then, embarrassed, she added candidly, "I didn't really think about it at all. I acted on instinct."

Roxanne's full lips curled ever so slightly in a smile. "Your instincts were good. At least as good as mine. I didn't think, either. I only knew I had to stop them stoning her to death...."

The smile faded, and Christina wondered if she had only imagined it in the first place.

Neither of them mentioned the gypsy Leonie, but each knew the other had been thinking of her. They walked, silent now and oblivious to the sunshine and the brilliance of the autumn leaves, back to the wharf.

It was Megan who spoke first.

"Look! She's made it into the harbor! There's the *Edwin J. Beaker*! Now we'll get our belongings back!"

Christina supposed she ought to be relieved, since the bundles and the trunks on board were all they possessed in the world.

Yet she felt shaken by their recent experience, and for the moment the clothes did not seem to matter very much.

Somehow she had not expected to encounter such prejudice and hatred here, and she was too disturbed by what might have been a real tragedy to be philosophical about it yet.

She stood with her sisters on the dock and watched the longboat from the *Edwin J. Beaker* move toward them across the bay. Even by the time it had reached the wharf, her heartbeat had not subsided to its normal pace.

CHRISTINA HAD IMAGINED this moment many times: the three of them would be faced and verbally examined by prospective masters, and some kind and wealthy benefactor would smile and accept them as indentured servants.

Occasionally she had indulged in the most pleasant daydreams—a romantic liaison for Roxanne, perhaps, which would settle her down, a good home for Megan where there were children she could serve and love, and for herself, simply an endurable period of indenture ending up with Vilas, too, wanting to settle down and marry her.

She knew these fantasies were only that. Listening to Roxanne spin her tall tales had perhaps stretched her own imagination further than it would normally have gone, yet a fantasy harmed no one.

Only now, faced with the reality of these sober-faced Boston citizens who evaluated them as if they were prize cattle, Christina was unable to control the tremors that ran through her. There were only four men in the room, in addition to Captain Stratton—who cared about nothing except collecting the passage money from one of them—and none was the smiling, genial, generous master she had conjured up in her wishful thinking.

A glance at Roxanne showed her to be scrutinizing the men as openly as she was being observed. Christina wished fervently that she'd thought to warn her to lower her gaze, to appear modest and retiring, yet there she was, boldly meeting the eyes of the least appealing of the quartet.

Not him, Christina thought, her mouth dry. She had thought the Puritans—and judging by their garb, each of them belonged to that religious sect—would be an ascetic lot, not given to the robust sins of the flesh demonstrated at home by such as Lord Windom—but this man induced in her no confidence of that. He was perhaps forty, rather heavily built and handsome in a suety way; his dark eyes rested hotly on Roxanne's face, then visibly traveled down over the straining bodice of her gown as if picturing what lay beneath the fabric of it. Even as Christina watched, he licked his lips in a manner that made her swallow hard.

Dear God, indentured servants were to earn out their passage money in respectable tasks, weren't they? No one would expect more than that of them?

Roxanne held her head high, and her expression altered ever so slightly, to one of dismissal. It was as if she, not these men, was the one in control, the one who would decide.

The man saw, correctly interpreted and flushed with anger, though he said nothing.

Christina felt Megan's hand creep into her own and was not certain whether the trembling was Megan's or her own or a combination of the two. All bravery felt in Cornwall had fled; Christina was frankly terrified.

Her gaze moved on to the second man, whose appraisal seemed of a less licentious nature, yet just as sober, perhaps censurous. The girls had worn the plainest gowns they owned, and it was too warm in the room to have concealed them under their cloaks. All of these masculine faces seemed judgmental, she thought. Found them wanting.

For all Daisy Meek's encouraging words about their youth, strength and good health, Christina felt a surge of panic: what if no one chose to take them on, thinking them worthless for servants?

"Well, gentlemen?" Captain Stratton prodded, breaking the silence that had gone on too long. "Do I have an offer? Sturdy, good workers, all three of them."

The third of the three men cleared his throat. "Don't look as if they're much used to scrubbing and chopping wood and all such. Gentry, ain't they?"

"Aye, quality stock," Stratton agreed. "Educated, even. Can all read and write. And what they lack in experience at menial tasks can soon be remedied. They're young and quick to learn."

The ensuing silence was not encouraging, and then the fourth man cleared his throat and stared at Megan. "I might could take the little one, be she good with younguns. Got no use for three of 'em, though."

Megan's hand jerked in her own, and Christina spoke quickly. "No, sir. My little sister and I stay together."

"I might could take on the other'n," the first man said, again running his tongue over his full lips. "I reckon she could learn kitchen work, has she any wits at all."

This time it was Roxanne who spoke. "Thank you, but no, sir. I've a mind to stay with my sisters. We none of us have anyone else but each other, and we'll not be separated."

Captain Stratton gave them a look of extreme irritation. "Hear, now! Nobody said aught about having to place all three of you together! I've a right to collect my money and go on about my business, without all this folderol about staying together! Nobody's going to take on the lot of you!"

Christina's throat constricted, but before she could come up with any reasonable response, a familiar voice sounded from the door on the far side of the room.

"I'm looking for servants. I'll engage the three of them."

Stratton sighed in relief. "Very good, sir. Step right over here and sign the papers."

Christina stared at the man who scarcely glanced at the trio waiting for their fate to be decided.

He was the man who had interceded on their behalf with the aggressive women in the street a few hours earlier.

"Your name, sir?"

"Adam Hull, of Boston and Ipswich."

"Master Hull, you've signed on for your money's worth," Stratton assured him. "Your signature right here, sir, and you've three females for three years' service."

The matter was done. For better or worse, the next step had been taken. Christina felt giddy and relieved and wondered if she dared ask where the nearest convenience was located, for her bladder was full to bursting after all this tension.

Adam Hull straightened from the table where he had laid the quill pen and stared at his new maidservants.

"Sisters, are you." It wasn't a question. "You don't look it, except for the eyes. Well, give me good service and you'll find me a fair master. 'Tis but a mile walk, and it's growing late; we'd best be about it."

He led the way out of the public building where the meeting had taken place, oblivious of anyone around him except to nod when he was greeted by name.

His mind was not on the passersby, nor even on the females he had just taken responsibility for. He was thinking of his daughter-in-law, who had begged—no, he amended in annoyance, she had *demanded*—that he find someone to help about the house since old Mary had become so crippled up they'd sent her home to her son to care for.

Well, he thought, she'd be taken aback by *three* servants, but the way Patience was continually taking to her bed and leaving the care of her infant to others, and Abigail herself had no motherly instincts whatever, no doubt there'd be work enough for three. It might take the edge off Abigail's sharp tongue if there was less to complain about.

And then Adam almost smiled to himself, recalling the episode in the street when these newcomers had faced down the small band of witch-hunters.

Abigail might meet her match in this batch, he thought in satisfaction. At the very least, they would provide a source of counterirritation.

He clapped his hat on his head and stepped out at a smart pace, leaving the girls to follow.

Chapter 18

"FOR AN OLD MAN," Roxanne muttered under her breath, "he walks mighty fast."

"And he doesn't talk much," Christina murmured in response, hoping Adam Hull hadn't overheard Roxanne. If he had, he gave no indication, striding ahead at a pace that required near running on their part to keep up.

Megan, who had seldom had the chance at home for lengthy walks because she'd been tied down with young Thomas, was getting a stitch in her side. She paused, though only momentarily, because Adam Hull was not waiting. "It says Cambridge Street. Isn't that where he said he lived? On Cambridge Street?"

"Not much farther, then," Christina encouraged her. She was tiring, too; her exercise had been much curtailed for the past weeks, with strolls around the deck of the *Edwin J. Beaker* limited to fair weather. "The homes here are nice ones, respectable looking."

The dwellings were, of course, more the size of the village cottages at home than of Kenwood, but they seemed sturdily built, mostly of wood with multipaned windows and high peaked roofs.

"That's because of the snow," Roxanne reported when Megan had commented on the uniformity of the roofs. "Daisy told me. They have to slant so the snow won't pile up and cause the building to cave in."

Startled, Megan had stumbled and clutched at Roxanne to catch herself. "That would take a tremendous amount of snow, surely!"

Snow was something they knew little of, having lived all their lives in the mild Cornwall climate. It was hard to imagine, walking through the afternoon sunshine that touched the skin like silk, and the bright foliage adding a feeling of additonal warmth, that winter could bring enough snow to crush roofs.

Of more immediate concern, though, was the family of Adam Hull, who strode ahead of them toward their new home. Christina was bursting with questions. How many were there in the household? What sort of people were they? But the man gave her no opportunity to voice them.

At least none of them had had to go with the man who had gazed at them while lasciviously moistening his fleshy lips; Adam Hull did not look the sort of man one would have to worry about in *that* way. In fact, it now occurred to her, he reminded her a bit of her father. She wasn't sure whether that was reassuring or not, for the earl of Kenwood had considered his servants to be on the level with his dogs, from whom he expected faithful service unto the death.

When Adam Hull stopped unexpectedly, turning back to face them for the first time since they'd set out to follow him through Boston Town, they nearly ran into him. Christina's heart thudded as she stared into the face with the big beaky nose and the thick white brows over startling blue eyes.

"This is it," he said. "Follow me."

A glance at Megan proved she, too, was nervous, and even Roxanne seemed subdued. Inhaling deeply, Christina led the way after Adam Hull into the frame house with the mullioned windows and the steep shingled roof. The die was cast. Whatever they came to here, it would be their lot for the next three years.

ABIGAIL HULL WAS FORTY-SEVEN, slight in build but overwhelming in presence; her eyes were a very pale blue, her hair gray under the plain cap, her lips thin and habitually compressed if one could judge by the lines around it.

"Three?" she asked, eyebrows rising, and not, Christina guessed, with delight. "Three? Father Adam, what are we to do with *three*?"

Surely, Christina thought, she imagined that amusement flickered in the old man's eyes. There had so far been no indieation that a sense of humor was one of his attributes.

"No doubt when we reach home there'll be work enough to go around," Adam stated, taking off his hat and hanging it upon the peg beside the door. "I doubt they've eaten since midday, nor have I. A meal would set well."

When they reached home? Was not this home, then? Christina was confused, and then she recalled that the old man had informed Captain Stratton that he was of Boston and Ipswich. Did that mean they were not remaining in Boston Town? Panic surged through her, though there was no time to dwell on it; if they left Boston for this unknown Ipswich, would Vilas find her?

"You know, Father Adam, that I have no servants here. A haunch is roasting for supper, but I fear it's not yet ready to eat." While her voice was carefully neutral, something in Abigail's eyes suggested resentment of his expectations.

"There's bread, and some of last night's mutton, is there not? A cold bite will do nicely for the moment, along with a good glass of ale."

He turned aside, leaving the newcomers to the mercies of his daughter-in-law, and moved toward the great brick hearth, where the joint roasted, sending out a savory aroma. The room, though large by Bay Colony standards, as they would learn, seemed very small to Christina and Megan as compared to the great hall of their childhood. The ceiling was low, low enough so that a man as tall as Adam would have to stoop to pass from one room to another, making the space still more confined.

Roxanne liked it at once. It reminded her of the cottage where she'd grown up. She had never taken a liking to stone walls and vast, cavernous, unheatable rooms. Here the floor was wide wooden boards, waxed and warm with handmade rugs. The furniture, though simple, was of richly polished woods: a table with a bench on either side, two chairs flanking the fireplace, which was large enough to have roasted an entire ox at one time. Open shelves displayed pewter plates and bowls, and on the face of the fireplace hung various pots and utensils. At the far end of the room, facing the fire, was a wooden settle padded with brown cushions, and a footstool placed before it.

Best of all, Roxanne saw with a lightening of spirits, was the bookcase above the settle, where two rows of books promised future hours of pleasure. A little of the tension she had managed to hide began to seep out of her, until she looked again at Abigail Hull.

She wasn't going to like Abigail.

The woman was staring at them, not moving. "Wherever are we going to sleep three more people, in a household already overflowing?" she demanded.

There was a bite to Adam's tone as he lowered himself into one of the chairs beside the fire. "Is there no satisfying you, woman? You wanted help. I've brought you help. Where is that cold joint?"

Abigail's lips flattened until they virtually disappeared. She crossed to a sideboard and began to set out food. "You, take this to the table," she said.

Christina cleared her throat. "I'm Christina, mistresss."

It was as if she hadn't spoken. Abigail gestured at Roxanne. "There's cider in the cask beside the door. Fill a pitcher."

"I'm Roxanne," the girl informed her, moving at no great speed toward the designated cask. The woman was a bitch, Roxanne thought. Indentured servant she might be, but there was no crushing the independence of spirit she had cultivated over the years. Three years stretched before Roxanne like decades; five minutes in this household and already she was feeling rebellion rising within her like mist from the moors.

The cider was good, however, the bread fresh and thickly spread with butter, the joint tasty and welcome after shipboard fare. At home, servants would have supped in the kitchen after the family had eaten in the great hall. Here, there was only one kitchen, which also served as the main room of the house. Servant and master shared the same table.

Christina wanted most urgently to ask about the rest of the family who overflowed the house—or was it another house, in Ipswich? She had no idea where Ipswich was; she could only hope that it was not far distant, though why would the Hulls require two homes close together? She could not, however, quite bring herself to ask. Not of Abigail, who chose not to eat with them but busied herself turning the spit and basting the joint roasting there. And not of Adam, who offered no conversational gambits of his own.

Roxanne, however, was impatient to know these things. When she had taken the edge off her hunger, she sipped at the cider and asked directly of the new master, "Are we not to remain here in Boston, then, sir?"

"Only for a few more days," Adam replied, wiping his mouth. "Then we return to Ipswich."

He would apparently have been content to leave it at that, but Roxanne persisted.

"We are unacquainted with this part of the world, sir. Where might Ipswich be?"

For a moment, when he hesitated with a bite of bread and meat halfway to his mouth, it seemed he might reprimand her for voicing her curiosity. He put the food into his mouth, chewed and swallowed before replying.

"Ipswich is some thirty miles to the north," he said. "Our family has many business interests in Boston, so we maintain a home here for our convenience. But we prefer to live in Ipswich. My son Ezra, his wife, Abigail, and I are here this week attending to various affairs, which should be completed within a day or two. We will be here over the Sabbath, and on Monday we sail for home."

"Sail?" Megan uttered the word involuntarily, and then flushed. When the man stared at her, she stammered, "We—we have been at sea overlong to look forward to another journey, but thirty miles? That will not take long, sir?"

"With good fortune no more than a day," he assured her dryly. "The weather can be unpredictable this time of year, however."

Roxanne set her mouth to ask more probing questions, but a glimpse of Christina's face dissuaded her, though she didn't see why Christina was so timorous about this. What was wrong with wanting to know what their lives would be like from now on?

She contented herself with another mug of the cider, which was delicious, and ignored Abigail until the woman addressed them once more.

"I have to go out. You may clear away the table and tidy up the house before I return. The spit will need tending, and there are vegetables to put into the kettle within the hour." She reached for a cloak from the peg and wrapped it around her shoulders; it was dark brown and, like her gown, the material was excellent; she gave the impression of subdued elegance. "Good day, Father Adam."

His only reply was a grunt. Then he, too, took down his hat from its peg and stood before the door. "I'll be back for supper in two hours' time," he said, and was gone.

The three of them stood for a few moments after the Hulls had gone, and then Christina began to smile.

"We're here, and while we don't seem exactly to have been welcomed with open arms, we have fallen into reasonably fortunate circumstances. We'll be adequately fed, it seems, and there'll be a sturdy roof over our heads."

"And we'll work ourselves to the dropping point," Roxanne added, though with commendable good spirits. "Which is what is expected of servants everywhere, no doubt. At least I don't have the fear that Adam Hull will creep into my bed at night and make demands I've no desire to accommodate."

A giggle worked its way up Christina's throat and escaped. "I wouldn't have been confident of that with some of the others."

Megan had walked to the doorway that led to an adjoining room. "This is one of the larger houses, but compared to Kenwood it's very tiny. Where are they going to put us to sleep?"

"Everyone's gone. Let's explore," Roxanne proposed.

"Maybe we'd better clear the table first," Christina demurred, "In case Mistress Hull comes back sooner than intended."

"Ah, she said she'd be gone for hours! How long will it take to look at the house? Come on," Roxanne said, and put a hand on Megan's shoulder to propel her into the next room.

It was nearly a twin of the one they left behind, though there was no fire on the hearth that stood back to back with its counterpart. There were two beds, several chairs, a chest for storing clothing and a long table that clearly served as a working place, for there were a ledger, pens and an ink pot and several books upon it.

"Doesn't look as if anyone spends much time here," Roxanne observed. "Come on, let's see what's up above."

Unlike the broad, shallow stairs at home, these were narrow and steep, with a sharp turn when they had nearly reached the top. The upper floor was much like the lower one, except that the ceiling was lower still, so that under the eaves no one but a child could have stood upright. Again there were back-to-back fireplaces of brick, each of them with wood laid ready to be lighted, and in each room were two beds and assorted chairs and chests. A few garments hung on wall pegs, but here, too, the house gave the impression of being infrequently used, for there were few personal items.

One exception was a book on a stand beside one of the beds: a Bible with a faint sifting of dust upon its cover. Roxanne made a face. "I'd have thought Mistress Abigail too fussy to allow anything to gather dust."

"She made a point of saying she had no servants here," Christina reminded her. She had opened up the Bible, to the page where family names were recorded in faded ink.

"Here! Look here, this may be the family we'll be serving!"

They stood together, reading through the Hull family history. Roxanne summed it up aloud.

"Adam Hull has buried three wives, the last of them less than a year ago, and he is . . . uh . . . seventy-two years old. Between the lot of them, they lost a total of eleven children. Three remain. Ezra, married to the admirable Mistress Abigail. No children to Ezra and Abigail. No wonder she looks so dried up. Ezra is . . . um . . ."

"Fifty," supplied Christina, who was quicker with figures.

"Yes. And the next son would be Wesley, who is . . ."

"Thirty-five."

"Yes, thirty-five. And he is married to Patience—no birth date given, because she's only a Hull by marriage—and she has lost two babes. Presumably the rest of these survive—your department, Megan."

Megan pushed between them to examine the page on her own, bending forward to more easily make out the bold handwriting. "Elizabeth, who would be eight. Nels, who is six. And a baby, Emory, who is less than a year old."

"And," Roxanne went on, not nearly as intrigued as Megan with the children, "there is Fitzhugh. Age twenty-five, no, twenty-four. I wonder if they call him Fitz or Hugh? He's the only eligible one. See, he was married to Hester, who died in childbirth last February."

"What do you mean, eligible?" Megan asked.

"I mean he isn't married. I wonder if the wealth is all his father's or if he shares in it? Well, he's been married, so he was able to care for a wife, obviously. I wonder what happened to the baby? It doesn't say anything about the baby; it must have died, too, though I'd think they might have said so."

"Maybe they just haven't gotten around to putting that in," Christina said softly. "So many babies dead. The same as at home."

And then she remembered that some of the deaths of the babies at home had been attributed to the curse of Leonie, Roxanne's mother, and she felt uncomfortable at having brought the matter up.

Roxanne, however, had not noticed. "I'll take a look at this Fitz. Or Hugh. Whatever they call him. It wouldn't do to have a daughter-in-law who was an indentured servant, would it? I don't fancy working under Mistress Abigail's thumb for three years."

"I thought you were taken with Captain O'Neal," Christina said without thinking, and then wished she hadn't.

Roxanne grinned. "Oh, he's handsome enough. But a female needn't confine her considerations to one man, need she? The thing is to make an advantageous marriage, and since no one here knows I'm the illegitimate issue of an earl—and neither of you is going to tell them—I might make my own choice of husbands. After all, that's one reason I left Cornwall, isn't it? I didn't fancy going to bed with Master Beaker or anyone else of his ilk. Captain O'Neal, now, that's a more interesting idea. And I don't know yet about this Fitzhugh. I'll wager he's attractive. I think the old man was, when he was younger," she added unexpectedly.

Megan blinked. It was hard for her to imagine Adam Hull as a young, handsome man. "I think we'd best clear away downstairs, so we don't get caught snooping around. We don't want to start out on the wrong foot with our new employers."

There was much lighthearted banter as they cleared the table and washed the utensils they had used. Roxanne had another mug of cider and began to do an impersonation of their new mistress, giving orders to the others, criticizing the way they wiped up the crumbs and swept the floor and turned the spit.

"No, no, not backward, but forward, you dolt!" she cried when Megan adjusted the position of the roasting meat.

They were all laughing when the door opened and a man walked in and stopped, his Puritan face frozen.

The laughter died.

They guessed his identity at once, from his resemblance to Adam. This would be the oldest son, Ezra. He was stockier than his father; the face was much the same: a big nose, brushy eyebrows—his were gray, rather than white—and penetrating blue eyes.

"And who," he asked with no hint of humor, "might you be?"

Megan was stricken dumb. Roxanne fell silent. It was left to Christina to find her tongue.

"We are indentured servants to Master Adam Hull," she managed.

The man's gaze stripped her of all assurance. "All three of you?" he asked, incredulous.

"Yes, sir. We're sisters, and we wanted to stay together."

Clearly he found this an insufficient reason for his father to have acted so rashly. "Here? Or at home?"

"Master Hull said we would all be going to Ipswich." Her voice was barely audible.

He considered that briefly, then removed his hat to reveal hair the color of his eyebrows. "Are you capable of pouring a man a dollop of cider?"

"Yes, of course," Christina said quickly, but it was Roxanne who moved to do it.

There was no more laughter, no more joking. They didn't really know what to do with themselves when Ezra Hull sat at the table with his cider, perusing a newspaper that had a well-worn look about it.

They finally took seats on the settle and remained, hands folded in their laps, until it was time to put the vegetables into the pot.

When Ezra rose and without speaking let himself out the rear door, Roxanne peeked out the window after him. "He's heading for the outhouse. I thought I'd choke, imagining it."

"What?" Megan asked. "His going to the outhouse?"

Roxanne's mirth escaped in a strangled laugh. "No. Him in bed with Mistress Abigail!"

Even Christina was convulsed, though afterward she thought it might have been more nerves than because it was so funny. Unfortunately, they were still trying to control their amusement when Ezra reentered the house.

His glare squelched them at once. Except that, for the next hour before his wife returned, every time any of their eyes met, they choked again, smothering the sounds in coughs and throatclearings, because they were all remembering the mental picture that Roxanne had painted.

Chapter 19

THEIR BRIEF SOJOURN in Boston Town was an illuminating and frustrating transition from the kind of life they had known to the life they would lead now in the Massachusetts Bay Colony.

Clearly the Hull home was one of the richest and most comfortable in the town of some nine thousand souls. Adam Hull was a respected and well-to-do businessman, with varied interests and a firm control over both his investments and his household. Had it not been for the latter, Christina feared they would have done even less well under the tutelage of Abigail Hull.

During the endless boring hours aboard ship, they had pumped Daisy Meeks about many aspects of keeping house, a subject on which they were, for the most part, abysmally ignorant. Roxanne had spent her early life in a small cottage where she had learned a few basic skills, such as tending a fire. Christina and Megan knew nothing of fires, beyond the fact that the warmth was welcome on cold days. Servants had kindled fires and kept them fueled.

"Now," Megan said ruefully, "*we're* the servants."

Their initial attempts to swing an ax, splitting the wood stacked in the lean-to at the back of the house, convinced them that many seemingly simple tasks were not only difficult, they could be dangerous. Christina shaved the end of her shoe and stared at it in dismay even after she realized she had not amputated a toe. Roxanne sent a chunk of wood flying so that Megan was struck in the shin, making a purple mark almost at once, even through her skirts and petticoats.

Chopping wood was done unsupervised. Their inexperience was apparent only to themselves. Inside the house it was a different matter.

"At least at Kenwood," Roxanne muttered once, "we didn't stand around watching and criticizing every move a servant made. We didn't all have to be in the same room at the same time."

Here, Abigail kept a critical eye on virtually every activity. When Megan chopped vegetables for a stew she was so intimidated by Abigail's pursed lips—"*Bite*-size pieces, girl, not chunks that would choke a horse!"—that she nearly lost a finger. Blood dripped onto the floor and had to be scrubbed up, and more water carried to rinse the carrots and the dripping finger, which fortunately stopped bleeding quickly once Christina wrapped a rag around it.

Megan was not the only casualty. Christina, in trying to maneuver a heavy pot off its hook over the fire so that its lid might be lifted for the addition of a forgotten ingredient, burned her hand.

The pain was excruciating. She broke out in a cold sweat, and her vision glazed with shock. It was Roxanne who came to the rescue with, first, cold water, and then an application of wet tea leaves. Those measures provided only minimal relief; the burn kept her awake that night, biting her lip to keep from crying out.

Although there were empty beds in the house, Abigail had them bring in pallets to place by the kitchen fire—"Take care it doesn't go out during the night, but keep it banked; there's no need to waste firewood this time of year, when we don't really require the heat,"—and Christina, nursing the injured hand, sat on the edge of the lumpy pallet, wondering how long the pain of it would endure. Many years earlier, when she was a small child, one of the maidservants at Kenwood had died of burns suffered when she had tripped and fallen into the fire.

Christina remembered how the woman had screamed and writhed and cried out mindlessly for several days before succumbing to the burns. Dear Heaven, she thought, what must it have been like, to have burns such as this over most of her body!

"Christina?"

The low voice brought her head around, to where Roxanne had raised on one elbow, visible in the faint light from the fireside. "Are you all right?"

The tears were audible in her voice, as well as dampening her cheeks. "It hurts so. If only there were some way to cool the fire of it!"

Roxanne sat up and crawled toward her. "I'll fetch some more cold water. That may help."

The water, from a barrel outside the rear door, had been chilled by the night air. It did bring temporary relief, and by the time her own body temperature had warmed the water Roxanne had prepared more tea leaves. Still, it was toward dawn when exhaustion allowed Christina to fall into a restless sleep.

By the following day the reddened skin had blistered. Abigail took one look at it, pursing her lips as if to indicate that the injury was the result of Christina's own ineptitude, but she'd produced unsalted butter to smooth over it. "You'd best work away from the fire today," she conceded. "The heat will make it burn worse."

Abigail watched as Roxanne bound another poultice of wet tea leaves over the burn, her pale eyes sharp. "You have some knowledge of healing?" she asked.

Roxanne barely glanced at her, intent on securing the poultice in place. "My mother knew a bit about herbs and healing. She died when I was but twelve, and I don't remember it all."

Abigail considered that, then changed the subject. "I'll be out this afternoon. There's a basket of mending, there, if you run out of the things I've asked you to do." She paused, then added, "With three of you, the chores should always be taken care of very quickly."

Roxanne stared at the door that had closed behind the woman a moment later. "Not if she works as hard as she has so far to think up things for us to do. Dusting! When we dusted yesterday, and there's no dust to be seen!"

Megan was already picking up the basket of garments to be mended. "We can do this, Christina. Why don't you try to rest? You didn't sleep much last night."

"I won't sleep now, either," Christina decided wearily. "I might as well do the dusting. I can do that with one hand."

Learning to cook would have had them laughing if it hadn't been for their apprehensions over the poor results. Listening to Daisy tell how to prepare something was a different matter from actually doing it.

"Did she say to cut the meat up first? And how long will it take for the joint to cook? What if it isn't done by the time Master Adam and Master Ezra are ready to eat it?"

"How much molasses should I put in this?"

"The biscuits are like rocks. What did I do wrong?"

"How was I to know the mush would swell up that way and overflow the kettle?"

"Well, at least mush is easy to cook once you learn how much to put in," Megan conceded. "And it seems a large part of the diet of these Bay Colony people. I like it, too, better than the porridge we had at home."

"It's not bad if you don't scorch it," Roxanne agreed. "I thought for a minute she'd say to dump it out, but I suppose she's too thrifty to waste food. At Kenwood it would have been fed to the dogs."

Abigail took several mouthfuls of the first meal they had prepared entirely on their own, in her absence, and put down her spoon. "Did any of you ever see a kitchen before you came here?"

"We're not particularly experienced in the kitchen," Roxanne admitted in a masterful understatement. "But we're doing our best, mistress."

Abigail's flattened lips suggested their best fell far short of her standards. It was Adam Hull who put an end to the discussion. "They'll learn. They're quick-witted enough," he said, and that was that, for the time.

"If Captain O'Neal comes for supper tomorrow night," Abigail stated, "it seems I'll have to do the cooking myself."

She did not notice the quick glances exchanged between the sisters, nor the sudden rush of color to Roxanne's cheeks.

"Captain O'Neal?" Christina echoed involuntarily. "The pi—the privateer?"

Abigail gave her a curious look. "The same. You have heard of him, then."

"Yes, he…it was his ship that rescued us when our own lost a mast."

"You will want to see that he enjoys his meal with us, in that case. After a time at sea, he is always hungry for fresh meats and fruits."

Roxanne had gone from flushed to rather pale. "He is . . . a frequent visitor in your home?"

"When he is in port, yes. He and my husband and my father-in-law do considerable business together. There are goods he has to sell, and I'm hoping that will include some European fabrics this time. The ones available in the Bay Colony tend to be rather coarse, and I've need of new gowns." Abigail pointedly scrutinized their clothes. "As will you, I suspect. Your garments are hardly suitable for females of your class."

Taken aback, the trio instinctively moved closer together. "Unsuitable, mistress? In what way?" Christina dared to ask.

"The fabrics are much too rich for indentured servants. And the colors are more appropriate to those of the higher classes."

Now it was Christina whose cheeks flamed. "I'm sorry, mistress. They are all we have, and we have no funds to replace them."

Was there envy in the older woman's face as she examined the gowns they wore? They were old—Christina's had, in fact, belonged originally to her mother—but it was true they were of good quality, and in a city where virtually everyone wore more sober colors, no doubt blue and green and dark wine-red did stand out.

"How is it," Abigail asked, "that you come to have such gowns as these?"

"They are what our father provided," Christina said.

"And who is your father?"

"He was the earl of Kenwood."

Disbelief flickered across the woman's face. "An earl? Yet you are here as indentured servants?" Incredulity shifted to the beginnings of anger, as she suspected that she was being made sport of. "Unseemly levity and untruthfulness are not only frowned upon here, but are punishable offenses," she said tightly.

Roxanne's response was hot and quick. "Calling people liars can cause trouble, where we come from."

Christina drew in a distressed gasp, wanting to smack her. "Mistress Hull, we *are* the daughters of the late earl of Kenwood. Upon his death, and the loss of his protection, we were forced to flee from England. You can verify this through our cousin, Vilas de Clement, when he arrives. He was to sail a few weeks after we did but on a much faster ship; he may be arriving any day now."

Abigail visibly weighed this, decided it had some grain of truth and sighed. "The fact remains that it is inappropriate for females of your class to appear in such garments. I will take it up with Father Adam and the matter will be resolved."

To Christina's vast relief, the subject was dropped for the moment. There was, however, another thing to be resolved. It was hours before she had a chance to bring it up with Roxanne in private, when they were carrying slop jars to the privy.

"Roxanne, please think before you speak. There's nothing to be gained and much to be lost by antagonizing the woman."

"I'd have said the same thing if I'd thought it over first," Roxanne said coolly, stepping first into the outhouse to empty her container.

Christina tried to suppress her exasperation. "Then don't speak at all!"

"Who gave you the authority to make all the decisions, even about what I say?"

"Nobody. I don't want to be the authority. But whatever you do or say reflects on Megan and me, as well as yourself. The woman is difficult, yet it's possible she may be won over if we try. Insulting or defying her isn't likely to be helpful."

Roxanne stepped aside so that Christina could empty her pot. "Well, maybe I won't be with you much longer. Captain O'Neal expressed an interest in my company. And I take it he's wealthy enough to pay off an indentureship."

Christina's mouth went slack. "He can't have proposed already! On the basis of one meeting?"

"I didn't say he'd proposed marriage," Roxanne said, nettled. "I said he was interested in me."

Christina's green eyes were wide under the thick lashes. "You'd not go to him except in marriage, surely."

Roxanne shrugged. "It might be preferable to leave Madame Razor Tongue in there under any circumstances. Come on, let's rinse these things out and go see what we're to do in preparation for Captain O'Neal's supper. We may have learned enough so that it won't be scorched, if we're lucky."

Christina followed her back to the house, not reassured. Roxanne had always spoken her mind without considering the consequences. Perhaps she should have been encouraged to go her own way instead of remaining with the other two. Well, there was little to be done about that at this stage.

Abigail spoke sharply as they reentered the house. "If you persist in dawdling over every chore, we'll not be ready when Father Hull returns with Captain O'Neal. Christina, we've need of a few items from the market. You should be able to find it easily enough; just retrace your steps toward the bay until you come to it. Can you remember half a dozen items?"

"I think so. But to be on the safe side, why don't I write them down?"

"You can read and write?" Again Abigail was distrustful.

"Yes. We all can."

"Very well. There are some bits of birch bark on the writing table in the other room; fetch them and make the list. And don't tarry along the way. Father Hull likes his meals on time."

It was advice Christina fully intended to take. Until, her purchases completed and stowed in her basket, she turned away from the market vendor and saw a familiar blond head that stood out above the milling crowd of shoppers.

Her breathing ceased, and a strangled cry caught in her throat. Then she was pushing her way through the women who had not yet made their purchases, toward the one person she wanted most in the world to see. Her body was flooded with warmth and vitality, her limbs infused with new strength, her heart with new courage.

"Vilas!" she called out. "Oh, Vilas, you're here!"

Chapter 20

VILAS DE CLEMENT had always stood out among other men: his stature and his fair good looks assured that. Here, among these Puritans, his garments were an additional guarantee that he would not pass unnoticed.

He wasn't wearing the scarlet cloak—the day was warm enough so that he didn't need it—but the rich deep blue of his doublet and knee breeches would have been enough to set him apart from all those black and brown homespuns.

He heard her call and turned with a welcoming grin and a shout. "Chris! I'd just asked directions to find you! I saw that old bucket with her broken mast and for a moment feared the worst!"

Christina so far forgot herself as to run into his arms for a hug. It was too cousinly for her taste; she had dreamed—admittedly building on no reality—of a lover's embrace when they were reunited.

However, the solid feel of his body pressed, however briefly, against her own sent prickles of delight through her. His arms were strong and eager, at least for a few moments.

Then he held her off, laughing down into her face. "You stand out like a rose among the thorns in this place! I always liked you in green; it brings out the light in your eyes."

"Mistress Hull finds green, and velvet, inappropriate to our new station in life," Christina responded. "No doubt within the month we'll be in brown kersey like everyone else. I'm glad you found me before then. How are you, Vilas? You had a good voyage?"

"Better than you did, from what I've been told." His hands still rested on her shoulders, burning through the fabric of her gown. "You look well enough, after what you've been through. How is Roxanne? And Megan?"

"Well. Though I don't know how we're going to fit into this society of Puritans. Especially Roxanne. She doesn't *think* before she speaks."

Vilas laughed, drawing the attention of the women at marketing chores around them. If there was disapproval or reservation about the garb of this pair, there was also interest in the eyes that rested upon this blond young giant.

"She hasn't changed, then. You have, I think. You've grown up a bit, Chris."

"I began to grow up when I realized my father was dying." No sooner were the words spoken when she saw something change in his face, a wariness come into his blue eyes. "What is it, Vilas? You have bad news?"

"Aye. It's young Thomas. Megan will take it hard, no doubt."

"Thomas? What's happened to him?"

"He's dead," Vilas said simply. "A riding accident, not a week after you sailed. Lady Jacobina will wed Lord Windom before the mourning period is decently observed, it seems, and his influence is already apparent."

Christina stood very still. Thomas had not been her favorite person in the entire world, but he had been only a little boy. And Megan had loved him dearly.

"What happened?" The words caused an ache in her throat.

"Lord Windom decided the boy must learn to ride, only instead of the pony the earl would have bought him, the child was set astride a stallion." Vilas's teeth closed with an audible click; the muscles in his jaws and neck bulged for a moment with his effort at control. "It was murder, pure and simple, if you ask me. Lord Windom wanted the child out of the way, and that's what he got."

She felt sickened. "Did he . . . was it . . . quick?"

"He broke his neck. He lived only a matter of hours."

Christina swallowed. She swayed slightly on her feet, putting her hands onto her cousin's chest, where he covered them with his own and held them. Not even that distraction, however, could divert from the horror of his tale. "And Lady Jacobina, how does she take it?"

"Prostrate with grief, at least for a day or two. Yet she turns to Windom for comfort."

"How will I tell Megan? She already felt guilty about leaving him." Tears blurred her vision; she leaned against him so that his arms went around her once more. No doubt this was improper behavior among these damned Puritans, too, she thought, not caring.

"Her staying wouldn't have helped. Windom would still have insisted upon riding lessons. The boy would still have been put upon a stallion, or an accident would have happened with a pony. Or the child would have fallen off a parapet, something. Thomas was doomed from the moment his father fell ill."

"From the moment Lady Jacobina poisoned him, you mean," Christina said bitterly. "Oh, I knew we must escape from her, but I'm not sure how well we'll do here, among the Puritans. So far we do not blend in very well, and it's not only a matter of clothes. They actually have laws prohibiting people of 'our station' from wearing fine fabrics or lace and embroidery!"

"An odd lot, I've heard," Vilas agreed. "Yet fair-minded in their business dealings, it seems. I've heard of a privateer who deals with them regularly—as a matter of fact, the Bostonians are surprisingly liberal in their views of dealing with privateers and even pirates, when profits are to be made—and I've a mind to seek him out and see if he needs another crew member. After working out my passage under Captain Loring I know I care not to sail with him further, but the sea and the ships draw me. I think I might like being on something other than a merchant ship."

Christina drew back, though they were still clasping hands. "A privateer? Not . . . not Captain O'Neal?"

"Shea O'Neal, the very same. You know of him?"

"He's the one who rescued us when Captain Stratton put us ashore on that island after the mast was broken. Roxanne is taken with him." She hesitated, then added, turning belatedly to rescue the basket she had set aside the moment she saw him, "He's to be a guest of the Hulls for supper tonight."

Vilas, who had laughed when she mentioned Roxanne, sobered at once. "O'Neal? Can you introduce me?"

"Vilas, he's . . . he's not the sort I'd seek out to sign on with."

"Why not?"

"Because he's ... well, he calls himself a privateer, but he's no more than a pirate! I'm grateful that he rescued us, though there was something between him and Roxanne that ..." She hesitated, then decided not to pursue that line of thought. "Anyway, before he rescued us, he attacked us at sea, and took a chest from Captain Stratton! When reminded that we sailed under the flag of England, he retorted that in his view a privateer might, at his own discretion, use the authority granted to him to right his own wrongs as well as those against the Crown. We thought our captain might well suffer a fatal seizure because of it."

Far from being appalled at this tale, Vilas seemed both intrigued and amused. "As well he might have! Old devil that he is, he's probably overdue for his just desserts."

"Captain Stratton?" Indignation rose within her. "You consider him a rogue, yet you sent us on his ship?"

"We had to get you out of Cornwall in rather a hurry, if you'll recall. His was the only ship available. And," Vilas added, selecting an apple from her basket and biting into it so that the skin snapped from the force of it, "he's going to be in hot water when he returns home. Not only for the cost of replacing a mast, and most likely for the contents of the trunk O'Neal carried away, but because Lord Windom eventually figured out that the three of you must have been aboard the *Edwin J. Beaker* when it sailed, since you couldn't be traced anywhere else. Beaker hoped to wed the fair Roxanne, and he was livid."

A chill ran through her, and Christina drew her shawl more closely around her shoulders. "They searched for us, then? They tried to find us?"

"Oh, indeed! Your stepmother might well have throttled you if she'd caught up to you. She did not inform me of the particulars, naturally, but I got the distinct impression that she had some sort of arrangement with Beaker and Hunnicutt that was to her advantage beyond just getting you and Roxanne out of Kenwood. She screamed and threw things, and Windom jumped. He, too, was angry over the wrecking of his coach and having to track down his horses, but he eventually decided that had been a false clue to your whereabouts. For a bit, there, I was afraid they'd lay your escape at my feet, for there were suspicions in that quarter. Luckily I, too, left England before their suspicions could be confirmed. Oh, this is splendid, I won't even have to seek O'Neal out in the usual places. A social introduction will be better than any other."

He took her arm, but Christina did not fall into step with him.

"Mistress Hull is not the most hospitable female I've ever encountered. I don't know if she'll welcome you or not."

"Ah, I've been told of the universal hospitality offered in the Bay Colony! Strict the Puritans are, and prim and proper, but they don't turn away anyone who is hungry. If supplies are short, they share. It's their Christian duty."

Christina stared pointedly at the blue doublet with its silver lacings. "You scarcely look a charity case."

"Looks are deceiving," Vilas said cheerfully. "I have clothes but no coin. I worked for my passage, not for a wage. Come along, they must be expecting you with this basket if you're to prepare a meal for Captain O'Neal. Let's go and meet this dragonness of yours, and after I've charmed her into inviting me to stay for supper, too, I'll handle matters with O'Neal myself."

"Your self-confidence is truly amazing," Christina said, but she could hardly regret that they were not met only to part at once. "You'll have your work cut out for you, though, with Mistress Hull."

"Trust me," Vilas said, grinning. "Here, let me take the basket."

"There'll be no apples left by the time I get home with it," Christina objected, laughing. With Vilas at her side, however briefly, everything else faded into insignificance.

Her heart soared, her lips smiled of their own accord and the lights sparkled in her green eyes as they began the walk back to Cambridge Street.

SHE OUGHT NOT TO HAVE BEEN ASTONISHED when Vilas did, indeed, charm Abigail into an invitation to supper.

While the older woman had greeted Christina with, "Well, mistress, it took you long enough," she acknowledged the introduction to Vilas with civility.

"This is the cousin of whom I spoke," Christina said, reminding her of the doubt she'd had about the girls being of the nobility. "He was my father's heir apparent until my little half brother was born." She remembered, then, what had happened to Thomas, and her voice faltered as she glanced toward Megan, who sat before the fire with a basket of mending.

"An earl, this was?" Abigail said. The tone of her voice suggested that she was, in spite of herself, impressed.

"The earl of Kenwood, yes, ma'am. I am relieved to find my cousins under such excellent supervision, Mistress Hull. They have been sheltered and kept innocent until their father's death, and I've been concerned about them. My worries have been for naught, it seems."

Abigail thawed slowly. Vilas was naturally adept at putting others at ease, however. He was careful not to carry flattery too far; his ingenuous manner was convincing. He drew her out by asking questions about the Bay Colony and her husband and father-in-law. He also told entertainingly about his own voyage to America, as an unskilled seaman.

"You learn quickly, though, under those conditions. And I find I've a liking for the sea, as well as for this new land. When my ship sets sail for Bristol, I'll not be on it. I've a mind to find a place here, where I can occasionally ascertain that my cousins are doing well."

Christina could have sat listening to him indefinitely, had it not been for her apprehension about how Megan would take his sad news. That, and Abigail's orders for the preparation of supper, which required that she go at once to work.

Roxanne, turning the spit with its burden of a haunch of venison, spoke under her breath when Christina came near enough to start the corn bread baking in the oven. "What is it? What's wrong?"

Startled, Christina glanced toward Megan, who was engrossed in darning a large sock, listening to Vilas and Abigail who by now were chatting with near amiability about Boston politics. How dare he, she wondered, when he knew less than nothing about the subject! "What?" She turned and saw concern in Roxanne's eyes.

"I'd expect you to be ecstatic about meeting Vilas, but there's something wrong." For a moment Roxanne forgot to turn the spit, and the hot grease spat as it dripped into the fire.

"He brought bad news, and I'll have to tell Megan." Christina kept her voice very low. "Thomas is dead. Lord Windom caused him to be put up onto a stallion for a riding lesson. There was an . . . an accident, and Thomas broke his neck."

Roxanne, who had considered the boy an unpleasant brat, was nevertheless taken aback. The epithet she used to describe Windom would have brought a sharp reprimand from Abigail had she heard it; Christina only nodded. "Murder, Vilas called it. It will break Megan's heart."

"She'll think she could have prevented it, had she stayed," Roxanne agreed. Her color was high, part of it from her proximity to the fire, part from recently kindled anger. And most of all from the prospect of seeing Shea O'Neal within the hour. "Maybe it would be best not to tell her."

Christina considered that. "I'm not sure I can conceal it, it upsets me so. And Vilas is sure to mention it, sooner or later."

Christina moved away to set the table as Abigail had instructed. That, at least, was something she knew about, though she'd never done it at home; she had eaten at a larger table, and more lavishly, all her life.

She had always daydreamed; listening to Roxanne's tales during their voyage had fueled her imagination in different ways. When she did not look at Abigail, it was easy to pretend that this was her house, that Vilas had returned here as a loving husband, that in a little while they would go up the stairs. They would undress before the fire she would have lighted earlier on the hearth, and she would see Vilas's body and he hers, before they embraced and made love on one of those beds that were too fine for mere servants to use.

When she turned from the table, however, away from the correctly set table with its pewter plates and candlesticks displayed on the linen cloth, there was Abigail, rising from the settle where she had been listening to Vilas.

"I believe that is my husband coming now," she said. "We would be pleased to have you dine with us, Master de Clement, and meet our other guest, Captain O'Neal."

The dream fell away. It was Abigail's house, and Vilas was not her husband, nor even her lover.

Yet the memory of the dream lingered, and Christina knew that she would make it come true, if she could.

Chapter 21

VILAS PROVIDED A VIVID CONTRAST, in his blue doublet and breeches, to the Hulls in their somber grays. But once Shea O'Neal arrived, it was he who outshone the lot of them, including Roxanne, who had chosen to wear—in a deplorable show of defiance, Christina thought—the jade velvet gown she had been allowed to keep.

O'Neal exuded confidence, and his finery would have done justice to King William himself. His coat was of scarlet, laced with gold and revealing a collar of white linen that dripped Brussels lace, which also showed at his wrists, and the buff breeches were secured with golden buckles just above well-polished French bucket-top boots.

Vilas caught her astonished gaze as Christina finally turned it from the guest, and he grinned. As for Christina, she felt resentment that the Hulls accepted the privateer in his gaudy garb while she and her sisters were criticized for far less lavish and colorful apparel.

"It's good of you to have me, Mistress Hull," O'Neal said, bowing low and sweeping off his hat with a lavish flourish of feathers. "I always enjoy your company and your table when I am in Boston Town."

Abigail nodded, smiling. "You are welcome, I'm sure, Captain. I believe you are already acquainted with our new bound servants. You do not know Master de Clement, I think?"

The two men measured one another in the way that young men do; sizing up, evaluating, then accepting. Adam Hull called for a tot of warming rum to be brought, for the evening grew cool, and the men stood at one corner of the room, talking, as the meal was set out.

At home, as servants, the girls would have been banished to another part of the castle for their own supper. Here, once they had brought the platters and bowls to the table, they sat down with the family. A chair was brought to the head of the table for Adam; its mate served opposite him for Ezra. The others made do with the long benches on either side.

Christina did not have to maneuver to sit next to Vilas; Megan was on his other side, while Roxanne and Abigail flanked Captain O'Neal, at Abigail's direction.

Heads were bowed while Adam intoned the grace—mercifully rather shorter than was customary, perhaps in deference to their guests, yet long enough so that Christina began to feel giddy from the aromas drifting beneath her nostrils. Or was it because she could feel Vilas's strong thigh pressed against her own?

She raised her head when the "Amen" was intoned and guessed at once that Roxanne was having similar feelings regarding O'Neal's proximity, for the girl's face was flushed and her lips curved in a smile.

The men, of course, led and dominated the supper table conversation. Little of it was of any interest to Christina: talk of tariffs and taxes, dissatisfaction with the way those matters were being handled by the British Parliament and the colonists' frustrations over the current lack of a Bay Colony charter. For a moment, when Ezra spoke of skirmishes with Indians, her apprehension rose, until it was made clear that the fighting took place well to the north and was not an immediate threat to the residents of Boston.

For the most part Christina was nearly unaware of anything except the presence of Vilas beside her, the warmth of his thigh, the way his elbow occasionally brushed her own as he maneuvered knife and fork. Even the food, delicious and varied as it was, was eaten automatically and without proper appreciation. She could not think of food when Vilas was so near.

His quick grasp of colonial affairs brought forth her admiration. The way his thick fair hair fell forward over his brow, the keenness in his blue eyes, the faint, almost invisible stubble on his freshly shaved jaw, the shape and strength of his hands all fascinated her. If only those hands would touch her with love, she thought with longing. And then went dizzy when he suddenly put a hand over hers on the edge of the table and said, "Isn't that right, Chris?"

She had no idea what he was talking about. She had been too raptly engaged in covert examination of him—without, she hoped, being obvious about it—to stay in tune with the conversation.

"Y-yes, of course," she murmured, and hoped that agreement made sense.

Across the table, Roxanne regarded her with sardonic amusement, and Christina flushed. Roxanne knew she hadn't known what she was replying to and undoubtedly had figured out why, as well.

Vilas removed his hand almost at once, but the touch had sent fire shooting through her, a heat so enveloping that it was difficult to breathe.

"You'll not be returning to England, then, Master de Clement?" Abigail asked. With two guests at the table, she seemed more pleasant, more relaxed, than at any time with only her bound servants.

Vilas had just speared a forkful of tender venison, which he now rested back on his plate. "No, ma'am, I think not. England has little to hold one with no financial prospects. There seems more opportunity to be had here in the New World. I've a mind to try the sea, for I took a liking to it." Now he ate the meat, and then spoke again. "In fact, I had made up my mind to seek out Captain O'Neal here and ask if he had room for another seaman."

Christina's heartbeat accelerated. She had hoped Vilas would look for adventure and his fortune on land, somewhere near at hand so that she could see him frequently. How could she make him fall in love with her if he was off privateering for months at a time?

Shea O'Neal shifted position on the long bench. Was Christina the only one who noticed the sudden change in Roxanne's face, a change so quickly masked? Her own recently heightened senses made Christina perceptive, and she made her own guess: When O'Neal stretched out his long legs, one thigh had come in solid contact with Roxanne's under the table, and the rigid control the girl was maintaining convinced Christina that he had not moved away; nor had she.

"As it happens, I might have need of a new mate. My present one has taken a fancy to a young lady whose father can put him in the way of a good living over in Salem. Do heights bother you, sir?"

Vilas turned his hands, revealing calloused palms. "I spent my share of time in the rigging, Captain." The marks of the ropes were there, proof of what he said.

"Come see me tomorrow aboard the *Revenge*," O'Neal invited. He fixed his smile on his hostess, the scar standing in sharp relief across his cheek. "You have never been aboard, Mistress Hull. Perhaps you, too, would care to visit. Along with your servants, if you like. I have many valuable goods beyond those I'm selling to Adam and Ezra. An especially fine gray woolen material that would make up into elegant gowns for Sabbath wear, for instance."

Abigail hesitated, though it was clear that she was intrigued. "The present gowns our servants wear are inappropriate for their station," she stated. "Though I scarcely think the fabric you describe is appropriate, either. Perhaps something of a coarser, more durable nature...."

Adam Hull helped himself to another serving of baked fish. "I see no reason to invest in expensive garments when they have gowns that can be made to do. When the present gowns are worn out will be time enough to consider replacing them."

"But Father Adam," Abigail protested, "the colors... greens, and blues, they'll stand out in meeting and attract unfavorable comment, most certainly! And they wear velvets and brocades, which you know are forbidden for the lower classes!"

"Waste and extravagance are also forbidden," Adam said dryly. "It would be wasteful in the extreme to discard wearable garments because of their color and richness. Can they not be dyed to more suitable colors?"

"Perhaps," Abigail said doubtfully, looking at Roxanne's green velvet. "At any rate, I would like to see the material of which you spoke, Captain. With my husband's permission I would accept your invitation to visit your ship."

Roxanne's pulse beat visibly at the base of her throat, though she sought to conceal her eagerness when she spoke. "Will you require our company, Mistress?"

"Yes, if there are parcels to carry, I may need all of you to help," Abigail decided. "It is decided, then, Captain. We will call."

"My men will be waiting with a longboat at midday," O'Neal said. "It would please me to return your hospitality with tea and cakes; I look forward to it."

Roxanne—fortunately unobserved by Abigail, whose attention was fixed on the privateer—was looking like a cat just offered a saucer of cream, Christina thought. Well, why wouldn't she? That she had developed a tendresse for Shea O'Neal had been plain from the start. Though if Abigail Hull realized this, it seemed unlikely that she would be a party to furthering Roxanne's desire to increase the opportunities in that direction.

Christina was more interested in her own prospects. Megan had risen to serve out hot slices of Boston brown bread, which she had just learned to make under Abigail's directions; it was dark and moist, rich with flavorful corn and rye flours and molasses, and the girls had taken to it as readily as had the Bay Colony settlers. There were appreciative murmurs around the table; under the cover of this attentiveness to the food, Christina stirred so that her arm brushed Vilas's elbow and spoke softly.

"And you, cousin? Will you be aboard the *Revenge* when we make our visit at midday?"

Vilas grinned. "I think I'll make my arrangements with Captain O'Neal before the ladies appear on the scene, so his attention isn't distracted from business."

Before her disappointment could fully surface, however, he added, "I've no doubt I can time my discussion so that I have not left before you arrive."

It was enough to carry her through the rest of the evening, while clearing the table and washing the dishes. The men sat around the fire in earnest discussion—how could they spend all their thoughts on such dull subjects as trading of merchandise taken from foreign ships by the privateer and the cost of Jamaica rum? For a religious sect that severely punished public drunkenness, the Puritans seemed inordinately fond of their rum, Christina thought.

Had it not been for the realization that she would have to tell Megan about Thomas, Christina would have been supremely happy that evening.

MEGAN'S EYES FILLED WITH TEARS, and she moved into Christina's embrace; her slim body quivered with the pain of the news, and Christina hugged her hard.

"You could have done nothing for him," she said softly. "And perhaps it's better this way than had he lived with a stepfather who did not want him, who would only have exploited him for his inheritance."

"And now Lord Windom will have it all," Megan said. "Everything that would have gone to Vilas, had Father still lived after Thomas's death. It isn't fair."

"I suspect very little in life is fair," Christina concurred, brushing her sister's hair back from her forehead. "But we did the right thing, I think, to sail for America rather than to remain in Cornwall. We are safer here, and even as indentured servants more in control of our destinies."

Later, when the household was abed and only the glow of coals on the hearth broke the darkness, Christina heard Megan's muffled sobs. She reached out a hand to comfort the younger girl and encountered Roxanne's hand there, as well. For a few moments the three of them were in communion, and then each withdrew her hand and the kitchen at last fell silent.

Tomorrow, Christina thought, putting aside all memory of Thomas, she would again see Vilas, and she fell asleep smiling.

Chapter 22

HAD IT NOT BEEN for the barely perceptible rise and fall of the ship as it rode at anchor, they might have felt as if they were having tea in some snug English cottage.

Sunlight streamed through the portholes to assist the lanterns that hung overhead from sturdy beams. The captain's cabin was barely large enough to accommodate all of them, but the small cakes and steaming tea were served by a burly seaman with an air of aplomb that made Christina wonder how often O'Neal did this sort of thing. Certainly he played the host to the hilt, and she watched the byplay between the privateer and Roxanne with mingled interest and uneasiness.

He hadn't invited them here for Mistress Hull's benefit, she thought. He could have brought the bolts of fabric to her house for examination, and far more conveniently for Abigail. He had chosen to do so because he wanted Roxanne aboard the *Revenge*, Christina decided.

She wouldn't have cared if they'd been more circumspect. Covert glances behind Abigail's back, smiles, a brushing of hands as this bolt or that was shifted for better viewing, all would eventually attract disapproving attention. Since the display was laid out on O'Neal's bunk, Abigail stood facing it— her back to the others—while she fingered the brocades and velvets and serges and even the laces that ladies other than Puritans would use to trim their gowns and their petticoats. Oblivious of observing eyes, Abigail even stroked a wine-colored velvet with one finger; so Puritan women, too, were drawn to the vivid hues that their leaders frowned upon.

Roxanne and O'Neal found numerous opportunities to make contact in the cramped quarters.

"Excuse me," Shea said, stepping around Roxanne to reach a bolt of rich, heavy woolen material in an acceptable rust color, and managed to bring the full length of his body against hers for a long twenty or thirty seconds while he lifted the cloth over her for Abigail's inspection. It was a measure of the latter's interest in forbidden treasures that she noticed nothing except the fabrics, but sooner or later, with such blatant displays going on behind and beside her, she was going to be aware of her host and her bound servant.

It was impossible for Christina not to imagine herself and Vilas in a similar situation. Her body felt warmed simply by the thoughts, and she regretted that the size of the cabin had made it impossible for Vilas to join them for tea. He was still aboard, however, having gone for an inspection tour of the ship. With any luck she'd see him again before they left. In fact, Christina decided, drawing in a deep breath, there was little reason to remain here and watch Abigail choose among the fabrics denied to the others. She spoke without emphasis, hoping her new mistress would be as undiscerning about *her* as she appeared to be about Roxanne.

"It's so close in here; I believe I'll step on deck for some fresh air."

Abigail was absorbed in the rust-colored wool and made no response. Roxanne was pinned against the captain's writing table as he reached for yet another of his plundered treasures, and if O'Neal's weight against her caused discomfort she concealed it remarkably well. Did his mouth slide across her cheek as he withdrew, or did Christina imagine it?

She turned and let herself out of the cabin, emotions churning. Roxanne was such a fool, and if her actions wouldn't reflect on Megan and Christina, as well, good luck to her. However, impropriety on the part of any of the three of them would reflect on them all, she thought with a touch of anger. And Abigail's displeasure, fully unleashed, promised to be awesome.

The moment she gained the deck, Christina forgot about Abigail and Roxanne. For Vilas leaned against the rail, looking out over the harbor and Boston Town. He straightened lazily, turning to greet her.

"Had enough of pretty things already?" he asked as she joined her.

"Since apparently we're to be allowed to keep our own gowns, so as not to be wasteful, there's no point in looking at fabrics. Why won't the Puritans let their women dress as other women do, in things that are pretty? Abigail is sharply against *our* colors, yet I notice she's drawn to them the same as we are."

Vilas shrugged. "Don't ask me to explain Puritans to you. I could live here a hundred years and not see eye to eye with them on most things, including this one. I like women in pretty clothes."

He stretched out a finger to stroke the sleeve of her blue gown, and the tremor began at the spot he touched and continued to spread throughout her system long after he'd taken his finger away.

"I do like the honesty of the Puritans. O'Neal says they're honorable to deal with, and they accept privateers and even pirates—who all say, of course, that they've raided only Dutch ships, or French, or Spanish—as business partners. If the New World is not impressed by my noble birth, neither is it put off by my lack of ready cash, and this is a place where every man may make of himself what he will."

She could have devoured him with her gaze, yet she was not Roxanne. There was no brazen courage in her. Christina smiled, leaning on the rail beside him, pretending to study a pair of gulls on the water below. It was exciting enough to be here, by Vilas's side, speaking with him, to see his bronzed hands carelessly resting on the rail beside her own.

"And what would you make of yourself? A privateer?" she asked.

"Why not? It's a respectable profession among these people, and a way to earn enough to give me other choices," Vilas stated. Even though she wasn't looking directly at him, she was vividly aware of his lean height, the breadth of his shoulders, the fair hair blowing in the breeze. "A year or two at sea could give me what I need to turn to something more settled, on land, but I've no desire to become a merchant or a shipbuilder like the Hulls, not for years yet."

The autumn sun was warm on her face; the red-gold hair escaped from its covering cap in bright tendrils, and she'd never felt more alive than she did at this moment. "No desire for a home of your own, a . . . a wife and a family?"

"There's plenty of time for those things," Vilas said. "I'm not even in a position to support a family until I've saved up some funds, not unless I go out in the wilderness and build a cabin and start plowing up ground. And I hear there are a lot of rocks in this country—some of them great granite boulders impossible to be rid of. No, with winter coming on and no provisions put by, the only sensible thing is to sign on with O'Neal and share in his takings."

"A man at least has choices," Christina observed. "A female has few, if any."

He turned to rest an elbow where his hands had been, bending over, looking straight at her in a way that made her disconcertingly conscious of her looks and possible shortcomings in his eyes. "Do you regret coming to America?"

"No. Only that we have three years of indenture before we'll be free to make any choices. Such as marriage." Her mouth was dry.

"The Hulls seem good masters. They'll see you're well taken care of, fed and clothed, protected."

A muffled burst of laughter behind them made Christina grimace. "As long as Roxanne doesn't do something that gets us into trouble. This is a very...rigid society. Even minor transgressions are severely punished, and she is so...so impulsive, so outspoken! The Puritans have no tolerance for anyone who violates any of their stringent standards, and she makes no secret of her contempt for what she feels is foolish!"

"Aye," Vilas said quietly, "there's much in what you say. They swill rum and ale with the best of Englishmen, yet doing so to excess will land them in the stocks or earn them a public whipping. 'Tis an odd thing: they fled England because they felt themselves persecuted for their beliefs, yet here where they have those freedoms they sought, they deny freedom to anyone else who thinks differently. Still, they are decent, hardworking folk, for the most part; you'll be safer here than you were at Kenwood."

"Yes. If only three years weren't such a long time." Her throat suddenly closed, and she struggled to speak around the ache created there. "It won't seem so long if I'm able to see you frequently." Then, feeling that might be interpreted just the way she had unthinkingly stated it, she added quickly, "Someone from home. A man, with a man's viewpoint on things. But you'll be at sea much of the time, I suppose."

"Oh, aye, O'Neal ranges from Newfoundland to Barbados, from time to time." He said it with rising good spirits. "I've a mind to see those places and to go adventuring."

Her throat ached worse than before. "He's signed you on, then? Captain O'Neal?"

His grin made her chest constrict with unnamed desires. "Of course! Did you think he could resist me? When we're in port I'll look up my cousins, naturally."

Cousins, she reflected dismally. Not *cousin*. "We won't be here in Boston. Not all the time, at any rate. It sounds as if we're to go to some place called Ipswich, to the north of here." Desperation made her bold. "Will you come, even there, to see us?"

"If there's time enough ashore, to be sure. The Hulls and O'Neal do business together on a regular basis, so there should be opportunities. Ah, this is a fair place, is it not? Puritans be damned, Boston is a tidy, bonny town, and prosperous. I like the look of it."

"I, too," Christina agreed, seeing him through a blur of tears. Vilas sounded like a brother, and she didn't want him to look upon her as a sister. Why couldn't he do the things that O'Neal did, arrange to see her, manage to touch her in those ways that brought the color to Roxanne's cheeks, the sparkle to her eyes?

"It may be I'll eventually settle here," Vilas said, oblivious to the pain he caused her. "Even with the Puritans. Though I've yet to see the other places in this New World...they say that Rhode Island is much the same as Massachusetts, and it's become a colony for the black sheep who are not welcome here." The grin flashed again. "That may be more to my liking."

"Do you know...how long it will be, before you sail?"

"O'Neal didn't say. Whenever it damned well suits him, I suppose. He defers to no one." One of the gulls suddenly took wing, and he lifted his head, following its flight. "When do you leave for this place, what is it, Ipswich?"

She had to clear her throat. "Monday week, I believe."

"Well, we've a few days, no doubt. Will you be marketing again? Perhaps I could accompany you, carry your basket,"

Vilas suggested. And then he ruined the entire thing, when her heart had only begun to lift. "I've a desire to ingratiate myself with the Hulls, as well as with O'Neal. Adam Hull, in particular, is an influential man in the Bay Colony. His help, if only in the way of a recommendation, could be most advantageous."

Still, anything that brought them together was an opportunity, wasn't it? Christina made her lips smile and hoped it was more convincing than she thought it was. "I'd be pleased to have you carry my basket. If I go to market, it will probably be in midmorning."

"I'll turn up, just in case," he promised, and with that small morsel she had to be content.

For Megan, the excursion was moderately tedious. When Abigail made her selections, they were handed over to Megan, for to put them down amidst so many bolts of fabric would have been confusing. After a time Megan's arms began to ache. She felt her mistress would have been as personally concerned with a bedpost as she was with the slim girl who stood patiently holding a gradually increasing burden of fabrics intended for someone else's pleasure.

She, too, was aware of Roxanne and Captain O'Neal. Even when they didn't touch, which they did often enough to make Megan tingle all over vicariously, there was a tension between them like that in the air before an electrical storm.

If she were to be granted one wish, she thought suddenly, shifting the heavy bolts of cloth to ease her weary arms, it would be to have a man look at her that way. Touch her that way. All her life she'd known that she would never bare her body to any man. At best he would find her disfigurement disgusting; at worst it could be dangerous if anyone with the mentality of the villagers who had stoned Roxanne's mother learned of the suspect birthmark. Yet even a maid who was imperfect had yearnings, had dreams. As long as no one knew of them, what was the harm of that?

Megan shifted her weight from one foot to the other and superimposed a blurred, half-defined, imaginary face over that of Shea O'Neal; she pretended that it was she whose cheek was brushed by that darkly tanned hand in the guise of judging how well an apricot brocade would look next to her face.

Unfortunately, Abigail turned in time to see that last gesture. Her lips compressed, though her voice remained civil enough. "I beg of you, Captain, do not tempt my servants. She could not possibly wear such material as you hold there."

"A pity," O'Neal said, unperturbed. "She has the very coloring for it, with those great green eyes and that mop of dark curls. Ah, well. Here, mistress, did you see this one? Dark blue, very fine, very warm. It would be most becoming with your complexion."

He had successfully diverted her; his dark eyes danced as they met Roxanne's.

As for Roxanne herself, she felt nearly drunk with the nearness of this man. She had had only tea, yet no wine could have set her spirits soaring in this way.

Part of her exhilaration came from the aspect of danger. She knew full well that Abigail Hull would be scandalized by her behavior, that this, too, would be "inappropriate." There was the element of danger from the privateer captain himself, as well. Shea O'Neal was no stableboy, to settle for pinch and grab or a stolen kiss. He was a man, used to women, used to getting what he wanted. He'd already made it clear that he wanted her, and while she'd not quite made up her mind that she was ready to relinquish her virginity, Roxanne knew she wasn't prepared to reject O'Neal irrevocably, either. After all, every woman needed a mate, and O'Neal was as fine a specimen as she'd ever encountered. One her mother would have approved, she thought with inward amusement, even if no one else did.

While she didn't precisely invite his advances, she did nothing to hinder them. With Abigail and Megan here, he would do nothing overt, nothing truly compromising. This was only a preliminary bout, and risks could be taken without immediate peril.

The brush of his hand as he tendered a bolt for her to examine sent tremors through her. The glint in his eye made her pulses build to a thunderous pace. And when, in leaning over her shoulder to reach something he had certainly placed on a high shelf with just such a maneuver in mind, he brushed his lips across her cheek, Roxanne felt a rush of euphoric delight; she gripped the edge of the table to maintain her balance.

God's blood, if he made her feel this way, and she fully dressed and in the company of two other females, what must it be like to share his bed?

Her mother had entertained many men, including the earl of Kenwood, though usually no more than a single protector at a time. Leonie had not considered herself a whore, only a woman with a woman's needs, both physical and financial. She had never taken a lover except when her daughter was tucked away for the night. She could not have known of the times that Roxanne lay awake, listening, striving to see through the blackness of the cottage, wondering about the noises, the groans that did not appear to indicate distress, the smothered laughter.

Many times she had imagined abandoning her own chastity. She'd been tempted once or twice to allow the liberties that various servants at Kenwood would gladly have taken. Now she faced a man who aroused her in ways beyond those imaginings, setting sparks along her nerves, sparks that could rapidly build to a full-fledged conflagration.

Abigail broke the spell.

"I do thank you, Captain, for showing me these things. I will take the ones Megan has here. You may present my husband with the bill. Come, we must be going. Roxanne, please follow us with those two bolts, if you will."

She swept out of the door into the passageway, Megan following. Roxanne, eyes suddenly demurely downcast, would have stepped past their host had he not put out a hand in an iron grip to grasp her upper arm.

"You leave so quickly, mistress, with scarce a proper good-bye."

"I follow orders," Roxanne reminded him. "I am no more than a slave to Mistress Hull."

He towered over her, the scarred side of his face in shadow, his voice soft. "There are many kinds of slavery. Including that between a man and a woman, a relationship desired by both."

He bent his head to capture her lips, and the breath stopped in her chest. His mouth was warm and firm and, after that first moment, demanding.

"Roxanne! Where are you?" The query was sharp, and she reacted as quickly as she was able, considering what she was experiencing. For long seconds she stared into O'Neal's dark eyes, uncertain of what was to be read there. Did he want her simply as a desirable woman, a woman to share his bed for an hour, a day or two? Or was there more than that? Was there an escape from everything her life had been so far, from loneliness and insecurity, from the repressions of society as a whole and these Puritan bigots in particular?

He let her go, smiling, and Roxanne stumbled after the others.

She had no way of knowing. Yet the thrill remained, for there would be more to follow, though what, remained a mystery. The choice, when the time came, would be hers.

Her own smile had resurfaced by the time she climbed down into the longboat. When Shea O'Neal lifted a hand in a farewell gesture as the boat pulled away, she did not wave back, but continued to smile.

Chapter 23

THE PURITANS DID NOT COOK, or carry on other normal activities, on the Sabbath. Food, therefore, must be prepared before sundown on Saturday evening.

Christina felt she was beginning to get the general idea about cooking, beginning to enjoy baking the rich Boston brown bread, the hearty corn bread, the pots of beans and stews and the meats and fish and poultry that made up a large share of Puritan diets. After nearly two months of dreary fare on the *Edwin J. Beaker*, any fresh foods would have been welcome. But in the Hull household there were luxury items, as well: raisins and figs and dates brought in on ships from distant places, oranges and all manner of spices and teas, as well as a plentiful supply of rum. Adam and Ezra drank the latter without showing any effects; the females in the house watered theirs down, and still Christina felt its potency; she was careful not to drink too much of it.

Roxanne quaffed more generously than the others. With her, it was difficult to tell whether it affected her or not, because she was always more exuberant, irrepressible, spontaneous. Whenever Abigail spoke sharply to them about their slowness to learn—though to the three of them it seemed that they learned very quickly, considering how ignorant they had been to start with—Christina held her breath, hoping Roxanne would not be provoked to some outburst that would bring Mistress Hull's wrath down on them all.

At least Abigail never struck anyone, no matter how furious she was. Even when Roxanne overturned an entire kettle of soup onto the freshly scrubbed floor, and Abigail went first red and then white, biting off her words with stinging force.

"Clumsy, stupid girl! Now what are we to put on the table for the men when they come in?"

For once Roxanne made no reply. She, too, had gone white, and Christina stepped forward in distress, seeing that the other girl's face registered pain and shock.

"Roxanne, did it spill on you? Have you been burned?"

"My foot," Roxanne managed through her teeth. She sank onto a bench and drew up her skirts, which gave off steam when Christina dropped down to help. Remembering the pain of her own burn only a few days earlier, she winced upon seeing the reddened foot.

Abigail's tirade dwindled. "There's butter to smear on it," she said to Megan, but before the younger girl could take a step, Roxanne shook her head.

"No. Cold water will stop the pain more quickly, and there was ice on the barrel this morning. Bring me a pan of ice water, Megan." A drop of blood showed where Roxanne had bitten through her lower lip.

Once the injured foot had been immersed in cold water, the color began to return to her face. Roxanne's tension relaxed somewhat as the ice lessened the pain. "I'll sit here for a spell, until it feels better," she stated flatly.

Abigail had watched the procedure with doubt, but there was no question that it was working. "How is it you know something of healing?"

Roxanne, as usual, spoke without thinking. "My mother was a gypsy. She knew about herbs and healing. Mud from a creek bank will serve when there's no ice, or wet sand from the sea. It eases the pain more quickly than smeared butter."

"A gypsy?" Abigail repeated. "An earl married a gypsy?"

For a few seconds there was silence except for the crackle of the fire and the sounds of their breathing. Once more Roxanne went rigid. It was Christina who spoke into the breach.

"Our father was married three times," she said quickly, "and so we are but half sisters, you see, mistress."

Though it was hardly the entire truth, anything seemed preferable to exposing Roxanne's illegitimacy to this woman; while the fact had roused little censure in England, where it was all too common among the gentry to produce offspring on the wrong side of the blanket, it was different among these Puritans.

Abigail considered this before she finally lost interest in Roxanne and her burned foot. "Clean up the mess, then," she told the other two. "Cut bread and meat for the table. She cannot put a stocking or a shoe over that for a time, so it will have to be you who goes to the market again today," she told Christina. "Your sister can attend to the mending."

Behind the woman's back, Roxanne made a face, accepting the basket Megan silently brought her. Her stitches were not neatly precise, like Megan's, nor competent like Christina's. She had not, after all, been introduced to sewing at the age of three, as had her sisters, and she had little liking for the task. Still, she picked up the shirt Megan had been mending and took a perverse satisfaction, until the ice melted and the water on her foot became too warm to keep down the pain, in seeing how irregular her stitches were compared to Megan's. With any luck Abigail would not ask her to sew again, once she'd examined this work.

Christina gathered up her basket, put on her warmest cloak—for the weather had turned crisp, and there was still frost in the shaded places—and set out for the market.

She was sorry they'd soon be leaving Boston. She liked the town, different though it was from her Cornwall hills, and it was where Vilas would be much of the time that he was ashore. What would it be like to be a goodwife here, to have money to make her own selections in the market and the shops, to keep her own house and kitchen?

With Vilas, of course. Her steps quickened. Would Vilas be there at the market?

And then, as if she'd conjured him up by thinking about him, there he was, striding toward her along Cambridge Street. Not quite the peacock Captain O'Neal was, but unmistakable in his blue doublet and hose, among the Puritans who glanced at him as he passed.

He greeted her with a smile as he took the basket. "You're looking rosy and lovely this morning." And then, before her own smile had fully formed in return, he added, "Anyone as pretty as you are, Chris, should have no trouble in finding a husband even in this land of peculiar ideas. The Puritans may have strange ideas about many things, but they appreciate a beautiful woman the same as other men, I think."

Hurt and disappointment surged through her, making her waspish. "I've no interest in finding a Puritan husband, I assure you."

"No? Well, there aren't many others about."

"Then I'll remain a spinster, I suppose." She had no such desire, but he had cut her to the quick. In England marrying cousins was not uncommon—especially when there were fortunes to be linked—so why could he not see her as other than a childhood playmate?

To her further chagrin, Vilas laughed, shortening his stride to accommodate hers. "That I'll not believe! Even with that cap, enough of your hair shows to reveal how spectacular it is, that extraordinary color that's neither red nor gold but somewhere in between. And you've a face like an angel and a form to match. No, no, cousin, among these people it is almost a sin to remain single, for either a man or a woman. It is their duty to populate this New World; I'm told even Adam Hull, past seventy, is being pressured by the authorities to take another wife, though he resists. It's a man's responsibility to care for a woman and rear a family, and a woman's responsibility to bear that family and keep his house. I predict you'll not last out your indenture."

Her insides were quivering. "I'll not marry except for love," she stated. "There's no one here to compel me to wed against my own wishes."

He was still in a teasing mood. "And what sort of man do you seek, then?"

"Someone who treats me well, who cares for me as I must care for him." Someone six feet tall, with thick fair hair and blue eyes, she could have said. Someone exasperating and too stupid to see what's before his very eyes, she might have added.

"Well," he said, continuing to be obtuse, "at least you think in terms of marriage or remaining chaste. I'm not sure that's the case with Roxanne."

Shocked, she came to a halt and faced him. "What are you talking about?"

"Roxanne and O'Neal. It's clear they've taken a liking to each other, but I can't imagine him marrying her. He's not the type to tie himself to one woman ashore."

"Are you suggesting that she would...would become his mistress? That's absurd!" Christina exclaimed, even as she realized that he was probably right.

"You think so? I pray so," Vilas said calmly, after setting off this storm within her, making her want to strike him. "Because I don't know how well she'd be received in Boston Town if she doesn't follow the rules, and while privateers and even pirates are welcome here, I doubt their mistresses would be tolerated by this society. If you've any influence with her, you might try to get some sense into her head."

"I've less than none," Christina said tartly, and now she was disturbed as well as disappointed in the way this day was turning out. Why did life have to have all these complications?

Still, she did have an hour or so to spend in Vilas's company. She tried to put down the unwelcome emotions and devote herself to enjoying it.

THE DAY HAD NOT YET finished with its setbacks. While marketing with Vilas, once they relaxed into their old friendliness, was enjoyable, Christina once more slid into mild depression when he left her at the front door with a casual, "I should see you one more time before we sail, cousin. Farewell," and he lifted a negligent hand.

Deflated, for she had done her best to be entertaining and amusing, Christina entered the house to find Roxanne standing at the window, looking after Vilas.

Christina tried to pull herself together. "How's your foot?"

"Not as painful as I'm sure it would have been without the ice water. I've put a stocking and a slipper over it; I'll wait a day or two for a shoe. You'll never get him that way, you know."

Stung, Christina swallowed hard. "What are you talking about?"

"*Cousin* Vilas, of course. You *do* want him, don't you?"

Denial leaped to her lips, then died, unuttered. "He thinks of me as a cousin, as a little sister. Even though," she added helplessly, eyes suddenly brimming, "he *says* I'm beautiful, and that other men will admire me, *he* remains a *cousin*!"

Roxanne regarded her with pursed lips. "How much do you want him?"

For a matter of seconds Christina hesitated, unwilling to reveal her very soul. And then, because the matter weighed so heavily upon her and Vilas was so recently departed from her, the handle of the basket still warm against her wrist from his own body heat, she blurted out the truth. "More than life itself!"

"Then go after him," Roxanne said.

Despair welled up, making her throat ache. "But I don't know how! What do I do, besides being pleasant and caring and being what I am?"

"You're more than he's seen," Roxanne suggested shrewdly. "Do you want him to kiss you? To take you to bed?"

Christina cast a wild glance around the room. Abigail was nowhere in sight and Megan was visible through a rear window, doing something in the backyard. Her face went crimson, yet again she was honest. "Yes," she murmured, nearly inaudible.

"Then show him that you do."

"How? How does a respectable woman—"

Roxanne laughed. "That's your problem; you've gotten stuck on the matter of respectability! A man may want a respectable wife, but in his bed or his arms he wants a mistress, and the more wanton the better!"

It never occurred to Christina to wonder how Roxanne came by this information. Nor did she question its accuracy. Her voice was a moan. "But I don't know how to be that way! I cannot be other than God made me!"

Roxanne shrugged, suddenly cynical. "Presumably God made me, as well, though I've seen little evidence of His interest since then. You want me to demonstrate for you what I mean? How to make a man look at you as a woman, not a cousin?"

Christina's hesitation this time was brief. "Yes," she muttered. And then, as Abigail entered from the other room, already forming a scowl because they stood conversing when they might have been working, Roxanne flashed her half sister a grin.

"Done," she said, and ignoring their mistress, limped toward the fire to turn the spit, leaving Christina so shaken at the conversation just concluded that she did not hear Abigail until the woman had repeated her orders for the third time, tone grown sharp.

Even then, the orders seemed not to matter. Bemused, Christina took off her cloak and hung it up, and then wondered exactly what it was she had been told to do.

Chapter 24

THE PURITAN SABBATH was a sobering experience.

Roxanne had mumbled under her breath about Abigail's orders the previous day concerning cooking. "The Lord didn't say anyone had to fast on the Sabbath, so He must have intended that food be prepared on that day," she said.

"It's their custom to prepare it ahead of time. I don't suppose eating only cold food will harm anyone," Christina offered.

She might better have remained silent. Roxanne only gave her an ill-tempered glare. There was, Christina thought dolefully as she sliced the bread that had been baked the previous day, no way of dealing with Roxanne if no attempt to soothe or sympathize was accepted for what was intended.

Yet the food was the least of the shortcomings of the Sabbath.

They breakfasted on bread and cold meat, and then they went to Meeting. Abigail had instructed them briefly about what they were to wear. Regardless of Adam's decision that they did not need to replace serviceable garments, she did not wish to attract attention to her servants, and it was not feasible to dye anything until they went home to Ipswich. She looked over the gowns in their trunks, her lack of words speaking volumes as she examined what they had brought with them. The worn old things they had worn for everyday at home would have suited Abigail just fine, Christina thought, but they had left those behind. When having to choose only a few things to take with them, they had naturally chosen their favorites, not the ones that seemed fit only for rags.

Abigail selected the plainest things they had, while her manner made it clear that the fabrics were still too rich for servants. That didn't stop her from hankering after the velvets and fine woolens, however; they could tell by the way she touched them and the covetous expression she could not quite conceal. What harm would it have done these women, to enjoy looking nice, as women had wanted to do since the beginning of time?

Christina was allowed to wear a russet wool, which was too rich in both color and fabric to be considered drab, and set off her pale red-gold hair to perfection, though that had to be nearly covered by her hood. Megan was respectable in deep blue, Roxanne less so in deep rose, which she was instructed to keep covered with her cloak.

Nothing could truly have disguised either their beauty or their slim, youthful figures. The cloak drawn firmly across her bosom only emphasized Roxanne's buxom charms. Abigail sighed and turned away.

They walked to Meeting, Adam in the forefront of the procession, Abigail and Ezra following, the girls trailing them. There was no casual conversation. When they encountered another Puritan family whose small son had paused to admire a squirrel that darted across their path, the boy was sharply reprimanded.

"The Sabbath is no time for such interests," the man said sternly.

The joy went out of the child's face until he saw Megan's smile and tentatively returned it, though carefully, so that his parents did not see. Apparently smiling was not acceptable on the Sabbath, either.

Attendance at Sabbath services was compulsory. Only illness was an acceptable reason for failure to appear, and each excuse would be verified by a church official. The sight of all the soberly clad Puritans walking to church—not too fast, nor yet too slowly, for even that was prescribed—made Roxanne draw her mouth into a droll mockery of their expressions, so that both Megan and Christina had to smother their amusement before it got them into trouble.

The meetinghouse was stark and simple compared to the churches they knew in Cornwall. The latter were built of stone, with colored glass in the windows, and had stood for hundred years; moss had formed on the rock and ivy climbed the walls.

Here, the structure was of wood, with no colored glass in the windows, and the backless benches were hard and unyielding, less comfortable than the pews to which they were accustomed. Not only that, but the men sat on one side of the center aisle, the women on the other, and not even glances were exchanged between them except surreptitiously. Little girls sat with their mothers; the boys, once they were old enough to be out of skirts, were consigned to the back of the unadorned room, where they could be controlled by the tithing man with his long stick.

To add to the general discomfort, the sermon was nearly four hours in length. Long before it was concluded, the three newcomers from England had lost interest in the minister's hellfire and brimstone warnings and drifted into their private daydreams. Toward the end, a reference to witches caught Christina's attention, and she roused from thoughts of Vilas to attend momentarily.

"I exhort you to struggle against the wickedness of the world," the orator thundered, "and to resist the lure of witchcraft. Let not your thoughts be drawn to demonology, but rather hold to a steadfast course as prescribed in the scriptures. I quote from Leviticus 20:27: 'A man or woman that hath a familiar spirit, or that is a wizard, shall surely be put to death; they shall stone them with stones; their blood shall be upon them.' Beware, for there is danger all around us."

Beside Christina, Roxanne stiffened, and instinctively the older girl put out a hand to still the involuntary movement. Roxanne was pale, except for a spot of color in each cheek; her full lips were compressed upon the protest that swelled her throat. It was not until they were at last allowed to stretch their cramped limbs and emerge into the crisp, cold sunshine, however, that she spoke.

"Damn their hypocritical souls," she said in a low voice. Christina glanced nervously around them, but no one appeared to have overheard. "It was a mistake to come here. They're even more bigoted and ignorant than the people at home."

"It won't do to let them know you think so," Christina told her urgently. "Think what you like, Roxanne, only guard your tongue! Remember that poor woman who was being stoned in the street when we first met Master Hull."

"I remember my mother," Roxanne said grimly.

"Of course. But it won't help to antagonize them. Perhaps it will be better when we get to this new place, this Ipswich. It's a smaller village, I think. In the meantime mind your words, I beg of you."

The trek homeward was as silent as the walk to church had been. How did they bear all this silence? Christina wondered. She had loved the quiet of the hills in Cornwall, with the muted sounds of the surf in the distance and the wind stirring her hair. It was totally different from this enforced Sabbath quiet, when there were people gathered together, not speaking. Reading was restricted to scripture. There was no conversation even with their midday meal except to say grace; they ate bread and cold meat and baked beans, which made up their entire Sabbath diet, in an oppressive hush.

Not only did they spend the morning in worship, the afternoon was to be continued in the same vein.

After the rather alarming sermon in the morning, Megan was aghast upon learning that they were to return to the meeting-house as soon as the crumbs were wiped from the table.

"The entire day? Every Sunday?" she said, and could not keep from showing her dismay.

"We observe the Sabbath very strictly," Ezra said, having overheard her. It was a masterpiece of understatement.

Roxanne, too, took the news with poor grace, though she refrained from saying so until they set out for the second time that day and fell far enough behind the Hulls to be able to speak without risking censure.

"If there were any interesting men in this place," Roxanne stated, "they wouldn't show up at the meetinghouse. Can you imagine Captain O'Neal or Vilas sitting through that tedious service? And listening to such rot! It's no wonder those stupid women were attacking that unfortunate creature we saw, when their ministers urge them to violence from the pulpit!"

Neither Christina nor Megan had any response to that, being as distressed about it as Roxanne was.

The afternoon sermon was no improvement over the morning one. And once more the subject eventually came around again to the matter of witches and witchcraft.

The minister had recently read a book, "Malleus Malefica-rum," written by a pair of Dominican monks nearly two hundred years earlier. He now plunged into its contents with enthusiasm. His congregation sat, inexplicably rapt, their faces eager for the news he imparted. Christina, unable to bear watching the minister himself, wishing to shut out his words, glanced cautiously to one side and found herself staring at a familiar face; it was one of the women who had held a rock, ready to hurl it, when Adam Hull had sent her packing. Christina shivered and drew her arms more closely across her breast.

"The purpose of witchcraft," the man in the pulpit stated, his bony hands gripping the lectern, "is to blaspheme against God and hurt his true servants. We must guard against it, therefore, and protect ourselves and our families. The witches threaten our little ones, especially, for children are sometimes sacrificed to the devil at midnight meetings, when all decent folk are asleep in their beds. It is not enough that we lock our young people behind our own doors, for a witch can fly in through the window in the darkness and turn them into animals or drive them mad."

Christina squirmed uneasily. Megan reached for her hand under cover of their full skirts. Roxanne cleared her throat loudly enough so that several people gave her disapproving glances. Though Abigail, seated directly ahead of them, did not turn, there would no doubt be a comment from her at the close of the service over the inadvisability of attracting undue attention.

"How may we know these blasphemers, you ask?" the minister cried, though no one but Roxanne had made a sound. "We can recognize them, by God's grace, if we know what we do look for. They call upon the powers of Darkness, bringing sickness and death, storm and trial. Not always do they do these things openly, so that we may know them and see that they are punished for their wickedness. But when they fail to conform to the laws of God and man, we may be suspicious. When they take mysterious measures to heal, in opposition to God's teachings or will, we will know them."

Healing, in opposition to God's will? Did that include putting tea leaves on a burn or using icy water? Christina's uneasiness deepened, and she could not look at Roxanne.

"We will know them, also, by other things," the minister went on, holding his audience apparently entranced. "Those who consort with the devil are known to wear his good-luck charms, of which the righteous have no need. One of the surest signs is a devil's mark, put on his servants' bodies to set his own apart from the rest, though you may be sure the mark will be concealed so that the witch may practice his or her wickedness in secret. These are dark spots that protrude from the skin by which their familiars may be suckled or other unnatural markings. Our leaders, as well as the scriptures, tell us that these witches must be sought out and eliminated from our society, for they are an ever present danger to us all.''

Megan was trembling, and Christina grasped her hand tightly. It could not be true, what the Puritan minister said! Megan was marked, but she was no more a witch than any of the babes in arms throughout the congregation.

There was a collective exhalation of breath when the sermon at last came to an end. Christina rose with the others, feeling numb and frightened. Leonie the gypsy had been stoned for witchery, but only after uttering threats and curses. In this place, however, it seemed that even the innocent, who attempted to provoke no one, were in danger from the witch-hunters.

The sermon left its mark on the Hulls, too. They discussed it as they walked toward home in the late afternoon. The air had grown chill, the sunlight thin and nearly gone for the day; they shivered within their enveloping cloaks. Ice would form on the water barrels again tonight.

"We must take care," Abigail observed in a righteous tone that made some of her listeners grind their teeth, "that we do not fall into careless ways. Even a member of our own household could be drawn into paths that lead away from God and His teachings, contaminating the rest of us."

Roxanne stumbled over a root that crossed their path, and Christina put out a hand to steady her. Roxanne seemed unaware of the touch; her lovely mouth had a grim set to it.

Adam's voice was deep-timbred, harsh. "I like not this thundering from the pulpit that stirs the populace to suspicion and hasty, ill-considered actions. It seems to me the clergy could better spend their time in instructing the citizens in proper behavior than encouraging them to directing their spite against their neighbors. A group of women set upon Goody Loring this week past, were stoning her when these young women stepped in.'' He jerked a thumb to indicate the girls walking behind him, and Abigail gave them a startled look over her shoulder—a look certainly not approving, though there had been no censure in Adam's tone. ''I sent them about their business and later inquired into the matter.''

''Goody Loring?'' Ezra echoed. ''She seems harmless enough.''

''That's what Reverend Parker was talking about,'' Abigail said eagerly. ''We must be watchful, because even our neighbors can be dabbling in witchcraft.''

Adam made a snorting sound. ''Aye, they could be. But on hearing the circumstances, I'd say it's more likely those women were being spiteful. There'd been a quarrel a few days earlier over some foolish matter, and then one accused Goody Loring of causing her milk to sour, and another joined in to say the woman had caused her hens to stop laying. Goody Loring was unwise enough not to attempt to placate them. When she cursed them roundly they decided she was a witch.''

Abigail turned her head to speak to her father-in-law, so that her profile was in sharp relief to the girls following. ''But how can we know they aren't right?''

''How can we know they are?'' Adam countered. ''Milk's been known to sour on its own and hens to stop laying. 'Tis hardly proof enough of a connection with the devil to entitle them to execute her. That's a matter for the magistrate, not private citizens.''

''There's too much gossip,'' Ezra decided. ''You'll not join that, wife. Nor encourage taking the law into other hands than those of the proper authorities.''

Rebuked, Abigail subsided. The girls listening to this exchange were not reassured, however. Not all the dangers in this New World came from savage Indians and wild animals.

The Puritans were dangerous in and of themselves.

Yet youthful spirits cannot long be dampened. Adam's announcement over their third cold meal of the day brightened their outlook.

''We leave at dawn for Ipswich, and we'll not take the shallop this time, nor ride through the woods at a time when the skies threaten snow; Captain O'Neal sails north on the tide; he's offered us passage on the *Revenge*, and I've accepted.''

Ezra and Abigail reacted with indifference to their mode of travel. Roxanne, however, smiled for the first time that entire day.

Of course, she'd welcome any chance to see Captain O'Neal, Christina thought. Her own heart was glad, as well, for O'Neal wasn't the only man aboard the *Revenge*.

With any sort of luck she'd have some time with Vilas, who was now a member of that crew. Christina, also, smiled to herself as she prepared for bed that night.

Chapter 25

THE BRIEF VOYAGE was not uneventful.

Had not Abigail taken ill, the girls might have spent their entire time aboard the *Revenge* sitting in the salon keeping her company, their fingers busy with the mending or stitching that she considered appropriate for every waking moment when they weren't engaged in anything more urgent.

As it was, the ship had barely cleared Boston Harbor when Abigail began to have a pinched look about the mouth. Roxanne, frustrated because she'd scarcely exchanged a word with their captain before they sailed, was alert for any further opportunity in that direction; she stood restlessly beside the small round window that gave a limited view of one small section of deck, hoping that Shea O'Neal would appear.

Megan had settled down obediently with a basket of stockings to darn. It was Christina who noted Abigail's growing distress: the chalky skin, the convulsive swallowing as the woman fought back nausea.

"Mistress Hull, are you all right?"

Abigail turned her face in Christina's direction, the pale blue eyes seeming unfocused. "I am *never* seasick," she stated, and then rose and made an unsteady dash for the door of the salon, and the rail.

When the spasms had passed, and she clung to the rail for support, Megan brought her a dipper of water to rinse her mouth. "You'd best lie down, mistress," she suggested.

Abigail's voice was thick. "Yes. Yes, I must. I cannot imagine why... I am *never* seasick! Run... run and ask the captain if I might ... use his cabin. There is nowhere to stretch out in ... there...."

Roxanne, who had come out on deck with the others, spoke quickly. "I'll find him," she offered. "I'm sure he will want you to use his bunk."

Captain O'Neal returned in person, to solicitously assist his guest to his quarters. By the time they got there, Abigail's teeth were chattering as she took a chill; her skin was clammy, and she requested a basin to keep beside her in case her stomach again insisted upon emptying itself.

O'Neal had an unexpectedly gentle touch as he settled the woman on his bed and drew a quilt over her. "Do you wish me to fetch your husband, Mistress Hull?"

"No. No." Abigail swallowed, started to shake her head, then thought better of it as the motion intensified the unpleasant sensations she was experiencing. She closed her eyes.

Roxanne spoke uncertainly from the doorway. "Perhaps some ginger tea. We used it on the voyage from England, for sickness."

"I'll have some sent to you," O'Neal agreed. "And perhaps your maidservants can take turns sitting with you, mistress. You won't want all three in here at once; listening to their chatter is probably not what you need now, but rest."

Abigail made no response, which they took for assent. Christina did not miss the quick glance between O'Neal and Roxanne: an opportunity for an unchaperoned meeting, for the male members of the family were occupied elsewhere and would pay little attention. It was not their responsibility to supervise bound servants.

"I'll sit beside her and tend her," Megan offered, and it was with a sense of relief that Christina departed the cabin behind Roxanne. Already it seemed to have taken on a sour odor, and the fresh air on the open deck was welcome, indeed.

Once the sails were set, the ship headed northeast along the coast that intrigued the newcomers with granite outcrops, small sandy inlets and blazing color amidst the deep green of pine and hemlock. It was truly a beautiful land, Christina thought, and then forgot the scenery when Vilas appeared at her side.

"What's wrong with Mistress Hull? The sea doesn't agree with her stomach?" This was asked with the cheerfulness of one who has never suffered the malady.

"She's ill, at any rate. She says she's never been seasick, so who knows?" Christina didn't want to discuss Abigail. "I can see why you like being on shipboard, if it is like this everywhere you go. But when you're on the open sea, beyond sight of land . . . and when the storms come up, with the water washing over the deck . . ." She shivered in the fall sunshine.

"Even then it's exciting," Vilas stated. He was smiling down into her face, sending those tremors through her again. *Go after him,* Roxanne had advised, yet how did she do it?

The lesson Roxanne had offered came quickly thereafter, as the other girl came briskly along the deck, dark hair blowing in the wind. She came to them with a smile, standing next to Vilas so that their arms touched and her billowing skirts brushed against his legs. Even her hair cooperated by blowing a strand or two against his cheek, while Christina, who was downwind of him, made no contact of any sort.

"How goes it as a sailor's life, cousin?" Roxanne asked, looking up into his face from only inches away, lips parted, green eyes lively and provocative.

Vilas made no move to step away from her, though he did put up a bronzed hand to brush her blowing tresses aside when they touched his mouth. "Nothing in Cornwall, except galloping across the moors on a good stallion, ever approached it. And then there was not the danger of the sea in one of its tantrums . . . nor the prospect of challenging an enemy ship, and perhaps making a fortune."

Roxanne turned her gaze toward shore, leaning more heavily into the man beside her. Just imagining that contact between Vilas and herself was enough to make Christina tingle, yet she could not take the step that would have put her in a similar position on Vilas's other side.

With seeming indifference to what effect the gesture might have on the man—or on the watching girl beside him—Roxanne reached out and took Vilas's hand, turning it palm up in her own.

He didn't resist this, Christina noted with a stab of jealousy, but allowed the maneuver with every indication of enjoying it as much as Roxanne appeared to do.

"A working man's hand," the girl observed, and ran a finger over the calluses. "A ship's rigging must be hard to handle."

He was grinning, Christina observed with a spurt of anger. Encouraging the silly chit. "The ropes took the hide off to begin with," he admitted. "My first week or two at sea I wondered if I'd made a mistake. The ropes were more savage than a horse's reins. But there's something about being up there...." He glanced upward, to where the canvas overhead was stretched to catch the wind. "It's exciting, and it's beautiful."

Roxanne followed his glance, her eyes widening in what any fool could see was exaggerated awe. She swayed even closer to him, pressing for a few moments against the full length of him until the motion of the ship sent her body slightly away again. "It's so high. I don't see how anyone dares scramble around up there ... aren't you afraid of falling?"

Vilas laughed aloud. "Why do you think I have the calluses? It's from hanging on for dear life! You get used to it."

Roxanne gave an exaggerated shudder. "I never would. I'd be terrified."

Liar, Christina thought savagely, knuckles turning white as she gripped the rail. She'd seen Roxanne climbing the cliffs and once had seen her standing boldly atop a parapet at Kenwood, gazing out over the countryside. How could Vilas be taken in by such a shameless misrepresentation?

"The *Revenge* is the finest ship I've ever been on," Vilas said. "I was lucky to find a berth on her. O'Neal's a firm disciplinarian, but he's a fair man. A kindred soul, I think, though we've had little time together as yet. But over our grog last night we talked, and I like the man. I think he likes me, too."

"We all like you, Vilas," Roxanne said, laughing. And then she released his hand and turned aside. "Before anyone decides it's my turn to sit with Mistress Hull, I think I'll see what our handsome captain is doing. He doesn't have to stay at the helm once the course has been charted, does he?"

"When we're in sight of land, he doesn't exactly need to chart a course," Vilas told her, amused. "I'm sure he'll have time for you, Roxanne. He makes no secret of having an eye for beautiful women."

His own admiration was evident on his face, Christina decided miserably as they both watched the other girl stride away. Now that she was not standing next to Vilas, Roxanne had no difficulty at all in balancing on the deck that rose and fell beneath them.

"That one's going to survive in this New World," Vilas predicted. "How about you, Chris? Are you feeling more at ease with the Hulls?"

Was she? The honest answer was no; her doubts about living under Abigail's domination for three long years were as great as ever. The Puritan society was rigid and intimidating. Yet what did Vilas want to hear? What could she say to make him look at her the way he looked at Roxanne, like a man admiring a woman?

She fell back on her customary honesty. "Not really, no. I had hoped we would be taken on by someone who would...like us. So that we would like them. Master Adam may, a little. I think he admired the way we faced those women who were stoning Goody Loring. He seldom speaks to us, however, and he's gone most of the time. Master Ezra—" She hesitated, wanting to be fair. "He isn't there much, either, and when he is he seems disapproving, or perhaps he's only reserved. Not friendly, anyway. As for Mistress Abigail—" She inhaled deeply, then sighed. "I think she'd be better satisfied with servants whose garments she didn't envy, someone not young and..."

"And beautiful," Vilas finished for her. "Well, there's not much you can do about that. Is she going to work your fingers to the bone?"

This time it was he who reached out for a hand to examine, sending prickles of excitement through her as he held it. "You've the beginnings of calluses yourself, it seems. And what's that, a burn? Still, if Mistress Hull is fair-minded and doesn't work you until you drop..."

"Well, she hasn't so far, though she's very particular, but the situation may be very different when we reach Ipswich, which is where they really live. There's a large household there, another daughter-in-law and two sons to deal with, and several young children. There is also, I believe, an old woman, a relative of the other daughter-in-law, Patience. No doubt there'll be plenty to keep us busy. It's not the work we mind, though I must admit it takes some getting used to. It's the Puritanical attitudes toward so many things, and all this talk of witchcraft is unsettling...."

Roxanne had disappeared, and Vilas returned his full attention to her. "Yes. I've heard it, too. These Puritans are no more forgiving of witches than our neighbors in Cornwall were. O'Neal told me of a case in Boston a few years ago, involving a Goodwin family, where the children were bewitched by a servant, a Mrs. Glover. The woman was hanged. The famous Reverend Cotton Mather took a hand in helping the children overcome their afflictions. Have you heard of the Mathers?"

"Ezra has referred to them, I think. They're in politics as well as Puritan leaders, aren't they?"

"The Puritan leaders *are* the political leaders in Massachusetts," Vilas confirmed.

She wasn't interested in the Mathers, whoever they were. "I'm concerned about the kind of thing that took place, the situation we happened on the day Master Adam met us. This Goody Loring had angered some women, and they accused her of witchcraft when their milk soured and their chickens stopped laying. Though as Master Adam said, those things happen all the time, without the aid of witches. They stoned her and might have seriously injured her or even killed her if we hadn't stepped in, and then Master Adam. *He* was the one who sent them packing. They might have stoned us, as well, if he hadn't come along when he did."

"Women can be irrational and violent," Vilas said, as if agreeing with her assessment as applying to all females.

Nettled, because that wasn't what she meant, Christina frowned. "Irrationality and violence can hardly be said to be limited to females," she said with an acerbic note. "What I'm trying to say, Vilas, is that I fear for *us* among these people. Anyone who doesn't obey all their silly rules, who doesn't grovel before their leaders, who crosses one of them in any way, may easily be suspect. It's difficult not to make mistakes with them. Even Roxanne's use of ice water and wet tea leaves instead of butter on a burn seemed to be suspect, and when she admitted her mother had been a gypsy... I don't know, but Abigail listens to that minister who talks about witches and their marks, and she makes me afraid."

"Roxanne tends to speak before she thinks," Vilas said, no longer laughing. "I hope she has wit enough to begin to watch her tongue. I've not noticed that a sense of humor rates high on the Puritan list of virtues."

"If she sets them against herself, they may be set against Megan and me, too." She longed to tell him the truth, that the great birthmark which had almost cost the girl her life at birth might present a similar problem now if it were seen; she dared not. She would ordinarily have trusted Vilas implicitly, but what if he mentioned his young cousin's imperfection during a rum-soaked evening with O'Neal and his men? It was the sort of thing that could explode like wildfire, with terrible consequences.

His attention had wandered. "Ah, I see that the fair Roxanne and my captain are deep in conversation up on the bow. A pity Mistress Hull has had to take to the captain's bed."

The implication was unmistakable. Christina responded more tartly than she intended. "Thank God for it, would be my opinion. The girl has no sense at all!"

Again she had roused his sense of humor. "Would you deprive them both of an hour of pleasure?"

She couldn't share his amusement. Instead her green eyes were sober. "Not if they harm no one. But everything one of us does reflects on the others, and the Puritans punish their citizens for such infractions as a child skipping on the Sabbath! Can you imagine how they'd react to fornication?"

Vilas refused to be serious. "On the Sabbath or otherwise? I'm assured—by those who've been here longer than I—that the Puritans have the same urges as ordinary men and women."

"Perhaps, but they've little tolerance for wrongdoing, and their laws allow stringent punishments. Besides, Roxanne is young and ignorant, for all her show of... of worldliness. *She* is the most likely one to be hurt. If a man offered her marriage and his love and protection, I would be the first to wish her well. My impression of Captain O'Neal is that he is looking for a romp, not a bride, though I don't think Roxanne is convinced of that."

"Shea O'Neal is a fine man," Vilas assured her unexpectedly. "He left England for much the same reasons that I did; his prospects there were dismal. He comes from an excellent family of considerable means, but he's the third son. He was reared as a gentleman, given no means to implement the standard of living he was accustomed to, and after a brief stint in the navy he decided to seek greater fortunes and more freedoms elsewhere. He sailed with another privateer, took his share of the plunder and bought the *Revenge*, which is a bonny ship." He stroked the rail beside him in a manner that sent a tremor through Christina; would he ever touch a woman—no, would he ever touch *her*—in that loving way?

"It's a fine ship," she agreed, "and he may be a gentleman born and bred. But he strays from the role of privateer from time to time, as when he boarded the *Edwin J. Beaker* in what could only be described as an act of piracy. He confiscated a trunk from Captain Stratton's cabin, and the poor man nearly suffered a seizure over it."

"I wouldn't agonize for long over Stratton's plight," Vilas said indifferently. "He's Beaker's man in more ways than one, and Beaker is an unmitigated bastard. He and O'Neal had some sort of run-in a few years ago. I don't know the particulars, but it involved a lady Beaker had taken advantage of. Whatever this last episode involved, I think it had to do with that earlier episode. O'Neal was, at least as he saw it, righting a wrong done the lady by Beaker."

"So now," Christina observed with a touch of asperity, "your chivalrous captain will commit his own wrongs against another female."

To her exasperation, Vilas met this with a wider grin. "I've heard chivalry described as the urge a man has to protect a female from every man but himself. There may be some truth in it."

"Oh, you're impossible!" Christina blurted. If Roxanne had been demonstrating how to win over a man, with her coy glances and her touching and leaning into him and letting her hair blow in his face, the method was beyond her. She wanted Vilas with a passion she had never felt toward anyone else; she dreamed about him constantly when they were apart. Yet when, as now, they were together, she found herself wanting to smack him.

Did he read some of that in her face? He was laughing down at her in a way that suggested he did.

"Come, take a turn about the deck with me," Vilas said, reaching for her hand to tuck it through the crook of his arm, instantly melting her irritation. "We enter Gloucester before we round the point and change directions for Ipswich, and I'll be needed to help change the set of the sails. Walk and talk with me a bit, tell me how it goes in the household of the Hulls."

His arm was warm and muscular beneath her hand. Her breathing was constricted, as it always was when he touched her, her emotions churning.

In the bow she saw Roxanne and the captain, and her mouth twisted wryly. Who was she to cast stones? If Vilas were to take her in his arms and kiss her, at this very moment, she would melt against him as wantonly as Roxanne could ever do.

Three years among these Puritans weighed heavily against her, but with Vilas's hand closing over her own to steady her when the ship rolled beneath them, Christina forgot about anything except the man beside her. For the moment, at least, she would simply enjoy his company and his touch, and she would bite her tongue to keep from saying anything to antagonize him.

ROXANNE AND SHEA O'NEAL were oblivious of the strollers on the deck. They were, instead, engrossed in each other.

Roxanne's color was high; the wind whipped her hair as it filled the sails behind her, and there was no coquetry in her delighted exclamation as she peered downward at the water rushing past the prow. "This is wonderful! On a ship like this one I could spend days at sea without becoming bored. With the proper company, of course." She flashed him a grin that, had she known it, twisted at his gut in a way that was familiar, yet oddly new.

"Aye, the company is important," he agreed, smiling. "One day I'd like to take you on a real voyage, not this insignificant little run. To Barbados, perhaps. I take it you've never been there."

"I've never been anywhere, except my home village in Cornwall and then across the sea to Boston Town." She had the unbridled enthusiasm of a child. "And so far I'm not thinking very much of the latter. Oh, the town itself is all right, and the countryside is lovely, but the Puritans..." She made a face, and O'Neal laughed.

"Fortunately they don't expect privateers to conform to their standards of behavior, not as long as our relationship is mutually profitable."

"Does it make you rich, being a privateer?" She put up both hands to confine her hair as she looked at him.

O'Neal shrugged. "Riches are relative, aren't they? My father—and now my oldest brother—was rich in lands and goods. There are those rich in gold and silver. And one of the richest men I know, in terms of what it took to make him happy, is a fisherman with his own small boat, a lovely wife and three healthy children. He never sees a sovereign from the beginning of the year to its end, yet there is always food upon the table, and his cottage is snug against the winter winds. He professes to require no more."

"And you?" Roxanne prompted. "What is your idea of riches?"

He lifted one brown hand in a gesture that took in the *Revenge*, the sea and the sky. "This. A deck of my own beneath my feet, the freedom to come and go as I please. If there is plunder to be had, why, I'll take my share of it. But the best of it is being my own man, bending my knee to no one but my king and queen."

She gave up on her hair and let it blow, so that she viewed him through a moving screen of it. "I can see that, the part about freedom. The happiest time of my life was when my mother was alive, when I ran free in the forest and along the beaches. That was before Himself took me, by force, to live at Kenwood Castle. Where they made me learn table manners and to read and write—"

"A terrible fate," O'Neal agreed, white teeth gleaming in his bronzed face. "And how fare you now, in the Hull establishment?"

Roxanne scowled. "At Kenwood there was at least a place to hide, to be by myself when I liked. I've a notion that we'll scarce have time to sit, once we reach our destination, let alone time to read or to write."

"And to whom would you write?" he asked, curious.

"Not *to* anyone. But my thoughts flow in a way that makes me want to put them on paper." She had never before revealed that to anyone, and she watched warily for any sign of ridicule.

There was none, only interest in the face that held such fascination for her. "And what form do these thoughts take? Poetry?"

"Sometimes. And sometimes stories form in my mind, romantic stories of adventures and love affairs...."

The thin lips softened in a half smile. "Love affairs. You write from experience, then."

He was teasing, though without malice.

"No more than I've had with dueling and the fighting of wars," Roxanne confessed cheerfully. "But my imagination is equal to it."

The smile deepened almost imperceptibly. "Think how much better you could do it with some actual experience."

"No doubt that will come, in time," Roxanne said. She sounded casual, but her heartbeat had quickened. "Even among the damned Puritans romance is allowed to flourish."

"Under their controlled conditions," O'Neal affirmed. "However, not everyone in the Bay Colony is bound by their strictures." Though he paused she had no doubt that he continued a moment later on the same subject. "We lie overnight off Ipswich, after we've unloaded cargo at Gloucester. I like to walk in the dusk, when we're close enough to land; the forests here are different from the ones of my childhood, but I'm drawn to them."

Roxanne went very still. Was that the invitation she thought it was? "From what I've seen so far, I do not think that servants will be allowed to walk out in the evenings," she offered tentatively, her heart suddenly racing.

"A harsh taskmaster, is she, your mistress? Well, even an indentured servant must sleep, must she not? Once dark has fallen, no doubt Mistress Hull is thrifty enough to send everyone to bed rather than burning candles. It's an easy enough path from the Hull house to the bridge in the center of town, even a stranger could follow it by moonlight, which there will be tonight. I shouldn't wonder but I'd find myself in that vicinity shortly after dark."

How much plainer could the invitation be? Roxanne gave no thought to the possible consequences of such a rash act, the first night in her new home. Pleasure was offered, and only a fool would refuse it.

"I shouldn't wonder but what I'd enjoy a stroll in the moonlight," she said recklessly, "unless, of course, the air is too chill. There's been frost in Boston these past few nights."

The thin lips were incredibly sensual when O'Neal smiled. "There are ways of keeping warm," he told her. "And you've a warm cloak, have you not?"

"I do," she affirmed, and did not really mind when O'Neal went away to attend to his duties as they approached Gloucester.

She had been certain the privateer was attracted to her, as she was to him. Poor Christina, she thought. She's afraid to take the steps that might lead to true happiness. She thanked God she was not Christina.

Chapter 26

THE ORIGINAL PLAN had been to unload cargo only at Gloucester. However, Abigail was so ill that it was decided the females should spend the night ashore with her, in the hope that cessation of movement might calm her. O'Neal had business that could be conducted at the fishing village, though the impression Christina had was that he was not overly pleased at the delay.

He did a great deal of business with the Hulls; they were important contacts, and he would go out of his way to ingratiate himself with them. If that meant lying overnight at Gloucester to enable Abigail to recover, why, that was the price one might be called upon to pay for the goodwill of an important family.

The females were installed in two rooms in a small inn overlooking the bay, which was filled with fishing boats. It was not unlike the village at home, with the tang of salt air and the familiar odor of fish, and cheerful fishermen drinking their ale during the evening in the main room of the inn downstairs.

Abigail did not, however, recover upon being taken ashore. She could eat nothing; even broth and ale refused to stay down. She did not like the bed; she wanted to sink into the stuporous sleep that was her only relief from the nausea and could not, for the bursts of laughter or profanity from the public room below made sleeping difficult. Alternately she felt chilled and feverish. Neither a fire nor the lack of one made her feel any better, and she spoke waspishly when she was able to speak at all, demanding services that left the other three worn out and resentful.

"Megan sat with her all day," Christina said when they had first gotten the woman settled. "You and I'll have to take turns tonight so Megan can get some rest."

The younger girl gave her a grateful smile and was asleep as soon as she'd pulled the quilts up to her chin. Roxanne stood in the doorway, gazing at the mistress in the adjoining room. "I suppose so. You take the first turn. I'm going to get some fresh air; I'll take over later."

"You've had nothing but fresh air all day," Christina protested, then fell silent as she realized she was talking to empty air as Roxanne walked away toward the stairs. Damn the wretched girl, anyway! No doubt she'd planned a rendezvous with the privateer captain or hoped for a chance to meet him, or one of those drunken louts whose laughter rose up the stairway from the public room.

Resigning herself, Christina stepped into the room where Abigail lay spent and miserable. The woman turned her head and said, "Draw the curtains; the light hurts my eyes."

Without speaking Christina obeyed, although it was late afternoon and it did not seem to her that the light was strong enough to have bothered anyone. She wouldn't have minded a chance for walking out—perhaps with Vilas—and certainly had no desire to spend the rest of the day and night in this room with a querulous sick woman.

It was nearly dark when a blowsy woman of middle years brought a tray containing bread and soup and lighted a fire on the hearth and a candle. When the food was offered Abigail groaned and turned her head away. Christina ate and wished she had something to read or even a bit of sewing to do to pass the time.

After a few hours of inactivity, during which her sole entertainment was gazing into the flames and daydreaming, Christina rose and moved restlessly about the confining room, until Abigail groaned. "Must you pace that way? You're enough to drive one to distraction!"

"I'm sorry. Would you like me to leave the room and let you rest more peacefully?"

"And then who would tend me if I need the basin or another quilt?" A volley of raucous voices raised in argument made Abigail press her hands to her temples. "Dear heaven, will they go on this way all night? I might as well have stayed aboard the *Revenge*. It was quieter than this!"

Christina resisted the impulse to point out that it was Abigail herself who had insisted upon being taken ashore for the night. She would be glad when Roxanne returned; she might take a bit of air then, for the room was close and confinement was tiresome.

But Roxanne did not return. Hours passed, and Christina grew sleepy and longed to crawl in beside Megan in the next room, and still Roxanne did not come.

THE FRESH AIR she had said she craved smelled of fish and salt and, as she passed through the public room at the foot of the stairs, damp wool and ale and perspiration.

In Cornwall there would have been gibes and suggestive remarks when a pretty young woman passed through their midst; here there was no such ribaldry, though the eyes followed her passage across the room. She had recognized two of the sailors from the *Revenge*, but there was no sign of the tall, lean figure she sought; Roxanne let herself out into the dusk, hoping that O'Neal hadn't already completed his business ashore and returned to the ship.

There were still men working on the beach, with nets and small boats. To a man, they paused to watch her progress; none approached her or spoke, however, as she walked toward the longboat in which she'd come ashore. The fact that it was here needn't mean O'Neal was somewhere about, though.

Roxanne stood beside the longboat and stared toward the ship anchored in the harbor. A single seaman stood watch on deck; nothing else moved on board.

She sighed. Well, better to sit here by herself, at least until it grew too cold for comfort, than in that stuffy room at the inn, listening to Abigail's whimperings. She'd no doubt the woman was truly ill—not even Thomas had been able, in an attempt to evoke sympathy, to turn gray and ooze cold perspiration from a clammy brow—but she'd little patience with sickness. Especially if the victim was someone she disliked.

She'd made up her mind, the very first day in Boston, that she disliked Abigail Hull. Being her servant for three years was simply not going to work. There must be some way out of her predicament, and she intended to find it, with Shea O'Neal or someone else.

She sat on the edge of the longboat, watching the waves lap about its stern, her thoughts wandering. She had made up stories about the princesses from the castle; now she had to make up a more realistic tale about herself and make it come true.

The hand on her shoulder made her jump. She had sat there longer than she'd realized, for the light was nearly gone. The man who spoke wore a leather jerkin and homespun knee breeches, looking neither sailor nor fisherman. "You lonely, mistress?"

Roxanne looked into a face that was quite ordinary except for the bad teeth. He was grinning, and the hand tightened on her shoulder, its warmth emphasizing how chilly it had grown.

"I'd be pleased to buy ye a bit o' food and a mug of ale," the man offered.

She shrugged off his hand. "No, thank you," she said. Only then did she realize that all the fishermen had left the beach and gone home; she was alone with this man whose muscles and hands suggested he might be a blacksmith. His breath suggested he'd already sampled the ale.

"Ah, lass, don't be shy! Ye're alone, as am I! Bryan Brady, at yer service."

She drew the shawl around herself and started to step around him. "You're very kind, Master Brady, but I don't allow strangers to buy anything for me. Excuse me."

The hand was back, on her upper arm this time, and with a strength that sent a preliminary quiver of alarm along her nerve endings.

"Ye're not of the Puritans," he stated. "Not in them clothes. And ye're new come to Gloucester. I'd have noticed if ye'd been about before." He turned his head to look out across the black water, to where a single light glowed on board the *Revenge*. "Is that the way ye came? On that pirate ship?"

"Captain O'Neal's a privateer, not a pirate," Roxanne said automatically. "Take your hand off me."

"Ah, no need to take offense, mistress! Are ye his woman, then?"

"I'm nobody's woman." She was becoming angry and wondered if anyone at the inn would hear her over the sounds of the customers if she were to scream. "Now let go of me, sir."

His face was a pale oval in the twilight, too close to her own. "No need to take alarm," he assured her. "No unattached females in this place, none as will talk to a single man without their pa gives his consent first. I wouldn't harm ye, I swear, I only wants to talk and maybe . . .''

Neither of them heard O'Neal's approach across the strand until he spoke. "The lady doesn't want your attentions, you oaf. Be on your way."

Brady stumbled backward when O'Neal shoved him, sprawling full length with a muffled cry as his head connected with some unseen object.

"Even in Puritan country it's not wise for a pretty woman to wander about at night by herself," O'Neal told her, but there was no real disapproval in his voice. In fact Roxanne had the impression that he was amused, which annoyed her; if he hadn't suggested a meeting, if they'd reached Ipswich this day, she would have had no reason to expect that he might be waiting for her out here somewhere.

"It seems men are the same everywhere in the world," she said, ignoring the man who was now on his feet and making his way off into the darkness.

"Ah, not so! Some of us are more charming, more gallant, more interesting than others. I was on my way to the inn, where supper is to be set out for me in a private room, mistress. Pray join me. They've promised a leg of lamb, as well as fresh fish, and a beaker of rum to warm my innards after hours of haggling with the local merchants. What do you say?"

He touched her arm, and her pulses leaped under his fingers. She *was* hungry, and not only for food; the company of these blasted Puritans had already worn thin, and she no more than a week in this New World.

For a fleeting moment she thought of Christina up there tending Abigail. But if the circumstances were reversed, Roxanne decided, she would understand why a girl would want to have supper with an attractive man rather than tend a nasty old woman.

"I would like that," she decided, and gave no more thought to either her half sister or her mistress as they walked up the beach toward the inn.

CHRISTINA CAME OUT of the hard wooden chair and stepped into the passageway when she heard the footsteps, lifting the candle high so that it highlighted Roxanne's face. Her lips tightened as she saw the heightened color, the half smile, the telltale grease at the corner of the other girl's mouth.

"Have a nice supper?" Christina snapped in a low voice.

The half smile deepened. "Yes, actually. It was very nice."

Christina leaned forward as Roxanne reached the top of the narrow stairs. "And rum with it, too. How lovely for you. Compliments of Captain O'Neal, I suppose?"

"What are you so waspish about? I'll take my turn with old Abigail now."

"How considerate of you! After I spent hours adjusting the window and the curtains and the pillows and smoothing the sheets and holding the basin for her! Listening to her complaints about everything as if it were all my fault, and sitting on a hard chair where I couldn't doze even after she finally did! She's asleep now; you can take the easy shift."

"Good," Roxanne said. "I've no wish to nurse the ill-tempered old witch."

"Don't use that word! For the love of Heaven, Roxanne, guard your tongue, especially in a public house!"

"Nobody up here but us, is there? Are you going to let me have that candle?"

"You might hold it for me until I find my way into the other room," Christina told her coldly, opening the door to the chamber where Megan slept. "And don't waken Megan before dawn; she spent an entire day looking after Mistress Hull, and she deserves to rest until then. Since you contributed no work time at all, it's only fair that you do it now, for the rest of the night."

Roxanne took the candle, shrugging. "All right. Is there a blanket I can put on the floor? No point in sitting up watching her sleep, is there?"

There was no provoking her, not in the mood she was in. Selfish wretch, Roxanne had given no thought to the others at all, but had simply gone off somewhere with Shea O'Neal and enjoyed herself. I wonder if he kissed her, Christina thought with a stab of jealousy. It continued to eat at her while she undressed in the dark and until she fell asleep moments after sliding into bed beside Megan.

ROXANNE DID NOT FALL ASLEEP as quickly. A single blanket to roll up in on the hard floor had not the comfort of a feather bed, and there was no pillow. Still, she did not mind over-much. She had her thoughts to keep her company.

The meal in the tiny side room had been excellent, and she had drunk freely of the watered rum. Shea O'Neal was excellent company, too. He was full of laughter, and he made *her* laugh. There had been precious little laughter in the Hull household this past week, a dismal forecast of the weeks and months to come.

He had touched her hand as it lay on the table, sending shivers of delight through her. And then, when the time came to say good-night, he had drawn her for a moment into his arms and held her in a way that sent her senses soaring, had captured her mouth for a too-brief kiss that was no more than a promise of delights to come, yet in itself left her reeling. She didn't remember climbing the stairs, having wafted to the top of them on a cloud of euphoria, and even Christina's fury had not lessened that.

She lay in the darkness, listening to Abigail snore, reliving that kiss, remembering how it had felt to have a man's strong arms around her, to have her breasts crushed against his chest, to surrender her mouth to his.

Abigail coughed and flailed about on the bed, providing only a momentary distraction. I'll not be serving you long, mistress, Roxanne promised silently. Not long at all, at all.

She turned her back to the woman in the bed, curled up and went contentedly to sleep.

Chapter 27

IN THE MORNING Abigail was no better. She was carried back to the ship and again took over O'Neal's cabin for the remainder of the voyage. She insisted upon Megan as her attendant for that time, to Christina's secret relief and Roxanne's open satisfaction.

They sailed out of Gloucester Harbor, headed north by northeast around the peninsula called Halibut Point and changed their course to almost due west. There was no dallying on deck today, for the fog obscured the shoreline and even, at times, their own sails. The men were busy elsewhere, and the girls sought refuge from the damp in the main salon, impatient for the journey to be ended.

An uneasy truce lay between Christina and Roxanne. Roxanne was unaware of how her inward-turning smile created speculation and envy in the older girl. And Christina could not bring herself to ask about anything Roxanne did not voluntarily reveal.

The fog rolled away at last, and they were at the mouth of the Ipswich River. The autumn foliage along the shore outdid the splendor of what they had seen at Boston, gold and crimson splashes against the landscape, offering what seemed to Christina a glorious welcome. Had it not been that Vilas would be sailing away with the *Revenge*, her spirits would have been high. She liked this land, wishing only that the colonists here were less rigid in their attitudes. And anything was better than having been left to Lady Jacobina's less than tender mercies. Poor little Thomas, not even he had been safe at Kenwood in her care.

"Lower the longboat!" the order rang out, and there was no time to think about Thomas or what might have been back home in Cornwall.

It was Vilas who helped them over the side and down the ladder. Christina treasured those few moments when he steadied her, when his strong hands held her, before he reached up for Megan.

The sea was calm, a far cry from the ocean they had crossed at such peril. There was no bay here adequate for large ships; the *Revenge* had to anchor offshore at the mouth of the river. The village itself was a goodly walk upstream, which Abigail refused to attempt. She had spent the entire voyage from Boston flat on her back, except for the times when she raised herself onto an elbow to use the basin Megan held. It was all she could do to manage the rope ladder down the side of the *Revenge*, and she had to be lifted out of the longboat when they reached shore.

It was difficult to tell whether Ezra was annoyed with his spouse or the circumstances that inconvenienced them all. "You," he said, poking a finger in Roxanne's direction, "stay here with my wife until we can return with a conveyance to get her home. Clearly she cannot walk the distance."

Abigail was not too ill to accept that dictum; though still pale and weak, she roused enough to speak decisively, making no bones about her own preference. "No, let Megan remain with me. Her voice is softer; it does not make my head hurt. Christina, see that there is hot food when we get there; I doubt that Patience will have prepared for us. And," addressing no one in particular, "warm my bed. I cannot bear the thought of damp sheets when I am stricken this way."

"I will have one of my men remain with Mistress Hull, as well," O'Neal declared. "I have business in the village with Master Whipple, or I would stay myself. De Clement, the ladies have need of someone to return with a cart; perhaps you could accompany them, so that Master Hull need not do so when he has pressing business after his time away from home."

Vilas joined the group with alacrity, though Christina was mildly provoked that he chose to walk with the men rather than where she could talk with him. Roxanne did not seem bothered by O'Neal's conversation with Adam Hull; when they came to a tree that had fallen across the path, he paused to assist both girls over it, meeting Roxanne's smile with one of his own that conveyed, at last to Christina's eyes, an air of intimacy.

It was a pleasant walk through the woods. Once they glimpsed a deer, startled at its browsing; it bounded away from them through a fall of scarlet leaves.

Walking in this forest would not be the same as her walks along the bluff overlooking the sea, but it would be pleasant enough, Christina decided, then wondered how much free time she would have to devote to her own needs.

Ipswich was much smaller than Boston, and with its own air of charm. There was little here of brick or stone; instead, the frame houses were built of native timber, as was the bridge over the river that bisected the village. The church, or meeting-house, was unmistakable atop its hill, encompassed by a low stone wall. Was there any hope that the compulsory services here would be shorter than those in Boston Town?

In the middle of the village a cluster of men stood talking. They turned as the small group approached; appraising eyes measured the newcomers, and an older man doffed his hat and waved it, calling out. "Adam! Ezra! It is good you have returned safely!"

"It's good to be home," Adam responded, pausing, so that the others paused, too. "What is this, you away from your forge, Denton, and George, there, not minding his shop?"

The speaker shook his head. "We like not what is happening these days, nor the news that comes. A wise man must sift and evaluate, and choose his way with caution."

"Ah? What's happening, then?" Adam didn't wait for a reply but waved a hand at his son. "Be you taking these young women on home, Ezra, to show them the way. I'll tend to a wagon for Abigail, and we'll have a warming cup until it gets here. My bones are too old for standing in the middle of the road. Let us sit, Denton, and you can give us the news."

Ezra did not seem overly pleased at being ordered about this way, but he made no verbal protest. "Come along," he said to the air between the girls, turning away from the other men.

To the chagrin of both girls, neither Vilas nor O'Neal gave them more than a casual goodbye, and they were left to follow Ezra on along the narrow main street.

Most of the houses were small, no larger than the cottages at home. A few were comparable to the Hull house in Boston, including the one at which they eventually arrived.

Constructed of narrow planed boards, softened to a silvery gray by the elements, it stood half a mile from the bridge in its own spacious grounds marked by a split-rail fence. The house was large by New World standards, and in the Elizabethan style. Its thatched roof was steeply pitched, the small windows with their diamond-shaped panes showing two and a half stories in the main part of the house. It had been added on to several times; there was a lean-to, and a privy on the edge of the woods. A thin column of smoke rose from the large central chimneys, the only sign of life.

Ezra led the way into the house, calling out. "Patience! Where are you?"

Somewhere a baby cried fretfully; there was no other response.

Ezra's large-featured face took on an irritable expression. "Patience? Wes? Mistress Wentworth? Where is everybody?"

Well, he might ask, Christina thought, entering behind him. Although it was late enough in the day so that they might have expected meat to be turning on the spit or a stew simmering in its kettle, there was no welcoming fragrance of cooking food. Instead there was the faint odor of wet diapers that made her want to throw open all the windows as well as the door.

The room they had entered was much like the kitchen in Boston, except that it was larger and had an untidy air at odds with what they knew about Abigail. The floor plan was much the same as that other house, with twin fireplaces standing back to back, probably two rooms upstairs and two down in the original building. The floor was of wide boards that had been scrubbed not long ago but now needed sweeping, for small muddy footprints crossed from door to fire, where someone had carried in a supply of wood.

Overhead, heavy oak beams supported the second floor; they had darkened with years of smoke and age. Strings of onions hanging beside the door gave off a pungent aroma; a row of dark green squashes and some large orange vegetables Christina didn't recognize sat along the nearest wall.

"Betta!" Ezra bellowed, walking to the foot of the stairway that rose from just inside a door opposite the one they had entered. "Where is everybody?"

The baby had stopped crying. A moment later a little girl, perhaps eight or nine years old, appeared carrying the infant, her blue eyes wide and wary. She was a pretty child, with long pale hair; she reminded Christina of Megan. "Uncle Ezra, I'm so glad you've come. Where is Aunt Abigail?" The blue eyes searched beyond the man and hesitated over the two unfamiliar females.

"She's waiting for the wagon your grandfather is sending back to the shore for her; she's ill. Where's your mother?" His voice was harsh, and the child shrank back a little; when she stopped patting the baby, it began to whimper again.

"Mama's sick, too. And Grandmother fell down the stairs day before yesterday and can't get up. I've been taking care of them, and Emory and Nels, but Emory cries so much. I think he's cutting a tooth, perhaps. I scorched the stew and we had to throw it out." Tears brimmed suddenly, and Christina wished that Megan were here. She knew how to deal with young children, and this one was very appealing.

"Maybe I can help you with the baby," she offered, reaching for the infant. He was damp, and his round face was flushed from crying, but he allowed her to hold him. She remembered cradling Megan this way, when everyone else would have left her to die; for a moment she felt a rush of emotion, holding the small body against her own. "Roxanne, why don't you have . . . Betta, is it? . . . show you where Mistress Hull's bed is, to be sure it's ready for her. Is there a warming pan? And we'll have to see about something to eat right away."

"Betta will show you," Ezra said, relieved that she was stepping in. "Where's Nels? Why isn't there more wood here? The fire's nearly out. Nels!"

"He's getting wood now, sir," Betta said. "He's been very good about helping, really he has. Only there has been so much to do, with both Mama and Grandmother abed and Emory fussing every time we put him down. . . ."

Ezra made a sound of exasperation and walked back out the door through which they had entered, leaving them to cope as best they might.

Christina smiled at Betta—short for Elizabeth? "I'm Christina, and this is my . . . my sister, Roxanne. Our other sister,

Megan, will be coming along with Mistress Abigail. We are indentured servants.''

Betta stared up at them. "You're both very pretty," she observed. She hesitated, then asked, "There are *three* of you?"

"That's right. Can you get me clean clothes for the baby? And then show Roxanne where Mistress Abigail sleeps?"

Betta gestured toward the room Ezra had entered. "Over there. I'll get the clothes; they're on the line yet, we just washed them this morning."

She ran past Roxanne and out the door, calling for her brother. "Nels! Where are you! Come quickly!"

Roxanne had not yet moved. Her gaze roved over the walls, hung with utensils and drying herbs and vegetables, to the open shelves of plates and cups, to the cushioned settle and the pair of stools before the fire—the latter made with three legs instead of four, so that they would more easily adjust to any unevenness of the floor—to the great long table that held the remains of a cold meal that had been eaten not long before.

"I think Mistress Abigail was hoping for hot soup when she got here," she observed wryly.

"I think she isn't going to get it," Christina replied, jiggling the baby, who had started to whimper again. "I wonder if that heel is all that's left of the bread? Roxanne, for heaven's sake, see to the bed, make sure that's ready. There's a warming pan on the wall; set it to heating! And get a broom to sweep before she sees that dirt, or she'll be railing at us all, no matter how sick she is."

"Who gave you the authority to give orders?" Roxanne asked, with more disgust than rancor. "There're books in the place and a writing table. They're civilized, it seems."

She left Christina cajoling the baby and entered the second of the ground-floor rooms, only to stop uncertainly when she saw that the bed was occupied.

There was less untidiness here, except for garments laid out across a clothes chest. No fire burned, and it was chilly. The only sound was the scratch of a tree limb against one of the windows beyond the bed with its tall posters and bright quilt.

Startled, Roxanne had not watched where she stepped, and her skirt brushed heavily against a poker leaning against the brickwork of the fireplace. It fell crashing onto the fire dogs, and the sleeper awoke and sat up, confused and unfriendly.

"Who the devil are you?" a querulous, high-pitched voice demanded.

"I...I'm sorry, I thought this was Mistress Hull's bedroom. I'm to prepare the bed for her."

Patience Hull sat up, adjusting the white cap that had nearly slid off her blond curls. She had been an extremely pretty girl; now, at twenty-six and after bearing five children—two of whom had died shortly after birth—her rather thin-lipped mouth had taken on a permanent flatness; selfishness and temper had taken a toll in her face. Gray eyes stared at Roxanne with displeasure. "Mistress Hull? I am Mistress Patience Hull."

Roxanne moistened her lips. "Mistress Abigail Hull, ma'am. I thought this was her bedroom."

Patience came wide awake then. "Is she here? Is she home today?"

"She's ill, and they've sent a wagon to bring her from the shore."

Patience slid her feet out of bed, then hesitated. "Are you the new bound servant?"

"Yes, one of them. I'm Roxanne."

"One of them?" Patience echoed, one hand clutching the neck of her sleeping garment. "There's another?"

"There are three. We're sisters." Roxanne evaluated the other young woman, deciding within seconds that she wasn't going to like this one any better than she liked Abigail. "Do I have the wrong room, then, mistress?"

The words were right, but she did not have the proper deferential tone. Patience Hull's mouth went even flatter.

"No. This is her room, but since she wasn't here and I was not feeling well, it was more convenient for me to sleep in this bed so that Betta didn't have to run up and down stairs so often when I had to feed the baby." The significance of what Roxanne had said finally penetrated. "Abigail is ill? But she is never ill!"

"She is now," Roxanne stated. "And she'll be here shortly."

Patience muttered something under her breath, reaching for the garments she had cast aside, gathering them up, along with her shoes. "Straighten the bed, then. And bring me something to eat, upstairs." She would have passed out of the room without further words had not Roxanne stopped her. "Am I to change the bedding, then?"

By this time they were side by side. Patience turned sharp gray eyes upon the new servant. "Change it? Whatever for?"

A lesser person would have quailed before Patience. Roxanne was not intimidated, only filled with dislike of both this person and her own situation. There was an insolence about her shrug that almost brought forth a protest, but Betta had appeared, again holding the baby. "Mama, Emory's hungry."

Patience gritted her teeth. "Bring him upstairs to me, then." She stalked out of the room, ignoring Roxanne entirely.

Roxanne could have given in to gritting her own teeth. She stared around the room, unwilling to do any more than she had to yet not wanting open warfare with Abigail the moment she arrived here. Make the bed, then, so Mistress Abigail didn't know her sister-in-law had been sleeping in it. Roxanne's lips quirked at the corners. Why should she care if Abigail knew it? She suspected there was no love lost between the two of them; if they fought with each other, maybe they'd have less time to criticize the servants.

"Servants," she said savagely, jerking the quilt into place and roughly plumping the pillows to erase the imprint of Patience's head. "I won't be one for long, I'll swear to that!"

When she emerged into the big kitchen, Christina was swinging a big kettle over the replenished fire.

"I don't know what to fix, except to heat water for tea. The squash take a fair amount of time to cook, I think. What are those orange things? Another kind of squash?"

"They're pumpkins," a small voice said, and they turned to find a little boy, perhaps six years old, standing in the doorway with an armload of wood. He was towheaded like his sister, with the same wide blue eyes and fair skin tanned from the summer just past.

"What's a pumpkin? What do I do with it?" Christina asked.

The child walked over to dump his load of wood. "It's to eat, but you have to cook it. It takes a long time."

Christina sighed. "That's what I was afraid of. Is there anything here that can be cooked quickly? Or cold meat? Or bread?"

Nels hunched his thin shoulders. "Betta doesn't know how to make bread. We ate the last of the roast last night, and nobody brought any more meat. Perhaps," he offered thoughtfully, "I could shoot a rabbit, if you like."

Christina's sigh was more pronounced. "I think that would take rather a long time. I wonder if the ingredients are here to make corn bread." She bent over the kegs set along one wall, lifting lids, wondering if Abigail would create a fuss if they couldn't feed her soup, and at once. It was hardly her fault if nothing was available to make it with, though. "Are you going to warm the bed, Roxanne?"

"I shouldn't think it necessary," Roxanne said with a touch of returning humor, "since Mistress Patience was in it. If that thing is hot I'll use it, though." She paused before she scooped coals into the warming pan. "Did you meet Mistress Patience?"

"Just barely, as she went up the stairs. She seemed in poor spirits."

"My guess is that she's always in poor spirits. I don't know about you, but I'm not going to be here for any three years, taking orders from such as those two." She grasped the long handle of the warming pan, swinging it about before she realized the little boy still stood listening. "You don't tell anyone I said that, or I'll make your ears burn, you hear, boy?"

Nels covered both ears with his hands as if to protect them. "Yes, ma'am!" he said, and ran outside.

Christina had located a bowl and cornmeal. "Do you have to antagonize even the children, the minute we get here?"

"With this family, it'll be impossible not to. I've no intention of lying down and letting them walk over me as if I were a rug," Roxanne asserted.

Christina was too anxious about feeding people when the rest of the Hulls came home to worry over Roxanne at the moment. She wished she had some assurance that there would be a way out of this indenture, short of a miracle. At the moment she couldn't think what it would be.

She began to mix the corn bread and had put it on to bake when she heard them coming. She looked out the window and immediately her spirits soared, for Vilas was still with them.

Chapter 28

ABIGAIL WAS GRAY with exhaustion as Megan helped her undress and get into bed. She did not ask for anything, nor give any orders. She closed her eyes and was so still that Megan dared to tiptoe out of the room, hoping she was granted a reprieve from her sickroom duties now that Abigail was in her own home.

Megan had scarcely taken in the house that was now her own home, as well, except to note the general similarity to the house in Boston. Now details settled in her mind: a comfortable house, snugly built, with rag rugs on the wide plank floors, cushions on the chairs in the big kitchen, a shelf of books behind the settle, a chest that served as both clothes press and seat, where someone had put down a basket of apples.

The main room was full of people, including two young children with towheads and a stranger who entered from the outside as Megan passed by the bottom of the stairs. She looked directly into his brown eyes and felt as if a bolt of lightning had slashed through her. Something in his gaze made her wonder if he felt it, too.

Fitzhugh Hull, she thought. The family resemblance was marked, yet he was far handsomer than either his father or his older brother Ezra. Of course Ezra was old enough to be his father, and Adam to be his grandfather; she remembered the calculations they had made from the Bible in Boston. Yet it was not only the differences in age; this young man would always be attractive, she thought, because he looked happy and good-natured.

Fitzhugh was twenty-four. His thick brown hair was cut short, like that of all the Puritans, a style that seemed peculiar to one recently come from England. He was nearly a head shorter than Vilas, who stood beside the fire drinking a cup of ale, and his garb was the sort she was getting used to: brown homespun knee breeches, a leather doublet, a plain Holland collar. And though slim, he was lithe and muscular.

He had stopped upon seeing her, seemingly caught in the same trance. Now, he made his way deliberately across the room to speak to her. "Good day, mistress. I am Fitz Hull, and you, I take it, are one of the new indentured servants."

Megan's breath caught in her throat. She was petite enough so that she had to look up into his face, which at close range was even more appealing than it had been from a distance. His mouth looked as if it smiled naturally and readily, as now, and the dark eyes were warm and friendly.

"I'm Megan," she said, sounding breathless.

"Megan." No one had ever repeated her name in quite that way before; it sent a shiver along her spine. "Welcome to the Bay Colony, Mistress Megan. Come, I believe everyone is having a refreshing drink. Can I get you a cup? Would you prefer ale or cider?"

It was if she were not a servant at all, she thought, dazed, accepting the cider. This man, dear heaven, had she come all this way across the sea just to meet this man?

And then she remembered, and her smile faltered. She was not an ordinary female, but one marked by a curse made years before she was born. Heat flooded her face, imagining what he would say were he to see that terrible disfiguring mark; of its own volition, her free hand rose to the collar of her dress as if to further conceal the imperfection.

Adam's voice cut through the murmur of conversation. "Is there nothing ready in this house to feed a band of hungry travelers?"

Christina, who had been smiling up at Vilas, jerked about like a puppet whose strings have been manipulated. "I...I have corn bread baking, sir. And there is a basket of apples, but there wasn't time to cook beans and I didn't find anything to make a stew..."

Adam's eyes raked over the assemblage, not finding the one he sought. "Where is Patience? Surely it isn't too much to expect a hot meal when we return."

The little girl cleared her throat. "Mama is abed, Grandfather," she offered timidly.

"Abed? At midday?" he asked, but with a resignation suggesting this was not a new situation. "What about your great-grandmother, child?"

"Grandmother Wentworth fell and hurt herself. She is all bruises and too stiff to get up, sir."

A frown began to form on the old man's brow. "And who has been looking after the household, then, with all the females abed?"

"I have, Grandfather. And Nels helped."

"And now Abigail, too, is indisposed. Well, we'll have to make the best of it. Fitz, is there no meat to be cooked?"

"Aye, sir, I brought in a young doe just now, though it needs butchering. Perhaps the liver could be cooked quickly."

Megan saw Christina's flash of panic. None of them had ever cooked liver; they had no idea what to do with it. Fitz, who had taken a step away from her, paused. He was perceptive, this one.

"Is something wrong, Mistress Megan?"

She moistened her lips, glad Adam had delegated the job and was done with it, concentrating on dipping himself another mug of ale. "How does one prepare liver?"

Fitz grinned, and once more shock waves ran through her. "I'll slice it, and then I'll show you. Find a bowl to put it in, and come with me."

Behind her, as she followed Fitz out into the late afternoon sunshine, she heard Adam ask, "Where's Wesley? If his wife is sick and his children are left to their own devices, what is he doing?"

Megan didn't hear the answer. She didn't care about Wesley or his sick wife. It was wrong, nothing could ever come of it, but for the moment all she could think about was here and now, and Fitzhugh Hull, who had smiled at her.

THE LIVER, fried with onions in bacon grease and the thick squares of corn bread made a hearty meal. They all ate together, with Patience coming reluctantly to table and even the old grandmother being carried downstairs in Fitz's strong arms to join them; only Abigail remained in her bed, and sipped at comfrey tea.

Cordelia Wentworth was Patience's grandmother. Nearly as old as Adam, she was much more fragile, a bent little woman with crippled hands, thin white hair and bright dark eyes that darted from face to face.

No one designated any particular seating order. Fitz stepped over the bench to place himself beside Megan; for the first time in her life, she felt a man's thigh pressed against her own as they made way for Vilas on one side and the old woman on the other.

As usual, the men dominated the conversation. Megan let it flow over and around her—politics, it seemed, overpowered everything else, with strong dissatisfaction on the part of the colonists regarding the suspension of their royal charter and their anxiety about replacing it.

Wesley Hull had come home as they were sitting down to eat; he inquired of his wife how she felt but scarcely waited for the answer before filling his plate. He was the middle brother, thirty-five years of age and handsome in a sharp-featured way, though not, to Megan's mind, as handsome as Fitz.

When the baby, Emory, began to cry, Betta was sent to fetch him. Balanced on her knee, he was given bits from her plate; Wesley paid him scant attention. Instead, Wesley's gaze returned again and again to the dark-haired girl across the table, and Roxanne looked him boldly in the face as she passed the platter of meat.

Trouble there, Megan guessed uncomfortably. Even if neither Wesley nor Roxanne ever passed beyond this stage, staring at one another, it was dangerous. Patience might not be feeling well, but she was present and she wasn't stupid. And she did not seem the sort of woman who would tolerate a servant's familiarity with her own husband.

Megan's emotions ran up and down like a seesaw. She was apprehensive about this new life, about Abigail and now Patience—who seemed to be inappropriately named to an extraordinary degree—about Roxanne's inability or unwillingness to conform to the standards of these Puritans, which might endanger them all. Yet most of all she was aware of the pressure of a muscular thigh against her own, the warmth of it even through their garments, and of a desperate wish that she could be unblemished and worthy of a man like Fitz Hull.

Wesley spoke, and attention focused on him. "I suppose you talked to the men in the village when you came home, Father?"

"I did," Adam conceded heavily. "I like not what I hear."

"The business of witch-hunting? Well, not everyone believes as you do, sir. There are those who feel that the creatures should be rooted out and dealt with."

Though tremors ran through two of those around the big table, he was not aware of it. "Surely you don't condone what they do, these devil's helpers?"

Adam snorted. "Not if they're true witches, no. But the accusations being hurled about are suspect when a woman who has quarreled with her neighbor for years suddenly decides her own misfortune is witchcraft at the instigation of that neighbor. It's as if a horse never threw a shoe without some satanic force being responsible, or milk curdled, or a hut burned down. Everyone knows Goody Felton is careless, not only of fire but of every other thing; if the tithing man didn't remind her that it was the Sabbath, she'd never even show up at Meeting. In fact, I recall another occasion on which she caught her skirts afire and was sorely burned. Why now, because fire destroyed her entire cottage, does everyone assume that Goody Marrow is a witch who caused it to happen?"

Ezra chewed thoughtfully, drank from his mug and speared another chunk of corn bread. "Goody Marrow has crossed swords with half the countryside, over one thing or another. Give them an excuse to call her to account for her bad temper, and it's human nature to do it."

"When bad temper becomes a crime," Cordelia Wentworth said unexpectedly in her frail, old woman's voice, "there's many a female will have to answer for it."

Though no one looked directly at Patience, it was notable that red spots formed in her cheeks. Fitz covered the uncomfortable silence with a cheerful, "And men, too, I should reckon. The corn bread is good, Mistress Christina. Is there more of it?"

The moment passed, but the significance of it hung over Megan. These people had fled England, at least in part, to escape persecution for their beliefs. Yet they had brought their dread of witches with them, and it took so little to convince them a person dabbled in witchcraft.

She was no witch, but there were those who would say she was marked as such. And in this household of so many people, where total privacy would be impossible, how long would it be before someone saw the birthmark?

CORDELIA WENTWORTH WAS SIXTY-EIGHT, which was a very great age for a woman of her time. She had borne nine children; all of them preceded her in death, as had her husband. Now there was only one granddaughter, Patience, and her three surviving children, Cordelia's great-grandchildren. The children almost made up for their mother's shortcomings, in Cordelia's mind.

She was too frail to lift Emory, but if Betta put him on her lap, baby and old woman entertained each other by the hour. Nels liked to come and lean against her, in a way he never did with his mother; Cordelia enjoyed the solidity of his sturdy little body next to her own. And Betta, why, Betta was willing and biddable, fetching shawls and spectacles, misplaced knitting needles and cups of watered-down rum; her young legs sped up and down stairs with ease, and her shy smile was a delight after her mother's sour puss, Cordelia thought.

Abigail ran the house efficiently, and she saw to the old woman's needs, but there was no affection between them. For the most part the men paid her no mind whatever. Only with the children did Cordelia feel needed and wanted.

And now there were three more females in the house, very different from one another, all of them beautiful. Already causing tensions, perhaps unknowingly.

Cordelia observed Wesley's hot gaze sweeping from Roxanne's face to her throat to the swell of her bosom under the green velvet. She saw Fitz—her favorite of that generation—lean forward so that his arm brushed against the shoulder of the little, quiet one. She observed Christina's nervous joy at sitting next to young Vilas De Clement, and that young man's oblivious good nature, which sat well with his astonishing good looks. Cordelia might be past the age of wanting to lie with a man, but she hadn't lost her appreciation of such things.

The old woman put an arm around young Nels when he pressed into her side, hugging him close, but her mind wasn't on the child. She was watching Roxanne. The girl was bound to bewitch men used to demure Puritan females, for no cap could hide that wealth of shining dark hair and no gown conceal the rich, full figure. As for the face, ah, there was no girl in the village who could match it for beauty.

Oh, yes, Cordelia thought, it was going to get interesting. She couldn't wait to see what would happen.

Chapter 29

THE HOUSE WAS LARGE, but so was the family. Megan's fears about a lack of privacy soon proved well founded.

Abigail and Ezra shared the bedroom on the ground floor. Fitz and his father had the one over the kitchen; Patience and Wesley slept in the remaining second-floor room, with Nels and Emory in trundle bed and cradle. Betta and poor Cordelia were relegated to the tiny space at the very top of the house, where Cordelia sometimes felt suffocated in the heat of summer and always frozen in the winter; besides which, it took her an interminable time, with the stiffness of her old legs and back, to get up and down the steep, narrow stairs.

This left little space for the three servants.

Abigail emerged that first evening, looking drawn and limp, to assist in making the decision as to where the girls should sleep. Patience, too, was there, as well as Cordelia, though the latter would be given no official voice in the matter.

"Three of them, for pity's sake!" Patience said, as if they were not there to hear. "Why on earth did Father Adam bring *three* of them?"

"Would you care to demand an explanation of him?" Abigail asked wearily.

Cordelia chortled. "The way you both went on about how much work there was to do, no doubt Master Adam thought to put an end to the caterwauling."

The other two ignored her; it was their only defense against an old woman on the edge of senility, who would not be silenced.

Roxanne regarded them with distaste. It didn't matter to her where they were relegated to sleep, so long as it was possible to keep warm. It would also be convenient if rising from bed did not necessitate padding through someone else's sleeping quarters, risking wakening anyone who would object to her leaving the house. She could hardly wait until the household was asleep so that she could retrace her footsteps to the bridge to meet Shea O'Neal.

She didn't understand why Christina and Megan wore such an air of anxiety. A bed was a bed, wherever it was placed.

"They could sleep in the lace room," Abigail said, considering.

Immediately Cordelia frowned. "There's no room there, my lace takes up the whole of it. They couldn't spread more than one pallet on the floor."

"Besides that," Patience said, for once siding with her grandmother, "they'd have to come and go through our bedroom. I hardly think Wesley and I would like that arrangement. It would disturb the children."

Again Cordelia laughed. "The children, is it! Well, mayhap so, for all they're sound sleepers. Nothing else occurs in that chamber, does it, since you've taken to being an invalid."

Patience turned fiery red, stung into retaliation. "You speak of matters that are none of your business," she snapped, "and of which you know nothing! I will not have them traipsing through my bedchamber! When I have one of my headaches or am otherwise indisposed, how would I get any rest?"

Abigail's mouth tightened, and she pulled an item out of her apron pocket. "Speaking of where anyone sleeps, may I inquire why this was in my bedroom? It belongs to you, I believe, Patience."

It was a stocking, which Abigail dropped onto the chair beside her as if it repelled her.

The younger woman's color remained high. "All right, so I slept in your bed while you were gone. It was much easier to direct the household from a ground-floor room...."

"Oh, I can tell that you directed it," Abigail said with an unpleasant smile. "It doesn't look as if anyone did a lick of work the entire time we were gone."

"And that's my fault, I suppose? I was ill, and left alone with three small children and an old woman who fell downstairs so she had to be waited upon and no servant."

The trio who waited for their fate to be decided exchanged wary glances. These sisters-in-law obviously were not friends;

would their servants be constantly caught between them, unable to win approval from both sides no matter what?

"Well, now you have three servants," Abigail told her. "No doubt if you are going to take to your bed every time you have the slightest indisposition, we will need that many. Especially if someone else is going to have to tend the baby—"

Patience was hot-faced and quivering with rage. "*You've* certainly never lifted a finger on behalf of *any* of my children, not even when one of them was in need and you were the only adult present! I remember when Betta—"

Abigail cut through the flow of words. "I assure you that had I ever had a living child to attend, I would have been there when I was needed. The point is, we now have three servants and a decision has to be made as to where they are to sleep. Mistress Cordelia has made a point, that the lace room will not accommodate three of them, so there is little use in putting one of them there. That leaves pallets on the kitchen floor, or the summer room." She gestured toward a doorway that led into the lower section of the added-on part of the house.

"The summer room, then," Patience said; her fair skin was mottled, and her prettiness was difficult to discern. "This room is too crowded as it is."

"Summer room's too cold," Cordelia asserted. "Fireplace never got built, and they'd freeze, come December. Ice on the buckets."

"There will be ice on the buckets in here, too," Abigail said, but she sounded less forceful. "Very well. Until it is too cold, you can spread your pallets in the summer room. As you may have assumed from its name, we use it primarily in warm weather. We intended to build a fireplace out there so that it could be used year-round, but the men never got around to doing it." Her expression suggested that there were a number of chores the men never got around to.

Abigail issued a string of orders about tasks to be undertaken at dawn, and then, professing herself too worn out to do anything but retire, she withdrew. Patience had a few commands of her own to make, regarding bringing her breakfast upstairs because she would be feeding the baby there, and then the girls were alone.

They stared at each other. "It sounds," Megan said in a small voice, "as if there'll be plenty of work for three."

"If we wait on that Patience hand and foot, as she'd obviously like, and those brats of hers, there certainly will be." Roxanne picked up one of the pallets that had been left out for them.

"They aren't brats," Megan protested. "They're nice children. Nels is a lovely little boy. Healthy and strong the way Thomas should have been." Tears formed in her gray-green eyes.

Christina spoke quickly to turn their thoughts away from Thomas. "No one has designated any particular person for any special chore. It may be best if we settle the matter between us, who will tend the little ones, who the fire, who do the cooking and so on. That way each can do what best suits her." She had already decided that she'd let Roxanne choose what she wanted to do, if she could; it would be less painful in the long run.

They took a candle into the summer room, which was indeed much colder than the rest of the house, and spread their pallets. The room was small, and held only table and benches and a storage chest where they could keep some of their belongings. The rest would have to remain in their trunks that had been brought ashore from the *Revenge*.

It had been a long and eventful day, and they were tired, yet none went immediately to sleep. There was too much to think about.

Vilas, sailing off for God knew how long, Christina thought. The chances were he wouldn't even wish her a decent farewell. An ache built in her throat, thinking about it. If only he had chosen to do something on land, so there was a chance of seeing him regularly!

Megan, too, had food for thought. She had only to close her eyes to see Fitz Hull's face, to recall his hand brushing hers when he handed her the bowl and the warmth of his body as it was crowded against hers at table. Was there any possibility, however faint, that a man would consider taking to wife a woman with such a blemish as her own? If only such things were not considered the mark of the devil! If only Fitz were different from the other Puritans....

Roxanne, unlike the other two, had no intention of going to sleep. The men of the family had gone out for the evening, presumably to a local tavern to meet with their friends and exchange what, among females, would have been considered gossip. It wouldn't do to venture out before they were safely in and abed. To meet them on the road could be disastrous.

Of the entire clan of Hulls, the one she liked best was Cordelia, Patience's grandmother. Outspoken, blunt and cunning, Cordelia reminded Roxanne of her mother. Leonie had been young when she died, but if she'd been allowed to live out her life span, she might well have been like Cordelia.

Roxanne gazed upward into the darkness that was unbroken except for the flicker of firelight on the wall opposite the kitchen. Abigail and Patience were impossible. The children were, she supposed, no worse than Thomas had been, and perhaps would be less trouble. At least they were accustomed to shifting for themselves, not being waited upon by servants, and they'd been taught their place. There would be no whining lazy children in this household, she guessed.

And then there were the men. Roxanne had disliked Ezra on sight; what could you expect of a man who shared the bed of someone like Abigail? He would probably be out of the house most of the time, working in the family businesses as a merchant or a boat builder; she would simply ignore him unless he issued a direct order, which so far hadn't happened often.

Adam was different. He was the one in absolute authority, when he cared to exert it, over his sons as well as over his daughters-in-law. He reminded her somewhat of Himself. For a moment, to her surprise, she felt a wave of nostalgia, of grief that her father was gone.

Young Fitz, she reflected, amused, had shown an immediate and marked preference for Megan. He was eleven years her senior, but that was of no matter. Nor was her youth. Here in the New World, as in Cornwall, brides were taken early. And worn out early, she thought, pursing her lips in the darkness. That was not for her.

No, she was her mother's daughter, half-gypsy, with a tug toward adventure as much a part of her as mothering was a part of Megan.

The last of the men was Wesley. She lay listening to Megan's quiet breathing beside her, thinking of Wesley. Handsome, robust and with an eye for a pretty face or a well-rounded bosom. He'd chosen Patience for her looks, rather than for her disposition; now, perhaps, her blond prettiness was wearing thin. From the remark old Cordelia had made, it sounded as if Wesley's wife was too frail—or pretended to be—to accommodate her husband in bed. Which quite possibly would make her husband, Puritan or not, look elsewhere for his carnal pleasures.

He liked her looks. Roxanne knew that; he's stared openly enough, in front of the entire family. Had anyone other than Patience noticed? Not that she cared.

Wesley had brushed against her, leaving the room after supper, in a way that could only have been deliberate. Though he did not excite her in the way Shea O'Neal did, there was something about a man's touch that sent shivers of pleasure through her. If it didn't work out with O'Neal, was Wesley a viable alternative as a husband? Providing, of course, that Patience truly was an invalid and that she did not live long. In this society, a man was encouraged to remarry as soon as possible if he lost his spouse. And Wesley would be well able to provide for a wife.

On the other hand, he'd expect her to care for his children, Patience's children, which held little appeal. Unlike Megan, she had no proclivity for adopting other people's strays. And Wesley would also expect her to remain in this household, under Abigail as the senior wife. *That* held no allure.

No, her interest held with Shea O'Neal, though it might be entertaining to play at cat-and-mouse games with Wesley during the boring times when O'Neal was at sea.

A man's laughter rang out, and she went rigid, then relaxed. The Hulls were returning, and soon they'd be asleep. Then she would steal out to her assignation with O'Neal.

She heard them come in, taking no particular care to avoid disturbing those presumably sleeping in the darkened house. She heard the soft sounds of a gourd dipper in the water pail as someone took a drink, the thud of a log dropped onto the fire, a cough, a muttered word she could not make out, but which

sounded profane. Did these Puritans swear like ordinary men?
She'd yet to hear them.

Boards creaked as they climbed the stairs. Silence overtook
the household, and still Roxanne waited.

A sliver of moonlight crept in through the single window,
making a ribbon of light across the floor of the summer room.
Roxanne reached for her dress and cautiously pulled it over her
head, then groped for her shoes, carrying them when she
stepped carefully around Megan's pallet and padded into the
deserted kitchen.

Christina had dozed into a light sleep after the men had retired; she heard the latch a short time later and then the closing of the door.

She sat upright. Someone going out again, in stealthy fashion, when all should have been in for the night?

Suspicion was confirmed when she rose to hands and knees
and crawled over to the pallet where Roxanne should have been
sleeping.

She knew at once where the other girl was. Damn her,
Christina thought furiously. Roxanne had seen the nature of
these Hulls, must have guessed the consequences should she be
caught at any illicit activity. Yet she had gone out, their first
night here.

Burning with resentment, Christina crawled back into her
own bed without disturbing Megan. If she had been honest with
herself, she would have admitted to envy, as well as to resentment.

It was a long time before Roxanne returned.

Chapter 30

ROXANNE SCARCELY FELT the night chill, though she drew her shawl closely around her as she moved away from the house. The village was asleep; there were no late-evening revelers in this society. A breeze stirred the trees, sending down showers of autumn leaves, making the moonlight shift and flicker around her.

There was plenty of light to walk by once she reached the road. The smell of woodsmoke drifted to her, and the lingering aromas of someone's supper. The poorest family here had plenty of meat, for game was free to anyone who cared to hunt it, and the sea provided an abundance, as well.

She had never felt more keenly alive than she did tonight. The Hulls were forgotten, as was her indenture to them. She was her own person, acting independently; she would do as she chose.

A scurrying sound behind her caused her to spin, heart suddenly pounding, only to see a gigantic maple leaf scudding along before the wind. She laughed softly and went on.

He was already there, at the bridge, boldly outlined in the moonlight. When he saw her, O'Neal came to meet her in long, easy strides. How graceful he was, how powerfully he moved!

In the open the moon provided enough illumination to read by, had that been their inclination. They both instinctively stretched out their hands, joining them. In the instant before she was drawn into his arms she saw the scarred side of his face and had the fleeting thought that anyone would take him for a pirate at this moment.

And then his arms came around her, hard and strong. His lean body was pressed against her, and she saw his dark eyes above hers before she closed her own and surrendered to the embrace she had craved.

His mouth was warm and demanding, and the kiss deepened, searing not only her lips but her very soul. Roxanne felt as if she were falling, falling through a darkness studded by exploding stars, a darkness that held no terrors, only an intoxication far greater than from the rum that lingered on his breath.

He released her at last, laughing. "I'd begun to fear you wouldn't come."

"I had to wait until the house was settled, and the men were late coming home." The words came with an effort; she was breathless, and she resented being dragged back to reality.

His teeth flashed in the moonlight. "I know. We drank together and talked. And I arranged to conclude my business very early in the morning, so that I might take advantage of the tide to be away at dawn. That made it logical that I should spend the night ashore, to save time on the morrow. The longboat will be on the beach for me at daybreak."

She fought for control of her breathing, for his hands held her firmly beneath the shawl, his thumbs resting on the soft undersides of her breasts. Tantalizing, paralyzing. "Where do you go? How long will you be gone?"

"We sail north. The French supply their colonists along the St. Lawrence, and the colonists send back furs and dried fish. Both bring a goodly price in Boston Town. As for how long—" he paused, shrugging "—one never knows as to that. A few weeks, a month. Perhaps more. If we are lucky, we'll be back before the snow falls. The North Atlantic in winter holds little appeal, not for French arms and food, nor for furs and fish. The tropics, that's the place to be when the winds grow cold, sailing jeweled seas rather than the sullen northern waters. Someday I will take you there, to the southern climes. We will swim in those warm waters and walk sandy beaches that stretch for miles—"

"A pity you don't leave for the south tonight," Roxanne managed. What she would give not to have to return to that house with those bitchy women to give her orders!

"You're trembling. Are you cold?" He drew his cloak around her at once, the fur lining soft and warming, as were the arms he once more wrapped her in. His breath was warm, too, against her temple. "There is no need to stay here in the cold.

I've taken a room, and it has an outside door of its own, so there's no risk involved.'' The laughter issued from deep in his chest, low and rich. ''These Puritans take a dim view of such things, at least in public, but they don't let their scruples stand in the way of the price of a night's lodgings.''

For all that she'd been responding to him completely, Roxanne now stilled. Meeting a man on a bridge in the middle of the village, even at night, was one matter. Accompanying him to his room was another, for that would mean only one thing. Was she ready for that?

''You are overbold, I think,'' she said, pulses leaping, trying not to sound as tremulous as she felt.

''Ah, milady Roxanne, I thought we had an agreement that we would play no foolish games,'' he chided gently. His hands moved on her back, stroking, caressing, and once more her breathing caught in her chest.

''I . . . I know of no such agreement,'' she stammered, fearing that if he continued to touch her this way, if his hands roamed much farther afield, she would not be able to speak at all.

''But surely we knew it without putting it into words!'' He drew back slightly, peering into her face, his hands now still though touching the sides of her breasts in a way that made her want to swoon. ''We are alike, you and I, milady.''

''Not quite,'' Roxanne countered. ''You are a man of broad experience, and I . . . I am only a country girl.''

''And a virgin? Is that what worries you?'' He didn't wait for her reply. ''I will prove a tender lover, I promise you. How better to be introduced to the pleasures of love than by one who knows them well and who will take as much delight in your pleasure as in his own? You need have no fear of me, milady.''

This time his kiss was gentle, yet it, too, sparked the fires within her. Fires, Roxanne thought dimly, that must have been burning already, though well banked, so quickly did the heat kindle.

When he swept her off her feet, the fur-lined cloak swirling out around them, his mouth still locked on hers, Roxanne made no protest. She was not even aware of the faint moan deep in her throat, only of the pounding heart, the racing pulses, the leap of anticipation deep within her.

O'Neal carried her swiftly toward the inn where he had taken a room. He must have left the door ajar, for he did not have to put her down but opened it with a foot. The warmer darkness enveloped them, and he kicked the door shut. A moment later she was lowered onto a bed that yielded to her weight, and his own pressing her into it.

The hands were freer now. While his lips traced the line of her throat, fingers worked expertly with small buttons. By the time his mouth had reached an exposed breast, the hands had gone lower still, pushing up skirts and petticoats, seeking out the moist, smoldering core of her awakening body.

Never had she experienced anything like the assault of this man's mouth and hands and body. Yet O'Neal was true to his word: he was a tender lover, teasing, coaxing, drawing back before there was pain, somehow managing to divest both her and himself of their garments without for a moment letting the tension lessen.

Roxanne had wondered if she would be embarrassed, not knowing what to do, but her body responded to his as instinctively as a bee finds honey in the depths of the rose. If she faltered for an instant, O'Neal was ready to guide her. Building, building, into an explosion that made her cry out at its peak and then subside, spent and trembling, knowing she could not have borne it for a second longer, yet sorry that it had ended.

God's blood, she thought, dazed, no wonder everybody wanted to do it.

Beside her, O'Neal chuckled in the darkness. "I did not hurt you, milady?"

She had a dim recollection that there had been pain, transitory and now nearly forgotten. She drew a shuddering breath. "It was worth it."

He laughed aloud. "Dare a gentleman say 'I told you so'?"

"You're no gentleman," Roxanne stated. She had a fleeting urge to push him off the bed, but he felt too good beside her, the lean body firm against her own bare flesh.

She liked his laughter. She would have liked staying here with him, in this bed, forever. Yet tomorrow he sailed for the mouth of the St. Lawrence and the hazards of attacking the French ships for their treasures. She would be sorry to see him go, while at the same time the possible dangers to come added an element of increased excitement to being with him now.

Gradually her breathing returned to normal. He moved his hand, which had rested on her bare stomach, lazily upward, cupping a breast so that the nipple hardened at once.

"Is it possible to do it again so soon?" she asked.

"Ah, I have made a convert to my way of thinking! But perhaps we should wait a few moments. A man must reload his weapon, so to speak. In the meantime, however, dalliance can be diverting."

He bent his head and found her mouth unerringly, the hand once more caressing, stroking, exploring.

Roxanne let herself go limp, let her mind float, giving herself over to sensation, and then a bold idea came to her. This time she would not be passive. Now she, too, would touch and experience through her fingertips this magnificent male body.

She heard his murmur of approval and smiled; though she could not see his face, she knew that he was smiling, too.

Chapter 31

IT WAS NONE of *her* business, Christina told herself, where Roxanne had been last night, nor what she had been doing.

Yet only a fool could look at the girl, even in the pale gray light of dawn, and not make an accurate guess, just from the dreamy expression in Roxanne's green eyes and from the little secret smile that kept forming around the full mouth as she went about her chores.

It chilled Christina's blood to consider the consequences if these Puritans determined that Roxanne was guilty of wrongdoing. They had laws against breaking the Sabbath, even by such harmless things as cutting one's hair, making a bed or cooking a meal. They had laws against drunkenness, against witchcraft, against fornication. Punishment for any of those things was swift and could be brutal.

The mush that had been simmering overnight in the big black kettle was ladled into wooden bowls for the men who ate it mostly in silence. A crusie, filled with oil and with a floating wick to carry the flame, was lighted in the middle of the long table, for it was still dim within the house. It flickered fitfully every time one of the women passed by close enough to create a draft, sending their faces in and out of shadow.

Fitz smiled at Megan as she refilled his bowl; Wesley's gaze followed Roxanne as she moved between table and fire. Ezra and Adam concentrated on eating once the grace had been said.

When the men had departed for the boat works near the shore, the girls ate their own breakfast. Roxanne laughed when Christina had hesitated over that. "You don't expect her holiness—or her Patience-less-ness—to show up momentarily and want something, do you? I'll be amazed if either of them is up for hours."

Christina glanced nervously over her shoulder. "Don't say such things where they can hear you. Why make them angry with you?"

"Who cares?" Roxanne said with a carelessness that would have won Christina's envy if it hadn't provoked her so. "We've agreed to work out our passage money, but we haven't agreed to be slaves. My thoughts and my words are my own."

"The words may not be," Christina cautioned, filling her own bowl and following the others to the table. "Not if they cause offense." Curiosity tugged at her, and she put it down. She would not give Roxanne the satisfaction of refusing information.

Megan, though, was not as reserved. She spoke with a confidential air between bites of steaming mush. "I heard you come back to bed very late last night, Roxanne. I hope no one else heard you."

The smile broadened. "So do I. Though what can they do, other than reprimand me?" She shrugged. "It will still have been worth it."

Megan's eyes were solemn. "Did you meet Captain O'Neal?"

The smile became a laugh. "Of course. Who else?"

"The way you were acting with Vilas on the ship," Christina said tartly, "and ogling Master Wesley at table last night, one might suspect an assignation with almost anyone."

Roxanne widened her eyes, mocking her. "Why, a body would think you were jealous! As I recall, it was Master Wesley who ogled *me*, and as for Vilas, why, I was only showing you how it's done, how a man is made aware of a woman. Not that most of them take much coaxing in that regard."

Her complacency and her apparent success in such matters did nothing to soothe Christina. There was little more to be said, however, and they finished their meal in silence. Christina wished miserably that Vilas had at least taken the trouble to wish her a private farewell, instead of the casual and impersonal words in front of the entire company.

Their first full day in Ipswich was a busy one and set the tone for the days to follow.

Patience did, indeed, remain in bed most of the morning, from which she issued a stream of demands and orders: a hot brick for her feet, an extra quilt, a cup of tea—after she'd finished her mush, so that Roxanne made two trips up and down the stairs instead of one—a book she'd left downstairs.

Roxanne took the latter to her, pausing on the upper landing to examine it. It was titled *The Tenth Muse* and consisted of poetry by someone named Ann Bradstreet.

Her interest quickened. Printed out, and by a woman! She would look more closely into this, when Patience had finished with it. In the meantime a romantic verse that had been forming in her head all morning might be written down, too, she thought. She had seen paper and pen on the large table in the room across the hall where Adam and Fitz slept.

She did not have time to put that plan into action at once, however.

Abigail was not a slug-abed, though she saw no reason to rise with the servants. She was feeling somewhat better now that she was home, though drained of energy. She rose and dressed, and came out into the kitchen to serve herself from the kettle, then issued orders as she ate.

"We will dye those gowns that are so unsuitable," she stated. "You'll have to get a fire going under the big kettle that sits in the corner of the summer room—you'll see the place in the side yard for it—and haul the water to be heated. Betta and Nels will show you where to gather the bark of the red oak to simmer in it."

Christina moistened her lips. "What color will that make, Mistress Hull?"

"Brown. A nice, practical brown. There is laundry to do, too, since Betta only washed out baby things while we were gone, but that will have to wait until the dyeing is done, since we'll use the same kettle."

Brown, Christina thought glumly. No doubt it would be the most drab color that could be managed, and every outer garment they owned would be dyed.

The loom in the corner of the main room was drawn out, and they were instructed to its use, to make material for the clothes that would be needed. None of them was in the least proficient in the use of a spinning wheel, either; they watched Abigail's deft fingers and despaired of ever matching her ability. Yet learn they would, they were told.

Cooking was an activity that took many hours every day. Meat was kept roasting or stewing almost constantly in the fireplace that, while not as large as those in the great hall at home, would have accommodated a number of standing men side by side. They learned to cut the tops off the orange vegetables called pumpkins and scoop out the pulp; the seeds would be saved for roasting, the pumpkins would be baked and were delicious when served with a sprinkling of cinnamon or drizzled with maple syrup.

Dried beans took a long time to soften and so were soaked overnight, then sat in the pot over the fire all day, to be eaten come evening with the cornbread that was baked for nearly every meal.

The apples were ripening, and they had to be cut and dried for use during the winter. Their hands grew sore and stained from cutting those and stirring the garments in the boiling kettle outside until they were the desired shade, after which the clothes were rinsed in cold water and then wrung out to dry. Brown, every item, though some of the deeper colors did not absorb the dye evenly or well and it appeared that the dried gowns were going to take on some peculiar shades.

It was late afternoon when Roxanne escaped from the aroma of apples and moved quietly up the stairs. Patience was resting, though from what was unimaginable. Emory had been put down for a nap, and the older children were cracking nuts on the back steps in the fall sunshine; she could hear their quiet voices and occasional laughter.

Roxanne let herself into the room where Adam and Fitz slept. It was not necessary to make up their bed; they had drawn up the quilts before they left the house. She crossed to the writing table, heartbeat quickening, and cautiously sat down on the wooden chair.

Writing paper was at a premium in the New World, having to be imported all the way from England, yet the Hulls kept a supply of it. There was a record book that she pushed aside, and she took a sheet of the precious paper, dipped the quill pen into the ink bottle and hesitated over the words. She could not waste any of these materials, so it must be right. The words had formed and reformed in her mind all during her tasks in the kitchen and the yard, and she knew what she wanted to say.

It amazed her that the words—no, the poetry—seemed to flow from the pen as easily as did the ink. Her handwriting was small and cramped, but legible. When she had filled the page, she read over the words and was filled with delight at her own work.

Sometime, perhaps, she would show this to Shea O'Neal. In the meantime, she would hide it away somewhere, to be taken out and savored when she needed a reminder of last night, of being in O'Neal's arms.

Her body ached, thinking of it now. Roxanne folded the paper carefully and put it inside her bodice, then made her way back downstairs.

"What have you been doing?" Abigail demanded, fortunately not waiting for a reply. "We need more wood chopped for the fires, and it's nearly time to peel the turnips and onions for the stew. I am going to walk over to visit Mistress Newbock, on the far side of the village. I will expect a meal to be prepared by the time the men return for supper."

Roxanne waited until the woman had left the house before she stepped out into the summer room, where she put the crackling paper inside her bedroll against the far wall, where it would be safe. She wondered if she could get away with enough paper to write an entire story, for now that the poem was out of her system, she felt the glimmerings of an idea. Not the dry sort of tripe that seemed to fill most of the books in this house— she'd already peeked into several of them and had no wish to read *The Bay Psalm Book*, nor Cotton Mather's *Memorable Providences Relating to Witchcrafts and Possessions*—but an adventure, a romance, of piracy and love on the high seas. She couldn't count on having the privacy of that upstairs room; she'd have to provision herself with pen and ink, as well, and seek out some other private spot in which to write. The idea excited her almost as much as thinking of O'Neal's return from the northern wilderness.

MEGAN FELL NATURALLY into caring for the baby, Emory, and looking after Nels and Betta. Actually Betta, though not quite nine, was a very self-sufficient little person who readily advised the newcomers and helped them avoid open conflict with her Aunt Abigail. She was already skilled in the use of both spinning wheel and needle, knew a good deal about running a household and cooking and did a considerable amount of the running and carrying for her mother, as well as doing her best to keep Nels out of trouble.

Both the children took to Megan at once. When she held the baby and crooned lullabies to him, the older boy and girl sat close beside her, listening. While they worked picking nuts out of their shells or stringing apples to dry, she told them stories that held them spellbound, for all their simplicity; there had never been storytellers in this household before.

Roxanne sometimes paused, overhearing. "Such tame tales you tell, Megan! Now I would give that one an entirely different ending!"

Nels stared up at her, his tasks forgotten. "How do you mean, mistress?"

"Well, instead of having Master Giles settle down to raising sheep—a boring occupation, to say the least—I would have the queen reward him with a ship and a commission to sail the seas in search of rich booty, so that when he returned home at last he could raise sheep or not, as he chose. He'd be rich enough to do nothing at all, if that's what he wanted."

Nels glanced at Megan, clearly unable to envision being able to do nothing at all. From the time he'd been able to carry the smallest chunk of wood he'd been expected to help hauling in a supply of fuel for the fireplace.

Megan was smiling. "I suppose it does make a better story your way, Roxanne."

From across the yard Christina observed them, unable to hear their words. Her back ached, her arms and shoulders felt as if they were on fire, and still she must use the wooden paddle to stir the garments that turned darker and darker in the kettle.

She lifted a gown, unrecognizable, ugly, on the end of the paddle, and felt a spurt of rebellion. Surely this was dark enough, hideous enough, to satisfy Abigail's demands. If the clothes were rinsed and hung to dry, the dye kettle emptied before she returned, the woman was unlikely to demand that the garments be processed again.

Christina gave the contents of the pot one last vicious stab and withdrew the paddle. "I need the cold water now," she called, and the children and Megan scrambled obediently to their feet to fetch it.

Roxanne crossed to look into the kettle. "She's going to see we don't attract undue attention, isn't she? I kept out the jade velvet, damn her. I may not be permitted to wear it to her church services, but I won't let her ruin it, either. When Captain O'Neal returns, I'll have one gown that won't turn his stomach."

"I kept back a blue one, too," Christina confessed, rubbing at the muscles in her neck. "I don't intend to live among Puritans forever."

"I decided that the first day," Roxanne said. She could afford to sound cheerful; she hadn't been stirring heavy wet clothes for hours over a steaming pot. "Where's old Mistress Cordelia? Were we supposed to be doing anything for her?"

Christina clapped a hand over her mouth. "Oh no! Did anyone take her anything to eat today?"

"I did," Megan said, dumping a bucket into the container that had been made ready for rinsing out the excess dye. "She had a bowl of mush. I don't think she had anything at midday, however."

"Yes, she did," Betta piped, emptying her own bucket. "I took her more mush. It was almost cold, but she said it was better than trying to chew meat. She doesn't have enough teeth."

Christina regarded the little girl with curiosity. "What does she do upstairs all day by herself?"

"She makes lace."

"Lace? When the Puritan women aren't allowed to adorn their gowns in any way?"

Betta glanced about in an oddly adult way, with the practice of one accustomed to considering who might hear her words. "It's true we aren't supposed to have lace. Aunt Abigail says it's sinful to take pleasure in such worldly things. But Mama has a petticoat with two rows of lace. She washes it out herself, so Aunt Abigail won't see. And Grandmother has one, too. She bastes it on and takes it off to be washed, since Aunt Abigail scolded her for it."

Christina considered this, puzzled. "Then why does she make lace, if no one is supposed to wear it?"

"She sells it. Grandfather ships it to England, where it brings a very good price. The ladies there wear lace on everything, Grandmother says." There was a wistful note in the young voice. "Many of the women in the village make lace to sell. In the winter it's too cold in the lace room, and besides, Grandmother's hands are too stiff and sore to work there. She gave me a little scrap of lace, once. I keep it hidden under my pillow."

The child flushed, then, as if expecting censure.

"I'm sure it's very pretty," Megan said, touching the little girl's shoulder. "In the part of England we came from, it is not considered wicked to wear lace."

"In Ipswich everything that's fun is wicked," Betta said sadly, turning away.

"Even coasting," Nels confirmed.

"Coasting?" The trio waited for enlightenment.

"Aye. You know, sliding down hills when it snows. It's a waste of time, according to the church," Betta said, pausing.

Nels laughed, again reminding them of Thomas in one of his better moments. "The tithing man is kept busy in winter, watching for coasters. And in the summer, for swimmers. Swimming is not allowed, either, nor even wading along the shore. Father and I went wading, once, and it was great fun." He stopped abruptly, putting his hands to his mouth. "I forgot. I wasn't supposed to tell anyone."

"We won't tell," Roxanne assured him. "As long as you don't tell on us when we do it."

Both children were convulsed with amusement at the idea of these grown ladies either coasting or wading. They hurried off for more water, and Christina began to lift clothes out of the kettle, letting the dark brown water run off before submerging them into the cold water. Not until they had cooled could they be wrung out without burning her hands.

But they will turn brown, she thought ruefully soon after her first attempt at wringing. Ah, well, Vilas was not here to see them. By the time he returned, no doubt the dye would have worn off.

The weeks stretched endlessly ahead of her, until that time should come.

If only, she thought, she had something to remember, as Roxanne obviously did.

The little secret smile was back on Roxanne's lips, and Christina made a vow to herself. The next time, when Vilas came back, she, too, would summon her courage to take steps to make him notice her as something other than a cousin, even if it meant emulating Roxanne's embarrassing tactics.

Somehow, she must reach Vilas in the way that Roxanne had obviously reached Captain O'Neal.

Chapter 32

THE DAY LEFT Abigail exhausted; she retired before the table was cleared away. Patience had emerged from her room for a desultory period of reading in the afternoon, had sat idly—but at least without giving orders—during the last hour of supper preparations, complained without vigor that there were too many turnips in the stew and the meat was tough, and also withdrew the moment she'd finished eating.

The men, as was their apparent custom, left for an hour of congenial company in the village; the children were dispatched to bed at dusk after Betta had begged a lighted candle, so that she might read to Grandmother Cordelia. "After making lace all day, her eyes are too tired," she explained.

Without the mistresses of the house present, the girls worked cheerfully at the clearing away. Christina brought inside the gowns she had dyed, examining them dolefully. "A fine lot we're going to be in these. Look at this. It didn't take the dye well, and the velvet is so matted it's hideous."

"No doubt that's what Mistress Abigail intended," Roxanne said. "Because she's a dried-up stick of a woman herself, she doesn't want us to appear attractive, either. May the devil take the woman!"

There was an indrawn breath, and they spun apprehensively to find Patience standing at the foot of the stairs in her nightgown. She was very pale, but even as they watched warmth grew in her cheeks. "I called you from the top of the stairs," she said sharply, "and no one answered."

"I'm sorry, mistress. We did not hear you," Christina apologized.

"No doubt! With all the chattering you're doing, you wouldn't hear a thunder clap if it were directly overhead. Surely you have better things to do than stand about jabbering nonsense."

Christina swallowed, accepting the rebuke, and Megan looked down at the floor. Roxanne, however, met Patience's hard gray eyes with a glint of spirit in her own.

"Are we not to converse together at all, then? After working all day at the tasks set to us—and still doing them, if you'll notice—do we not have the freedom to exchange a few words? We understood we are indentured to do your work, not be your slaves for the whole of the day and night!"

The heat grew in Patience's face. "You are impertinent, I think!"

"Perhaps so," Roxanne said with lazy insolence, taking off her apron and tossing it over the back of a chair, "but I, for one, have done my share of work for one day, and I long for some fresh air and a few moments to myself. I'm going out for a walk."

She turned aside to the summer room and had brought out her cloak before Patience found her voice again.

"Out! After dark?"

"I've no fears of the dark," Roxanne assured her. She drew the cloak around her and opened the door, leaving behind her a strained silence.

Megan reached for the broom and swept up the crumbs from the floor, not looking up. Christina felt compelled to cope on her own with the angry woman.

"What was it you wished, Mistress Patience?"

For a few seconds it seemed Patience had forgotten, so great was her rage at being spoken to in this way. Her memory was jogged by the cup she carried in her hand. "My tea," she said at last. "I like a cup of mint tea before I go to sleep. It soothes my stomach."

Christina took the cup. "Of course, mistress. Will you wait for it, or shall we bring it up to you?"

Patience curled her shaking fingers into small fists. "Bring it up," she decided, and turned on her heel, going soundlessly up the stairs in her bare feet.

A lesson to them, Christina thought, getting down the mint leaves to put into the cup. Without shoes on Patience could approach them without notice. She had not commented on Roxanne's remarks about Abigail, but there was little possibility that she would forget them.

She hoped when that time came, she and Megan would not be included in the consequences.

Christina would have liked a stroll herself; she missed the walks she had taken along the bluffs and the shore at home. Yet tonight she was very tired, and she did not really want to encounter Roxanne for fear she would say too much and worsen the situation between them. She was beginning to understand that opposing Roxanne was the poorest way to deal with her, though it was hard to see how one could do otherwise.

"I'm going to bed as soon as I deliver the tea," she said, dipping hot water from the kettle over the fire. "Have you finished?"

"I'll take the tea up," Megan offered. "I think I'll take some to Mistress Cordelia, too. I feel sorry for her, the way she's neglected, left up there alone when she isn't well enough to come down. Go on to bed, Chris."

She was glad enough to go. Her shoulders felt as if they were on fire. Would her muscles become accustomed to such things as stirring clothes for hours on end? It was depressing to think that all that effort would only result in having to wear those dreadful garments, some of which had not taken the color evenly.

She thought of Roxanne and Captain O'Neal. Had he made love to her or only kissed her? Either way, it was more than she and Vilas had ever done. A few tears of self-pity trickled from beneath her lashes before she fell asleep.

Megan carried up the tea, earning a stony look from Patience and grateful thanks from Cordelia.

"It's thoughtful of you, girl," the old woman said, sipping at it.

Megan glanced around the attic room. The roof was so low that standing erect was impossible near the walls. Though the quilt on the bed was a warm one, it was obviously old; it was much more faded than the ones on the other beds in the house. Betta slept on a trundle bed, her pale hair in disarray, and Megan smiled.

"Aye, she's a bonny child," Cordelia said, nodding.

Megan bent to pick up the bit of lace protruding from under the little girl's pillow. "She told me you'd given her this. She treasures it.'' She held the scrap closer to the candle to examine it. "It's very fine, very beautiful. Did you make it?"

"Aye, that I did. Brings a good price in England, they say. Would you like to see how it's done?"

Megan replaced Betta's lace and straightened. "I'd like that. Though I don't know if I'll ever have time to try it."

Cordelia nodded. "Hard taskmasters, those two. Keep you running."

Megan hesitated before she asked her question. "Is she really ill? Mistress Patience?"

Cordelia sipped of the mint tea, her old face shrewd. "That's a problem I've wrestled with ever since she was a babe. Her mother was a good child, much like Betta, there. But Patience . . . she was sickly, true enough. Nearly died at least once every winter from the year she was born until she was eight, and then . . . well, she never did anything she didn't want to do. When she rolled her eyes back in her head or fainted or turned very pale and had trouble with her breathing, why, no one pressed her. I believe she is frail. But I suspect she uses her weakness to escape things she doesn't want to do. She's scarcely done a lick of work about the house since the first few months she was married. Once she was with child, she wasn't well enough. *That* was real; I've watched her throwing up her insides many a time. And I've felt sorry for her, losing two of the babes. She grieved sorely, I believe, as I've grieved for my own losses."

Cordelia drained the cup. "Abigail has grieved, too, that the Lord did not see fit to send her children at all. It's a cruel world, girl. Yet that makes some more compassionate, and some more selfish, and I fear Patience is one of the selfish ones. Wesley has been a reasonable man, but he's a man, nonetheless. For all that he expects his wife to be demure and proper in society, he wants a responsive woman in his bed."

"And Patience isn't, you think?" Megan murmured, glancing at Betta to be sure the child still slept.

Cordelia's cackle made Betta flop over on her stomach, so that her long hair made a silken curtain over her small face.

"No guessing about it, mistress! When all is silent in the house, there's little I don't hear from the room below. The snores and the words, unless they're whispered. Wesley isn't much taken to whispering."

Megan wondered if the reverse were true, if the woman below would know they were in conversation up here. They had kept their voices low, however, so as not to disturb Betta.

"I'd better go," she decided.

"Well, I thank you for the tea. Tomorrow, if you'd come up and assist me, I may try to get downstairs for the day. I don't want to fall again. I fear breaking a bone, and I've no wish to die ahead of my time of a broken bone that won't heal." Her grin revealed her sparsity of teeth.

"I'll come up early, shall I? Good night, then, mistress."

Megan made her way down the stairs, past Patience's closed door, down the lower flight and into the darkened kitchen. The coals still glowed on the hearth, enough to illuminate in silhouette the figure stripping off garments before it.

Megan halted, heart leaping into her throat. It was Fitz, she could tell that, and for the first time she viewed an adult male naked, limbs gleaming in the reddish glow.

Emotion, sensation, surged through her. A hand crept to her throat in that characteristic gesture as she froze, not daring to reveal herself.

No doubt he thought the servants all asleep. She ought to have turned her head away—remounted the steps and come down more noisily, perhaps—but she remained fixed where she was. She had entertained the usual curiosity about men, though caring for Thomas as an infant had educated her as to the anatomical differences between the sexes. It had not occurred to her, however, that a man could have such a beautiful body, such lean yet muscular limbs, such grace of movement.

She stood spellbound as Fitz discarded garments that dripped audibly on the floor and pulled on a pair of dry breeches he must have taken from the basket Christina had brought in just at dusk.

She was foolishly unprepared when he turned from the fire and saw her. Of course he would see her, with her white apron and cap, even in the dimness; his eyes had adjusted to the poor light.

If he was taken aback, he hid it well. He came toward her across the room. "Mistress Megan, is it? I thought you all abed."

"I . . . I took tea up to Mistress Patience and Mistress Cordelia," she said. Surely he could not tell that her face was flooded with color, yet anyone could have detected the tremor in her voice. "I did not think anyone was here."

"I came back early after a tussle sent me into the river. It's too cold a night to sit around in wet clothes. I've set them to dry over the bench."

She had no more words. The memory of that fire-lighted body was too vivid, and he was too close, less than a yard away.

"No doubt you're weary and ready to retire," Fitz observed.

Still tongue-tied, she stood mute before him.

"Good night, then, Mistress Megan," he said softly, and went around her and up the stairs.

She stood there for a long time, unwilling to move, tingling all over, breathing more quickly. Until Roxanne came in, and the spell was broken, and they both went to bed on their pallets in the summer room, neither of them speaking.

Chapter 33

LIFE SETTLED into a pattern of early rising, chores that made their backs ache and chapped their hands and falling asleep the moment their heads touched the pillows.

The good moments were those they managed to find for themselves, which were few enough to be highly valued. Only Christina's suspicions were roused by Roxanne's blithe assumption of all duties on the second floor, even to setting Patience's room to rights with her present much of the time. Christina did not know what took so much time up there, and no one else questioned it. Abigail did not like Roxanne, and as long as the girl stayed out of her sight there was minimal friction between them.

For at least an hour a day, divided into shorter segments when necessary, Roxanne withdrew to the bedroom where the other women didn't come; she wrote her stories and her poems, carrying every page away with her to be hidden, hoping without serious concern that no one would notice how rapidly the supply of paper was diminishing.

Allowing her imagination to pour out onto the pages sent it soaring. No sooner had she captured an ode to the autumn woods than another on the way the frost made a jeweled circlet of a gigantic spiderweb came to mind; she could not rest until she had put the words into writing, to reread and savor later on.

No one objected to her taking down any of the books from the shelves in the main room, as long as she read them when she was not neglecting her duties. Sometimes she read by the dying firelight after the others had gone to bed, for read she must, and the compulsion to write down her thoughts was increasingly strong.

Megan fell naturally into the tasks that involved Cordelia and the children. The latter intuitively knew that Megan had more affection—and time—to devote to them than anyone else in their lives. Their mother was often unwell and did not want to be bothered by them. Their father spent long days at the boat works and seldom did more than ruffle their towheads with a hand as he passed by them when he returned. Betta was her Grandfather Adam's favorite; he would put an arm about her and listen to her recite her lessons, but he, too, was busy, away from the house most of the time.

The children responded eagerly to the things Megan set about teaching them. The older two attended the Dame School in the village when the weather permitted the long walk; on bad days, they were content to sit with Megan before the fire, reading from the primer they shared.

"Young Timothy learnt sin to fly. Whales from the sea, God's voice obey," Nels read aloud. Then Betta took her turn. "Xerxes must die, and so must I. While youth do cheer, death may be near. Zaccheus he did climb the tree our Lord to see."

Roxanne, overhearing as she passed through, grimaced. "Wonderfully uplifting material they learn on," she commented. "Even the Bible has more cheerful stories than that, if one looks for them."

"Are you criticizing the Bible?" At the incredulous voice, they looked around to find Patience staring at them. Her habit of moving soundlessly up and down stairs made them all nervous.

"Not at all," Roxanne denied glibly. "I'm going out to pick the last of those apples," and she rolled her eyes at Christina as she passed, a book hidden in her skirts for the half hour or so she would remain outside after the fruit had been gathered.

Megan filled most of her daytime hours with nursery chores, and running up and down stairs on errands. It didn't occur to her to wonder that she so seldom encountered Roxanne when they were both above stairs; her own thoughts were on Fitz.

She tried to be out of doors when it was time for the men to return from the boat works, for often Fitz was the first home. When that was the case, he invariably delayed to speak with her. To begin with he would ask some simple question about her day, an impersonal question. By the end of the second week, he would comment with a smile on how prettily the wind tangled her long fair hair or how becomingly the chill had put color into her cheeks. Shortly after that he was asking her opinions on all sorts of things, in a way that suggested he cared how she felt about life in this strange new place.

He was surprisingly easy to talk with. Not even Vilas, who had been as near older brother as cousin, had put her so at ease, while at the same time Fitz's presence created an inner excitement that permeated her entire life: she either anticipated this, or took hours to recover—reluctantly—from the latest encounter.

Only Christina moved through lonely days, missing Vilas, cursing herself for not having been brave enough to jolt him into recognizing her as a woman rather than as a taken-for-granted cousin. She worked methodically in the kitchen, taking what satisfaction she could from learning the skills of a housekeeper, against the day when she might display them for Vilas.

On the whole, their new lives were not unduly harsh, with the exception of the Sabbath days.

No one went away to work on the seventh day of the week. No chores were allowed at home, and leisure activities were restricted to reading from some appropriate religious publication.

Not much time was allotted even to that limited activity, for the Sabbath was spent primarily in church. This consisted of a four-hour session in the morning, a walk home to eat cold meat and beans, and another similar session in the afternoon.

The minister, Christina decided, was an improvement over the one they'd heard in Boston. The Reverend Drayton was a rawboned man in his mid-thirties, earnest and well-spoken. And while the subject of witchcraft did come up during his lengthy sermons, he begged for tolerance, for prayerful thought, rather than accusations and vengeance.

"Let not Ipswich be caught up in the madness of witch-hunting such as goes on now in Salem," he pleaded. "While it is true that the Bible warns against witches, it also counsels us to refrain from false witness against our neighbors. Take care, lest you be overzealous in one area and careless in another."

Wrapped in her own concerns, Christina gave little thought to what was happening with her sisters, except on the occasions when Roxanne clashed with one of the mistresses of the house. If she retired to the summer room with a book half-concealed in her skirts, half an hour before she and Megan had completed *their* duties, what did it matter? It kept Roxanne out of trouble.

She was pleased that Megan had accepted her own lot so easily. She was clearly contented with the children, for they were always with her, and she smiled so much. She was spending more time out of doors, in the crisp fall air, than she had ever done when she was responsible for the sickly Thomas; her color was high, and she grew prettier by the day. Christina did not see how often Fitz paused to speak to the younger girl, nor note that Megan's ear was attuned to his footsteps.

Christina planned strategies as she stirred the boiling concoction of lye and fat to make the year's supply of strong soap or bent over the candle molds, ignoring the tiredness in her arms and shoulders as she contemplated what she might do to make Vilas notice her as a woman. One after another she discarded the plans as being too bold or too foolish or simply beyond her capacity to carry out. At night, when she dreamed of Vilas, he was hers, to love and care for. She imagined him on the decks or in the rigging of the *Revenge*, scarlet cloak billowing, and prayed for his safety.

The days grew shorter, and every morning now there was heavy frost everywhere when they awoke. Abigail, though up early and heavy-handed with her orders, seemed tired, and took to afternoon naps.

They all took advantage of that. With neither Abigail nor Patience hanging over them and issuing orders, free time increased, though there was some risk of being taken to task about the quantity of spinning or weaving that had been done. As far as the men were concerned, if the floors had been swept and they were greeted with the aromas of roasting meat and baking bread, the servants were fulfilling their obligations.

Having the privacy of the summer room for their sleeping quarters had allowed Christina and Megan to grow lax in their concern; they undressed in the dark and dressed the same way. Several times Christina was on the verge of revealing Megan's secret to Roxanne; each time, at the last moment, uncertainty held her back. Roxanne would not deliberately endanger the younger girl, but she was so heedless of her words in front of others!

Though they knew there were other bound servants in the village, they had little opportunity to become acquainted with them.

"These Puritans aren't much for entertainment, are they?" Roxanne asked ruefully one rainy afternoon as they sat around the kitchen with baskets of mending and knitting. "Kenwood Castle was a far cry from what I've heard of London, but at least there was an occasional feast, and guests came to hunt in season. There was a chance to dress up and attend a ball if you were an adult, and we could watch the festivities from the gallery. Now look at us!" She ran a hand over the skirt that had once been a lovely shade of blue and was now a disgusting brown. "We're so ugly!"

Megan looked up to smile at her. "You couldn't be ugly no matter what you wore, Roxanne."

Unmollified, Roxanne rolled up the sock she was darning and hurled it away from her, into the fire, where it sent out the odor of burning wool.

For a moment horror held them suspended, and then Roxanne began to laugh. "It was past mending anyway."

Within seconds they were all laughing. Until Patience's voice cut through their merriment.

"What is going on out here? What is that awful smell?"

Roxanne met her gaze guilelessly. "I can't imagine, mistress. We're sorry if we disturbed your rest." Since it was mid-afternoon, there might have been a touch of sarcasm in her tone.

"Your boisterousness is unseemly," Patience stated.

The wise thing undoubtedly would have been to bow their heads in acquiescence. Roxanne, however, seldom considered what was the wise thing. "No? But the Good Book tells us to make a joyful noise unto the Lord, does it not? What is that, Christina, your memory is better than mine. From the Psalms, I believe."

"The sixty-sixth," Christina murmured, surprised that Roxanne was even remotely correct on such a matter.

Patience had very fair skin, and when she was angered it became a mottled pink and white. "Don't quote Scripture at me, girl. *What* is that stink?'' She walked over to the cavernous fireplace and peered into it, but the sock was indistinguishable in the flames. She lifted the lid of the stew pot, then replaced it, turning to face them. ''You have been making enough noise, and not to the Lord, so that you've failed to hear Abigail calling you. *I* heard her clearly enough, from overhead.''

In the startled silence they heard her now, and also the wail of the baby. Patience compressed her lips. ''Now she's wakened Emory, as well. Please tend to her at once.''

Her back was ramrod stiff as she left them.

Roxanne stood up, making a face that imitated Patience's in every particular except coloring, and both the other girls broke into giggles, hastily smothered. ''I'll see what she wants. Don't throw any more of those stockings on the fire. Mistress Patience is right; it *does* stink.''

She emerged from the bedchamber a moment later to announce that Abigail was feeling queasy and had requested mint tea to soothe her stomach. ''I'll fix us some, as well,'' Roxanne offered.

The door burst open as they were sipping at it a few minutes later. Nels pulled off his cap, his cheeks ruddy and glowing with good health. ''It's snowing!'' he declared, blue eyes happy.

They all moved to the doorway to peer out at the hard, dry flakes, shivering in the icy wind.

''It's winter,'' Betta said, tugging at her mittens. ''I love it when it snows, don't you? When all the ground is white and beautiful?''

Christina closed the door, shutting out the cold. ''It didn't snow very much where we lived. Does it really cover everything and build up on the roofs?''

''Oh, yes!'' the children told her. ''Last winter it was up to our necks, and Nels fell down and was nearly buried!'' This was related as if the experience had been a thrilling one.

''Mama hates the winter, though,'' Betta said, hanging up her cloak on the peg beside the door. ''She says she never gets warm enough.''

''Come have some hot tea,'' Megan offered, and the pair eagerly followed after her.

Roxanne pursed her lips. ''It will give her one more reason to stay in bed,'' she said. ''To keep warm.''

"Shh! Oh, dear, now what?"

For Patience again appeared at the foot of the stairs. "Can't you hear her? She's ill, and she could die for all the attention you lazy sluts are paying!"

For once Patience was not raising a tempest over nothing.

Abigail was indeed ill, vomiting over herself and her bed and onto the floor, moaning in distress.

After a moment of indecision both Christina and Megan attended to her. When the spasms were over, when Abigail lay spent and clammy, they changed her gown and her sheets and sponged her face.

Roxanne, who had remained in the kitchen where the children sat sipping their hot drinks, turned from putting another log on the fire to find Patience almost on her heels.

This time Patience was deathly pale, almost as pale as the sick woman in the next room. Her lips trembled as she spoke in a choked whisper.

"What did you do to her?"

Roxanne, bewildered, said nothing, and Patience reached out with small hands—the skin soft and creamy, because she did none of the chores—to dig her fingers into Roxanne's upper arms.

"Answer me, you wretch! What did you put into Abigail's tea?"

Chapter 34

BEWILDERED, ROXANNE FACED the other woman. "The tea?" she echoed.

Christina, turning from the bedside, fighting revulsion at the thought of dealing with the mess of soiled bedclothes, thought of Sadie, back home, spending all those days beside the earl as he lay dying; this was part of being someone else's servant, having no choice in the matter of performing even the most distasteful of chores. She stopped when she reached the pair at the foot of the stairs between the two rooms.

By this time Roxanne had detected something other than bad temper and anger in Patience's face. She recognized it at the same moment that Christina did and heard Christina's indrawn breath.

The something was fear.

"What is it?" Christina asked sharply.

Patience was scarcely audible. "She put something into the tea."

"What are you talking about?" Christina glanced beyond her, to where the children were at that moment draining their cups. "Everyone had mint tea. That's all Mistress Abigail had."

"It made her ill. She was not nearly so bad before she drank the tea."

Indignation sparked within Roxanne. "And you think I gave her something to make her sick? How absurd! I mixed the tea right here in front of everyone else, the same as we all had."

"She did," Christina agreed quickly, though she was frightened by what she read in the woman's face. "It was mint leaves, only mint leaves."

"She carried it to Abigail by herself, however, did she not? Can you guarantee that it was still only mint by the time Abigail drank it?"

Christina's heart was pounding with dread. "You are mistaken, mistress, if you believe anyone wished your sister-in-law harm. She became ill on the ship, coming home, and has not really recovered since then. It has nothing to do with some foreign substance in her tea."

"She has always been a healthy person. I've never known her to be ill, before this. Before you came into our lives."

It was a ridiculous accusation, yet they both saw that Patience believed it.

"She asked for the tea because she had an upset stomach," Christina said quickly. "She was ill *before* she drank the tea."

Might it have ended there, at least for the moment, if Roxanne had kept quiet? Christina would never know.

"You're a fool," Roxanne said. "Your own children drank the same brew, and there's nothing wrong with them. Or with us, who shared it. Where are your wits?"

"You will not speak to me in that manner," Patience told her in a tone that boded ill for the lot of them. "You forget your place!"

"And you display a lack of rationality," Roxanne countered, obviously stung by the now fully developed understanding of what Patience was saying. "Even healthy people suffer indispositions from time to time. Every one of us is eventually going to die, no matter how healthy we have been throughout our lives!"

Patience's lips were pale. "Are you threatening us?" she demanded.

Roxanne cast her half sister an exasperated glance, though not for long enough to grasp the unspoken message Christina tried to convey: *Let it go, don't further exacerbate the situation.*

"How could I threaten you or her? I'm only saying what any person of intellect knows, that everyone sooner or later takes ill and eventually everyone dies, with no other reason than that it's the will of God!"

"Or the work of the devil," Patience said in a strained voice. Her hands had knotted into fists so hard that her knuckles showed white. "And if it is the latter, be assured that you will not get away with it. Betta! Nels! Come upstairs at once!"

She swept them away, but there was no relief for those remaining when she disappeared from sight. Megan, anxiety clearly written across her countenance, came to put a hand on Roxanne's arm. "What was she talking about? She can't seriously think you tried to poison Mistress Abigail!"

Roxanne's face was expressive. "She doesn't like me. She's a troublemaker and an idiot. Who cares what she thinks? I'm going to take a walk and get some fresh air."

"In this weather? Christina asked.

Roxanne took down her warmest cloak, wrapped the hood over her head and grimaced. "Another moment in this place and maybe I really will poison one of them—or knock Mistress Patience in the head with a poker."

Christina stood looking at the door after it had closed behind her. "I wish she wouldn't say things like that. She doesn't mean them, but someone may think she does."

Megan reached for her hand. "Don't worry, Chris. The people of Ipswich are not witch-hunters like those others we hear about. The ministers are the community leaders, and they're sensible men."

Not all the citizens were sensible, though, Christina thought a few minutes later as she went on with the preparations for supper. Patience certainly wasn't.

Patience didn't like Roxanne—had, indeed, given little sign of liking any of them, even Megan who took so much of the responsibility that should have fallen upon Patience—and Patience wasn't especially bright.

But she had been genuinely frightened at the thought that Roxanne might have given Abigail something to make her so violently ill. And if she believed that, she might believe other ominous things, as well. There was no question that the Puritans, like their counterparts in Cornwall, believed in demonic possession, in witchcraft. There were those who cautioned against bringing false witness against the innocent, who pointed out that catastrophes did occur without the implication of the devil and his minions. Yet those rational heads seemed not to be the ones whose voices were most often and persuasively heard.

If Patience truly believed Roxanne guilty of such wickedness as she'd accused her of, it was chilling to think of the damage she might do.

IT WAS TOO MUCH to hope for that Patience would keep her nasty thoughts to herself. In spite of what she had suggested, she left Abigail to the servants to care for, and the older woman dozed fitfully through what was left of the afternoon. Megan looked in on her several times, but neither girl wanted to offer her anything else to drink.

Christina stood in the doorway once while Megan was at the bedside, remembering how her father had died. Slowly, starving to death because he could not keep food or drink down, wasting away. Poisoned.

What Patience had said was monstrous, impossible. Yet did it matter whether it was true or not, if Patience believed it? If she spoke of her suspicions to others?

The big kitchen was too quiet without the children chattering in a corner over their lessons. Upstairs, the baby cried and was immediately soothed into silence. Down here, Christina and Megan worked without speaking, each lost in her own apprehensive thoughts.

Roxanne returned only moments before the men arrived from work. The cold had heightened her dark beauty, and a few snowflakes lingered briefly on the thick lashes before she brushed them away.

"It's bone chilling out there," she said, sounding perfectly normal, spirits restored by her excursion away from the house. If Christina had not known that Captain O'Neal was far away, she would have been certain the other girl had met her lover. She was sorry she'd had the thought, because it reminded her that Vilas, too, was far off in the north.

Megan had set out the plates upon the table for the family, though God knew if they would peacefully sit for the evening meal after Patience had spoken to them. Christina tasted the stew and wondered absently if she hadn't overdone the turnips again; they tended to have a strong flavor if they outweighed the carrots and onions.

Roxanne crossed the room to hold out her hands toward the fire, staying to one side out of the way of the cook. "How is she?" She tossed her head toward the other room, and her black hair, mussed by the wind and her hood, lifted and fell around her shoulders.

"Fitful, but resting," Christina said. "You might have come back a little sooner. It's taken both of us to prepare a meal. If Mistress Abigail had continued to be ill, we'd have had a difficult time without you to help in some way."

"If I'd come back any sooner," Roxanne rejoined calmly, "I'd have thrown something at that other one's head. Clearly I'm not cut out to be a house servant. I'm better suited to pouring ale in a tavern, dealing with rowdy males who attempt to pinch my bottom as I go past, than with the likes of Mistress Patience."

As usual, she made no effort to modulate her voice. Did the words carry to the adjoining chamber, or was Patience on the stairs?

Christina held her breath at the sound of a creaking step until she saw that it was Cordelia, not Patience. The old woman advanced toward the hearth, seeking its warmth.

"Getting too cold up there to do the lacework much longer," she said. "Did I hear my granddaughter in another of her tirades a bit ago?"

For a moment there was naught to be heard except the crackle of the flames. Then Christina cleared her throat, resenting the fact that Roxanne obviously did not intend to respond.

"She was upset when Mistress Abigail became ill, and we did not hear her."

The bright dark eyes were close to her own and knowing. How much had she heard? To Christina's relief, Cordelia did not press the matter, instead turning her backside to the fire and lifting her skirts immodestly to allow the heat to reach her limbs.

A moment later, the men arrived home in a noisy group. Wesley and Ezra were arguing some point having to do with the boat they were building. Fitz knocked snow off his hat onto the floor before hanging it on its peg, his eyes seeking out Megan's slim figure as she sliced bread at the table. Adam was the first of them to reach the fire, where old Cordelia moved aside to make room.

"Cold," he said, and Cordelia nodded. "Ice on my pitcher this morning," she agreed.

Perhaps, Christina thought, handing Roxanne the big bowl to hold while she ladled out steaming stew, this afternoon's ruckus had all blown over and they'd done with it.

It was a vain hope.

Patience came down the stairs with the baby on her hip and the other children trailing her. She addressed the room in a strident, high-pitched voice. "Has anyone seen to Abigail?"

Creases appeared at once in Ezra's forehead. "Is she ill again?"

"Violently so," Patience stated, handing Emory to Betta. "After she'd drunk some concoction that vixen took her." She was looking at Roxanne.

There was a moment of silence, and then Ezra moved toward the room he shared with his wife. It was Adam who voiced the question Patience was provoking. "What sort of concoction?"

"Mint tea, sir," Christina said quickly. Damn the girl, why couldn't *she* take the responsibility for handling this crisis she had, however inadvertently, brought about? Instead Roxanne held her head high, her green eyes flashing dangerously, her mouth stubbornly mute.

"Never knew mint tea to make anyone ill," Adam stated.

"She was feeling poorly and asked for the tea," Christina inserted again, when it was clear Roxanne did not intend to speak in her own behalf. "When she'd drunk it she became very ill for a time. She's been resting quietly since then, this hour past."

Ezra returned, the frown deeper on his face. "She's asleep, but she looks gray and exhausted, and she's been vomiting."

"She was not violently ill until after she'd taken the tea," Patience said.

Now Adam was also frowning. He hated these confrontations between the females who made up the bulk of his household, and the fact that he'd listened to them for years made them no more palatable. "What are you getting at, woman? Do you say that there is wrongdoing here?"

"There's been nothing but trouble since *that one* came," Patience told him. "Abigail was never sick until *she* appeared. She put something into the tea; Abigail would never have become so violently ill otherwise."

"That's not true." Roxanne finally spoke in her own defense, but with an unfortunately insolent air that would do nothing to improve the situation. "It was mint tea, the same as we all drank. My sisters, the children—all of us the same."

Patience changed tactics. "You are rude, Mistress Roxanne, and arrogant, both highly inappropriate in a servant."

"Am I servant," Roxanne asked boldly, "or slave? I do the work I am told to do. No one ever informed me that in becoming indentured I was to give up my own thoughts, nor that every moment was to be devoted to waiting upon others, with not a moment to myself. Nor did I expect false accusations to be brought against me, accusations completely without foundation." She paused before adding, "I've no experience in dealing with irrational females; I confess to a lack of taste for it and an inability to deal with it."

Christina swore mentally. Why could she not have left off that final thrust? Roxanne might have won Adam over by being reasonable and calm. Now the thick white brows drew together in a scowl.

"Insulting me," Patience said with rising heat, "does not alter circumstances. You are—"

Adam's deep voice cut through her words with an authority that silenced his daughter-in-law immediately. "Enough! I will not have my supper ruined because of this bickering. I will speak to you—" Roxanne did not flinch when the pale blue gaze settled briefly on her "—at a later time. Right now I want to eat."

Only once more that evening did Patience speak. Wesley had talked earlier that day with an ironmonger from the works at Saugus, who brought news in the only possible way in a country without newspapers, except for those few that came all the way from England.

"They've arrested two more women on charges of witchcraft in Salem," he related. "The jails grow full, and still we have no charter and no one is authorized to deal with these matters. There is much concern on the part of the magistrates there, though some of the people seem caught up as with some new form of sport: several women were themselves put into the stocks after pelting the prisoners with rotten vegetables. We can be grateful that we in Ipswich are of a more temperate nature.''

Patience put down her spoon and leaned forward. ''Temperate, or foolish? When there are signs that the evildoers are in our own midst?''

Adam's big fist hit the table in a thump that set cutlery jumping. ''Enough, by God! We have been warned of the dangers of promoting dissension and violence! I cannot control what others do—I can only advise—but in my own household I will have order and harmony!''

The remainder of the meal was eaten in silence.

During the night Abigail again was taken ill. The girls were called to tend her.

Roxanne sat up, brushing hair back from her face. ''You two go,'' she said. ''It will only stir up the furies again if I go near the woman.''

Christina stared down at her in anger. ''That's probably true, but you can get up with us and be available to empty basins and carry away soiled bedclothes. You aren't going to use the situation as an excuse to lie warmly abed and avoid all unpleasantness.''

For a moment it seemed that Roxanne would resist. Then she rolled over, revealing a flash of shapely legs before she got to her feet. ''All right, all right. Just keep that Patience away from me.''

Pulling on her wrapper, Christina spoke with some bitterness. ''Never fear, she won't get up to investigate no matter what she hears. Not when she's safe and warm under the quilts.''

So it proved. The episode was much like the earlier one, in that once Abigail had violently emptied her stomach she fell back in a gray exhaustion, clammy to the touch, shivering so that they brought hot bricks to place around her and piled extra quilts over her.

Christina was half-frozen by the time she crawled back into her own pallet. She left the door open into the kitchen in the hope that some faint bit of heat would enter the summer room, for it was cold enough where they slept to have put a skim of ice on the pitcher already.

At home, she thought with longing, she could have rung for a servant to bring her additional covers and waited in bed on a cold morning until Sadie or Hilda had built up a fire in her room, before she rose and dressed. Home. How she missed the moors and the path along the cliffs, the broad sandy beaches and the tiny coves where she had wandered at will for her entire sixteen years!

But Lady Jacobina was at Kenwood. It was home no longer, nor ever would be.

Still shaking, curled up to conserve her own body heat, Christina wondered bleakly how she would bear the coming three years of indenture and what awaited her beyond that.

Chapter 35

WINTER CAME in earnest. Snow fell in blinding quantities, driven by a howling wind that threatened the thatching of the roofs and stung any exposed skin. The snow covered everything that was familiar, leaving an alien ye` beautiful landscape.

The wood in the lean-to diminished rapidly, so that more must be cut and split and carried inside to dry so that it would burn more readily. All four fireplaces now were kept burning day and night, and still the cold crept in so that water buckets froze, while frost made intricate patterns on the glass of the windows. One morning Megan slipped on an icy spot just inside the back door, where melted snow from the men's boots had refrozen during the night. She skinned her arm and twisted her back, so that for a few days she was stiff and lame.

Cordelia gave up making her pillow lace in the unheated little room upstairs. She took to spending most of her days huddled near the fire in thc main room of the house, a quilt over her knees and a heavy shawl around her shoulders, and still when they took her a cup of tea or a bowl of soup, her fingers were icy to the touch.

Cordelia seldom complained, however. Her bright brown eyes watched everything, and it was clear that she found being in the middle of the activity far more entertaining than making lace. Not that she was idle; her blue-veined hands were seldom at rest, for they turned out a succession of stockings and mittens, knit caps and scarves.

Patience seemed to feel more energetic; although her afternoon-nap time remained one of welcome respite for the rest of the household, she spent less time in her room and more beside her grandmother, with whom she actually carried on more or less congenial conversations.

Though she took no part in caring for Abigail, she took a solicitous responsibility for overseeing that care. "Have you seen to her fire? Has she had her tea?"

It was tacitly understood that Roxanne would have no part in carrying food or drink to the older woman who, though intermittently improved, could not regain her strength. This added to the burdens of the other two and a growing resentment on Christina's part.

Roxanne had a genius, Christina thought, for making herself unwanted and untrusted, eliminating for herself some of the less agreeable chores. It bothered her not a whit that someone else must then assume them.

In fact, Roxanne grew bolder about taking time for herself. Every day she walked out, sometimes even at dusk—preparing for the day when Captain O'Neal would return, and no one would question her absence from the house when she went to meet him?—while Christina had difficulty in taking half an hour here or there to escape into the fresh air.

Roxanne grew bolder as well in the matter of reading. Instead of retiring to the summer room—which had become almost unbearably cold at night—for that pleasurable activity, she brought her book to the fireside. Sometimes she read aloud to the others as they went about their duties. Christina enjoyed the readings, for the most part, though more of them than she liked pertained to the detection and punishment of witches. Yet there were times when she longed to be the one warming her feet on the hearth rather than having been standing up on them for an entire day.

Christina decided that somehow she must manage at least a brief, brisk walk once a day. She needed that kind of exercise not only to feel at her best, but to have some time to herself, to think, to dream.

Winter in the Bay Colony was far more harsh than the winters in Cornwall; it was also more exhilarating, for beauty lay all around her. She had never seen snow like this, where one's footsteps broke the virgin white blanket in a peculiarly satisfying manner; where every bush and tree and weed transformed the landscape into a fairyland.

Most of the time, while she walked, Christina thought about Vilas. He was so far away, in a place where the winter was probably more severe than it was here, and he was seldom out of her mind for long. Perhaps he would get the yearning for adventure out of his head, and when he returned he would be ready to settle down on land. Perhaps he would miss her as she missed him and realize that they belonged together. As she strode briskly through the cold, clutching her cloak tightly around her, she was unaware of the freezing temperature, warmed from within by the daydreams in which anything seemed possible.

Building boats out-of-doors in this weather was not feasible. Discomfort would not have mattered, but frostbitten fingers and toes might have to be amputated, should there be anyone around to perform such surgery. Physicians were few and far between, for they all had to be trained in England; there was no school in the New World, not even the college called Harvard in Cambridge, outside of Boston, where a medical education could be had. Frostbite meant being crippled, perhaps even dying. The men either moved indoors, where they were a constant trial to the women trying to go about their customary duties or changed to different outdoor activities.

Chopping and hauling wood for the insatiable fireplaces consumed many hours for all of them. Even Adam did his share of it. But their favorite occupation was hunting.

There was no way of preserving the summer vegetables, beyond storing carrots and turnips and onions in a root cellar; corn was made into meal, fish was salted and dried, apples and berries were dried or made into jam if sugar could be obtained from England for their making. But during the winter months the Puritans relied heavily on wild game, which could be had at no cost other than time that would otherwise have been wasted.

Every female in the house heaved a sigh of relief when the hunting parties left them alone. As much as they appreciated the meat, they welcomed the relative peace of a household without men and their wet boots, their loud voices, their needs that must be met.

Megan fought against the attraction she felt for Fitz, knowing all the while that it was a losing battle. Why had God cursed her with a shameful blemish, then brought this man into her life? It would have been painful had the attraction been one-sided, with her longing for him from a distance. The realization that he was also drawn to her brought both joy and anguish.

Common sense dictated that she discourage him, for nothing could come of this feeling between them. Yet she was incapable of turning aside the growing affection Fitz displayed, an affection she had never known from anyone save Christina.

Affection, no, Megan thought. It was stronger than that. She was coming to love Fitz Hull, and even before the day they met unexpectedly in the middle of the village, she knew that he was beginning to return that love.

She had become accustomed to finding his warm brown eyes upon her across the room. Accustomed to his strong hands easing the burden when she went to lift a heavy pot off the fire. She was familiar with the tingling that went through her when he smiled across the supper table.

She had not yet grown complacent about the way pulses raced and the heart hammered in her breast when he looked at her or touched her, however casually.

Her dreams were exciting and disturbing, and she often woke in the freezing dawn, reluctant to relinquish the satisfaction to be had only in those dreams. On this blowy afternoon she had been dispatched on an errand for Patience; while the woman scarcely ever left the house herself except to attend Sabbath services, she had no hesitation in sending anyone else out for the most trivial of reasons.

Megan had no objection to going, for all that the wind flung the snow into her face in a fury that made her duck her head against it as she made her way home. She could scarcely make out the road, so heavy was the snow; the footprints made half an hour ago had vanished in the drifts that in places reached her knees.

"Megan! Is that you?"

The blood congealed in her veins, then surged again in a hot, happy flood that made her forget the way her toes were going numb.

"Master Fitz! I thought you were hunting."

"There are more things to hunt than deer," Fitz told her, grinning. "I hadn't thought to be lucky enough to meet you here, however."

The fluttering in her chest was disconcerting, though not unpleasant. "Mistress Patience sent me for—"

"Mistress Patience has a singular lack of consideration for anyone but herself," Fitz said, as if agreeing with her own similar assessment. "On the other hand, had she kept you by the fireside we wouldn't have the opportunity to meet and walk together. Here, let me take your hand so you don't slip and fall."

In truth, the snow was not in the least slippery. Yet she was only too glad to allow her hand to be engulfed in his larger one while his other arm encircled her waist to draw her against his side.

"I've spoken to my father about you," Fitz said abruptly as they walked over the bridge and headed for home.

Startled, Megan missed her footing and felt his arm tighten more firmly around her. "About me?" The flutter in her chest became wilder.

"Yes. I've told him that if you're willing, I'd like to marry you."

For a moment Megan did not credit her hearing. There was a roaring in her ears and then an ache in her throat that grew until she could hardly bear it. "Marry?" The word was a whisper, born quickly away on the wind.

Fitz came to a halt. "You know I've had an eye for you from the moment you came. You know I'm alone, since Hester and the babe died. The church presses me to find another wife...." For a moment amusement brightened the face so close to her own. "It's a situation Father and I share, for they would have him wed again, as well, so he has understood when we talked about it. He resists, and so have I...up to now. I've no wish to wind up tied for life to a woman like the wives of my brothers, church orders or no. But the right woman, one of my own choosing, that would be a different matter. I know you are very young, yet Hester was only a year older than you when we were wed."

His face, so dear, Megan thought helplessly, so beloved, was only inches from her own; their breaths, visible in the frigid air, mingled between them.

Now was the time to tell him that she couldn't marry him, ever. That she couldn't marry anyone. That she was terrified of what he would think and do if he knew about the blemish that would condemn her in the eyes of many of those church officials who pressed him to marry.

She could not speak. Her throat worked and her eyes blurred, yet the words refused to be spoken. All her dreams, even the wildest of them, could not have prepared her for this moment. And while she knew she dared not accept his proposal, she was incapable of rejecting him.

Fitz misinterpreted her stricken expression and the tears. He smiled and cupped her face between work-hardened palms to hold it while he bent to kiss her.

Megan knew it was wrong, that nothing could come of this. It had been drilled into her since she was scarcely able to toddle about holding onto Christina's finger: *You must let no one see the purple stain.* She had not understood, then, why the blemish was so shameful. It was only years later that she heard about the gypsy's curse that had called down the devil's wrath upon the offspring of the earl of Kenwood, the curse that had caused his sons to die, and this daughter to be branded forever in such a way that anyone seeing the mark would know her as the devil's own.

Why was she, though? She had done nothing to deserve the role of outcast. And as Fitz's lips claimed hers, as his hands slid beneath the warmth of her cloak to draw her body close to his, she knew that she had never wanted anything as much as she wanted to belong to this man.

"I love you, Megan," he said huskily into her hair. "Hester was chosen for me and I came to care for her, but I never felt anything for another woman such as I have for you! Say you feel the same for me!"

A sob rose in her throat. Speech was beyond her, and her arms tightened around him as if of their own accord.

She had asked little of life, so far. Now she pleaded silently with God for the privileges He gave to most females, a right to marry and live with this good man and have his children and keep his house until she was as old as Cordelia.

If the devil had marked her to begin with, was it possible that God could take the stain away? Why hadn't she thought of that before? Why hadn't she been praying all these years that the blemish would be lifted from her, instead of resigning herself to the fate of an outcast?

With a fierceness she had never known she possessed, Megan returned Fitz's kisses, standing on the deserted street with the snow blowing around them, settling on hair and lashes, icy, yet not cold enough to cool their ardor.

There must be a way, Megan thought desperately, to take what had just been offered. She clung to him, fusing her body to his, trying to think of a way. It was impossible, however, to think at all while in his embrace.

Let herself go, then. Give herself over to his touch, his kiss, the male strength of him. Pretend that all is well, that this could end happily for them both.

And all the while, in the very back of her mind even as his kiss deepened and drew a sharp response from the most secret depths of her young body, Megan knew it was pretense, and she despaired.

Chapter 36

CHRISTINA KNEW THE MOMENT that Megan entered the house—with Fitz only moments behind her, carrying a load of wood that didn't fool her into thinking they had not been together—that something momentous had occurred.

How was it possible for the girl to look simultaneously ecstatic and terrified? Christina stiffened, forgetting to stir the pot of beans as Fitz noisily dropped his load of wood and threw an unnecessary log onto the fire.

She caught a glimpse of his face before he turned away from her, and saw that Fitz wore a broad smile indicative of...what?

Christina returned her attention to her younger sister, hanging up her cloak by the door, stamping the snow from her shoes. Megan had always been quietly pretty, but now she was radiant. She was, Christina realized in surprise, beautiful, as beautiful as Roxanne, in a more sweet and wholesome way.

It had been obvious that Fitz and Megan were drawn to each other, but somehow Christina had taken it for granted that the girl would not allow matters to progress any further than that. Megan, of all people, knew how impossible her own situation was. The witch-hunters were more bloodthirsty here than they'd been in their own corner of Cornwall at home.

Yet if Megan hadn't just been thoroughly kissed, Christina missed her guess.

There was no time to dwell upon it now. She must have supper upon the table shortly; she could hear the rest of the men coming. Patience was talking quietly to Cordelia, the baby on her lap. The other children sat with their lessons in a corner so far removed from the fire that they must be straining their eyes to see the printed pages. Even Abigail had come to join them at table, looking gaunt and pale.

Once the men arrived the house seemed full to bursting with their wide shoulders and deep voices. Christina and Roxanne dished up food into bowls and onto platters, carrying it steaming to the long table. At home, food had been eaten mostly lukewarm, since it had to be carried some distance from kitchen to the great hall where they dined. Here, it was only a few yards from fire to table; eating truly hot food had taken a bit of getting used to, welcome though it was in these winter temperatures.

The fare was good and plentiful, and as a rule Christina ate as heartily as anyone. Tonight she was distracted by the subtle byplay between Megan and Fitz: modestly lowered eyes, then a shooting glance and a heightening of color, the beginnings of smiles that Megan tried to repress and Fitz allowed full reign. Did anyone else notice?

Christina was too alarmed at the implications to have an appetite. She liked Fitz; he seemed a decent young man, but he was one of these Puritans; they had not known him long enough to be certain how he would feel about the crucial matter of a mark that might be taken for the devil's. He usually only listened to talk of witchcraft, contributing no thoughts of his own, though Christina's impression had been that he leaned toward his father's moderate views rather than Patience's radical ones.

Had Megan told him about the birthmark?

No. The answer came at once. Had she done so, now knowing she had nothing to fear on that score, Megan's joy would not be tempered by that barely perceptible fear. Dear Heaven, where would this lead?

Christina's glance slid around the assembled company. A brisk discussion was under way between Ezra and Adam about ironmongers and their prices. Fitz ate with customary gusto while spending an inordinate amount of time watching Megan. His father and brothers paid him no mind, nor did Patience and Abigail, both of whom picked at their food. The children, as always, stood at the end of the table, not speaking, lowering their eyes when anyone looked directly at them. Only Cordelia seemed aware of the undercurrents: her brown eyes were bright and alert.

Roxanne, absorbed in her own thoughts, finally came out of them as the meal was concluded and they rose to clear away the dishes. "Megan's uncommonly happy tonight. Has something happened that I don't know about?'' she asked under cover of the general milling around that always followed the evening meal.

"She hasn't confided in me," Christina said, wrapping the leftover bread in a cloth so that it wouldn't dry out. "I assume it has something to do with Master Fitz."

"Really?" Roxanne brightened, turning to seek out the pair of them, who had gravitated to a far corner and were in earnest conversation. "How marvelous, if she should have found a suitor! It would lift our responsibilities, would it not, if she married?"

Since when had Roxanne ever taken any responsibility for the younger girl, Christina wondered bitterly? "It would if she could marry him. She won't," she stated with a flatness that made Roxanne's green eyes narrow.

"Why not?"

"She won't," Christina repeated, and moved away, leaving Roxanne looking after her with mingled bewilderment and annoyance.

"They'll hang her for certain now," Wesley said into a momentary silence.

Immediately everyone in the room came to attention. Christina held her breath, dreading the words to follow.

"Who's that?" Patience demanded.

"Some woman in Salem who was imprisoned for causing her neighbor's chickens all to die," Wesley told her. He was washing down his supper with an extra mug of ale. "She denied it, of course, but when the women stripped her down to examine her they found unmistakable evidence of her connection with the devil. She has an extra teat, albeit a very small one, only a nipple, apparently. When they spied it they exclaimed over it, and the woman attacked them with fingernails and her teeth, drawing blood. If Mather ever returns with a new charter so the officials can be about their business of emptying the jails and disposing of such cases, the gallows will do a thriving business for a time."

For once Adam did not defend the victims of the witch-hunters. He sighed heavily instead, as if resigned to the truth of Wesley's statement.

A third nipple? Christina broke out in a cold sweat, though she stood near the fire. Did it look anything like the mole on her own breast? Was it any more compelling as evidence than Megan's purple stain?

Had it not been for the flickering firelight, Megan would have been pale enough to attract attention. Her eyes met Christina's across the room, and all animation faded from her face. When Fitz spoke to her she seemed not to hear, instead walking over to the water bucket to take a long drink from the gourd.

Did anyone other than Christina notice that her fingers were trembling?

"The sooner we're rid of the troublemakers, the better," Patience opined.

Ezra sighed. "Too much time passes without that charter. If we had a stronger governor, no doubt he'd be able to take some reasonable steps to handle what becomes a growing morass of legal problems. Simon Bradstreet's more useless than no governor at all."

His words brought nods of agreement. The girls had learned early on that almost no one in the Bay Colony held much respect for Governor Bradstreet; not only was he nearly ninety years old and so enfeebled by illness that he was excused from the usual compulsory attendance at Meeting but he was known also to be soft on witchcraft. He had once gone so far as to refuse to hang a witch condemned to the gallows, so no one expected any help from that quarter.

"Well, let's hope our own magistrates are allowed to continue to operate on a local level," Wesley said. "Old Ferguson is in stocks again for public drunkenness. He's become a disgrace."

"In the stocks? In this weather?" Abigail, who had not opened her mouth to speak all evening, registered shock. "Surely he will suffer frostbite and perhaps lose his toes or his fingers!"

"Then he'd best learn his lesson and stop drinking too much," Patience snapped. She saw her daughter's face and added sharply, "It's time you two were in bed. Off with you now! And don't forget to say your evening prayers."

"Aye," Adam said heavily, "'tis profitless to speculate on matters over which we have no control. We'd all best be abed, preparing for tomorrow, when there will be plenty to do. The best we can hope for is to manage our own household according to the laws of God and man."

"Grandfather," Betta asked in a soft voice, "will you hear my prayers?"

The big gnarled hand rested briefly on the child's towhead. "Aye, girl. You too, Nels."

Within minutes the rest of the household also began to drift away. Abigail was notably frail and weak, though she had been up only briefly, and leaned heavily on her husband's arm as she left the room.

Patience stared moodily after her sister-in-law. "I do not understand it. She has always been such a sturdy person, and now suddenly she fails so badly!"

Fitz, having banked the fire for the night, rose from the hearth. "The household suffers for lack of her direction, does it not? Our new servants are hardworking and efficient, but they admit to being new at their present occupation. They cannot be expected to learn what there is no one to teach."

Patience flattened her lips, staring at her brother-in-law with distaste. "Is that a reference to *my* shortcomings, pray? You know I do the best I can, considering the delicate state of my health."

"Of course. I had no intent to cast aspersions on anyone, only to state the obvious: that Abigail's presence as overseer of the household is sadly missed. Until she's better I'm sure you'll do the best you can. Good night, all."

With an especially warm—and open—smile at Megan, he departed for the room he shared with Adam.

Unmollified, Patience stared stonily at the girl. She did not, however, ask the question that she so clearly wanted to ask. Not with her husband's hand on her shoulder, urging her toward bed.

"Fat lot of good it'll do him when he gets her there," Roxanne observed when the couple was—Christina hoped—out of hearing.

Christina didn't care whether Patience was responsive in bed or not. What she cared about was her younger sister.

"Are you going to tell us?" she asked Megan softly, determined that none of *her* words should carry beyond the three of them. "Or must we guess what transpires between you and Master Fitz?"

Megan was torn between smiles and tears. "He's told his father that he wishes to marry me."

Christina stood motionless, hearing the crackle of flames, the wind howling around the eaves and the chimneys, and the painful thudding of her own heart.

Roxanne laughed and reached for Megan's hands to squeeze them. "That's wonderful!"

Christina's throat ached, and her words came slowly. "It's impossible, Megan. You know that."

Roxanne dropped her sister's hands and spun toward the other girl. "Impossible! Why, for the love of God? It's a chance to escape from this indenture, to be her own mistress, and it's clear from the look of her that she loves him! What do you mean, it's impossible?"

If Roxanne had really looked, she would have seen that Christina's distress was genuine, and in no way a selfish reaction, as Megan had recognized at once.

Megan's lips trembled. "I . . . I could not refuse him."

"But you can't accept him, either. Unless he knows . . . ?"

Megan shook her head. Her long, silky hair swirled around her shoulders from beneath her cap. "No. I didn't have the courage to tell him, either."

"Tell him what?" Roxanne demanded, exasperated with them both.

For a few seconds there was only silence. Megan's hand rose to the neck of her dress. Slowly, reluctantly, her fingers worked the buttons. And then, turning toward the fire after checking to see that there was no one else present, she folded back one side of her bodice.

Roxanne drew in a sharp breath. "God's blood! What is it?"

"I was born with it," Megan said, almost inaudible.

"After your mother cursed the progeny of the earl of Kenwood," Christina couldn't help adding with some bitterness, though in truth she did not hold Roxanne responsible for Leonie's maledictions.

"Sweet Jesus!" For once Roxanne's utterance was not blasphemous. "No wonder you keep your throat covered. And undress in the dark," she added, finally making the connection. "Who knew about it?"

"My mother and father," Megan said, swallowing. "Christina. They would have let me die, I think, it it hadn't been for Christina, who insisted that a servant nurse me as an infant, when my mother refused to do so."

"And servants," Christina added. "Cook and old Elspeth knew. Our father swore to see them hanged if the secret was ever revealed, and to the best of my knowledge neither of them ever spoke of it."

Roxanne swore again, this time less reverently. "How extensive is it?"

Megan did not further bare her breast, only gesturing with her fingers.

Roxanne inhaled deeply, exhaled and groped for words. "If he loves you, he may not mind. He might be willing to ignore it. After all, you keep it covered. And it wouldn't be visible in the dark."

A spark of hope leaped in Megan's face. "I kept it from you, and Daisy Meeks, all those weeks we were crossing the ocean."

Christina felt her eyes stinging. "It's not the same, Megan. You couldn't conceal it from a husband. You couldn't sleep in the same bed with him for years, making love with him, without his finding out. There would be children, and you'd have to nurse them—how would you hide it then?"

"Then tell him," Roxanne said. "Let him decide."

"And if he is as horrified as you were, those first moments after you saw it?" Christina asked softly. "Then what?"

"I *was* horrified, for a moment. But it doesn't make her so grotesque that I reject her as a person. She's the same Megan she's always been," Roxanne said with some vigor. "If she simply refuses him, she's given up love forever. If she tells him, there's at least a chance he'll want to marry her anyway."

"In this household? Where they talk of hanging a witch because she has a spot they've taken for an extra nipple? Where Patience finds it reasonable that a man should be held in the stocks in freezing weather for drinking an extra mug of ale? Where she accuses you of poisoning Abigail because you took her tea just before she became violently ill? What if he takes the same view of witches and witchcraft as so many of the others in this place? What if he reports her to the authorities?''

''But she's done nothing to make anyone think she's a witch!'' Roxanne protested. ''Everyone likes her, respects her!''

''Would Patience, if she knew? Would any number of others, if they seek a scapegoat for their pigs running off, their chickens stopping laying, their relatives taking sick? Think, both of you, before Megan speaks out to anyone, even Master Fitz. They are probably going to hang those unfortunate women in Salem who've been accused by that group of children! Can we risk that, with Megan?''

Roxanne searched both their faces, accepting at last that Christina spoke from love and concern, and that there was much to what she said.

''What's the alternative, then? To renounce love and happiness?''

Christina had no answer to that. Megan's eyes brimmed over.

''I do love him,'' she said.

''Then perhaps there will be a way,'' Christina said, though she could not imagine what it would be, without taking a horrible risk. Yet she could not bear to crush every scrap of hope in Megan's heart, no more than Megan could tell Fitz she did not want to marry him.

Megan lay awake for a long time after her sisters slept, listening to their quiet breathing in the frigid room and the scrape of a naked branch against a windowpane.

It was a relief to have told Roxanne. The shock in her face had hurt, but not as much as she'd been warmed by the immediate support that followed.

Could it be that Fitz would react in the same way? If he truly loved her, would he reject her because of a blemish that no one except himself ever need be aware of? Was it at least remotely possible that he would consider it no more a detriment to marriage than a delicate constitution like Patience's or a lame foot or weak eyes?

There was no way to be certain except to ask him.

And if she guessed wrong about entrusting Fitz with her secret, she might endanger not only herself but Christina and Roxanne, too.

Sleep brought no relief. In her dreams she saw their faces, those women in Boston who had stoned another. Only this time the victim was not a stranger, but Megan, and in the dream she felt the stones thudding into her flesh, bruising it, cutting it.

Killing her.

Chapter 37

MORNING BROUGHT NO SOLUTIONS. Yet Fitz was there at the breakfast table, searching out her gaze, smiling. And Megan smiled back.

It's hopeless, hopeless, Christina thought, watching. He'll never marry her if he knows, and if she married him anyway and he found out, he could condemn her as a witch solely on the basis of that mark she carried; he could say she had bewitched him into the nuptials, and they'd all agree, and throw her into prison.

She felt like crying, and with her grief for Megan came concern over the matter near to her heart: Vilas. What could she do to awaken him to her own existence, not as his cousin but as a woman who loved him?

Abigail did not rise that day, nor the next, nor the next. She tried to sip the broth that Megan brought; nothing solid passed her lips. It seemed to the watchers that she shriveled before their very eyes, losing flesh, losing her very will to live.

The minister came to see her. Friends from among the villagers came to see her. Abigail was too weak to converse or to make the effort to smile. By her third day in bed the visitors no longer asked to see her; instead they paused just inside the front door and asked about her in hushed tones.

She's going to die, Christina thought with dread. And when she does, are they going to blame Roxanne? And, by association, Megan and me, as well? Will they throw us into jail and strip us as they did the woman in Salem and find the witches' marks?

Winter held the Bay Colony in an icy grip. Where the snow melted on the floor from the boots of those who had been outside, it refroze even during the day now if it was not quickly wiped up. Any water left standing more than a few yards from the fireplaces froze solid during the night. The summer room became unbearably cold; the girls dragged their pallets into the kitchen at night, as close to the fire as they dared, and privacy was no longer assured. In the early morning darkness they scrambled into their outer garments—having slept in petticoats and stockings—before any of the family should emerge into the kitchen.

The children developed coughs and runny noses, and for a few days no longer attended the Dame School on the other side of the village; Patience worried about their being lost in the blinding snow. Cordelia complained that she slept under so many quilts that she could not turn over for the weight of them and sleeping so immobilized made her ache all over.

There was no more word of the witch-hunting in Salem Village; the weather was so bad that no travelers carried the news from one place to another. It was a relief not to hear, yet none of the three sisters totally forgot the situation. Even Roxanne seemed to be aware of the potential for disaster, now that she knew about Megan's disfiguring mark; for her, she was reasonably thoughtful before she spoke, even to Patience, who was admittedly difficult enough to try the patience of a saint.

Which none of them could claim to be.

It wasn't until they were kept inside for five days running because of frigid temperatures and heavy snows that Roxanne and Christina fully realized how much their daily walks had served as a safety valve. With everyone cooped up together around the clock, tempers wore thin. Small things were magnified into major aggravations.

And Abigail sank into a semistupor from which she could be roused only with effort to sip a bit of broth or tea. Her husband read the Bible aloud at her bedside, whether for her benefit or his own was uncertain.

They discovered the true meaning of servitude. If there was an unpleasant task to do, one of the three girls did it. During the worst of the weather, use of the privy was virtually abandoned in favor of chamber pots. These, however, must be emptied at least once a day, which meant that someone had to venture out into the wind and the snow.

The fireplaces took a seemingly endless supply of fuel, and much of it had to be carried up the narrow stairs to the fireplaces above. Patience would even call one of them from downstairs to replenish her fire rather than getting out of bed to do it herself. Megan found herself hating the woman after the dozenth time she'd run up and down the stairs in one afternoon to fetch and carry for her mistress.

The children, bored by the enforced inactivity, became cross and mischievous. There was more needling and hair pulling than normal. Megan set them to playing every game she could think of, to reciting their lessons until they were letter-perfect, and told them every story she'd ever related to Thomas, plus a few more she made up.

"You tell them a story," she begged Roxanne. "They've heard all of mine, and they are too tame. You make them up better than I do."

Roxanne, as bored as the children, welcomed the opportunity. It had been virtually impossible the past week to slip into the bedchamber upstairs to write down any of the words that filled her head; the men were around too much, and Adam had spent considerable time at his own writing table, which held the only source of paper, pens and ink. Stories were bursting in Roxanne's head.

"Sit down," she told them briskly. "I'll tell you a tale of pirates and ships on the high seas and adventures such as you've never heard of! And Megan will pop some corn, and we'll have a bowl of it while we drink our cider, all right?"

The tale was, indeed, one such as they'd never heard. Betta and Nels sat spellbound, forgetting to torment each other, blue eyes wide in wonder at the pictures Roxanne painted. When Megan brought the popcorn—a treat native to the Indians in this part of the world, and one the girls had heard of but never sampled at home—they nearly forgot to eat, so vivid and so exciting was the story.

Megan was smiling over it herself, and Christina, though her hands were busy with her knitting, was engrossed in the tale, as well. She hoped that Vilas wasn't engaged in such hair-raising adventures—or would it be better if he *was* and got the need for such things out of his system?

Even old Cordelia, huddled within her quilts, never took her gaze from Roxanne's face, enjoying every word.

The interrupting voice was shrill with outrage. "What is this nonsense? These...these *lies*? What do you tell my children?"

Roxanne stopped speaking in midsentence. "Lies?" she echoed, incredulous.

"'Tis but a story, mistress," Megan said quickly. "My sister but tells a tale for the amusement of the children...."

"Amusement?" Though it hardly seemed possible that her voice could grow more shrill, Patience managed it. "Men hacking one another to death with swords until the decks run red with blood? Seek you to send them into nightmares for weeks to come?"

"Nightmares? Nay, only to stir their blood during these days while they must stay indoors and go mad with boredom," Roxanne protested. "A bit of adventure and romance surely do them no harm."

"Adventure? Romance? Is that what you call it, this ill-considered recitation of matters best kept from young ears? Kissing, did I not hear you mention embracing and *kissing*?"

Roxanne moistened her full lips, unaware of how her very looks enraged her persecutor. "Men and women do embrace and kiss," she said, striving to control her own rising indignation. "And your menfolk deal all the time with pirates and seamen. Is this something shameful?"

Patience allowed her voice to rise in a full-fledged shriek. "I will not have you putting such ideas into my children's heads! I forbid you to—"

None of them had heard the door open. It was only when Adam's deep voice cut through Patience's strident one that they realized he had entered the house.

"Enough, woman! By the good Lord, is there no peace to be found in this household? 'Tis no wonder I've no wish to re-marry, regardless of what the church says, when I'm already surrounded by caterwauling females!"

He stomped snow off his feet, and while Megan scurried unobtrusively to wipe up the mess, Adam advanced to the middle of the room, his bulk filling it.

Patience had allowed him to speak, but her mottled pink-and-white skin revealed the extent of her anger, and she did not accept his rebuke in meek silence.

"You do not know what this wretched creature has been telling my children," she accused, and proceeded to inform him.

She had, Christina thought with a sinking feeling, obviously been listening for some time before she broke in upon Roxanne's tale. In the retelling, it did indeed sound bloodthirsty and salacious, though in truth Christina had not seen anything in it to corrupt the children. Why did it sound so much worse when Patience told it?

"Enough! Enough, enough," Adam said, holding up a hand to stop the spate of words. "Hold your tongue. Have you forgotten there is a sick woman in the next room? What must she think of this commotion? You, girl, see to her."

His nod indicated Megan, who hastily moved to obey.

Adam's ire had so far been directed at Patience; it did not, however, exclude the rest of them. He addressed Roxanne with impatience. "Where did you come by this tale?"

"I made it up, sir," Roxanne replied promptly. "'Twas naught but a fable, a narrative to entertain the children."

Adam considered for a moment, glancing at his overwrought daughter-in-law and back to the servant, who displayed far more calm. "Aye," he said finally. "Well, let's have no more of it, if it upsets their mother." His head swiveled as Megan returned. "How is she?"

"The same, Master Adam. Scarce aware of what transpires around her," Megan reported.

He sighed. "Very well. That fire needs another log."

As a matter of fact, it did not, yet no one argued with him when he threw another length of wood into the fireplace. Nels, seated on a low stool, lifted his small face.

"Grandfather, aren't we going to hear the end of the story? We don't know whether the pirate was killed or not!"

"My stories all end with the heroes living happily ever after," Roxanne said quickly.

Adam's mouth flattened. "Be still." He gestured toward the stairs. "Find something to do upstairs," he told the children.

"But Grandfather, it's so cold up there!" Betta protested. "We would have to go to bed to keep warm, and we've not had our supper yet!"

"Then put on your mittens and bring in some more wood. There's not enough here to last out the night." With that directive, he stalked past Patience and climbed the stairs, no doubt to the sanctuary of the room where the others hesitated to disturb him.

Patience met Roxanne's gaze with loathing. "You have not heard the last of this," she said, keeping her tone low so that it should not carry beyond the room. "Stay away from my children, or you'll regret it. Should any harm come to them, I'll know whom to blame."

Roxanne did not flinch away from her, speaking only when Patience, too, had fled up the stairs.

"Good Christ preserve me," she said then, "from such ignorance as that woman has! Be damned to her!"

"Don't say anything to worsen the situation," Christina pleaded. "She can make it miserable for us all."

"It's already miserable, isn't it? Don't expect me to lie down so she can wipe her shoes on me. I'll be glad when the *Revenge* returns!"

And what did that mean? Christina wondered. Did she think Captain O'Neal would marry her and take her out of bondage?

She did not dwell on that, however, for her thoughts led naturally to Vilas, who was with O'Neal in the frozen north. When the *Revenge* returned, so would Vilas, and she clung to the thought and the hopes that rode on that event.

When Megan took in afternoon tea an hour later, Abigail was dead.

Chapter 38

"SHE NO LONGER BREATHES," Megan whispered. "We'll...
we'll have to tell Mistress Patience."

Christina stared down at the woman in the bed. She did not
want to touch her; neither did she want to announce to any
family member that Abigail had died if this was not, indeed, the
case.

She stretched out a reluctant hand toward the emaciated
cheek. Despite the fire that was kept burning day and night, the
room was cold. Not cold enough, though, to account for the
way the flesh felt against her hand.

Christina had a vivid memory of her father as he lay dying,
and she jerked back, wiping her fingers on her apron. "She's
gone, right enough. I'm not sure Patience is the one to tell,
however."

Understanding disturbed Megan's face. "You think she'll
cause trouble? She can't blame Roxanne for this, can she?"

"With that one, who knows? Is Mistress Cordelia downstairs?"

"I'll fetch her," Megan said quickly, and fled the room.

The old woman came quickly, standing beside Christina at
the bed. She touched the younger woman matter-of-factly, then
nodded. "Aye. She be gone. Seen plenty of dead ones, I have.
They won't be burying her until the ground thaws."

Apprehension prickled up and down Christina's spine. "Will
you tell Mistress Patience?"

The bright brown eyes held Christina's for long seconds.
"Might be better to wait until some of the menfolk are here. I
believe my granddaughter is taking a nap. Patience was never
one to be disturbed during a nap."

Christina felt a small measure of relief. "Yes, we'll wait until at least one of them is here before we tell anyone," she
agreed.

The move was a wise one, though it could not have been said to be entirely successful in defusing the expected reaction. Patience had come downstairs carrying the baby just as Adam, Wesley and Ezra came home from hunting; they had brought in a brace of rabbits and a young buck for the pot and were feeling jovial and expansive.

Until Cordelia dropped the news like a stone into a pond. "Abigail's dead. Died in her sleep."

Silence congealed the laughter and conversation of moments before. Ezra was the first one to move, without speech, quickly crossing the kitchen to the room where his wife's body lay undisturbed.

Adam dominated the room, both in size and in presence. "She go peacefully?"

"Seems like," Cordelia agreed. "Just went to sleep."

"Did that slut give her something else in her tea?" Patience demanded, staring at Roxanne, who had not been previously informed and was therefore considerably taken aback.

How had this family put up with the woman's unbearable voice all these years? Christina wondered. Quite aside from the question of how they'd lived with her as a personality. Patience sounded like a harpy even when she wasn't annoyed about anything, simply because of her extraordinarily high-pitched voice.

"I have given her nothing," Roxanne said hotly. "Does no one die in this godforsaken place, as in England, without the intervention of some human hand? Why would I wish her ill?"

"Why indeed?" Patience demanded. "Why do you corrupt my—"

Adam's words held thunder. "Wesley, silence your wife or remove her from the room."

"You aren't here all day to observe the things she does, the things she says," Patience protested before her husband could reach her. "Why, once there was even the smell of brimstone in the air...."

"Brimstone?" Adam's voice was sharp.

"I asked what the stink was, and they denied there was one—"

"It was a stocking," Christina interrupted quickly. "Only a stocking that was thrown into the fire, not brimstone!"

"A stocking? Why would you burn a stocking?" Patience was incredulous, and the frightening thing was that she, too, appeared sincere, and was genuinely afraid.

"It was badly worn, and I thought it not worth darning," Roxanne told her. She might have done better, Christina thought, to have sounded less defiant. "I pitched it into the fire instead."

"Even a worn stocking is of some use," Wesley said, frowning, though there was no vehemence in the words. "How is it you take it upon yourselves . . ."

Adam spun upon his son. "Stockings, brimstone, let's hear no more about it! We have other matters to attend to!"

The moment passed, but the girls were under no illusions. Patience was not done with her convictions, and probably not even Adam could permanently still her tongue. Especially if she was to learn of what she would certainly regard as witches' markings on the bodies of her servants.

Even the children were subdued for the rest of the day. Ezra, his big, plain features showing the strain, went out to assemble what he needed to make the box in which Abigail would eventually be buried.

Christina, glancing out the window, felt as cold and as bleak as the day. She prayed that Vilas would return soon, that he would realize he had missed her as much as she had missed him. That he would provide a solution to the ever-growing problems in the Hull house.

With Abigail gone Patience was now the only mistress, and there was no doubt whatever in Christina's mind that she was a danger to them all.

ROXANNE'S ONLY REGRET over Abigail was that her coffin must be stored in the lean-to until weather permitted burial, and even that didn't bother her too much when she went out there to bring in wood or cut off a haunch from the hanging meat.

She had not liked Abigail. She liked Patience even less, while dismissing her as an unreasonable female of the worst sort, the kind of woman who would be disregarded by anyone of any common sense. Unfortunately, these Puritans seemed devoid of any such quality.

Christina's fears that Patience would spread her suspicions in the community seemed of little significance to Roxanne. They were, after all, entirely in her own blond head. The clergy in Ipswich preached against the hysteria displayed in other parts of the colony. True, the villagers gossiped and speculated over the stories that came out of Salem, where a small band of young girls accused three women, including a black slave, of witchcraft. There was little else of such interest to occupy their minds, and whenever a traveler came from afar, the first thing the local people wanted to know was what was taking place in Salem.

There had been, however, no demonstrations of demonic possession in Ipswich. No children screaming in convulsions, eyes rolling back in their heads, no shrieking with pain said to be inflicted by witches.

Idiots, Roxanne thought.

She was more concerned with her own needs, her own future.

Her introduction to the delights of love by Shea O'Neal had only whetted her physical appetites. Her dreams at night often brought her awake in a state that warmed her even in the freezing kitchen. She could not wait for O'Neal to return, and in her naïveté she was convinced that he must offer her marriage and take her away from this place.

She had grown up, to the age of twelve, in a simple household without servants. This caused her no feeling of deprivation; the cottage was snug enough in winter—warmer than Kenwood, when she finally was taken there—and there was always enough to eat. That various men came and went in the night hours was of little concern.

At Kenwood there had been servants, so that she need no longer search for fuel for the fire, nor set snares for rabbits to stew. She had been forced to learn to read and write and had had leisure time beyond imagining, yet except for the books then made available to her she had not been happy in the castle.

She was even less happy as an indentured servant to the Hulls. A kind and reasonable mistress would have been a help in that direction; Patience was neither. And Roxanne was too independent a spirit to bow easily before a superior, even if she'd recognized anyone as such.

There was plenty of work to do, and Patience became more demanding than she had been while her sister-in-law lived. Yet there was no reason, Roxanne decided, why she could not have time to herself.

She would have liked to sit before the fire with pen and paper, creating romantic tales of swooning maidens and dashing heroes. She dared not. Everyone would have had to know what she did, and this would have provided more fuel for Patience's fires.

And so, instead, she roamed the outdoors, sliding on the ice, struggling through the snow which at times drifted to the height of her waist, living the stories in her head until she was driven by the cold and wet back to the fireside.

Once in her wanderings she came upon a hill where a group of boys were sliding. The impulse to join them leaped within her, but they ceased their activity and stood staring at her. Coasting was forbidden. No doubt they feared she would report them to the tithing man, who would see that they were stopped and punished.

Roxanne lifted a hand in salute and turned away. What a miserable religion this Puritanism was, she reflected; anything that offered diversion was forbidden, no matter how harmless it was.

Perhaps she'd been a fool to leave Cornwall. True, she had been unable to find employment close at home, but she was young and strong. She could have walked or gotten a ride on some farmer's cart, to Truro or Falmouth or to some even more distant place, like Plymouth or Exeter, where no one knew her. She'd proved these past few months that she could empty slops and scrub floors, turn the spit and stir the stew, as well as anyone else. There would have been hostelries where her looks would have worked for rather than against her. She knew she was beautiful; the words Shea O'Neal had whispered, with lips pressed against her bared breasts, had assured her of that, and warmed her blood now as she strode along the track that passed for a road on the edge of town.

"Mistress Roxanne! Wait a bit!"

Roxanne stopped, recognizing Wesley Hull when he emerged from the woods. He carried his musket over one shoulder, and there were several rabbits at his belt. "You wander far from home," he said upon reaching her, though there was no censure in his voice that she could detect.

"I like the exercise." She began to walk again, and Wesley fell into step beside her, matching his stride to hers.

"The cold does not keep you indoors."

"No. It's invigorating."

"I find it so, too. I wish my wife would try it and see if it did not improve her health." He shot a sideways glance at her. "She has always been frail, however. After Abigail's death I fear for her health."

Roxanne's private thought was that Patience would enjoy poor health for another fifty years; it did not seem prudent to say this, however. "She is much younger than Mistress Abigail was. I doubt you've overmuch to worry about."

"If I were to lose Patience," he said, as if she had not spoken, "we would be without a woman to direct our household. Not an enviable position for four men, and with three young children to care for."

"You have three female servants," Roxanne pointed out reasonably. Who manage now with no help from your wife, she was tempted to add.

"And you do very well, considering that you were not born to this sort of life. Is it true that in England you were the daughters of an earl?"

"Yes," Roxanne admitted shortly. What would he think if he knew she was the illegitimate daughter of that noble gentleman?

"You learn quickly. And you have some . . . some sensitivity for my children. I would hope that would carry over to a husband, as well."

Illumination flooded her. He wasn't concerned about someone to run his household; old Cordelia could do that with the aid of three servants. He wanted someone in his bed, the devil. Someone not cold, nor always sick, like Patience.

The thought amused her. Too late she realized that he might have misinterpreted her small smile.

"You know, I'm sure, that in our society every man is encouraged to marry. It is pure necessity. If Patience were to take ill..."

There was something about the way he was watching her that turned her amusement to uneasiness. God's blood, did he *want* something to happen to Patience? Not that she'd blame him if he did, but the idea was disconcerting, especially when another speculation crept into her mind.

Did the man think his wife's accusations were true, that she'd had something to do with Abigail's death? And that she had the power to rid him of Patience, as well?

"You are a very attractive young woman," he said tentatively.

"And an independent one," she told him with haste. "I've no wish to marry as yet. Puritan society is far different from what I'm used to. I don't think," and now she spoke with deliberation, "I could ever conform strictly to the kind of life your church asks of you."

Wesley *was* good-looking when he smiled. "You are very young. Wisdom comes with the years. And marriage to a mature man has been the making of many a woman."

No doubt, Roxanne thought sardonically. Well, Shea O'Neal was a mature man, too, only a little younger than Wesley Hull. And far more exciting.

Nevertheless, it was impossible not to wonder what it would be like to be Wesley's wife. Certainly she'd be more responsive in bed than that pallid stick of a Patience; perhaps Wesley, too, knew the meaning of passion.

What would it be like, making love to Wesley? Would his fingers and his lips find all the secret places, know all the ways to caress a woman into a frenzy that could be quenched only by that final, incredible explosion of sensation?

Was it possible that Shea O'Neal was not the only man who could carry her to such heights?

Roxanne watched Wesley from then on, often encountering his gaze in return. He was wary in the presence of others. Yet she knew he was thinking thoughts similar to her own, and quite of its own volition, her pulse would quicken.

Chapter 39

EVERY NIGHT BEFORE SHE FELL ASLEEP Megan told herself that on the following day she would settle the matter, one way or the other. She would tell Fitz why she had so far not accepted his proposal of marriage.

Every morning her courage leaked away, simply because she lived in this house of Puritans. In this house where Patience Hull was now mistress.

Fitz attributed her hesitancy to shyness. He did not press her, being content to court her gently, sweetly. When the tears came to her eyes, as they frequently did, he kissed them away, if they were alone. "Surely you are not afraid of me, are you, Megan?"

"No," she said, almost truthfully. If it were not for the matter of the witch-hunters and the mark that condemned her she would not have been afraid of anything.

The news that filtered through to the village—more easily now that the blizzards seemed to have blown themselves out—gave her no comfort. In Salem, Sarah Good, Sarah Osburn and a slave called Tituba had been accused of bewitching two young girls in the household of the Reverend Samuel Parris. The children were nine and eleven years old, too young, in the opinion of most, to have invented their tales of being tormented by these women, who protested that they were innocent. Not everyone could be telling the truth; the growing conviction was that the women, not the children, were guilty of lying.

The number of young girls involved grew to nine. They ranged up to twenty years old. They came from good families, while those accused were a slatternly woman with no permanent home, one who had recently given up going to church, and a slave. It was little wonder that the afflicted girls were believed, rather than the accused, particularly when they screamed and writhed so convincingly.

On a morning when the sun made a blinding blanket of the snow and a slight rise in temperature had created gigantic icicles at the eaves, Megan looked out on the sparkling world and drew a deep breath.

The glorious day gave her hope and strength. Only last night, in a stolen moment on the stairs as everyone else gathered for supper, Fitz had kissed her: gently, yet with a controlled passion that was unmistakable, a kiss that infused her with determination. He loved her. He would still love her after she told him.

She had climbed to the top floor with a tray for Mistress Cordelia, who had trouble getting out of bed on these cold mornings. It was a pity the old woman could not sleep in one of the rooms that boasted a fireplace, for the chill made her stiff in the joints. Though a chimney rose through her chamber, the heat it provided was inadequate for this time of year.

Cordelia gratefully accepted the hot tea and the bowl of mush. "You're a good girl to think of me," she said, nodding.

"I'll wait for the dishes," Megan offered. "Then you won't have to carry them down later."

The old woman nodded again. "Lean against the chimney, girl, so your feet don't freeze to the floor while you wait," she suggested.

By the time Cordelia had finished, they heard voices from the chamber below. Wesley's, deep and gruff, said something about having gotten wet so he'd had to come home for dry clothes.

Patience's voice carried with startling clarity to the listeners above. No wonder Cordelia was aware of the marital state of those two, Megan thought.

"You find many excuses to come home these days," Patience said.

"What's that supposed to mean?" There was an irritable note in Wesley's voice. "There's no satisfying you. A few months ago you complained because I was never here."

"That was before *she* arrived."

"She? Who?" Wesley demanded, yet even the pair listening from above knew who Patience had meant.

Megan watched the vapor from her breath form on the icy air. She was eavesdropping, and the fact that it was unintentional did not alleviate her sense of guilt. Yet she stayed where she was, pressed against the faint warmth of the brick chimney.

"Do you think I don't notice the way you look at her? The way you contrive to be around her?" Patience spoke savagely, for once dropping her voice, but not enough to prevent the listeners from making out the words. "I want her out of here, Wesley. Abigail is gone, and I'm mistress now. I don't want that harlot in my house."

"She's not a harlot," Wesley countered, any pretense of not knowing of whom she spoke forgotten.

"She's bewitched you. I know things about her you don't."

"Patience, my father has warned you—"

"His reluctance to see what is under his nose will only delay the inevitable. She is evil, husband. I overheard Abigail talking to Ezra, and you cannot accuse *her* of being foolish in her speech. The girl is a gypsy! You know what gypsys are! They dabble in magic, in witchcraft! She healed her own burns with nothing more than water, and you know that's impossible! At least it is without the assistance of the devil!"

There was a silence, during which Megan wished she could see Wesley's face. Then, heavily, he said, "I've no time to listen to this. Give me my scarf."

"You will listen, now or later," Patience insisted. "I want her out of this house! I do not trust her, and if she's around I cannot even trust my husband."

"I think you forget yourself," Wesley told her gruffly. "You may be mistress of this household now, but you are not master of the house. My father signed the indenture papers and paid the fees. If any of them is sent away, he will be the one to do it, not I."

They heard footsteps on the board floor as she followed him to the doorway. "You don't want to get rid of her! It isn't your father who stands in the way of it; you simply won't ask him to get rid of her!"

Wesley's voice, muffled but still audible, came from the landing. "No, I won't," he said.

Megan and Cordelia stared at each other. They barely heard Patience, talking now to herself.

"Then I will," she stated, and Megan felt the chill run from her feet up through her limbs and along her spine.

Fitz was there in the kitchen when she went down, but the conversation she had overheard was too frightening. Her resolution to reveal to him her secret had wilted away, and she was filled with despair.

ON FEBRUARY 29 warrants were issued for the arrest of the accused Salem witches. On the following day the tavern where they were to be questioned by the magistrates was surrounded by people who had happily put aside their own business to follow this exciting examination.

By the time the magistrates arrived the throng was too large to be accommodated at Ingersoll's tavern; the proceedings were delayed until the authorities, the accused and the avid onlookers could make their way to the larger meeting house.

What followed was related almost verbatim to every other part of the Bay Colony. Considering the fact that the news was relayed by mouth rather than the written word, it was conveyed in remarkable detail. Even in the Hull household, where Adam frowned upon furthering speculations of witchcraft, the entire story was told. It was legitimate news.

Magistrate John Hathorne, who clearly believed the woman guilty, had questioned Sarah Good in a bullying fashion, demanding to know what evil spirit guided her, what contract she had made with the devil and why she hurt the children. When she denied any such doings, the magistrate turned to the waiting girls.

"Is this woman one of those who have tormented you?" he asked.

At that, the girls cried out as if in pain and began to have seizures that set the onlookers to murmuring among themselves. This was far more entertaining than chopping wood or scrubbing floors, and the populace was eager to milk the situation of all possible drama. Many of them had never seen the girls demonstrate their bewitched state: they watched, goggle-eyed and impressed. Nothing this interesting had happened within most of their memories.

Sarah Good not only denied the accusations but also made one of her own. "'Tis Sarah Osburn is the guilty one," she said.

While Sarah Osburn also denied her guilt, she admitted that possibly the devil went around in her likeness, tormenting people. She herself was innocent.

The slave, Tituba, was last to testify.

The last, and the most fascinating.

For while Tituba initially denied her guilt, she soon gave in to the battering ram of accusation and confessed at some length. Tituba was articulate, and she held her listeners spellbound. Even the girls who claimed to be bewitched fell silent as the slave woman's story unfolded.

Yes, the devil had bidden her serve him, she admitted. She had signed her mark in his book, along with nine others. A tall man in black had threatened to harm her if she did not torment the children. He had urged her to kill them. Sometimes his spirit came not as a man but as a huge black dog or a hog. She said that she and the other witches on trial with her rode through the air on sticks to do their evil deeds.

When she fell into convulsions of her own, the magistrates and the audience were convinced. It must be true. There were witches in their midst: the three women on trial and six others.

Who were the others?

Salem Village was like a boiling pot, with the scalding fluid running over and touching everyone with hysteria.

For five days the women were questioned. The young girls testified against them: they had been tortured, bitten, pinched, pricked and choked.

Now other townspeople came forward, given courage by the testimony already admitted. Suspicion became conviction. Grudges were remembered. Sarah Good had cursed those who refused her food or shelter: now those people recalled how shortly thereafter their cattle had died or their hogs disappeared. They had suffered illnesses and accidents themselves. Even episodes that had taken place years earlier were dredged up and became part of the record against the witches.

On March 7 the women were put into jail for their crimes, and their story traveled with the speed of wildfire to the distant villages, where they were discussed in every kitchen, every tavern, every street corner.

In Ipswich there was much disquietude, and nowhere more of it than among the indentured servants in the house of Adam Hull.

Chapter 40

THE MINISTERS WERE the primary leaders in the Puritan community. In Ipswich, unlike other places such as Salem Village, the clergy urged caution. They, too, were concerned about witchcraft and evildoing, but at least so far cooler heads had prevailed. From the pulpit the citizens were warned to beware of overzealous pursuit of the sinners.

"Let us not be misled into sins of our own," Reverend Parker pleaded, "by bearing false witness against our neighbors. Not all catastrophe can be attributed to witchcraft. The fact that someone has done us wrong is not sufficient to allow us to state that it occurred at the instigation of the devil. It is not enough, because an individual has cursed us, to assure that person's conviction as a witch. Human nature has always been weak, and we must be certain that it is not only this weakness that leads us from the paths of righteousness."

Christina listened and was not reassured. Not when Patience maintained a tight-lipped silence most of the time, when she forbade the children to be alone with the servants, when Megan had reported the conversation she had overheard between Patience and her husband.

They had decided not to tell Roxanne about it. It might only inflame her to further destructive conduct.

As far as Christina could tell, Roxanne did nothing to encourage Wesley's attentions. It seemed unlikely he had the opportunity to go beyond watching the girl. Perhaps Patience thought that a witch was capable of creating time as well as trouble.

The icicles first grew longer from the eaves, then melted and fell off. Patience was furious when Nels and two neighbor boys were caught fencing with some of the larger ones, with all the enthusiasm of six- and seven-year-olds.

"'Tis what comes of telling children wild stories of pirates and such," she stormed, jerking Nels inside, his icicle sword smashed upon the doorstep.

Christina longed for spring, when she could spend more time out-of-doors, away from the critical tongue of Mistress Patience.

Spring came, though slowly. The first thaw was temporary, and there was another flurry of snow, though this one did not build up into drifts. The earth softened enough so that a grave could be dug, and Abigail was buried, to the relief of those who had had to pass by her remains every time they entered the lean-to.

Bare spots appeared on the ground, the snow shrank into the shadowed areas and pussy willows budded out. Betta and Nels picked armloads of them, Betta to put into vases and Nels to sail on the puddles in improvised boats.

So like Thomas, Christina thought when the little boy suddenly pelted the boats with pebbles and sank the pussy willow sailors. Boys were the same everywhere, whether highborn or low.

Soon, she thought with intense longing, the *Revenge* would return from its voyage to the mouth of the distant St. Lawrence. Would it drop anchor at Ipswich, or would it sail on by, to Boston? How many days remained before she would see Vilas again? With every passing day, as buttercups and violets opened their tender petals and the breezes grew warmer, her hopes rose that Vilas would suddenly be there on the bridge the next time she walked into the village. She could close her eyes and see him in the scarlet cloak, his fair hair shining in the sun, a welcoming smile on his face.

She had not talked further with Megan about Fitz. Any idiot could see they were smitten with each other; Christina thought only she detected the underlying anguish as Megan struggled to deal with her difficulties. Had it not been for those crazed by the word *witch*, in a village none of the sisters had ever seen, Megan would probably have dared to speak out to Fitz. As it was, the ongoing list of horrors in Salem Village kept her poised on the edge of an abyss, never knowing when the next second might send her over the edge.

Now that the trails were clear of snow, news reached them more rapidly than before, and all of it was bad. In the middle of March one of those young girls accused a different sort of woman of tormenting her, a woman of excellent repute, a devout churchgoer named Martha Corey.

From what they heard, Mistress Corey was more sensible than most. She had refused to attend the witch trials, condemning them as foolishness, uncharitably skeptical about the girls who claimed to be bewitched. Even members of her own family complained about her attitudes, which they did not share. Martha Corey, in spite of her protestations of innocence and the sensibility of her replies to her questioners, was arrested.

The meetinghouse was crowded when she was brought there on a Monday morning for further questioning. All normal activity was suspended in the village; no one wanted to miss a word or a gesture from any of the principals of the drama.

When Martha Corey suggested that they must not believe the children, the girls went into the now-familiar yet ever fascinating antics. When the woman bit her lip the girls cried that they were being bitten; when she involuntarily clenched her hands in her lap, they insisted they were being pinched. One of the girls claimed to see the specter of a tall dark man whispering his orders to the defendant.

Although no one else in the crowded room saw anything of the sort, the electrifying tension was overwhelming. Martha Corey, too, was thrown into jail for the crime of practicing witchcraft.

Was there to be no end to it? Christina wondered pensively, staring out over the bay where no tall sails yet announced the return of the *Revenge*. Where would it all end? Only last night Adam had commented with some bitterness that it appeared half the colonists would not be satisfied to return to their daily tasks until the other half had been jailed or hanged for imagined crimes if no real ones could be proven.

Even arranged marriages in Cornwall might have been preferable to swinging from the gibbet in this New World.

"You are sad, mistress? We had hoped you would come to like it here in Ipswich."

The voice was unexpected. Christina turned, startled to find Ezra Hull beside her. It was the first time he had directly addressed her since his wife had died, and there was something in his eyes that set her immediately on guard.

"There is much that disturbs me here," she said in a masterful understatement.

"You do not worry for your future, I hope? In Massachusetts we have need of healthy young women to help us build a strong colony." His features were large, not ugly, but certainly not handsome. He smiled, and she realized with astonishment that she had never before seen him smile. "Homesickness can be a painful thing."

"I'm not homesick," Christina said truthfully. She had not meant to come so close to the boat yard owned by the Hulls; in her eagerness for a glimpse of the bay, she had not paid attention to where she walked. She would never have expected Ezra to leave his work to approach her. "I'm not completely at home here either, though. All this talk of witchcraft . . . is dismaying."

"It is," Ezra agreed. "I do not think the fever to search out witches will come to Ipswich. Our clergy are sensible, intelligent, in their leadership."

But all the citizens weren't, Christina thought. One of the worst of the lot lived under his own roof.

She had never really carried on a conversation with this man, despite having eaten at the same supper table with him for an entire winter. It occurred to her now that over the past month she had noticed his gaze upon her a few times. He had never made her uncomfortable, however, until now.

She'd lost track of whatever he'd said to her. "I suppose I'd better get back. We're airing the bedding today, because the sun is so warm."

"I'll walk with you," Ezra offered, and fell into step as she started along the path.

Alarm tingled along her nerve ends. She didn't want him to walk with her, talk to her; she wanted her private time, to dream her dreams, to release the tensions of living in the same house with Patience and her suspicions and ill temper. How did one get rid of a man who was also a master, when she was the servant?

"The winters here are severe," Ezra was saying. His fingers touched her elbow, to help her over a fallen branch, sending further apprehension through her. "You'll like this country better in the spring and summer. There is no need for you to remain a servant in someone else's house, Mistress Christine. You would be happier, I'm sure, as mistress of your own establishment."

Good heavens, was he suggesting what she thought he was? She could not look at him, for fear that was what she would read in his face. Instead she concentrated on choosing the best place to put down a foot so as not to trip or step into a boggy spot and wet her shoes.

He was not put off by her lack of response. Again he took her elbow to guide her, though there was no need for it, and this time he did not let her go. Christina felt panic rising within her as they moved through the woods. They were alone, and even this touch seemed inappropriate for a man so recently bereaved.

As if he'd read her mind, Ezra said, "Already the elders are pressing me to remarry. There are several widows..." Did he know how heavily and eloquently he sighed? "It is a man's duty to act in the best interests of the entire community, of course. I've no wish to rush into matrimony; Abigail's too recently gone, but I wanted you to know."

His voice dropped to a more intimate level, and Christina's stomach dropped, too. She inwardly willed him to stop speaking, with no results whatever.

"I've been noticing you. You're the sensible one, the mature one of the three of you. You've taken hold very nicely; in fact, we've hardly been aware of a disruption in the running of the household since you took on the entire burden of it. I'm aware that Patience hasn't shouldered much of the responsibility. I will have to take a wife, and you are an excellent choice, it seems to me. Perhaps..." He faltered, and this time she did look at him. His color, already ruddy from working out-of-doors in the wind and the sun, deepened in hue.

Christina's mouth was dry. Why did he cling to her arm? Why didn't he let her walk away, as she wanted to do? She would have covered her ears to keep out his words if he hadn't stopped in the middle of the path, still gripping her arm; they stood amidst the white barked birches, as yet only lightly touched with pale green foliage, the sun warm on their faces.

"You know that Abigail and I had no children," Ezra said with painful earnestness. "We did not even lose a babe, as Patience has done. The Lord, in His wisdom, did not see fit to bless us with children."

She wanted to jerk free of him and run. Perhaps she tensed her arm to do so, for his fingers tightened. His face was close to hers, too close.

"Perhaps I've been given a second chance to father a child," Ezra said. "My friend Richard Alberts fathered a son at the age of nearly seventy. He had a young wife, of course. A young, healthy girl. Like you."

Revulsion rippled through her. He didn't care about her as a person, she thought wildly, trying to pull free of him. A seventy-year-old husband—or a fifty-year-old one, like Ezra—would not disgust her if the husband were Vilas, if she'd married him as a young man and they'd grown old together. The idea of going to bed with this man who was nearly as old as her father had been, however, solely to give him the satisfaction of producing an heir, a son to carry on the family name—no, never. She would end up like the despised Patience. Christina bit her lip and tasted blood.

"I'm not asking you to decide now," Ezra stated. "Only to think about it. To consider the advantages for you, as well as for me. You would always be well taken care of—"

"Please! I must get back! The clouds may be carrying rain, and I cannot allow the bedding to be soaked."

"They are only little clouds and not the sort that carry rain," Ezra objected, but when she tugged against his restraining hand he finally released her.

Christina stumbled and nearly fell, catching herself against one of the birch trees before he could touch her again. "I'm sorry, I really must go," she panted, and fled.

For a moment she felt he would pursue her. He did not, though his words drifted behind her as she ran. "Think about it!" he called.

She thought about it. She couldn't stop thinking about it. She'd die first, she thought. It would be no better than having stayed at home and been forced into a loveless marriage with master Hunnicutt.

Her breath came in sobbing gasps when she slowed her headlong pace; she had a stitch in her side and pressed a hand against it to break the cramp.

When she married it would be for love, she swore aloud to the silent woods. Oh, Vilas, Vilas, when would he come?

Chapter 41

It appeared there would be no end to the accusations and arrests in Salem Village. The first thing asked of any traveler coming to their own village was news of the witches, and it was usually related with considerable relish.

For once Christina was relieved to have a visitor in the house, holding everyone's attention with the latest information. Otherwise the others would surely have noticed her discomfiture.

Roxanne had done so anyway, while food and drink was set out for the newcomer. He was a small wiry man of middle years; he had had business dealings with Adam for as long as both had lived in the Bay Colony. His name was Charles Exeter.

He offered his condolences to Ezra, and for a moment Ezra's face was blank, as if he did not know the reason for the sympathy being extended. Then his face shifted into planes reflecting an appropriate grief. "Yes, thank you. 'Tis a grievous loss," he said.

Roxanne, dashing up the savory baked beans heavily flavored with molasses and fat pork, spoke under cover of the hubbub of greetings. "What did he do to you?"

"Who?" Christina asked, damning the girl for noticing.

"Don't be coy. Master Ezra, what did he do to you?"

Christina hoped her color would be attributed to working close to the fire as she hacked a slab of venison from the meat on the spit. "He didn't do anything."

"Try to do, then. Or say. Did he get you in a corner and pinch your behind?"

Christian gave her an angry glance. With Roxanne there was no point in dissembling; the girl would keep at her until she learned what she wanted to know. "He's indicated that he would like me to take Abigail's place." She didn't further humiliate herself by recounting all of it, of Ezra's idea that she was young and sturdy enough to give him the sons he and Abigail had been denied.

To her annoyance, Roxanne laughed. "I take it you surprised him by not being delighted?"

She didn't wait for a reply, instead bearing the loaded plate to the table to place before Charles Exeter. Adam waved a hand at her, and Roxanne went on to pour out rum for everyone.

Christina drank her own—well watered down—standing close to the fire, having no desire to sit where anyone could observe the emotion that must be revealed in her face. She could hardly bear to look at Ezra; to do so conjured up an image of him hovering over her in bed, prepared to kiss her, to do unspeakable things to her body. Revulsion rose, sour, choking, in her throat.

For the time, at least, no one paid her any attention. Even Ezra, seated opposite the guest at the long table, concentrated on Charles Exeter.

Patience was at the table, too, beside her husband. She leaned forward avidly, moistening her lips. "They've arrested more witches, then?"

Exeter took a long swig of rum before he answered. "Oh, aye, there's no end to it. Some of them have confessed—I heard the black woman, Tituba, myself, and it made the hair rise on the back of my neck, I can tell you!—and others stubbornly maintain their innocence. Some, like Martha Corey, cause me uneasiness. I've known the woman for years and cannot but struggle with the idea that she is an evil person. If the devil has claimed her as his own, he did it without her consent, to be certain."

There was silence in the room as they waited for him to partake of the beans and meat and corn bread, which he ate with enthusiasm. To no one's surprise, it was Patience who urged him on at last.

"Will they all hang, do you think?"

There was an eagerness in her words that chilled at least three of the listeners. Christina moved closer to the fire, wondering what she had done to offend God, that He should have led her to this place. She might have taken refuge with Vilas's mother—except, of course, Vilas himself would have been here in the New World. She tried to take comfort from the knowledge that they were at least in the same hemisphere, though listening to Exeter's ominous words allowed precious little solace.

"Oh, they'll hang, all right," the man replied to Patience's question. "Once that charter comes back from England, so our magistrates have some authority again, I've no doubt of that. And quite a spectacle it will be. Takes place during the spring, won't nobody plant their crops. And if it takes until fall, it'll be a miracle if the harvesting is done. Nobody thinks of anything but the witches, the trials, and looking forward to the executions."

Adam drank deeply of his own rum, which did nothing to lighten his mood. "It troubles me greatly, the way each one accused goes on to accuse someone else, as if to spread the misery around. If we'd as many witches as they'd have us believe, the colony would be in total chaos."

"You think it's not?" Exeter asked. He lifted his plate toward Roxanne. "Could I have another helping of those beans, young woman? Very good, they are."

As soon as she'd taken the plate, he went on. "The worst yet, I think, is the arrest of Goodwife Nurse. Known her, too, I have, for years. Nice old woman, God-fearing, gentle. The whole family is shaken to its boots—big family, she has, and they swear she's not guilty. Yet those girls declare she's one of those tormenting them. We got the word from the pulpit this Sabbath past: we are to do all in our power to check and rebuke Satan. We must root out the evil in our midst and rid ourselves of these damned witches, or we will surely *all* be condemned to perdition."

There was a murmur of approbation. Even Adam, much as it distressed him, had to agree: they must put an end to this business.

"It's down to arresting children, now," Exeter said, polishing off the remainder of his meal. "They carried off the daughter of Sarah Good, a mere babe of five years, after the child admitted she and her mother were both witches, that she has a snake as a familiar and showed them the places where it sucks the blood from between her fingers. I don't know if they'll hang her along with her mother, but what are we to make of the guilt of such a little one?"

Patience, who as the mother of three might have been expected to sympathize with the latest victim of the witch-hunters, hung on his every word, unwilling to have him come to the end of the recital.

"Tell us about the trials. You were there, were you not? You saw the witches themselves and the tormented girls?"

Christina's stomach was churning. Coming on top of the unsettling episode with Ezra, the account—and the way Patience reacted to it—were more than she could bear. Quietly, unnoticed, she took down her cloak from its peg and let herself out of the house.

The day no longer seemed as fine as it had, though the sun continued to shine. She strode briskly away from the village, wanting to meet no one.

Was it true, that all those convicted were actually guilty of witchcraft? Or were some of them innocent of any wrongdoing, as they claimed to be? As she and Megan, and even Roxanne, were innocent?

Should Patience openly and publicly accuse them, though the accusations be false, would the townspeople listen? Or would they be caught up in the hysteria that swept Salem, putting their lives in danger?

It occurred to her, as she walked through the peaceful woods, that marrying Ezra might afford her some protection against the witch-hunters. As being Fitz's wife might also protect Megan—at least if no one knew about the blemish.

Her stomach churned, a wave of nausea swept over her. It was not until she had leaned against a tree trunk for support and been thoroughly sick that Christina was able to go on walking. Today there was no healing touch in the woods around her, in the hint of spring in the air.

It was all she could do to force herself to return to the house at dusk.

HAD CHRISTINA BEEN AWARE of the continued heights of emotion, of the fear and suspicion that consumed the town at the center of the controversy, she would have been even more disturbed than she already was.

It took a strong person to publicly denounce the idea of witchcraft in their midst. One of those who did was John Procter; his servant, Mary, was one of the afflicted girls, and he shouted his opinion that if she and the others were allowed to go on, no one would be safe from their accusations.

One of the few besides Procter to show displeasure with the generally accepted attitudes was a sister of poor old Rebecca Nurse, already languishing in the overcrowded jail; when the sister was angered by a sermon that encouraged the witch-hunting and, she thought, cast aspersions upon Goody Nurse, she angrily slammed the door behind her as she left the meetinghouse in the middle of the service.

It was a mistake. She, Joe Procter and his wife were all accused by the young girls and were arrested. The accusations grew more detailed: these three had drunk the devil's sacrament, in wine like blood.

There seemed no end to the credulity of the citizens of Salem. Common sense had completely flown. New magistrates were brought in from the highest Colonial court in Boston to investigate the latest events, and any hope that the matter might be confined to Salem Village vanished.

The accusations and the arrests went on.

MEGAN, TOO, had listened to Charles Exeter with trepidation. So upset was she that she did not notice when Fitz left the other men at the table, where even on the second day the visitor was being urged to expand upon his original concise story, to come to her side. When he took her hand Megan started as violently as if some magistrate had come for *her*.

"You are distressed by this talk of witches," Fitz said quietly. "Do not be. It has no bearing on us. Our clergy and our citizens will not allow the poison of Salem to contaminate us."

Megan's throat worked. She had only to look at Patience to be disabused of his optimistic assertion. Fitz followed her gaze.

"My sister-in-law will submit to the authority of her husband and my father. They are not rabble-rousers."

"It takes only one small rivulet to begin a flood," Megan said.

"How can I reassure you?" His face hinted at what he would *like* to do. "You trust me, don't you? You know that I would never allow harm to come to you."

Megan made no response to that. If only there were some way to gauge his reaction to the truth! "You believe they're guilty, though, don't you? Those unfortunates who've been thrown into jail?"

"Since some of them have confessed, 'tis impossible not to."

"But the others? The ones who swear they are innocent?"

"If they are innocent, surely God will protect them. At any rate, they've nothing to do with us. I am in sympathy with your tender heart, though I fear it causes you undue distress. Come, they are going to be here for hours. Let's get some air, away from this depressing talk."

Outside the house it was easier to let her fears slide into the back of her mind. With her hand warmly held in Fitz's, a little of the hope crept back into her heart.

And when he drew her into his embrace, when his mouth claimed hers in a sweet and sensuous kiss, Megan could blot out everything except the lean young body pressed to her own and the hands that caressed her.

It was only when they drew apart that the uncertainties pressed in once more. Time and again she shaped the opening words with her lips, only to have her courage fail her at the last moment.

Another day had passed, and still she agonized over her own situation. What would it take to give her the courage to tell him?

FROM THAT DAY FORWARD, Christina determined never to walk near the boat works and to keep a sharper eye out for Ezra. That he sought her out, though discreetly, was beyond question. She would simply have to become more elusive, she decided.

The walks became all important, however. The atmosphere in the house, under the domination of Patience, was unendurable without an occasional break from it.

Besides, it was April. The ice had gone from the creek, the trees were greening, the air took on a balmy softness. Any day now, the *Revenge* would surely drop anchor in Ipswich Bay.

It was possible, of course, that Captain O'Neal had already sailed his ship on by this place, for it was not a true harbor, and his primary business would be with the citizens of Boston. Yet Christina could not allow herself to believe that the ship would not at least pause here briefly, so that she would know Vilas had returned.

Roxanne, too, showed increasing signs of restlessness. She, also, sought out a vantage point from which she could observe the bay. She, too, stared out to sea with a longing that might have touched a familiar chord in Christina had she seen it.

On the eighteenth of April, as yet unknown to the inhabitants of Ipswich, four more warrants were issued for another quartet of witches. One of them caused a new round of speculation and excitement, for she was Mary Warren, servant of John Procter who had been incarcerated with his wife and the previously convicted witches.

Mary had been one of the accusers. Now she was accused herself, by the girls with whom she had formerly been in alliance. Before it was over she would have confessed to witchcraft, implicating her former masters and others. Luckier than they, she would eventually be released and return to her role as one of the stars of the drama, an accuser.

It was not witchcraft that caused excitement and dismay in Ipswich that day, however.

Christina had strolled through the village, greeting several people whom she knew from Meeting, and down toward the shore, keeping a careful eye out for Ezra should he allow himself to be distracted from his work. Since he conducted some business unconnected with the boat works, he had more excuses than the others to leave the work on the latest construction.

The water came into view and Christina stopped, heart in her throat, pulses suddenly racing.

For there she was, the *Revenge*, even now lowering sail and dropping anchor.

Joy rushed through her so that, unknowing, she cried aloud. "Vilas!"

She forgot her fear of meeting Ezra and raced toward the beach, stopping only when the surf would have wet her feet. They seemed to be having trouble lowering something into the longboat; she couldn't quite tell what was happening, but she urged them on aloud. "Hurry, hurry!"

"They'll come soon enough," Wesley said, and she realized that a group of men and even a couple of women and children from the village had gathered around her. "It looks as if they've lowered someone in a hammock, someone who couldn't climb down the ladder. Someone's ill or hurt."

Hurt?

The word struck terror into her very soul.

Clearly there was nothing wrong with Shea O'Neal. He sat in the bow of the longboat as his men pulled upon the oars, and he was the first one over the side, wading through the water to the shore.

But Vilas, where was Vilas? Frantic now, the dread growing so that she felt suffocated by it, Christina pressed forward with the others. Willing hands helped haul the boat ashore far enough so that the hammock could be lifted free.

O'Neal called out to Adam, and his words set Christina reeling. "De Clement is grievously wounded. I don't know if he'll last long enough to get him to Boston. Can your womenfolk take him in hand? Perhaps with skilled nursing care he may have a chance, and Mistress Abigail has always—"

"Abigail is dead," Adam said bluntly. "But there are the others. Of course, bring him to our house and we'll do our best for him."

Christina thought she would surely faint. Her vision blurred, darkened and spots danced before her eyes. Grievously wounded . . . dear God!

The men carrying the hammock tramped up the shingle, and she caught a glimpse of the beloved face—scarcely recognizable beneath several months' grown of dark blond beard—between a cap of dirty, blood-stained bandages and the blanket that covered him from the chin down.

Adam saw her and waved an imperious hand. "Run ahead, girl, show the men the way and have a pallet prepared for him! Hurry!"

"Put him in my bed," Ezra offered. "'Twill be easier to care for him there. I'll be going to Boston soon, anyway."

She was so blinded by tears that it was a miracle she found her way but Christina ran, and as she ran she prayed. Beseeching the mercies of a God she was no longer sure was listening.

Chapter 42

BEING JOSTLED AROUND while he was carried through the woods from the sea had set his head to bleeding anew; there were fresh stains on the soiled bandages when Vilas was eased from the improvised stretcher onto the bed in Ezra's room.

Christina thought her heart would burst with the anguish of it. Her breath continued to come in painful gasps; only now did she realize that her legs were shaking and there was a pain in her side from running so far.

Patience had come to the doorway, standing to one side. She was curious rather than concerned.

"Who is it?" she asked petulantly. "Why have they brought him *here*?"

"It's Vilas," Roxanne told her. "Our cousin, de Clement. What happened to him, Christina?"

Christina shook her head. "I don't know. They sent me ahead. Nobody explained anything." The sailors who had carried him here were backing away from the bed, so she could approach it.

"A bloody fight," one of the men said. "He got a bad slash on the leg and the head wound. He's been unconscious for near a week. Odds are he won't make it, but the cap'n said bring him here for the best chance." He sidled past Patience, whose mouth turned downward at the prospect of having a seriously injured man in the house.

"Captain O'Neal wasn't injured in the fighting?" Roxanne demanded.

"No more'n a scratch," the sailor replied, retreating through to the kitchen. "I don't suppose you'd have a drop of grog?"

"Megan will get you some rum," Roxanne told him. She herself joined Christina at the bed to look down at Vilas. "God's blood! I've seen corpses looking better than this!"

Christina swallowed hard. "I wish there were a physician to call for him."

Roxanne gave her a wry glance. "After the way old Amesbury helped Himself? We'll do better on our own, more than likely. At least he'll be spared the physicking and the blood-letting."

"He looks as if he's lost plenty of blood already," Christina agreed, looking down on him through a blur of tears. "We'd best get that bandage off and see how bad the damage is."

"And those filthy clothes. Is that more bloodstains on his left arm? Where are your scissors, Megan? We'll have to cut away his breeches and doublet."

Patience tapped one small foot, the silver buckle on her shoe flashing in the light. "Are you taking charge, then, *Mistress* Roxanne?" Though she didn't add *in my house*, she might as well have.

Roxanne didn't bother to look at her. Vilas still wore his boots, and she began to tug at the nearer one. "Do you want to cut his breeches off, Christina, or shall I?"

Patience's eyes held a dangerous glint. "It may be Christian charity to take in an injured man, even though he is only a relative of our servants. However, I expect at least to be spoken to in a respectful manner by my inferiors."

Roxanne was working with the second boot, which resisted her initial efforts. "Inferiors be damned," she rasped, then stumbled backward with the boot in her hand. "Where are the scissors?"

Christina, gingerly unwinding the wrappings on Vilas's head, was bracing herself for the shock of seeing the actual wound; she paid little attention to anything else. The last part was stuck; perhaps if she dampened it with some warm water it would come off more easily. She feared setting the wound to bleeding profusely again.

She turned from the bed and heard Patience, taut with anger. "Are you claiming *not* to be inferior? You forget yourself, Roxanne."

Indifferently, Roxanne went to pass her for the scissors she needed; Megan was still serving rum to the appreciative sailors, for this was not watered down like the grog they had aboard ship.

Patience, however, blocked the doorway, eyes blazing. "You will not speak to me in this way!" she insisted.

"The devil take you," Roxanne told her thoughtlessly. "If you cannot assist, mistress, then kindly get out of the way of those who try to be of some use!"

Patience had gone very white. She stepped aside so that they could pass through the opening, her voice was low. "Do you invoke the powers of the devil against me, then? Openly, this time?"

Her words and her attitude finally penetrated the cocoon of anxiety in which Christina moved; the anxiety shifted outward. "'Twas only a figure of speech, Mistress Patience," she assured the other woman, but Roxanne had not sense enough to leave it at that.

She had returned with the scissors and was unwise enough to say, "If anyone in this house is allied with the devil, it is surely one who cannot be bothered to behave in a civilized way."

"You speak to me of the devil? As one who knows him well?"

This time Roxanne ignored her, beginning to cut away the blue velvet breeches at the knee after pulling off Vilas's stockings. His legs were pale, and there was a superficial cut above the level of his boots. She scarcely noticed it, in comparison to the one on his thigh.

She cursed, not quite under her breath. Christina, returning with a basin of water, spilled a little of it. "Dear heaven! They nearly hacked off his leg!"

"It'll be a wonder if he doesn't lose it," Roxanne agreed dourly. "It's putrifying."

Indeed, the stench that rose when the flesh was exposed was enough to turn their stomachs. Patience quickly withdrew, nursing her fury, leaving the two girls to deal with Vilas de Clement.

The man himself showed no sign of returning consciousness, which was probably a mercy. His pain would surely have been intense.

Christina fought nausea as she turned her attention away from the wound Roxanne's scissors had exposed. She clenched her teeth as she soaked the head bandage, then began to work it free.

The injury to Vilas's head had bled freely and now only oozed. It did not look nearly as bad as the wound in his thigh, but it was this one that had rendered him unconscious. To have remained that way for such a period of time emphasized the seriousness of it.

"Do you think I should bathe it or simply put another cloth over it? I've had no experience of such things?"

"Nor I," Roxanne said. "I'm only guessing." She hesitated, examining the mess her cutting had revealed. "Here, help me get the rest of his clothes off, and then instinct tells me to wash away the putrification. If we had leeches we could put them to him, but since there are none, washing would seem the best way to clean away the foul matter. I don't know if I can do this without getting sick."

Christina didn't reply to that, fearing that she'd be the first to set an example that her half sister would then follow. Had the injured man been a stranger, she was not certain she could have done what followed, for in truth she felt more ill by the moment.

But this was Vilas, her beloved Vilas. What they did or did not do might well mean the difference between whether he lived or died, and if by some miracle he lived, it might determine whether he survived with both legs or lost one of them.

She gritted her teeth and began to clean away the blood and the pus and told herself that she could not allow her heart to break before she had done all that she could for him.

WHEN THE BLOODSTAINED CLOTHING had been cut away and he had been bathed and left naked beneath the sheets, Vilas presented a less appalling appearance. Patience felt it inappropriate for unmarried females to attend a man this way, but since *she* had no desire to take on the task, she had chosen to remove herself from the scene and ignore it.

Her ire had risen, however, and it had to come out somewhere. She scowled at the rolled pallets in the far corner of the kitchen. "Surely, since there are no longer snow drifts to the eaves, those could be returned to the summer room. The kitchen is so crowded."

Megan murmured acquiescence and carried the offending pallets—knowing it was those who slept on them who were truly the offenders—back into the unheated summer room.

She was horrified and appalled at what had happened to Vilas and felt guilty about the way her own spirits had risen because Fitz had accompanied the sailors who carried the injured man here.

The latter had taken their rum out into the afternoon sunshine, where Megan also supplied them with cold meat and bread. Only Fitz remained inside, and he'd moved to follow her into the summer room.

Megan realized he was there only when she had deposited the pallets on the floor and turned to leave, finding Fitz blocking the door. The quickened tempo of her pulses was familiar, now, though not something she had grown complacent about. She would never become complacent about Fitz, she thought, even if they married and grew old together.

"You're distressed about your cousin," Fitz said, drawing her into his arms. "I wish I could reassure you that all will work out for the best. We can only trust in the Lord to heal him, if that is His will."

"Do you truly believe that? That everything can be left in God's hands and that whatever happens is for the best?" There was an uncharacteristic note of bitterness in her voice, though it already softened at his touch.

"What else can I believe? Man is such an insignificant creature, with so little control over his own destiny. We do the best we can and take what happiness is possible. Megan, you are young and innocent, and you do not realize how my torment grows, waiting for you to say yes! How can I persuade you to marry me, to let me love and protect you...."

"There are some things you cannot protect me from...."

Fitz brushed his lips across her forehead, then allowed his mouth to slide down the side of her throat to the place where a pulse was leaping wildly. The blemish was concealed under her drab gown, yet he was so close to it that she was panic-stricken.

"Let me try, in whatever ways I can," Fitz insisted. "We'll do better together than apart. I love you, I want you as my wife!"

His hands roamed over her back, dropping to her waist to draw her close again in an embrace that nearly crushed her. "Please, Megan, say we will wed, and soon!"

"You don't understand! I am not . . . not perfect, I cannot . . ." The words would not come, no matter how she tried. Her eyes stung even as her body responded to the pressure of his.

"We are none of us perfect, who expects that? Megan, Megan, don't put me off any longer!"

Never had he kissed her with such intense fury, and after a few moments she stopped thinking, giving herself over to the wondrous euphoria that his touch evoked. So complete was her loss of contact with reality that she did not even realize his fingers had sought out her buttons until they touched the skin of her breast beneath the dress.

The birthmark was not raised; it was as smooth as the rest of her skin. His fingers seemed to burn into her, igniting a spark that flamed and would not be quenched. Oh, dear God, she thought wildly, how could she have been so cursed, that she was not to be able to know this man's touch forever?

The door into the kitchen was closed. When had Fitz managed that? Did the others realize she and Fitz were in here, together?

He was murmuring her name, over and over, as he carried her down onto the pallets. Megan wanted to resist, but a strange lethargy held her limp yet inwardly churning. A single coherent thought manifested itself: let him find the blemish himself, and she wouldn't have to tell him. And then she would know, one way or other, whether the rest of her life was worth living.

For the moment, then, there was no longer fear or shame or apprehension.

All was sensation and joy as Megan surrendered to his need, and her own.

Chapter 43

HAD NOT CHRISTINA BEEN SO overwrought about Vilas, and Roxanne in a fever of excitement to see Shea O'Neal, they could scarcely have failed to notice the difference in Megan.

The girl was bemused, distracted, biting her lip one moment, smilingly unaware of her surroundings the next. When Fitz and the sailors had returned to the shore, only old Cordelia was left to observe, and her eyes were perceptive. A smile tugged at the corners of her mouth; she remembered when she had been young, many years ago. She sighed, but she was not really sorry that her days of passion were so long gone. There was something restful in simply sitting by the fire, the little ones near her feet, watching the others. There had been much pain, as well as joy, in loving a man.

Cordelia's amusement faded when she considered her granddaughter. Patience did not entertain her at all. While she did not doubt that the girl was in frail health, she was also convinced that Patience took what advantage she could from it. Even in her best moments she had never exerted herself on anyone else's behalf.

And Cordelia feared that if Patience's tendency to dwell on witchcraft was not curbed, she would make serious trouble there.

Cordelia believed in witches. The Bible spoke of them, after all—"Thou shalt not suffer a witch to live"—and in recent months enough of those wretched women in Salem Village had admitted to everything from flying in through open windows to tormenting innocent children to burning down the houses of their enemies. Yet Cordelia maintained a healthy skepticism about many of the accusations being bandied about by the young girls who went into convulsions at the merest suggestion that they might be in trouble themselves. And in her granddaughter she suspected a nature much like those girls.

The baby, Emory, tugged at her skirts, trying to draw himself to his feet, and Cordelia put down a bony finger for him to cling to, smiling into the small face. For the children's sake she hoped she was wrong about Patience's capacity to foment trouble.

THE MEN RETURNED FROM WORK at suppertime, with Adam and Fitz looking in on Vilas as he lay in a stupor in the ground-floor bedroom.

Neither commented upon his appearance as they came to the table. Roxanne had hoped Captain O'Neal would accompany them for an evening meal; her disappointment was acute when he did not appear, and she could not quite bring herself to inquire about him. There was little to be gained by calling attention to her interest in him.

Patience, having worked up a fine headache because of her anger and discontent at the idea of having an injured man in the house who would take much of her servants' time away from their household duties, did not come down to eat. No one paid any attention when Betta was sent up with a tray.

Roxanne ate heartily without knowing what her fork carried to her mouth. Would O'Neal be waiting for her tonight on the bridge? Perhaps, she thought in mounting expectation, he would have brought her something taken from some French ship—a gown or a lace-trimmed petticoat or even jewelry. She would never dare wear any of those things in this Puritan society, but in her mind she had built up those last hours she had spent with O'Neal; she was confident that he would marry her and take her away from this place, to where she could do as she pleased.

Megan, too, was in a world of her own. It was a measure of the preoccupation of the others that no one noticed she scarcely touched her food.

A lingering physical discomfort reminded her of the culmination of that lovemaking session in the summer room. She could not truthfully say that she had enjoyed that part of it, though Fitz's satisfaction had been nearly enough for two. It would be easier after this first time; he had assured her of it.

What came before, however, had been wonderful, far sur-
passing anything she might have imagined. Being kissed and
caressed was a totally new experience for Megan, and she knew
she would never be the same. Now it would be harder than ever,
if she were to be deprived of this physical side of loving.

To her chagrin—she did not know if she was relieved or disappointed—Fitz had not discovered her secret on his own.
While his hands roamed inside her bodice, baring one delicate
nipple to kiss, the blemish had not been exposed at all. Fearing they might be missed at any moment, Fitz had not dared
delay for undressing and dressing. That, he told her, laughing,
would come when they were wed and would make the entire
matter easier and better.

All she could think of now was that if they were not able to
wed, if Fitz did not accept her as she was, she would surely
shrivel and die.

Christina, too, had little appetite. She had tried to spoon a
little broth between Vilas's lips but he did not swallow, and she
feared to choke him. That he needed sustenance was clear: the
flesh had fallen from him quite visibly. Yet if he could not take
it, what could she do?

She blushed again, remembering how his body had looked
when they cut away his torn and stained garments. A man's
body, a magnificent, muscular chest with its tangle of fair hair,
the flat stomach, and below that . . .

She had seen Thomas naked as an infant, but never a grown
man. And now Vilas might be dying. She rose from the table,
stumbling because she could not see clearly for her brimming
eyes, and went to carry more wood for the bedroom fire.

Vilas lay as she had left him. His chest rose and fell faintly
under the quilts, and there was a flicker of movement where the
blood pulsed at the base of his bronzed throat.

Christina stood looking down at him, reaching out to brush
back the blond hair that had grown overlong since he had sailed
away last fall. "Vilas," she said softly.

There was no response, only the continued frightening silence.

"Vilas, please don't die! Please hear me and wake up! Get
better!"

Her whisper hung in the air, impotent, helpless. But not hopeless. No, if there was anything that tender care could do to restore him to health, Vilas would live.

There had been nothing she could do for her father, nor even for Abigail. But this was the man she had loved since she was a little girl, and he had not been poisoned by an unfaithful wife, nor stricken by some mysterious illness beyond the knowledge of men to cure. Others had lived through grievous wounds; Captain Stratton had lost a leg to an injury probably much like the one Vilas had sustained.

The thought of Vilas missing a leg was daunting, but the thought of Vilas dead was unbearable. She had decided earlier that God did not listen to ordinary people, that she could not trust Him for guidance and protection. Yet she heard her own words, murmured in the quiet room.

"Please, God, help me know what to do for him. Please, please, let him live!"

EZRA HAD DECLINED Christina's offer to put down a pallet for him in the room where Vilas occupied the bed.

"No, I do not care to be disturbed if there is the necessity of caring for the man during the night. Besides, the *Revenge* sails on the morning tide, and it will be easier if I go aboard tonight. I've business in Boston and will be gone several weeks, most likely. By the time I return it's to be hoped the situation will be resolved."

That Vilas would either have recovered or died? Christina wondered angrily, but she said nothing.

Roxanne, sweeping up the crumbs, heard only the words "sails on the morning tide." So soon? She had hoped the privateer would be around longer than that. She, too, was concerned about Vilas, but she was more engrossed in her own expectations at the moment. As soon as the household settled down for the night, she would stroll into the middle of the village.

To her annoyance, settling down took longer than usual. Ezra had to pack his belongings for a fortnight's journey, and since he was accustomed to having his wife handle that chore for him, he was awkward and slow. He kept reappearing in the kitchen to ask where various items might be found, to confer with Adam over the business to be transacted—he had not expected to go quite this soon, but could not pass up the opportunity to avail himself of Captain O'Neal's generosity in the matter of transportation—and to squabble with Wesley over something Roxanne neither understood nor cared about.

Then Patience, after having been too "ill" to descend the stairs at suppertime, came down to make tea. Unaccustomed as she was to waiting upon herself, she succeeded primarily in getting in everyone's way.

"We will brew it and bring it up to you, mistress," Megan offered, causing Patience to fix her with a stony glare.

"I have little reason to trust anyone to see to my needs," she said, and got down a cup and saucer, turning her back to the room.

Did that mean she thought someone would try to poison her, as she had indicated she believed had happened with Abigail? Roxanne grimaced at the woman's back. Why didn't she go to bed and be done with it, so it would be possible to leave?

Ezra finally left, and having no desire to walk with *him*, Roxanne delayed a bit longer. Megan and Fitz were exchanging meaningful glances—had they come to some understanding that Megan had not yet conveyed to her sisters?—and no doubt would be glad when the kitchen cleared out. Was Christina going to keep running back and forth checking on Vilas, though? Or would she eventually go to bed?

She did, after making sure that Vilas was warmly covered and his fire banked. A crusie was left burning on the chest beside him, so that if he regained consciousness he would not be alarmed at where he found himself. Since the vessel did not hold enough oil to last out the night, Roxanne assumed that Christina would probably get up to refill it before dawn, meaning she would be moving around and perhaps aware of the fact that Roxanne's bed was empty.

Well, she was going to meet O'Shea, regardless of what Christina thought. Roxanne brushed out her dark hair and waited.

THE NIGHT WAS ALMOST BALMY, for April. Roxanne wore a shawl as she hurried along the road. There was no moon tonight, only a heavy sprinkling of stars, and under the trees the footing was treacherous; she could see nothing.

She moved at a confident pace, however. She'd walked this way often enough. Her entire body tingled in anticipation of her lover's touch. Would he have been without a woman all those months, as she had been without him? She remembered, smiling, what he had said about a man having to reload his weapon, so to speak.

In the months he had been gone, O'Neal should have built up a considerable charge.

There was no flamboyant figure on the bridge, however, when she reached it. Roxanne walked on, more slowly, thinking that any moment O'Neal would step out of the deeper shadows and take her in his arms. In her imagination, her lips grew bruised with the pressure of his, then parted to admit him to the deepest of kisses, and within a short time she would allow him full access to her body.

There were still lights at the tavern, and male voices. She stopped, hidden from view under the trees when any should depart. It was later than she'd intended, but not too late, surely. He would know she was coming, and no doubt was passing the time with a drink or two.

Yet she stood there until she grew cold, and the shawl drawn tightly around her did not warm her. Why didn't he come?

When at last the door was flung open and the last of the customers streamed out of the tavern, her heartbeat quickened. Now, now he would come, and . . . ah, exultation surged through her, there he was, tall and dark and even more exciting than she remembered.

For a moment, when he turned his head to speak over his shoulder, his swarthy face was thrown into bold relief, the scar standing in a ridge across his cheek.

"If he can't walk, carry him, then. It won't do to have these Puritans putting him into the stocks and depriving us of our first mate, now, will it? Let's go, let's get back to the ship and a night's sleep before we sail on the morrow. Then we'll divide the spoils, and you'll have a week's furlough in Boston Town to court your ladies, drink your rum and spend your loot before we sail again.''

As he turned back again, she saw that he had a new mark, this one nearly healed, above his left eye. He was lucky the swordsman's aim had not been more accurate.

There was a babble of tongues loosened by copious amounts of unwatered rum as the seamen moved toward her in a wave. One of their number was clearly the worse for wear and had to be supported by two of his mates.

The men did not see her. O'Neal did not so much as glance in the direction of the bridge, and he was surrounded by the others; there was no way she could attract his attention without alerting them all to her presence. Roxanne bit her lip until she tasted blood. Damn him, why did he not look this way? Would he see her if he did so? Or was she lost in the darkness?

They were only yards away, now. ''I thought maybe you'd be staying ashore tonight, Cap'n,'' one of the men said with sly innuendo.

''There's much to do in Boston,'' O'Neal said, coming abreast of the girl waiting beside the road. ''I've no time for dallying; the only reason we dropped anchor here was to see that de Clement was cared for.''

''Those cousins of his provide considerable temptation,'' remarked a man she could not make out; indeed, she could not see anything now that the tavern lights had been put out. Roxanne's mouth was dry, and her fingers curled into small fists.

''There're women aplenty in Boston, same as everywhere else,'' O'Neal said with a carelessness that left Roxanne reeling from the shock of it. ''Come on, get Dunning on his feet, damn him. He'd better sleep it off, or I'll feed his ears to the fish. We're too shorthanded to let any man wallow in his bunk.''

She heard no more, though the voices continued to drift toward her on the air that no longer felt balmy.

He wasn't meeting her. He hadn't intended to meet her. He spoke of women in Boston and ''everywhere else,'' as if he'd taken them by the dozens, in every port.

Her breath caught painfully in her chest. He hadn't even thought of her! She had dreamed of him day and night for months, and the bastard hadn't even thought of meeting her on his return!

Rage rushed through her in a white-hot heat, making her forget the chill.

Did she mean nothing to him, then? Was all she had felt only on *her* side?

Her teeth ground audibly together.

Damn him to hell, she thought, nearly choking on the emotion that twisted her guts. He'll be sorry, oh, yes, he'll be sorry!

She turned, stumbling off through the darkness, only by a miracle keeping her footing across the bridge, and headed for home.

She didn't even know that she was crying.

Chapter 44

CORDELIA'S JOINTS ACHED, and the room where she had spent so many days making her pillow lace was still too cold for her old bones. She stayed in the kitchen, as close to the hearth as she could get without being in the way of those who must work there with the cooking, soaking up the heat. She entertained herself by watching the others.

The children often sat near her feet as they worked on their lessons, though they escaped to the outdoors whenever they could. The baby was beginning to toddle around now, and Cordelia enjoyed putting down a finger for him to cling to or holding a cup that he might learn to drink from it.

She could only guess at what went on in the heads and hearts of the three indentured servants. They were like no others the family had ever had.

For one thing, they were so young. For another, they were all exquisitely beautiful, each in her own way. It was a pleasure to watch Christina, fair skin often flushed by her proximity to the fire, her red-gold hair gleaming beneath the white cap, her classic features troubled now that she cared for that de Clement fellow. Cousin he might be, but it was more than cousinly affection that kept the girl running to him as she did, Cordelia surmised. There was a romance in the making in that corner; the old woman hoped that the lad would return the feelings, if he somehow managed to survive his wounds.

And Megan. She was fond of the children and gave them much of the attention they might have expected from their mother had she been in better health and spirits. Megan was the same age Cordelia had been when she married. All her life, which no doubt seemed to stretch endlessly before her at this time, to look forward to. She was in love with Fitz, and the boy clearly doted on her. Why had they not announced their betrothal? Adam would release the girl from any indentureship,

Cordelia was sure of that. Such a pretty little thing, and the way her eyes shone when she looked at Fitz was a delight to watch. There was something else there, however. The child was troubled, and Cordelia had not figured out why.

And then there was Roxanne. A wild one, that. No idea of how to deal with someone like Patience. Headstrong, and so beautiful that she turned men's heads everywhere she went. Cordelia had seen them eyeing her at Meeting, even the married ones who had no business watching anyone. Wesley watched her, as well, and that was dangerous, because Patience watched them both. She might not enjoy her marital duties—indeed, as Cordelia well knew, Patience avoided lovemaking on the pretext of ill health to the fullest extent possible—but she would never tolerate adultery on the part of either her husband or her servant. To believe that Roxanne was unaware of Wesley's attraction would be a serious mistake, though as far as Cordelia could tell the girl did nothing to encourage him.

Roxanne had been excited, yesterday. Today her eyelids were reddened as if she'd been crying, and she'd turned sullen and unresponsive. Christina, run frantic at carrying the burden of keeping the household going and at the same time caring for a seriously injured man, snapped at her. They squabbled and Megan gently interceded, calming them both, though neither had improved in disposition as yet.

Very interesting, Cordelia thought. The household was much livelier than it had been in years. A pity Abigail was not here to see it, though she might have been less appreciative than Cordelia was.

ROXANNE WAS STAGGERED by what she had heard the previous night. She had been so certain that O'Neal had fallen in love with her, as she had with him. She had convinced herself that he would rescue her from the absurd charade of being a bound servant to these intolerable people.

If she was mistaken, and it appeared that she was, another two and a half years of servitude remained, and no prospects at the end of it except the possibility of marriage to some fool of a Puritan who would probably be no more entertaining in bed than he was out of it.

She mashed her thumb trying to get the heavy iron kettle through the doorway and swore immoderately at the pain of it. And somehow that pain blended with the other, the internal anguish that had kept her sobbing half the night, unable to sleep.

She finally maneuvered her way free of the doorway into the sunlit yard. The cold weather had ruled out boiling clothes for months, and every garment the family owned required laundering. Roxanne affixed the kettle to its chain to be suspended over the fire she would next prepare, and then she would spend the rest of the day stirring with the wooden paddle until her shoulders ached and her back felt broken and her hands had been chapped and reddened practically beyond redemption, she thought resentfully.

When Patience had issued orders about washing the clothes, Roxanne had scarcely listened. It was Christina who had handled that chore before. But the moment Patience had left the room, Christina had spoken with firm authority.

"You'll have to do it, Roxanne. I'm too busy with Vilas, and all the cooking that must be done. I can't spend the day in the yard."

Her anger and frustration had spilled over, and not until Megan stepped in with conciliatory words had Roxanne gotten her fury under control. Inside, she continued to churn until she felt sick with O'Neal's betrayal.

She hated him. She would like to claw his eyes out. She would like to stick a knife into his black privateering heart. She could pick up one of those blazing sticks of kindling with which she was starting the fire, and blind him with it.

That made her remember the healing scar over his eye and then she thought how a black patch over a blinded eye would only add to his attractiveness.

Damn him, damn him, Roxanne thought, and wept as she went about the tasks she loathed, as much as she loathed O'Neal.

IT DID NOT SEEM POSSIBLE to Megan that she and Fitz could have made love without his discovering her secret. Perhaps it was a sign from God, she thought hopefully, that all would be well, that she would be able to marry him after all.

Briefly, very briefly, she considered the possibility that she could simply marry him and contrive to keep the blemish hidden as she had done for her entire lifetime up to now. Then she remembered how his fingers had stroked her breast, his lips teased at the exposed nipple, and knew that neither he nor she would be content to forgo the pleasures that offered.

No, Fitz would have to marry her knowing the truth. Yet if she could not speak the words to reveal it even in a moment of love, how could she do it otherwise?

He greeted her this morning with a broad smile. "Do we name the day soon?" he asked, pulling on his boots before he left the house. "May is a good month for marrying. The weather is fine, and the celebrating can take place largely out of doors."

Megan hesitated, and his tone took on an affectionately mocking note. "I may have left you with child. In that case, we will announce our betrothal as soon as we know for certain. There is no disgrace in conceiving a babe before a wedding; there are many who do it, but the authorities take a dim view of those who do not marry at once."

Megan's heart lurched. It had not occurred to her, after a lifetime of trying to console herself at the thought that she would never have a child of her own, that she might become pregnant after one episode of lovemaking. A flood of joy rushed through her, only to be tempered immediately by the old fears.

"We must talk," she murmured, aware that others in the room might hear if she spoke in a normal tone. "There is something I . . . I must tell you. Then you may not . . . want to marry me."

There, she had committed herself to it.

Fitz laughed. "There is nothing you could say that would make me not want to marry you. But I agree, we must talk. I cannot delay now, the others are ready to go. This evening, after supper—'tis not so cold now that we cannot walk out once the meal is done. We will go, openly. If anyone asks, I will tell them we are courting."

He was gone before she could respond to that. She felt hot and cold all at the same time. When Nels asked her about his lessons, he had to repeat his question, for she had not heard.

She walked around during the rest of the day in a daze that alternated between happiness and sheer terror, with a tumultuous hope giving happiness a slight edge.

Cordelia watched with bright, speculative eyes.

"VILAS? Can you hear me?"

Christina bent over the bed, anxiety warring with the overwhelming desire to believe that she had, indeed, heard him make a small sound.

"Vilas? It's Chris, you're here in Ipswich, where we can take care of you. Do you hear me?"

This time there was no mistaking it. Vilas groaned.

Dear God! Were her prayers to be answered, after all? She pressed the hand that lay flaccidly on the coverlet. There was no responding pressure, but she had heard him groan.

"I'm going to bring you some soup, and you must try to eat it," she told him. A minute later, she was holding the spoon to his lips, letting the rich broth trickle between his teeth.

For a moment there was no reaction, and then Vilas swallowed convulsively.

He hadn't choked. Her eyes stung with tears of gratitude, as she dipped another spoonful. "Here. Swallow again," she urged. She kept feeding him until the cup was empty, then knelt to lean against the bed, unable to control her weeping, clinging to the hand that was so warm, yet so lifeless.

She forgot that she had given up on God, that she did not trust Him to answer her prayers. The words were a litany in her mind. *Please, God, let him live. Please, God.*

IT WAS LATE AFTERNOON when Roxanne lifted the last of the dripping clothes from the kettle of hot water into the rinse water. In her depressed state she could imagine herself doing this miserable chore periodically for the rest of her life.

Halfheartedly she doused the garments in the water that had started out cold enough to turn her hands bright red and was now tepid. Then she lifted a pair of breeches and began to wring them out.

It was hard work. No matter how she twisted the material, it continued to drip. She swore at the offending garment, then jumped when Wesley spoke beside her.

"What's the problem, Mistress Roxanne?"

She was in no mood to remember that she was a servant of the Hull family. "I can't get them dry enough to hang out," she said, sounding surly.

"Here. Let me do it."

To her astonishment, Wesley grasped the laundry and gave it a powerful twist. When he handed it to her, it no longer dripped.

"Thank you," Roxanne offered, and hung it up to dry. Wesley finished wringing out the rest of that batch and even hung up the last item himself, something she'd have wagered he'd never done before in his life.

He *was* handsome, she thought. Not as spectacularly so as Shea O'Neal, but Wesley was paying attention to her, which was more than O'Neal had deigned to do last night. By the time they had emptied out the iron kettle and Wesley carried it to the house, he had made her laugh.

Neither of them noticed Patience observing from the window above.

Chapter 45

CHRISTINA'S SEVENTEENTH BIRTHDAY passed unnoticed. She was too busy to think about such things.

Vilas remained in a semicomatose state, and the wound on his thigh remained inflamed, though she thought it helped when she cleaned it and changed the bandages. The latter stank to high heaven; she burned them as soon as they were removed.

His flesh was hot to the touch, and she spent considerable time bathing his face and chest with cooling water. When Roxanne brought her willow bark to make tea to bring down the fever, Christina sat beside his bed for extended periods, giving him sips of it slowly enough so that he could swallow it without difficulty.

The ability to swallow and the moaning sounds he made from time to time encouraged her to think he might be getting better. Once he threw out an arm and struck her in the breast. She ignored the momentary pain; it was the first vigorous movement he had made, and that, too, she took for a good sign.

She would have given her soul for a competent medical advisor; there was none nearer than Boston, and even there was no assurance that a physician would be an improvement over old Amesbury. Cordelia had nursed numerous victims of illness and accident, but for the most part they had all died, she confessed. She claimed no expertise to share.

Megan spent less time with the children and more assisting with the cooking, in an attempt to help.

Roxanne was no help whatever. She was sullen and uncooperative and sometimes went into the summer room during the day, closing the door, to do God knew what, leaving the others to struggle with the endless round of preparing meals, spinning, weaving and mending.

Megan's planned walk with Fitz had not transpired, for heavy rains over the next several days made outdoor activities impractical. She knew he expected her to reveal some foolish hindrance to their marriage, one that he would easily overcome with his masculine logic; he smiled at her so warmly that sometimes she managed, for a few minutes at a time, to believe it could happen that way.

The Sabbath came, and in a firm tone Christina announced her intention of staying home from Meeting, hoping that would be sufficient excuse to satisfy both the family and the tithing man. "I cannot leave Vilas alone all day. He's going to be waking up any time now, he moves more restlessly, and once he's conscious he must be fed something solid as soon as possible."

To her relief, no one cared, one way or the other. The house was still when they had gone. Rain rattled against the windowpanes, and even had it not been for Vilas, Christina would have been glad to be indoors. By the time they'd walked the mile to church and sat in their wet clothes for hours, they'd be lucky if they were not all sick by the morrow.

As it was, she was oddly content to be here in this dim room with the crackling fire to take away the dampness. No doubt it was against Puritan policy to heat broth even for an invalid on the Sabbath, but she did it anyway. At times she shared Roxanne's attitude of Puritans be damned, though she wouldn't have admitted it.

Vilas had taken nearly a cup of broth today, moving about more than at any time so far. When she put the cup aside and he fell back into an uneasy sleep, Christina pulled her chair closer beside him and rested her head on the edge of the bed. She had slept so badly the past few nights, she would appreciate some sleep herself.

She didn't know how much time had passed when something woke her with a start. The day had grown even darker, and thunder rumbled overhead. She wondered if she should get up and fetch the crusie against total darkness, though it could not yet be dusk. The family had taken food with them, rather than return home at midday through the downpour, but surely she had not slept all day.

Suddenly she sat upright, then bent over to make sure Vilas still breathed. She was sharply aware that her hand touched his, and he was no longer burning with fever.

The second shock came seconds later, when she looked into his face.

Vilas opened his eyes.

She cried out and stood up, overturning the chair. Vilas's gaze drifted toward her, but she did not think there was recognition in his eyes.

"Vilas, it's me. Chris. Do you know me?"

His lips moved, and she put her head down to hear the whisper. "Hurts."

"I know it hurts. You were sorely wounded, and you've been unconscious for days. Oh, thank, God, you're better! Do you think you could eat something?"

"Hurts like hell," Vilas reiterated, wincing when he attempted to shift position in the bed. "Grog. Where's the grog?"

Of course! A stiff dose of rum would dull the pain. She ran to bring it, and he gulped at it eagerly while she held his head, then fell back against the pillow. "Leg," he muttered indistinctly.

"Your leg was badly injured, but it's healing," she assured him. "Rest, now, and I'll fix you some soup, a good hearty one that will build up your strength. Sleep a bit."

She needn't have told him that. He was already sinking back into a stuporous state, but she didn't think he would relapse into unconsciousness again. God was answering her prayers.

Christina decided, from the rumbling of her stomach, that it must be well past time for the midday meal. She heated some of last night's soup, thick with corn and barley and carrots and onions, and ate some herself before she went back to Vilas.

He was in a deep sleep. There were beads of moisture on his forehead, which was clammy to her touch. He flinched when she wiped his face, but did not waken.

Again she sat beside him, content for the moment simply to watch him. He was pale—so pale!—but he would surely get better, now. Though the leg was not healed, it certainly was not worse. The odds were that he would not lose it, after all.

"Cold," Vilas said after a time. "I'm so cold."

She leaped to bring another quilt, and then, when he began to shiver, she brought heated bricks wrapped in towels to put against him. Still the shivering went on, until his teeth chattered, and her alarm returned. Was this some terrible manifestation that the end was near, after all? If only someone else were here to share the responsibility, even Roxanne or old Cordelia!

"Sweet Christ," Vilas whispered. "I'm freezing in this godforsaken climate! Is there no way to get warm?"

A log fell in the fireplace, sending up a shower of sparks that emphasized the near darkness in the room, as well as the silence of the house that was deserted except for the two of them.

His hand closed with unexpected strength around her wrist. "Hold me," he said hoarsely. "Help me to be warm."

Christina heard the blood thundering in her ears.

"I'm so cold," Vilas said, his strength suddenly gone. His fingers went slack; his eyes were closed, and she heard his teeth chatter.

He did not stir when she put out a hand to touch his face above the blond beard. It was true, he was having a chill.

She hesitated, and then her fingers worked swiftly with her buttons. No one would be home for hours, and they were alone in the house.

She dropped her gown over the chair beside the bed, bent to remove her shoes and stockings and slid under the covers beside him.

Vilas didn't stir, except that he was shivering. Her single garment covered much of her body, but there was skin to skin contact where her feet and her arms touched him. He *was* cold, and she had that horrible notion that it might be because he was dying, after all. Her father had grown cold before he died, as if the blood slowed in his veins and could no longer keep him warm.

After the first few moments, when she was dry-mouthed and half-paralyzed at her audacity, concern for Vilas reasserted itself. He must be warmed, he must be kept alive!

Christina turned toward him and put an arm across his bare chest, drawing him close, fitting her body to his, willing her own warmth to envelop him.

She had no intention of falling asleep. She meant only to comfort him, to make him feel better. The interrupted sleep of the past few nights had taken their toll, however. Gradually Vilas stopped shivering, and they both slept.

Christina wakened from confusing, exciting dreams. Vilas, she had dreamed that Vilas held her in his arms and caressed her, kissed her....

It was not entirely a dream.

She came wide awake, remembering, but she did not move. For a heavy arm lay across her body, just below her breasts, and the breath that stirred her hair was deep and steady.

A jagged bolt of lightning showed at the window, followed by a roll of thunder. The storm still raged. How much time had passed? What if the others returned from Sabbath services and found her this way? Would they believe that Vilas had been unconscious, or asleep, the entire time?

She moved, slowly, tentatively, and Vilas stirred. He groaned, burying his bearded face against her shoulder, and shifted position so that his hand moved on her belly, searing her flesh through the shift.

Her throat closed, and she struggled for breath. He had rolled over, halfway over, anyway, the first time he had done so since they'd carried him here. And he was neither chilled nor feverish, which was surely a good sign.

His hand moved upward, coming to rest on one breast. Christina thought her breathing would cease altogether. Never had she been so acutely aware of anything as she was of that hand, though it was not moving, not doing anything.

The touch was enough to send tremors through her, and she fought the impulse to turn toward him and kiss the lips so close to her own.

Cautiously she eased away from the long, lean length of him, so that the hand slid off, though she continued to feel it there long after she'd gotten out of the bed and hastily pulled on her gown.

She turned then to look down at him, almost fearing to find Vilas with his eyes open. Instead he continued to sleep, and even as she bent over him to see better, a smile curved his lips.

Her heart constricted. Dear heaven, how she loved him! Would he remember, when he recovered, how she had warmed him with her own body? How he had touched her, however inadvertently?

Probably not. There had been no indication that he was aware of her.

There was the sound of voices in the adjoining room.

Frantically Christina put on her shoes and hurried out to meet the returning family.

It would not have surprised her if they had looked at her and read guilt and emotional upheaval on her face as she began to set out the cold bread and meat. In fact it seemed impossible that Roxanne should speak to her in such a normal, truculent, unseeing manner.

"You were well advised to remain at home today. We were wet through, and any barn would have been warmer than the meetinghouse. The only interesting thing that happened all day was the gossip when the sermon was interrupted for the midday meal."

"Oh? What was the gossip?" Christina asked, not really caring.

"Everyone's aroused by the latest news from Salem Village. They've arrested a man, this time, a George Burroughs, and since he once lived in Ipswich, indeed was a minister here, practically everyone's in a state of agitation about it."

It was all Christina could do to draw her thoughts back to the ordinary world. "And he's been accused of witchcraft too?"

"Yes. That Ann Putnam claims that his specter appeared to her and tortured and choked her. She says he admitted to having murdered his first two wives, and though he denies it, they've thrown him into prison with the others. A movement is afoot to send a group from Ipswich to protest his innocence. I think they must be mad. It's not possible that so many should truly be witches."

Christina had finally come out of her reverie. "Did you think your mother was a witch? Could she truly cast spells? Was she actually responsible for the curse over my father and his children?"

Roxanne shrugged. "Who knows? Sometimes when she cursed someone they had bad luck. Other times nothing seemed to happen. And even those who were not cursed fell ill or broke their bones or had their cottages catch fire. I'll tell you this, if I thought she *was* a witch, and the power was hereditary, I'd put a curse on Mistress Patience. A less aptly named individual I've never met! She whines and complains until even a saint would be tempted to throttle her."

There was no way that Patience, on the far side of the room peeling off her infant's damp clothes to exchange for dry ones, could have heard.

Yet when Christina lifted her gaze and found the other woman watching her, an involuntary chill ran through her.

There was hatred in the glance, and nothing could be more perilous in this place of Puritans and witch-hunters.

Chapter 46

THE SUPPER TABLE DISCUSSION was livelier than usual. For once the Sabbath attention was focused on something other than Bible readings and the subject of the day's sermons. Today, since a fellow minister and a friend to most of the villagers was the latest victim of the young girls in Salem, the discourse from the pulpit had dealt with the subject uppermost in the minds of the listeners. It appeared that the girls were going to continue forever, with each charge wilder than the ones that had preceded it, until there was no one left judged innocent of the crime of witchcraft.

Adam was a thundercloud as dark as the ones overhead. "It's absurd! No one will make me believe that George Burroughs killed anyone, let alone his wives, nor threatened a living soul! If they don't put a stop to this soon the turmoil will spread through the entire colony and destroy it!"

Wesley agreed, though less vehemently than his father. Of the women, only Patience was imprudent enough to interject a question into the discussion. "But if there is no truth to what they say, why would the girls speak out in this manner?"

Adam's thick white brows drew together in a frown. "There are those, especially among young females, who will do anything to attract attention to themselves."

Was there a hint of personal animosity in his tone? If so, Patience did not consider it directed at *her*. She leaned toward him, her pretty face intense and earnest. "But surely, Father Adam, that is not the situation here. So many of those the girls have accused have confessed, which means they have been justified in those cases!"

Since this was irrefutable—and unexplainable—Adam went no further in his argument in that direction. "Nevertheless, there are many who profess to innocence, yet are punished with the others—"

Patience so far forgot herself as to interrupt him. "As why would they not, pray? When confessing will send them to the gallows? There is no way to tell who lies and who does not!"

"Exactly. And I do not believe George Burroughs lies, which therefore indicates the accusations against him are false." He glared fiercely around the table, though as far as Christina was concerned he should have directed the quelling look solely at Patience. "I will have no loose talk in my household. Nothing to fuel this fire that threatens to burn out of control. If it is allowed to do so, Heaven help us all."

Christina was glad they were worked up enough to discuss something like this with a vigor that kept them from noticing her. She could not put down the memory of that masculine body next to hers, of that hand resting, however innocently, upon her bosom. She felt as if guilt was written as clearly on her own countenance as anger and frustration were upon Adam's.

Fitz left the table when the meal was over, throwing open the door to look out into the night. "The rain has stopped, and the stars are coming out. Tomorrow will be a fine day."

Nobody replied to this remark. Cordelia sat beside the fire, evaluating Fitz's smile, Megan's bitten lip, Christina's flush, Roxanne's petulance and the zealous gleam in Patience's eyes.

Ah, yes, life was interesting even when one viewed it from the sidelines, the old woman thought with satisfaction.

THE INTERVENING RAINY DAYS had drained away Megan's courage once again. By the time she and Fitz walked out on an early evening, she no longer wanted to tell him anything. She would be content to spend the rest of her life tending the children of others, she told herself. So deeply ingrained was the necessity for secrecy that when Fitz smilingly faced her in the twilight, she was once more convinced that her cause was hopeless. If an admired and respected minister who had lived in this community could be falsely accused and branded a liar, how could *she* hope to survive with what so many would assume was a witch's mark?

"Well?" Fitz prodded gently. "What is this matter of which we must speak, before we make our plans to be wed?"

"I—I cannot marry you!" The words were blurted out in an agony that was clearly written on her face. "I'm sorry, Fitz, but it's impossible!"

His smile faded, though the softness was still there. "Oh, no, after we've come this far I won't accept that without a full explanation. What is it that troubles you, little one? I'll admit I was impulsive and perhaps should have waited until the lines have been read over us, but even we Puritans are not so rigid as to insist that a betrothed couple must wait for the marriage bed. In many communities there is no regular minister, and lovers cannot be wed until one comes around to perform a ceremony, but when blood is hot . . ."

Megan shook her head, desperately interrupting. "It has nothing to do with that! Your making love to me only makes it more difficult to refuse you."

"Then don't refuse me. I love you, Megan. What can be more important than that, important enough to keep us apart?"

There. He'd put it in such a way and at such a time and place that she had the ideal opportunity to respond truthfully. Could rejection hurt any worse, she wondered, than what she was already feeling?

For the first time in her memory, she lifted her hand to her throat—a familiar enough gesture in itself—and slowly undid the buttons there to reveal the blemish to another.

"I do love you," she said earnestly, "but I fear you will not want me when you know . . ."

He misunderstood her reason for exposing herself, at first; the smile was tender and triumphant all at the same time, until she folded aside her bodice with fingers that shook.

The light was fading, but not so dim that he could not see what she had exposed: the purple stain that marred the creamy perfection of her throat and bosom above the whiteness of her chemise.

Megan winced under the shock she saw written across his face. He slowly lifted a hand and stretched it out as if to touch the mark, and then his fingers gradually curled inward until he let his hand fall at his side.

"What is it?" The words were husky, strained.

"I was born with it," Megan said through the misery that threatened to close her throat. "My parents would have let me die as an infant if Christina hadn't rescued me and made sure I was fed."

Visibly, Fitz drew himself together. This time when he extended his arm his fingertips brushed the disfiguring mark, though not quite in the way that a lover caresses a breast. "It feels the same as the rest."

Megan swallowed, unable to reply.

"And all this time…" It was filtering through his mind, now, how she had been so strangely reluctant, so elusive and upon occasion, tearful. "You've always had it."

She could not bear to look any longer into his face; she closed her eyes in unspoken agreement.

She still held the neck of her gown to one side. She did not object when he brushed away her hand and rebuttoned the bodice. And then he kissed the tears that oozed down her cheeks and drew her into his arms, cradling her as a parent would hold a child.

"Poor Megan," he murmured. "You must have been through hell. Does no one know, except your sisters?"

She could only shake her head as she clung to him.

"And you feared to tell me, feared to have anyone else aware of it." He sighed, his chest rising and falling heavily under her cheek. "In the present climate of witch-hunting, it seems wise to make this revelation to no one, though I'm glad you've made it to me."

Megan pulled away from him, trying desperately to regain her composure. "I was afraid it would drive you away. That it would kill what you felt for me."

For a moment he cupped her face with one large hand in so tender a way that the tears spurted again. And then he took her hand and began to walk toward home. "Nothing could stop me from loving you, Megan," he told her, with every evidence of sincerity.

But he did not mention marriage again.

CHRISTINA HAD NOT KNOWN what to expect in the morning when she entered the room where Vilas lay abed. Would he retain any memory of those hours when they had lain together, giving and receiving warmth?

It did not matter that nothing had happened between them, that all had been innocent. She felt guilt and embarrassment.

Yet when she brought in the broth she felt would be more nourishing than tea and set her tray upon the chest beside the bed, she was as much disappointed as relieved to find that he had slid back into the half stupor of the day before.

"Vilas?"

His only response was a groan.

"I've brought you some broth. It's from the venison bones, and it has a bit of barley in it. See if you can take it."

He did not open his eyes nor speak. When she put the spoon to his lips, however, he swallowed, and she gave him the rest of the cupful.

When she drew back the covers to inspect his thigh—careful to expose no more than the injury, though she was tinglingly aware of what lay hidden a few inches away—it was gratifying to discover that the wound was healing at last. Now if only the head injury that had rendered him unconscious would diminish, too.

At least she would not be humiliated, she thought, by having Vilas remember she had crawled into bed with him while he lay naked and shivering.

Throughout the day Vilas moved restlessly, muttering mostly unintelligible words. Once he said clearly, "Thirsty," and she brought him water. He sipped at it, then grimaced. "Hurts," he added, and then, with as much vigor as if he strode the decks of the *Revenge*, "Where's the rum, damn it?"

Of course. If he could handle broth, he could handle rum, and it would help to deaden the pain that made him thrash about the way he did. Christina brought unwatered rum, and he drank it eagerly.

She emerged from the bedchamber into the midst of another of the scenes she had come to dread. Patience was glaring into Megan's face, and the younger girl appeared to have been crying, though perhaps some time ago. She held Emory against her shoulder, patting his small back. What was the matter now?

"The basket is full to overflowing," Patience was saying. "Why are none of these things mended? What is a person to put on, if there are no buttons and the seams are ripped? With three of you in the house, I do not understand why there should be any mending left undone!"

Megan lifted her head, and her reddened eyelids were clearly apparent. "I'm sorry, Mistress. I have been busy with the baby; he's teething, and very fussy. He cries if he is not held and cuddled. I thought you were sleeping and would not want to be disturbed." She sounded matter-of-fact, not subservient, and Christina wondered at this, for Megan was the meekest of them all before Patience's ill temper.

"What about the rest of you?" Patience spied Christina, then, whose tray told plainly enough what had kept her busy. "How long is this to go on, taking up all your time tending that sailor?"

Anger sparked in Christina's heart, though she kept her tone level. "Until he either gets well or dies, I suppose. Master Adam bade them bring him here," she reminded, not too subtly. She had become thoroughly tired of Mistress Patience, and those months still to be served stretched dispiritingly before her.

"Where's the other one?" Patience did not like to speak Roxanne's name. In fact she ignored the girl's presence in the house except when she was angry with her. "What's she doing when she should be working?"

"I don't know, mistress," Megan said, keeping her voice even. The baby began to wail, pushing away from her, and she turned to carry him toward the table, jiggling him in an effort to soothe him. "Perhaps if I rubbed a bit of rum on his gums it would ease the pain."

Megan had simply walked away from the mistress, and Patience's face flamed as her teeth came audibly together. "Where is Roxanne?" she demanded.

Megan concentrated on the baby, not answering, and Christina could only shake her head. Even as she inwardly cursed the girl for being the cause of this unpleasantness, she envied Roxanne's ability to avoid it, and as much of the work as possible.

"Is she in there? Reading or sleeping?" Outrage sent Patience to the door of the summer room, which she flung open so hard that it hit the wall and bounced back. "Are you in here, you lazy slut?"

The room was empty; this did not stop Patience's rampage but sent her nearer to frenzy. Christina, pausing in the doorway, saw the mistress kicking at the sleeping pallets which they had not bothered to roll up.

"She comes here to read; I know she does. There, there's one of Father Adam's books!" Patience swooped on the volume and snatched it up, then hesitated, bending to retrieve something else that had been hidden by Roxanne's pillow. "What's this?"

She turned with a sheaf of paper in her hand. "Where came she by Father Adam's writing paper? She's taken it for her own use from his room!"

She came into the kitchen, the book forgotten as she let it slide onto the corner of the table, engrossed now in the papers she had found.

"What is all this? Poetry, she's copied out poetry from the books..." Her voice trailed off, and the room was silent except for the baby's hiccuping sobs against Megan's shoulder. Old Cordelia said nothing, as usual, though her eyes missed no detail of the scene.

"What sort of poetry is this? She did not take this from any decent Christian book! It's filth, pure filth!" She started to crumple the top page in disgust, then thought better of it. "We'll just see what Father Adam thinks of it! Where did she get this?"

Christina reached out for the offensive paper, realizing at once that it was indeed a poem, and not copied from any Puritan book. Though she'd never seen it before, she recognized it for what it was: a love poem that Roxanne had composed herself. She even realized that the paper had been damaged by water spotting—by tears, perhaps, though it was hard to imagine Roxanne weeping over a poem.

Patience had gone on to the succeeding papers. "No wonder she spends so much time in there by herself! I thought the tales she told my children about pirates and fighting and...and her idea of romance...were bad enough! But this! I would throw it into the fire except that I need it for evidence against her!"

On that dramatic note, Patience left her son to Megan's devices and for the first time they could remember, except when attending Meeting with the family, swept out of the house, the forbidden papers tightly clutched in her hand.

Chapter 47

ROXANNE HAD NOT ACTUALLY BEEN as derelict in her duties as everyone believed. She had seen the mending basket, but mending was not her strong point. She was barely competent to replace a button, and her stitches were such that not even she took any pride in them; no matter how she tried, they did not come out a uniform size, the way Megan's and Christina's did. It simply did not seem worthwhile to perform the task knowing she would be castigated for the way she did it.

She had, therefore, undertaken without express orders the cleaning of the muddy boots assembled in the lean-to, which could be done sitting outside in the sun, free to daydream without interruption.

Not that daydreaming was the pleasure it had been in the past. The hours spent thinking about Shea O'Neal, imagining his homecoming, were among the most pleasurable she had known. Now her thoughts ran more toward revenge than romance.

Had Leonie been a true witch? Had the curse she had spat upon the house of Kenwood been the cause of the infant deaths, and Megan's terrible blemish? Had it even caused Himself to be poisoned by the woman he had taken in marriage instead of Leonie?

There was no way of telling for sure at this late date, she supposed. She wondered if, as the daughter of a true witch, she might have hidden powers of her own. Could she control any of the events around her?

Those who had confessed their guilt in the matter of witchcraft admitted to all manner of fascinating things: flying through the air in the night skies to torment their victims, changing their human shapes to those of cats or birds, biting and pinching the innocent without touching them, drinking wine that might have been blood drawn from murdered infants. How did they do those things?

She forgot the muddy boot in her lap and closed her eyes, feeling the sun warm against her face. Was it simply a matter of will? Could she wish something done and have it happen? Or were there spells to cast, ingredients to be brewed together, magic incantations to chant? One thing she would wish, she thought, was to have Shea O'Neal at her feet, begging for her favors, dying for them, and to spit in his face. To flaunt before him her attention to... to someone as yet nameless, to make O'Neal curl up with envy and desire for what he could not have.

She heard the door slam and opened her eyes to see Patience striding with astonishing vitality away from the house toward the village. She'd never known the woman to walk anywhere other than to Meeting, and she wouldn't have done that if she hadn't been forced to. She professed not to have enough energy even to carry her own empty dishes from the second floor to the first, yet there she was, rushing as if to meet a lover.

That made Roxanne think of Wesley. He'd made it clear enough that he found her attractive, that if anything were to happen to his wife he'd be receptive to marrying *her*.

She could entertain herself for hours imagining how Patience might meet her end, Roxanne thought with grim humor, beginning to ply the brush again to the muddy boot. She might be overtaken by a runaway horse and crushed. Or lean over at the bridge to look at her own reflection, to fall and drown. Or stumble at the top of the narrow stairs and break her neck. Or she might sicken and die slowly, as Abigail had died. In some ways the latter might be the more satisfactory demise, since Patience did not deserve a quick end, even a satisfyingly violent one.

"Roxanne, there you are. Where have you been?"

Christina stood over her, for once looking more anxious than annoyed, though there was some of the latter in her expression, too.

"Right here. Why? What's amiss now? Where was our dear Mistress Patience going in such a hurry?"

"She didn't say, but there's a good chance she intends to announce to the village at large that you are deserving of being put in the stocks with the drunkards and the fornicators."

Roxanne's fingers stilled on the boot. Patience couldn't have learned, at this late date, about the night Roxanne had spent with Shea O'Neal at the local inn. Could she?

Unlike the attitudes that prevailed at home in Cornwall, such things were taken very seriously by these damned Puritans. It was seldom anyone came to serious harm for being sentenced to the stocks, but being locked into an uncomfortable position, helpless against the onslaught of verbal assault or pelting with rotten vegetables, was something she had observed often enough to know she didn't want to experience it.

"Why? What's she angry about?" Roxanne stood up and brushed the dried mud from her skirt. Maybe she should attempt a hex of some kind that would take effect before the stupid chit reached any of the neighbors.

"She found some things you had written and hidden under your pillow. Poetry, and other things. She said they were... filthy."

Roxanne was totally unprepared for her own reaction to this invasion of the privacy of her innermost thoughts, poured out in the written words. Righteous indignation sent heat surging through her. "She has them? All of them?"

"All that I saw. In her hand, ready to show to whomever she meets, I'd guess. And to Master Adam, when he returns. You must have taken paper from the supply on his writing table."

"Where else would I have gotten any?" Roxanne asked. "Damn the wench, anyway!"

"I fear what she will do," Christina told her soberly. "She frightens me, Roxanne. You must think very carefully and keep a cool head when Master Adam speaks to you. You may be able to outwit or outtalk her." She hesitated, then added, "If you do not keep a level head, however, it may go very badly with you. These are perilous times."

Perilous and frustrating. Roxanne gritted her teeth. How dare the woman read what was not intended for her eyes? Her own most private thoughts had been expressed there, so that she could remember and savor them. She had almost burned some of them after O'Neal's betrayal, but she had not quite been able to do it. There was something heady about seeing the words in written form, knowing they had come out of her head and heart, she who had not known how to read and write until she was twelve.

And now Patience had them, was going to show them to... whom? Was there time to intercept her? Roxanne's intent and determination must have shown on her face, for when she took a few steps Christina put a hand on her arm to stop her.

"Don't make a bad situation worse. Anything you say to her will do that. Stay silent and think what you're going to say to Master Adam."

"It wasn't *saying* anything I had in mind, but rather to throttle her," Roxanne stated, but she had halted. There was sense in what Christina said.

She knew Patience posed a danger, but that aspect of the matter bothered her less than knowing her personal writings were in the woman's hands, being displayed for God knew whom. She'd rather die, Roxanne thought passionately, than have Shea O'Neal read them, for he'd surely know he was the lover to whom the poems were addressed.

She ground her teeth and tried to concentrate on how much she loathed and despised him, even more than she despised Patience.

PATIENCE WOULD HAVE CAPTURED more interest in her confiscated papers had it not been for two things, the second in reaction to the first.

Only minutes before she reached the village, the news came from Boston, carried by Captain O'Neal of the *Revenge*, that the new royal governor had arrived in the Massachusetts Bay Colony to take office, ousting the doddering and ineffectual old man who had lost the confidence of virtually everyone.

Sir William Phips and the new charter were the topic of considerable conversation and speculation so loud and controversial that few were inclined to listen to a mere female whose babbling seemed insignificant in the face of the important news they had been anticipating.

Some had long felt that the devil, so obviously abroad in their midst, had been working against them in the matter of government. The charter that gave them the right to govern themselves to a large extent had been stolen from England, carried with them to prevent precisely what had now happened: once it was in British hands, it had been revised.

The revisions were not to their advantage, for the new charter did not confirm many of their old and taken for granted privileges. Chief among the grievances was that the colonists no longer would be allowed to elect all their own public officials, thus retaining power in the hands of the Puritan leaders where they felt it belonged; anyone who was not of their faith had not previously been allowed to vote, assuring that everyone in the colony was forced to adhere to Puritan doctrine.

William and Mary, on their distant throne, had now sent a governor of their choosing, not a man picked by the colonists themselves, and resentment ran high. Others pointed out that the choice could have been worse: Phips had, at least, some knowledge of colony affairs. He was not a stranger who had no understanding of their needs or desires. Cooler heads urged that he be given a chance.

Patience had been confident that she would find a ready audience for her grievances against Roxanne, and that if public sentiment was aroused against the wench, even Father Adam would agree that they must be rid of her.

Instead the villagers were gathered around Captain O'Neal, eager to hear the latest news from Boston. No one cared, for the moment, about an indentured servant, nor that she had written some imaginary tale revealing knowledge beyond what one might expect of a virtuous maiden.

More important by far was the fact that the new governor had in his first official act appointed a court of judges to try the witches. William Stoughton, of Dorchester, the new deputy governor, was made chief justice of the court, from which there would be no appeal.

The entire colony was abuzz. At last this vexing problem would be dealt with. Most had no doubt that there would be scores of executions, and to many the situation took on the aspect of a circus: the trials should prove most diverting, and the executions would surely put an end to what had been a most disturbing series of events.

If a few voices were raised in protest at the prevailing thirst for the blood of the witches, they were drowned out by those who looked forward to the proceedings.

The citizens of Ipswich, traditionally conservative, were perhaps less eager for hangings than others, but just as disturbed about the basic situation. An end to it would be welcome, provided the trials were conducted with decorum and fairness. Already some argued that justice would not truly be served when there was to be no appeal.

Vexed beyond words, and already failing in energy, Patience turned away from the group that had ignored her. Eventually the family would hear her story, she thought grimly.

She did not have to wait until evening for that moment to arrive. That was where the second factor came into play. For O'Neal had landed near the boat works, and the Hulls had dropped their tools and trooped into the village along with everyone else to listen to an accounting of the latest news.

Adam saw his daughter-in-law first, standing on the edge of the crowd with a scowl on her face. What a trial the woman was, and since Abigail's death he found her even less likable. He was more determined than ever that he should not be coerced into another marriage. The last thing he needed in his life was another female.

Adam poked Wesley in the ribs with an elbow. "See to your wife, sir. Whatever's amiss at home, and from the look of her something is, need not be aired in public."

Wesley, caught up in the discussion and now annoyed by this unexpected interruption, made a disgruntled sound, then obediently worked his way through the crowd gathered around the privateer. What extraordinary catastrophe had brought Patience into the village?

She began to tell him as soon as he reached her. Wesley's heart sank at her first words.

"Enough, woman. We'll discuss this at home; it is not a matter to share with the entire populace."

Patience twisted against the grip of his hand. "The girl's a troublemaker, and I won't have her in my house any longer! From what I've just heard there'll be an end to this wickedness soon, and if I have any say about it, she'll be punished with all the others!"

He gave her a shake and forcibly drew her back out of the gathering. "Go home. At once. And don't talk to anyone on the way," he said, a muscle bulging along his jaw. "That, wife, is an order."

He thrust her away from him and turned his back on her without waiting to see that she complied. Patience stared after him, chewing on her lower lip, then strode angrily back the way she had come.

Today the village was consumed with excitement about a new governor and a tribunal to judge the witches. But when the excitement died down, there would be those intrigued by what she had to tell them and show them.

No one had heard the last of this, Patience thought defiantly. One way or another, she would be rid of Roxanne, no matter what she had to do to accomplish it.

Chapter 48

PATIENCE, WAITING WITH the accusations on the tip of her tongue, was not the only one to be disconcerted by the arrival of Shea O'Neal with the men of the family.

Taken off guard, Roxanne turned first fiery red and then, as the impact of his presence took effect, went deathly pale.

To her angry chagrin, the privateer captain did not even appear to notice that she was present. He accepted the rum that was handed to him and drank with gusto, wiping his mouth on his sleeve when he had drained the cup and handed it over for a refill.

How dare he come here and act as if she were no more than an insignificant serving maid! It was abundantly clear that the night when he had introduced her to ecstasy had meant nothing to him. She had been only another in a series of women to be exploited for his own physical pleasure.

Roxanne looked at the wickedly sharp knife Christina was using to carve the joint and longed to use it upon the appropriate area of Shea O'Neal's undeniably magnificent body.

The man turned abruptly to Christina. "How is de Clement? Does he survive?"

"His wounds are healing," Christina said. "He's not yet said anything that makes sense, and I believe he is unaware of his surroundings. But he takes broth and shows evidence of pain, for which I've given him rum."

"Good. Good. He's sturdy, and if the putrification is clearing, no doubt he'll get better. I'll be glad to have him back aboard the *Revenge*. We lost four hands in the skirmish when he was injured, and I was only able to take on two replacements in Boston. Once a fellow has worked out his indenture, none of them want to work for someone else. They're all set on going into business or farming on their own, leaving no one for a sea captain to sign on. I need a man of intelligence, which de Clement has above the average.''

Fitz drank thirstily of his own rum. ''We never heard the tale of that, Captain, how he came to be injured. Fought you the French?''

''Nay, not this time. It was a galleon commissioned by Charles II, perhaps blown far off course by the winds, perhaps seeking booty from the French. A fine vessel, she had been, but much damaged both by storms and cannon before we encountered her off the Nova Scotian coast. We never learned the facts of it, since their captain had apparently been killed some days earlier, whether in a confrontation with the French or by his own men is unknown. Certainly,'' O'Neal said, accepting the refilled cup, ''I would not have envied anyone trying to sail her back to Spain without major repairs that would have been difficult to come by along the desolate northern seaboard.''

He reached out to help himself to a slice of the savory roast Christina delivered to the table, chewing with relish before he continued. ''She carried a rich cargo, and I've never seen a more scurrilous crew, those few surviving the engagement they had had earlier. De Clement may know more, when he is able to tell it; he lay amidst them, sorely wounded, for some time before we were able to save him and dispatch the rest of them, for they fought like the devils they were. If he did not learn anything, we can only surmise as to why a handful of men remained of the crew and the ship was where it had no business to be. 'Tis possible that mutineers had taken over and intended to set themselves up in the New World rather than returning with the treasures to their king. At any rate, none of them lived to tell us. They did not cost us four men without paying the price themselves.''

Roxanne joined Christina in serving the others as they took their places at table. While grace was said she watched O'Neal—who had bowed his head in tacit respect for the Puritan custom—with mingled hostility and pain. He neither knew nor cared that he had humiliated and devastated her.

A few seconds before Adam intoned the "Amen," O'Neal opened his eyes and stared straight into hers. Incredibly, he grinned and winked.

Her jaw went slack. Did he, by God, think so little of what he'd done to her that he believed she would welcome him back as a friend, let alone as a lover?

Before her face could convey her true feelings, he leaned toward Wesley to say something that made them both laugh.

Roxanne's chest ached from forgetting to breathe. She could have joined the others now, to eat, as Christina was doing, but food was the last thing on her mind.

Roxanne turned and walked out into the dusk. She nearly tripped over an ax that had been put down hastily when the men appeared, early for supper. In the murderous rage that consumed her, she seriously considered picking it up and returning it to the kitchen. She imagined the blood spurting from O'Neal's shoulder as she sank the ax into it.

And then her eyes flooded with tears, and she hurried away from the house, not caring if she was missed or not.

CHRISTINA WENT ABOUT her evening tasks in the hope that O'Neal would stay until it was so late that Patience would not be allowed to begin a harangue about Roxanne and her writings. She would not dare to speak out while there was a guest in the house.

When she went in to feed Vilas his final cup of soup for the day, the privateer broke off his conversation and followed her into the bedchamber, looking down thoughtfully on her patient.

"He's looking better, indeed. You must be doing the right things, Mistress Christina."

Inexplicably, for he could not know about the way she had responded to Vilas's plea to be kept warm, she flushed. "I hope so, Captain." She hesitated, then asked, "Will you be sailing again at once? Should he regain consciousness, he's sure to want to know where you are and when you return."

"The *Revenge* suffered some damage in the fighting. We could have undergone repairs in Boston, but I thought it as well to return here and have the Hulls do the work. They're experts, their prices are fair and besides," a grin transformed the taciturn face, "there is less trouble for my men to get into here in Ipswich than in Boston Town."

"You'll be here for a few days, then. Perhaps he'll waken before you leave."

"Send word to me when he does," O'Neal requested. "It may cheer him to know his share of the spoils from the Spanish galleon remains locked in my sea chest. Where has your sister gone? She isn't in the kitchen with the others."

"Megan is putting the children to bed—"

"The other one. Roxanne." He sounded casual, careless, as if it didn't really matter very much, and Christina felt a pang of sympathy for her half sister.

"Out for a walk, I suspect. She often walks, when she can get away."

He had been scrutinizing Vilas; now he headed for the door. "I may take a stroll myself. After months on the deck of a ship, I need to readjust to a surface that doesn't pitch beneath me. Good night, mistress."

She echoed his words, then drew up the chair beside the bed. Except for swallowing the broth, Vilas gave no sign that he lived. For the moment that would have to be enough.

IT WAS SO WARM that Roxanne didn't need her shawl, after all. She pulled it off and carried it over one arm, then folded it to sit on, on a granite outcropping beside the road. It was a place where she sometimes rested on returning from a walk, when she was not yet ready to reenter the house and face all those critical people.

So far Patience had not had the opportunity to spread her seeds of destruction; it was only a matter of time before she did so. Probably Wesley would not be allowed to sleep until Patience had made her charges and shown him the writings.

Damn the woman, anyway. She wondered if there was any possibility she could get the papers back. She had been foolish to leave them in such an obvious place as under her pillow. Next time she'd search out a better hiding place.

O'Neal approached her soundlessly across the ground, which was moist enough to cushion his footsteps, drawn by the white blur of her collar and cap in the light that was almost gone. By the time he reached her and she sprang to her feet upon realizing who he was, it was too late to escape.

"A pleasant, peaceful evening," O'Neal commented, as if they had talked on friendly terms only moments earlier.

For a matter of seconds Roxanne feared she would not be able to speak for the fury that filled her. "It was, until you came along. I've no desire to speak to you, Captain O'Neal."

"Oh, come now! When I've been away for months, what sort of greeting is this?" he chided.

"Aye, for months! And when you were in Ipswich *last*, no more than a week ago, you didn't even bother to seek me out to tell me you'd returned alive! No, you were on to Boston, where there were plenty of women, *the same as everywhere else*! Wasn't that the way you put it?"

Too late, she realized she had given herself away; he knew, now, that she had waited for him that night, outside the tavern, and overheard his words. Well, she wouldn't stay here to be further shamed. Roxanne swung away from him, prepared to run even in the dark, and found her arm captured and held.

"Let me go, or I'll scream! I'll say one thing for these damned Puritans, they take a dim view of any men molesting their women!" she spat at him.

O'Neal chuckled. "But you aren't one of their women, are you? Nor want to be, unless I miss my guess. We had a beautiful evening together, and you enjoyed it as much as I."

She felt choked with the need to hurt him as she had been hurt. "What, even though you've had so many women, you can't tell when one of them is using *you*? Surely you don't flatter yourself that I *cared* about you? A renegade, a *pirate*?"

"A privateer," he corrected, but there was a different note in his voice. "Are you saying you weren't a virgin then? Don't try to fool an expert, mistress. No man had ever touched you before I did. And," he added shrewdly, driving a stake into her already aching heart, "I'll wager there's been no man since, even though I was gone the whole of the winter. There's no blood in these Puritans, to leave a woman like you untouched.''

The truth of that assertion made her angrier than ever. Roxanne lashed out in what was intended to be a slap; he intercepted it with steely fingers immobilizing her wrist, crushing it.

''Ow! Let go, damn you! I despise you, I hate you!''

His words were low and deadly. ''Have you not heard, milady, that hate is akin to love? We don't waste either on one who is unimportant to us.''

''You're not the least important to me,'' Roxanne hissed, twisting against his grasp. ''You've said there are plenty of women everywhere; go find one of them and leave me alone!''

He drew her close to him by the wrists, held tightly enough to hurt. His mouth was just above her ear, and his voice was harsh. ''Listen to me. A man has things he must do, and I had to sail on to Boston at once. My business lies there, not in this village. Where my business takes me, I go. My personal life is secondary to that, and it probably always will be. That doesn't mean that there is no personal life, nor that I do not appreciate a beautiful woman in my bed.''

She jerked her face aside when his mouth brushed her hair. ''From time to time, no doubt? Well, I've no intention of being your plaything when the mood strikes you, and sitting on the shelf between times! Confound you, let me go!''

She brought up her knee in a gesture she'd once seen her mother use on an unwelcome suitor; the original results had been gratifying indeed when the fellow collapsed upon the cottage floor and had lost his ardor before he dragged himself to his feet.

Either Leonie was more practiced in such matters, or O'Neal was more adept at dodging what was perhaps a familiar maneuver.

''Ah, we're going to play dirty, are we! Very well, turnabout is fair play.''

He released her wrists, but gave her no time to escape. Instead she was jerked into a brutal embrace that crushed her ribs and flattened her breasts against his chest. His mouth descended upon hers, ravaging, teeth drawing blood as she struggled.

She wanted to kill him, to tear out his eyes, to split him open from gullet to belly with the knife he wore at his side, but he held her in such a viselike parody of a lover's embrace that she was helpless. The only thing she could move was her mouth.

This time the blood she tasted was his, not hers. He jerked back with a profane oath, but only momentarily. "Vixen you are, then expect to be treated like one," he told her in a voice so cold that a trickle of fear started, far back in her mind.

"I've never raped a woman," he said, his own strain revealed in his voice, "and you've nothing of that sort to fear from me now. I told you that before. But you're going to listen to reason if I have to hold you here all night."

"Then reason and see how much it gets you," Roxanne rasped, wondering if he felt the tremors that ran through her.

"I will," O'Neal assured her. And then suddenly he was kissing her in a different manner altogether, the way he had kissed her that night at the tavern: slowly, tenderly, with a rising intensity that no longer hinted at violence, only at passion.

And in spite of herself, Roxanne felt herself responding to it.

She had lied to herself. She didn't hate him, at least not entirely, and she didn't want him to go away, out of her life forever. She wanted him with a hunger greater than any need for food had ever been.

Her body was inflamed by his touch, her will fading quickly. She heard the groan and did not know until he made a similar sound that the first had come from her own throat.

"I dreamed about you, during those frozen nights," he told her, melding his body to hers so that every inch of her seemed afire. "There were no other women in the north country, no one to compare to you."

There had been women in Boston, she thought with one tiny remaining particle of sanity. But the same particle warned her to say nothing of that.

"Let me love you," O'Neal whispered. "Say you want it as much as I do."

She said nothing, allowing him to carry her backward onto the hard surface of the boulder, to move over her, his weight upon her though not too heavily so, and surrendered to the depredations of his hands and his mouth.

Tomorrow, she thought dimly, I will hate him again, and myself most of all. Tonight, however, she must have this man, and it did not matter that the shawl was a poor cushion or that the night air grew chill.

I will hate him tomorrow, she thought again, and parted her lips to his.

Chapter 49

"I TOLD YOU, I don't want to hear about it." Wesley's voice was flat and tired.

Patience, the sheaf of incriminating papers in a clenched hand, blocked his way to the bed. "Pray look at these, at least! They might have been found by the children! Betta could read them as well as I!"

"The children," Wesley told her coldly, "would not have been poking around in someone else's belongings."

Patience flushed, holding her ground. "I was looking for the girl. She has a way of disappearing when there's work to be done, and sometimes she goes into the summer room and closes the door. That isn't the point. The point is that she's written this . . . this dreadful stuff that no decent woman would know about, or think about—"

"Patience, I am weary enough to sleep on my feet. It has been a difficult day, and the morrow promises to be even worse. Father may be one of those going to Boston to confer with the magistrates over this tribunal that is to judge the witches. There is much concern over the matter of no appeal, and Sir William Phips has not stayed in town to oversee the whole affair. He's already left to take charge of a military operation against the French and the Indians on the frontier, leaving all else in the hands of a judge with no legal training beyond the law as it is set down in the manuals on witchcraft. It is a considerable responsibility the man bears, and it may determine the fate of the entire colony. It is of far more importance than your petty problems—"

"Petty!" Indignation swelled her bosom, but Wesley did not pause.

"—and if Father leaves with the delegation, and Ezra already gone, it will mean only Fitz and I and that dolt of a Worthington to make the repairs to the *Revenge* and finish the boat we're building for Haverstock. We'll be lucky if we have time to eat, let alone to sleep. Leave me alone, woman, so I may rest while 'tis possible.''

''And you expect *me* to rest while this slut is under my roof, contaminating my children, my marriage?''

Wesley brushed past her to sit on the edge of the bed so that he could pull off his boots. ''She poses no threat to your marriage or your children. Come to bed and cease this unseemly tirade.''

''Very well, if you refuse to read for yourself, then I will read it to you.'' Patience tilted the papers so that they were better illuminated by the crusie they had carried upstairs with them. ''Listen to this.''

Wesley had never struck his wife. He seriously considered doing so now. Never had Patience been more annoying than at this moment, and what he had said was true. The next few weeks or perhaps months promised to be exhausting, and there was much to arouse his concern.

Concern was not the only thing to be aroused, however, as he listened to the words Roxanne had written.

It was a poem, the outpourings of a young woman to her beloved, and in spite of himself Wesley listened to the words. Even read in his wife's antagonistic tones there was a lyric quality, an eroticism in the writing that penetrated the shield of indifference he attempted to maintain.

He would not have known the word *erotic*, but he knew how the words made him feel. And this time, by God, he thought, he would not be set aside by protestations of illness or fatigue.

He rose, stripping off the rest of his clothes and dropping them on the chest beside the bed. He took the papers forcibly from his wife's hand and set them aside, then bent to blow out the flame in the crusie. ''There is nothing wrong with our marriage that cannot be mended in bed,'' he told her thickly, and carried her there at once, ignoring the sounds he muffled with a hard, eager mouth.

Overhead, Cordelia peered down at Betta to make certain the child was asleep, then put out her candle with a smile. After she had crawled into bed, however, the smile faded.

There was trouble ahead, trouble serious beyond the ordinary. And she feared that her granddaughter would be of no help in defusing it. On the contrary, Patience seemed likely to add fuel to what threatened to be a terrible conflagration.

ROXANNE HAD NOT RETURNED to the house when her sisters retired. Megan knelt overlong at her prayers, said some time after Christina had crawled into her pallet bed and lay staring up into the darkness.

For what did Megan pray? A miracle, a prayer most unlikely to be granted? Christina didn't know what the problem was, for Fitz continued to watch the girl, to smile when he caught her eye. It was no wonder if he was not as amorous tonight as he had been; he had much on his mind, with these new developments. Christina's own prayer was that they would overshadow the matter of Roxanne's writings, and that by the time the greater problems had subsided, much of the wind would have gone out of Patience's sails.

Christina was extremely tired, yet her mind refused to let her sleep. Vilas was improving, she thought. Any day now he would come to himself; his mind would clear, and he would realize that she had nursed him through what might have been a fatal illness. Would his gratitude perhaps turn to love during his convalescence? Especially if he had missed her, had thought about her, during the months he had been away? It might happen, she told herself.

Megan had finished her devotions and slid into bed. She was asleep within moments, judging by her deep, even breathing. It was later still before Christina heard the latch at the back door. Well, finally, Roxanne had returned. Had she simply been walking off her frustrations, or had she been with Captain O'Neal? Something had gone amiss there, though since Roxanne had not confided in her Christina could only guess at what it was. Had they spent this evening together?

Christina got up and without reaching for a wrapper—the rest of the household was asleep and unlikely to stir now before morning—went out into the kitchen, dimly lighted by what remained of the fire on the hearth. Roxanne was hanging up her shawl; she turned, and Christina could not read her face well enough to tell which surmise was correct. There was tension there, perhaps excitement, but it was guarded, or perhaps overlayed with something else impossible to discern.

"I expected you'd be asleep," Roxanne said, and the something was there in her voice, as well. Controlled, yet intense, whatever it was.

"I thought I'd get up to give Vilas one more cup of broth before I went to sleep. He still hasn't eaten anything solid, I've been afraid to urge it on him for fear he'd choke, so he needs all the soup he can handle."

Roxanne walked to the fire, which highlighted her dark beauty. At the moment she looked every inch a gypsy: black hair tumbled about her shoulders, cheeks touched with a ruddy glow, lips full and soft and looking as if they'd just been kissed. Had they? Christina wondered with a tinge of envy.

Roxanne reached for the gourd dipper and lifted the lid on the kettle that simmered before her. "Go on to bed, I'll do it. I don't feel sleepy yet anyway."

Christina hesitated, then nodded. "All right." It was unlikely that Vilas would awaken fully for the first time yet tonight.

She was halfway across the room when Roxanne asked, "Did Patience get a chance to talk to them about me?"

"Not that I heard. To Master Wesley, perhaps, after they had retired."

"Well, maybe they'll be too busy to listen for a day or two. There's a great furor over this panel of judges appointed to settle the witchcraft trials. Who knows? Between now and then, perhaps Mistress Patience will have a fatal accident."

On that cheerful note, she carried the cup of soup into the bedroom.

Christina, vexed, stared after her. One of these days Patience, or someone else, was going to overhear one of those remarks and, if there *was* an accident, blame Roxanne. For a moment she wished heartily that she had encouraged the girl to seek a placement of her own, away from the other two. That way Roxanne's rashness would have endangered only herself.

ROXANNE DREW UP A STOOL beside the bed and looked down at the sleeping man. "Vilas? Wake up, cousin, lest I choke you with this soup." She tested it for temperature and decided it would not burn him. "Vilas? Do you hear me?"

He stirred and threw out a hand that grazed her thigh, setting up a tingling that had not yet totally subsided from O'Neal's touch. More importantly, however, his eyes opened, looking dark in the poor light.

"Roxanne?" He rolled his head, taking in the room with its leaded windows, the big fireplace and the girl who was quite ravishingly beautiful. No wonder the earl had been so taken with her mother; Roxanne was the spitting image of Leonie as Vilas remembered her. "Where the hell am I?"

"In the land of the living again," Roxanne told him brightly. "In Ipswich, in Master Ezra's bed; he's gone off to Boston."

"Where's Mistress Abigail?" He twisted his head as if expecting to find her beside him, and Roxanne went off into a fit of giggles.

"She died. Don't worry, you're alone in bed. Here, I've orders to get this into you. Are you truly recovering? How's your head?"

He lifted a hand to touch the bandage. "It aches, and I'm cold, and my leg feels as if it's been cut off—" Horror etched itself across his face, and he threw aside the covers.

"Don't worry, it's still there. Cover yourself, your immodesty is embarrassing." Her grin belied the words, but he fell back against the pillow, drawing the quilts over him. "What do you remember of what befell you?"

Vilas stared up at the ceiling. His words came slowly, as if he must dredge them up from distant memory. "We boarded the *Marguerite* and there were only a dozen men, but they fought like demons. I ran the first man through, and another caught my leg with his sword. I lay on the deck in my own blood. . . ." He raised himself on an elbow, turning toward her. "How long have I been here?"

She told him, lifting the spoon.

He accepted the soup, then demanded, "What happened to the *Revenge*? To O'Neal and the others?"

"The ship is at anchor, awaiting repairs. They lost four men. O'Neal escaped with no more than a scratch. They brought you here fearing the worst, but it seems the devil has been cheated of his due. I believe you'll recover."

Even this small effort had exhausted him. He dropped once more to the pillow, shivering. "I'm cold. Is there another quilt?"

"You've half the quilts in the house now. Drink the rest of this, and I'll bring you a couple of hot bricks," Roxanne promised.

She was settling in for the night ten minutes later when Christina's whisper came from the adjoining pallet. "Did he rouse enough to take the soup?"

"The soup and a bite of bread, and then he called for more quilts. I didn't think there were any, so I took him heated bricks. He seemed quite rational, remembered lying in his own blood on the deck of that Spanish ship..."

Christina came bolt upright. "You mean he's conscious? He's talking?"

"That's what I just said, didn't I? He didn't say much, and it wore him out. He was sound asleep before I left the room. I'd say the crisis is past, as far as Vilas is concerned. He's on the mend. No doubt by morning he'll be ready for a meat pie or a bowl of stew and a few dumplings."

Roxanne lay down and pulled the covers over her, leaving Christina alert and trembling.

Vilas had awakened, and she had not been there. Hers was not the first face he had seen, the first voice he had heard. He had talked, not in dream fragments but in rational fashion, only not to her.

She fought the impulse to get up and go to him. Common sense held her where she was. He slept, and he needed the rest. It was part of what would enable him to wholly recover.

Regret that she had allowed Roxanne to take that last cup of soup to him made her ache. She was the one who had nursed him, fed him, cared for and prayed over him. She should have been the one beside him when he opened his eyes, when his mind had cleared.

She dozed, woke, dozed again and finally woke once more. A sound somewhere in the house brought her to her feet to investigate. If Vilas was restless it might take a drop or two of rum to calm him.

It was impossible to judge the time. There was as yet no faint hint of dawn. The fires in both kitchen and bedroom burned low, and she replenished them, then approached the bed. She carried no candle or crusie, for she did not want to disturb Vilas, only to be assured that he was all right.

He groaned as she bent over him, not really waking. "Cold," he muttered. "Damn this cold!"

Christina's hesitation was brief. She had warmed him before with her own body heat. The only other solution was to bring her own quilt to cover him, and she was beginning to shiver herself.

Roxanne must have been mistaken, or perhaps Vilas had only roused momentarily from his stupor. At any rate, she would be gone by morning, once she'd gotten him comfortable. No one would ever know what she did.

She lifted the quilts and slid in beside him.

Vilas made a sound and turned away, and she curled around him, against his back, putting an arm beneath his to hold him close.

What must it be like, she wondered, to be free to sleep this way every night with a man one loved? The texture of his flesh, the muscularity of him even during this enforced time in bed, sent tremors through her.

She had no intention of sleeping. It would not do to be caught here, not even by Roxanne or Megan, let alone by Mistress Patience. She must be away before the first stirrings at dawn. In the room above she heard Wesley snore and was reminded of the need for quiet. Neither Wesley nor Patience had apparently been disturbed by the nocturnal care she had given Vilas before, but she would take no chances.

The dreams came, and in them she was warm and happy. When a hand brushed her breast she sighed and snuggled deeper within the embrace.

And came wide awake.

They had both changed position, so that now she lay with her back to Vilas, and he had turned to fit against her, as a spoon nestles into its mate. Instead of her arm encircling him, it was now his that rested upon her rib cage, and through the material of her night shift his fingers slowly moved upon her breast, sliding over the mole, finding the nipple.

Sensation radiated through her, and she became aware of the hard pressure against her of a man who, asleep or awake, was becoming sexually aroused.

"Vilas?" His name came in a whisper, breathless, wary yet thrilled.

He made a moaning sound, deep in his throat, and she rolled over to face him. Was he fully awake or not?

It was too dark to tell anything. Turning had perhaps been a mistake, though, because it brought their faces close together, their bodies in startling frontal contact. Vilas moved his head; his lips brushed her temple and then, as she lay unable or unwilling to resist, sought out her mouth.

The kiss was at first dreamy and langourous; it quickly heightened, intensified, and became devastatingly passionate. It was as if quicksilver ran through her veins, and her breath came in audible gasps.

His hand slid up her thigh, carrying the shift with it. The touch on bare skin was electrifying.

A moment later she knew that whether he was awake and in his right mind or not didn't matter; his intentions were clear.

"Vilas, no!" The whisper could have carried no farther than to his ears, but she had a moment of heightened perceptions, of the sounds as something fell in the fire, of a tree branch scratching at a window, of his breathing, and her own.

"Wanted this . . . for a long time." The words were muffled in her hair, and then his lips traveled the length of her throat, nuzzling aside her shift, seeking and finding the nipple that had gone taut and erect even before he touched it. At the same time his hand roamed over her body in a way the dreams had only hinted at, setting every nerve to singing.

She had only seconds to decide and too little will to do what common sense dictated. She had wanted this for so long, and she could not, would not, hold him off now.

"Be careful, your leg," she murmured, remembering at the last minute.

"My leg be damned," he told her, and then it was too late. Christina gave herself up to euphoria, to bliss beyond any prior expectations—to a moment of pain that made her cry out, then quickly faded—and heard her own raspy breathing as it mingled with his and felt the sweat upon their naked bodies.

Vilas fell back, trailing his hand over her nakedness to plunge his fingers into her hair. "Sweet . . . I shouldn't . . . didn't think you'd still be . . . virgin. I'm sorry if I . . . hurt you."

Why would he not think she would still be a virgin?

She sat up, groping for the night shift entangled around her neck, shivering as the covers fell away. "No man has ever before touched me," she told him fiercely, but it was clear he hadn't heard. He had already gone sound asleep.

As her skin dried she scrambled out of bed, really cold now in the morning air. It *was* coming on morning; the window-panes showed a perceptible gray. She felt chilled and feverish at the same time, and even after she'd gone back to bed for what remained of the night, the question would not be put down.

Why did Vilas think she would no longer be a virgin?

Chapter 50

CHRISTINA'S HEART WAS THUDDING as she entered the bedroom that morning. She was not really sorry that she had allowed Vilas to make love to her in what she supposed was a shameless fashion; it was something she had longed for for years, and though a mild discomfort lingered, that was surpassed by the pleasurable emotions.

She was, however, somewhat embarrassed. What did one say to a man after such a session of lovemaking, when there had been no declaration of love between them? Would he propose marriage at once? Or would there be a deliciously prolonged courtship? At least she knew he wouldn't be leaving immediately. He wasn't well enough yet, even if his ship had been sailing, to rejoin O'Neal's crew.

Vilas still slept. Instead of lying flat on his back, however, as he had done ever since they'd brought him here, he lay sprawled facedown with one hand trailing over the edge of the bed. The leg wound she had considered so briefly during the night must be considerably less sore to allow him to sleep in this position.

Christina hesitated, then lowered her tray to the chest. She hated to wake him, but there was a good deal else to be done, and if she did not feed him now it might be difficult to get back until much later. "Vilas?"

He stirred, rolled over, winced and opened his eyes.

"How—how are you feeling?"

He yawned and stretched. "Chris? God, it wasn't a dream. I *am* in Ipswich. How long have I been here?"

She stared at him in consternation. Had he no recollection of what had transpired between them only hours earlier? How could that be? He had spoken sensibly to Roxanne, and certainly he had seemed to know what he was doing when he roused from sleep and found Christina in his bed.

This was worse than being embarrassed. Which obviously was not troubling Vilas. He looked at the tray. "What have you brought? I feel as if I haven't eaten for a month." He scratched through his beard. "Is there a razor about? I could get rid of this without missing it. Where's my ship?

He didn't remember. Christina's throat was dry, and relief intermingled with disappointment. He had, though, told her during those intimate moments that he had wanted this for a long time. Perhaps it was better this way. "Anchored offshore, awaiting repairs."

"Was it badly damaged?"

"Not as badly as you were," she told him. "How do you feel?"

Vilas considered. "I've all the strength of a newborn kitten, I think. And the appetite of a horse. What is it, mush?"

She didn't have to spoon it into him this time; he sat propped against the pillows and fed himself. When he had done, however, he showed signs of fatigue. "Lord, how long will it take me to get back into fighting shape? Have you had a physician for me?"

She shook her head. "There is none nearer than Boston, and Captain O'Neal feared you would not live long enough to get you there."

"Well, whatever you've done on your own seems to have been what I needed," he said, and perhaps did not notice when her face flamed. He was peeling back the covers to examine his thigh. "Hah! I'm going to have an interesting scar." He grinned. "I won't be able to display it as freely as O'Neal does his. Something about scars seems to attract the ladies."

Stung and confused, she sounded waspish. "I shouldn't have thought you'd need of scars for that."

He flopped back onto the pillow. "Oh, attracting them's never truly been a problem. The way I feel at the moment, it's strength I need, and I've damned little of that! God's blood, I'm sweating with the effort it took to eat a bowl of porridge, yet I'm chilled enough to make my teeth rattle. Would it be possible to have another log on the fire?"

He had been sweating with that earlier effort, too, she recalled. Her mind was a maelstrom, making her dizzy.

Christina drew herself together as best she could. "I'll bring more wood and something hot to drink. That should help."

"Thank you. When I've recovered from the exertion of eating a meal, I hope you'll have time to talk, Chris. I want to know everything that's been going on."

She murmured something noncommittal as she turned away. There were some things she'd be damned if she'd tell him, she thought, and felt the prickle of tears.

PATIENCE WAS, as usual, the last one down to breakfast. She sat at the table while Megan silently served her; only when she had finished did she issue orders for the day. She concluded with, "And one of you will have to take food to the boat works at midday; my husband says there will be no time to stop for a meal, with the press of all that needs be done."

"I'll go," Roxanne volunteered, eager for any excuse to escape from the house. Going down to the shore might also afford an opportunity for meeting O'Neal, though she was not entirely sure she wanted to see him yet. She had unrestrainedly enjoyed his lovemaking, but she had much to sort out regarding her feelings for him.

"No," Patience said flatly. "Megan, you go. Take something hearty, and plenty of it, for they will likely be late for supper, as well, until the repairs to the *Revenge* are completed. It seems Captain O'Neal is eager to have them finished and be away again."

Megan murmured assent, though her heart leaped. She, too, struggled with mixed feelings. She was more conscious than ever of the blemish hidden by her clothing, and whenever she found Fitz's gaze upon her she wondered if he saw her or only the blemish. His smile was as tender as it had ever been, yet on the brief occasions when they had been together in private, he had made no move to do more than touch her hand. There had been no more kisses or embraces, and certainly no repetition of lovemaking. Since there had been little opportunity for conversing except in the presence of others, she had no way of knowing what he was thinking. It was driving her wild, though she preserved her usual outwardly calm demeanor.

The hours dragged until it was time to go. She carried a pot of the rich, sweet baked beans in one hand, thickly seasoned with the last of the fall ham; in the other, a basket of fresh corn bread wrapped in a towel and dried-apple pie. The pot was heavy, and she paused several times to shift her burdens. It was a relief when the boat works came in sight, and she saw Fitz coming to meet her.

The tiredness fell away instantly. He greeted her with a smile and reached for the kettle. "You're only just in time. We're about to expire of starvation."

"I shouldn't want that to happen," Megan told him, smiling. She glanced toward the ship anchored offshore. "I thought you might be aboard the *Revenge*, and I'd not see you."

"No, Wesley and Worthington are there, though they're to come ashore for their share of this when I run up the signal flag. Father was here with me, working on the boat. He went into the village half an hour gone. Something about the delegation that's being made up to go to Boston. They're deeply disturbed about the upcoming trials, and this Stoughton who heads the judges. The man has no knowledge of law, he was a minister in England and 'tis said he has no sympathy for those accused of witchcraft and has sworn to rid the colony of this evil. In the minds of some, it does not bode well for fair trials."

She walked beside him toward the boat that was taking shape beneath the experienced hands of his family. "I wonder if there can be such a thing as a fair trial in this matter. There is so little evidence in many cases, one person's word against another's. When a man like this George Burroughs can be thrown into prison, a minister himself, and always well respected, it makes one... apprehensive," Megan admitted.

"It does, indeed. The trials begin next week. Bridget Bishop will be fighting for her life, and from what we've heard she's long been rumored to be a witch, even her husband has accused her. I fear that if she is convicted by this new tribunal, there will be many others to follow."

Megan looked to speak of something else, to regain the footing she and Fitz had had before she showed him the blemish; she did not know how to begin. Fitz was friendly, he was courteous, he insisted that she share the meal before she carried the empty kettle home, but there were no words of love, no caresses.

Megan's heart felt achingly hollow as she retraced her footsteps through the village an hour later. She knew nothing to do except to wait for whatever would transpire.

THAT AFTERNOON Vilas sat up before the fire while Christina changed his bed. He made casual talk, about the voyage northward on the *Revenge*, of the ships they had seen, the people they had encountered, and of the last encounter with the ill-fated *Marguerite*. He was convinced the crew were mutineers, though it was unclear whether they had lost their captain in some engagement or killed him themselves. "At any rate, they had a galleon heavy with treasures. They were heading for the Gaspé to live out the rest of their miserable lives on the proceeds of it, as near as I could make out from the little I heard while I was lying there watching my life run out, as I thought, on the deck of their ship."

"The Gaspé?" Christina echoed. She was back at the beginning, she told herself bleakly. Vilas did not remember having made love to her; he was no more than a friendly cousin, and she knew nothing to do save follow his lead there.

"'Tis a great long peninsula in Quebec, at the mouth of the St. Lawrence. Pirates have retired there, we've heard. At the very end of it stands a great rock they call Percé, like nothing I've seen before. Monstrous large, and in the sun it looks painted orange-gold against the brilliant blue of the water. The settlers are mostly French—O'Neal speaks the language well, and we traded with some of them for fresh water and food."

"French? I'd think they'd be your enemies, you with an English ship."

Vilas laughed. "They're an independent breed, the men of the Gaspé. Though they pay lip service to Louis XIV, they are mostly a law unto themselves. They make their own enemies and friendships. They're fishermen, for the most part, or trappers. That's a business I've a temptation to investigate, trapping. There's a wealth of furs in that part of the New World, and a man doesn't need a fortune to get into the business. Not that I'm penniless any longer; my share of the booty from this voyage should be considerable, if they didn't write me off as dead and share my portion amongst the survivors.''

He rose from his chair, then steadied himself with fingertips resting against the back of it. ''God's blood, 'tis mewling useless I am at the moment. Here, be a good girl and prop me up while I get back to the bed, or I may fall on my face.''

She did as he bade her, stiffening her back under the weight of the arm he draped around her neck, willing herself not to succumb to the sensations provoked by his touch as he came close against her. He staggered the last few steps, collapsing on the fresh sheets with a gasp.

''Damn me, it seems I'll be a day or two before I'm up to climbing the rigging of the *Revenge* again,'' he admitted. ''Red meat, that's what I need to get me back in shape.''

''There'll be a haunch of venison tonight,'' Christina promised. Her heart was pounding as if she'd carried him across the room. Yet she spoke with an outward calm. ''Rest, now. I'll be outside most of the rest of the day; there's wash to boil.''

She gathered the soiled sheets, startled at the stains on them, for his thigh no longer bled. And then she realized the blood was her own, and crimson flooded her face. She fled, turning the soiled sheets in upon themselves so that no one else might see, and wonder.

ADAM HULL and several others left, overland, for Boston the following morning. Their concern was deep, and the news that preceded the men home proved the validity of their concern.

Bridget Bishop was convicted of witchcraft and the twelve-man jury found her guilty. She was hanged on Gallows Hill on the tenth of June.

After this first execution, however, the judges displayed uncertainty. Much of the evidence against the accused consisted of accounts by the afflicted girls that the witches' specters had tormented them. While everyone viewed—mostly with relish—the way the girls writhed and cried out in their supposed pain, there were those who were doubtful. No one saw these specters except the girls.

Was this enough evidence on which to pronounce a sentence of execution? Some of the accused offered the notion that the devil might take the shape of some innocent soul rather than one of his own, and if that were the case, would not the innocent be condemned along with the guilty?

The esteemed clergyman, Cotton Mather, urged restraint in relying upon such testimony, and suggested as well that for some witches there might be a suitable penalty other than execution.

While the masses clamored for the excitement of trials and public hangings, a growing number of more responsible citizens began to express their dissatisfaction at the way matters were proceeding.

"At this rate," Adam said bitterly upon his return home, "there won't be any colonists left outside the prisons." He sank into a chair and accepted the rum Megan hastened to bring him. "I fear I grow old for journeying back and forth, and Boston loses its appeal for me. Half its citizens are mad with a thirst for the blood of witches, and I've no patience with their stupidity. The judges asked for opinions from leading clergymen, and what they got was sound, I think, much to the order of what Cotton Mather recommended: less hysteria and more common sense. What an *uncommon* thing is common sense! All are agreed that the practice of witchcraft must not be allowed, but there accord ends. No one can say who is and who is not a witch."

He drank of the rum and offered the cup for a refill. He looked old and weary, in mind and spirit as well as in body. "Ezra stayed behind to attend to our normal business there. When he follows, in a few days, I hope the news will be better."

It was a vain hope. Ezra's news was not encouraging that there would be a swift end to the problems that plagued the Bay Colony.

"The judges studied the recommendations and quarreled among themselves," he reported. "Judge Saltonstall resigned from the court when Stoughton insisted spectral evidence be allowed. Since Stoughton is chief justice, his will prevails, and I fear he's intent on clearing the jails by hanging everyone in them."

The news from Boston and Salem Village did nothing to settle matters in Ipswich, and at least among the Hull's indentured servants, the tension grew unbearable.

Patience had given up, for the time being, her insistence upon being immediately rid of Roxanne. If Wesley would not listen to her now, she would wait until the opportunity presented itself to show the hated writings to Father Adam. He, at least, would not wind up every argument by hauling her off to bed and insisting upon claiming marital rights, as Wesley had infuriatingly taken to doing.

Adam gave her little opportunity to advance her cause in his direction. He was needed at the boat works and came home so tired that he ate his supper and went directly to bed, as did Wesley and Fitz. Patience bided her time and watched both her husband and Roxanne with the keen eye of a hawk, taking care that the girl had little occasion to leave the house when Wesley was also away from it. She did not understand why Wesley failed to share her revulsion with the writings she had discovered, nor why he had suddenly seemed, in spite of the long hours he worked, to have enough energy to put aside fatigue for the time it took to force himself upon her in bed.

In the meantime Vilas increased in strength. Every day he ate more heartily and stayed out of bed longer. By the fourth day, which was clear and sunny and warm, he ventured out into the backyard. By the end of the week, though limping notably, he had made his way to the village, where he met with Shea O'Neal and they talked for an hour over several tankards of rum.

When he returned to the house he was pale and his jaw was clenched against the pain that shot through the injured leg. Not even another ration of rum and lying down on the pallet he'd taken in the corner of the kitchen—having relinquished Ezra's bed to its rightful owner—was enough to ease the lines from his face for a matter of hours.

"You've overdone it," Christina chided. "The village is too far for you to walk so soon."

"I want to be ready to go when the *Revenge* sails," Vilas told her, and she subsided, hurt and apprehensive about the damage he might do by taking on too much, too soon.

Further news from Salem Village was not good.

When the old woman, Rebecca Nurse, was acquitted by the jury, the courtroom was induced into pandemonium. Her accusers howled and fell upon the floor. Judge Stoughton, however, was unwilling to accept the verdict. In his subsequent continued questioning of the poor creature, her deafness and his misunderstanding of her replies led him to demand reconsideration of the verdict. The jury complied; she was sentenced to die with the other four women, and the mania went on.

Withcraft was the subject uppermost in everyone's minds when Patience discovered another excuse to put forth her cause, and this time she found listeners.

Chapter 51

"'TIS CLEAR," Vilas said as Roxanne brought him a rug to drape over his knees as he sat on the back stoop, where the afternoon shadows grew long, "that I'd never have survived if it hadn't been for your expert nursing care. Did you learn it from your mother?"

Christina, stirring sheets in the iron kettle a few yards away, stiffened. *Her* nursing care? Was the wretch not going to enlighten him as to who had done the major share of the nursing?

Roxanne laughed. "I learned a thing or two from her," she said coquettishly. She adjusted the rug, as if he couldn't do that much for himself, as if he was an invalid instead of only suffering from the chills that continued to plague him.

Christina forced herself to resume stirring, not missing the twitch of curtains overhead signaling the fact that Patience wished to make sure she did not shirk her duties.

It seemed that the woman was determined to work them into a state of exhaustion. Whenever one of them paused for even a moment, Patience was there with orders to do this or that, from the moment they crawled out of bed until they were able to return there at night.

Roxanne, of course, managed to avoid the more arduous tasks, such as the one Christina was presently engaged in. She flitted in and out on smaller chores that gave her plenty of time to exchange words with Vilas, and though she was not allowed to carry meals to the men at the boat works, she always managed some time to herself, to wander the woods on solitary walks—or not so solitary, Christina thought darkly.

Jealousy surged through her as she watched Roxanne hand over a tankard of rum, which Vilas accepted with a smile that cut through Christina like a knife blade.

"Ah, you know what a man needs to warm his cold bones," Vilas said, and drank. Roxanne's provocative laughter made him laugh, too.

A horrible possibility presented itself. Christina felt a chill of her own, and her legs were suddenly unsteady.

The way to warm a man's cold bones. Hot soup and rum were the least of what had warmed him. He'd never said a word to *her* about any of what she had done, including comforting him in the middle of the night in the way that only a woman could do.

Was it remotely conceivable that Vilas did not know who had shared his bed that night? The room had been dark, she had spoken only in a whisper and though he had seemed clearheaded enough at the time and also when she went to him after daylight, he had given no sign that anything had happened between them.

Shock held her rigid as she considered the implications of this. *Did Vilas believe it was Roxanne, rather than Christina, who had given herself to him?*

Dazed, she leaned upon the paddle so that the steam rose around her face, making the tendrils of red-gold hair curl at her temples.

I didn't think . . . you'd still be a virgin, he had murmured afterward. The words had been incomprehensible, yet now they stood out with stark clarity, and she had no difficulty whatever in understanding them. Not if he'd thought he was speaking to Roxanne.

It was as if her heart was crushed in a vise, squeezing the life and breath out of her. Dear God, no, don't let it be that, she pleaded silently.

And then, to make her misery complete, she remembered something else he had murmured in the darkness, his lips brushing her throat. "I've wanted this . . . for a long time."

Roxanne. Not her. Roxanne.

She could not staunch the tears that began to slide down her cheeks.

She let go of the paddle, and it fell into the ashes of the fire, where only the fact that the paddle was soaked through prevented it from burning with the rest of the wood. She was not even aware it was in the fire.

She didn't care if Patience watched from the window. She only knew that she could not allow Vilas to see her this way, and that she must be alone, must seek a solitary refuge like some wounded animal, to lick her wounds and perhaps to die of the pain.

"Christina? Is something wrong?"

She ignored Roxanne's call, plunging into the woods beyond the house, running so blindly that it was a wonder she didn't break her neck.

"What happened?" Vilas demanded. "All of a sudden she bolted like a rabbit pursued by the hounds."

"Who knows? She's a moody one," Roxanne stated, sinking to the stoop beside him.

"And you're not?" There was a teasing note in his words, quickly gone. "You'd better rescue that paddle and finish the job for her, or Mistress Patience will see your neck stretched."

Reluctantly, Roxanne rose and went toward the fire. "She'll see it stretched anyway, if there's a way she can contrive to do so. She thinks I'm a threat to her children and her marriage, among other things." She stared at the ashes stuck to the paddle, then wiped it off on her skirt, leaving dirty smears.

"And are you?" Vilas was back to teasing. "After her husband, I mean?"

"God's blood, no! I've a better opinion of myself than to settle for an illicit relationship with a married man, and a Puritan at that!" She jabbed viciously with the paddle and saw with a perverse satisfaction that it left a smear of ash upon the sheets.

"I rather thought there was something with Captain O'Neal, before we left Massachusetts last fall," Vilas mused. "You had the look of a sheep that's been poleaxed."

Quickly, lest her innermost feelings no longer remain a secret, Roxanne countered that. "Surely you jest! There's little future in becoming enamored of a privateer captain who's more devoted to his ship and his crew than he'll ever be to any woman." Her heart was racing, and she turned partly away from him, so that he should not read her face if she was unable to keep it from revealing the thoughts behind it. "Captain O'Neal is not a man to come to heel for any female, I suspect. And I've no interest in one who offers me less than I want in life.''

Vilas nodded. "You're wiser than I thought. He was in love, once, with a young woman he met as a youth.''

A knife twisted in her gut. "Oh? He didn't marry her?''

"He would have, I gather, if she hadn't died. Died, rumor has it, as a result of bad judgment on the part of our old friend Edmund Beaker and his employee, Captain Stratton. Something about a ship that was wrecked upon the rocks off the Irish coast, when Stratton saved himself at the cost of his passengers. She left a widowed mother and two young brothers in genteel poverty; the tale is that she and O'Neal were to have been married, and the men say he was wild with grief at the time and merciless with his enemies since then.''

Roxanne forgot the laundry. "Is that why he boarded our ship and confiscated something in a chest from Stratton?''

"He hasn't confided in me," Vilas admitted. "But I know he sent the trunk, containing whatever it was, back to England. My guess is that it was cash money, probably to provide for the widow and her sons. No doubt he held Beaker equally responsible with Stratton for the actions that sent his betrothed to her death.''

Roxanne did not quite know how to deal with the churning emotions she was experiencing. "He must have cared for this young woman very deeply, to take on the responsibility for the rest of her family after this long time.''

"Aye, I believe he did. He has taken no vows of celibacy, however. He's a normal man, and he buries his grief well now. If I had not listened to others of his crew, I'd be aware of none of this.''

"I suppose there are women aplenty in the life of a privateer, wherever he finds them.'' She hoped she revealed no personal interest in O'Neal, though her breathing had quickened.

"And that's the truth," Vilas confirmed, putting aside the rug. "The females find him from Barbados to the Gaspé. There, I think the rum's done the trick; I've stopped shivering. I've a notion to try a short walk. It's the only damned way I'm going to get my sea legs back.''

He headed off in the direction Christina had taken, limping, leaving Roxanne to stare after him broodingly. She hoped she hadn't given herself away to Vilas; she had no confidence that he would not joke over the matter with O'Neal, and nothing had ever seemed less a joke than what she had been going through these past few weeks.

When she saw O'Neal he was his usual audacious self. If the men of the family were present, he talked business—either his or theirs, or a combination of the two. On the rare occasions when he could tweak her under the chin, bestowing upon her that roguish grin, he did so. His banter gave her no reason to think she was any more special than any of those other women, from Barbados to the Gaspé. Wherever the hell *they* were, she thought in angry disappointment.

When she'd slapped his hand aside, O'Neal only laughed, as if it meant nothing to him whether she was annoyed or not. When she scorned his careless invitation to meet him one evening on the bridge—after agonizing over the matter for hours— he didn't even mention the matter the following day. She hoped he'd been there, and waited in vain, but she had no hope his wait had been unduly long. Even in a village of Puritans, there were maidens who would be flattered by the attentions of a privateer with a smooth tongue and considerable accumulated riches.

She alternately longed for his touch and hated herself for the longing. Especially she despised herself for allowing him to make love to her in that disgusting fashion, like some scullery maid tumbling in the hay with a stablehand, after she'd learned what sort of man he was.

And she hated Vilas, too, she thought now, for giving her so little to hope for. It was Christina's fault for talking her into coming to the New World, where the only interesting men were rogues, indeed. Certainly she'd met no one, except the priva- teer and his crew, who did not adhere to the principles of the Puritan religion, and she'd never tie herself to one of those, no matter how wealthy he was. If she'd stayed in England she might never have married into the nobility, but she'd have found a reasonably prosperous merchant or perhaps taken herself off to London to find a rich man who wasn't above ac- cepting an earl's illegitimate daughter as a mistress.

Even a wealthy man lived in austere circumstances here, compared to the ones in London, she thought sourly, and decided the clothes had been boiled and stirred enough. She hoped Christina would come back to attend to supper and wondered what had ailed the other girl.

"Mistress Roxanne! Is Vilas de Clement about?"

She turned to face one of the sailors from the *Revenge*. "He went off that way, a short time ago." She gestured toward the faintly discernible path.

"Ah, well, I've no notion to spend the rest of the afternoon tramping through the woods when there's a tankard of grog waiting in the village." The young man, who was known as Spiker, gave her a broad smile. "It's not often we get a chance to spend a few days ashore, to meet with young ladies and the like."

There was something about the way he looked at her that suggested he'd make that into an invitation if she gave him the slightest encouragement. Which was discouraging in itself. For if Shea O'Neal had given his crew the slightest clue that he was interested in her, above and beyond any of the doxies he encountered anywhere in his travels, they wouldn't be daring to approach her themselves.

"What are you wanting with Vilas?" she asked shortly.

He reached into his doublet and pulled out a folded paper. "Brung him a letter, I did. Cap'n sent it, brought in today on one o' them little boats as came up from Boston. It's from England."

"I'll give it to him." Roxanne took the missive and tucked it into her bodice, noting that Spiker's gaze lingered on the swell of her bosom. "Would you be wanting to wet your throat before you head back? Master Adam keeps a prime grade of rum."

"Aye, that he does! I helped unload the last batch," Spiker said eagerly. "I'd be much obliged, mistress."

Roxanne did not see the face clearly visible at the second-floor window. She would not have cared if she had. "Come inside and I'll get it," she offered.

It was there that Patience found her a few minutes later, seated at the table resting her elbows, sharing a pint with the sailor from the *Revenge*.

Before Patience summoned the sharp words she had in store for this ill-gotten excuse for a servant, however, there was a commotion in the corner of the room, where Megan had sat listening to Betta and Nels recite their lessons.

Nels suddenly sprang up, stumbling so that he nearly went into the fireplace, and Megan grabbed for him only just in time. Roxanne, turning, saw the little boy's face wreathed in terror or pain.

"What's the matter with him?" Patience cried, diverted by this emergency.

"He's choking," Megan said helplessly. "He's turning blue!"

"It's a walnut, Mother! He put a whole nut into his mouth, and it must have stuck!" Betta contributed, her blue eyes wide with fear.

Even as they watched, they saw Nels take on a perceptibly bluish tinge.

Patience rushed forward and grabbed the boy's arms to shake him vigorously. "God save him!" she shrieked, only to have the child slump between her hands, so that she went to her knees with him.

Betta and Megan clutched each other in distress, and Roxanne rose from the table, overturning the bench with a clatter.

"Bend him forward," she said, "and hit him on the back!"

"He's dying! Oh, God, don't let him die!" Patience was hysterical, still shaking the boy whose eyes rolled upward in an alarming manner.

Spiker was at Roxanne's side within seconds as she grabbed Nels out of his mother's hands. "That's the right idea, smack him on the back," he encouraged her.

But Nels was limp and not breathing, his color so dreadful that everyone in the room believed it was too late. Patience folded forward on the floor, wailing in grief, giving up.

Roxanne had not given up, however. "Hold him up," she said fiercely, and put a finger into the small mouth. "I can feel it, but I can't get under it . . . tip him forward, and I'll try again!"

Roxanne's face was screwed into a grimace of concentration and she probed once more. "The devil take you, come out of there!" she ground out between her teeth, and that time, when Spiker struck him sharply once more between the shoulder blades, Roxanne felt the foreign object give slightly. At the risk of pushing it farther into the child's throat, she dug into the soft tissue and got a fingernail below the nut meat.

A moment later it popped out onto the floor.

Almost immediately, the bluish skin faded into pink. Nels gasped and began to cry. Roxanne, perspiring heavily, sat back on her heels and let Megan and Betta drop forward to embrace the sobbing little boy.

"Good show," Spiker said approvingly. "What we need now is another tankard o' that rum."

Patience was breathing as loudly as her son. She made no move to take him from the other two into her arms. She was staring agape at Roxanne, who did not notice.

"I'll second the motion about the rum," Roxanne said, and drank off a full draught to ease the trembling in her limbs. "That was a close call if I've ever seen one. Help yourself, Master Spiker."

Gradually Nels' sobs subsided, and he clung to Megan's neck, face buried in her bosom. Patience rose from the floor, very pale now, moistening her lips.

She said no word to anyone, merely touching Nels upon his towhead for a few seconds, before sinking onto a stool as if her legs would no longer hold her up.

"My throat hurts," Nels said plaintively at last.

"I'll give you some rum and honey," Megan offered, brushing back the damp hair from his forehead. "Betta, dear, put the bench upright again, will you?"

It wasn't until she was preparing for bed hours later that Roxanne remembered the letter Spiker had delivered for Vilas.

Chapter 52

CHRISTINA'S FLIGHT through the woods ended when she tripped over a root and sprawled headlong.

For several moments she lay there, the wind knocked out of her, until gradually pain brought her out of her dazed state. She sat up, looking at the dirt and small stones embedded in the heel of her hand.

The tears she had not wanted anyone to see had dried on her cheeks. She got up and brushed the bits of grass and pine needles off her gown, then concentrated on picking the debris out of her hand.

"Chris! Where are you?"

She spun, wiping hastily at her eyes, hoping she wouldn't give away having wept over *him*.

"Here," she said, and waited as Vilas came between the birches, his brown leather doublet contrasting with the white tree trunks. He looked less flamboyant than the old Vilas in his scarlet cloak, but even with a limp and dressed little differently from the Puritans, he was the most attractive man she'd ever known, and the most endearing.

Except that her doubts and confusion made her angry as well as upset. He was bright enough about most things. Why was he so obtuse about *her*?

"Do you mind if I walk with you? This damned leg stiffens up every time I sit for a time. What's wrong?" He'd come close enough to see her reddened eyelids.

Wordless, unable either to tell a lie or to challenge him, she extended her hand, palm upward.

He took it in both of his own, sending signals throughout her body, signals she tried desperately to ignore, since nothing could come of them.

"Here, let me get the rocks out of it. There's no great damage done."

Not to my hand, Christina thought, but damage aplenty to my heart, you dense oaf.

Yet she did not draw her hand away until he had cleaned it the best he could without water for wetting a corner of her apron.

"I need to get back into shape," he said. "The *Revenge* will be ready to put to sea in another few days. I'd have moved back aboard before this if my quarters hadn't been among those needing repairs."

She had known this must come, and soon, yet the actuality made her heart constrict. "Where do you go this time?"

"Back to the Gaspé. He hasn't said so, but I've a notion O'Neal is as much taken with that part of the New World as I am. There's money to be made dealing with these Puritans, but their ideas are not much to our liking. All this rubbish about witches, when it's clear to any thinking man that most of the accusations are false, merely the means by which a woman rids herself of an unpopular neighbor! Some of those who've confessed have done so only after inhuman treatment in their wretched jails, and the best way to stay out of them seems to be to accuse someone else. At any rate, we were all intrigued by the north country, even if it is under the control of the French. They're a more understandable lot, different language or no, than the religious zealots here who accuse their own mothers of unspeakable acts and thereby send them to the gallows."

She was looking up into his face, hoping her own didn't reveal the depth of her dismay at his words. She encountered another root and stumbled slightly, and he caught her arm and continued to hold it as they moved on along the path.

"You're not...are you saying you may *stay* up there? In that...Gaspé place? But surely as a privateer Captain O'Neal can't prey upon French ships and then expect to...to live among the French colonists?"

"I'm not sure he intends to continue as a privateer. We've talked a bit, and I know he never intended to spend the rest of his days at sea, seeking out enemy ships to plunder. A share of whatever he takes goes back to England, to William and Mary, to support the throne. Even so, he's accumulated enough to keep him for the rest of his life in less dangerous circumstances. In our next to the last engagement, before the one in which I was injured, he had a very close call himself. As I can testify, it gives a man reason to think out his priorities. He said to me at one point, with that devilish grin of his, that he'd begun to think there might be something to spending a winter at his own fireside in a snug cabin, rather than facing high seas and foreign cannon."

He paused, rubbing at his injured thigh. "Damn, this thing either hurts, or itches, or both at once. I suppose I'd better turn back. It hasn't been much of a walk. Do you want to go on or return with me?"

After what he'd just said, each remaining moment seemed precious, though what good they were doing her Christina couldn't have said. She was no more than his little cousin, ready to listen, demanding nothing. "I'll go back, too. I've chores to do," she said, sounding as subdued as she felt. "Then you may sail away and never come back here?"

The very thought made her feel giddy and ill. What would be worthwhile in a life that held no further promise of seeing Vilas?

"I don't know. I think I'd have a liking for trapping, and I'd like to try it for a season. The French established fur trading stations in Quebec nearly a hundred years ago, and the men we met who engage in it seem well satisfied with it. I found them most admirable fellows, taking their strength and daring for granted in a way unlike any other I've met, except for O'Neal. He's past his thirtieth birthday, so it's time he considers his future, if he intends to strike out on a different course."

"I shouldn't think they'd welcome Englishmen," Christina said. "There's always been much animosity between the French and the English."

"The French who were bold enough to come to the New World are for the most part men of imagination as well as courage. They are not as narrow-minded as their counterparts in Europe. No, I have no fears on that score. A man up there will be accepted on his own merits, I think, regardless of his ancestors. God, I wonder how long it will be before this miserable leg stops aching at the least exertion?"

They had emerged from the forest near the house, and Christina adjusted her pace to his slower one. She wished now he hadn't recovered enough to leave with the *Revenge* when it sailed; she'd rather have him crippled, even permanently, than in some far-off place where she'd no hope of ever seeing him again. And then she felt guilty at the selfishness of the thought, though it was true enough.

Betta came bounding out of the door as they approached the house. "Nels choked on a walnut!" she announced excitedly. "And he turned all blue and stopped breathing, until Mistress Roxanne made it come out of his throat!"

The child danced around them, providing details that were repeated by Megan when they entered the house. Megan then gave Christina a compassionate look. "I have supper cooking. Roxanne said you were taken ill or something. Are you feeling better now?"

"Yes," Christina said untruthfully. "Did the washing get hung to dry?" she added quickly, changing the subject.

Patience, for once, had little to say during that evening. Cordelia was the only one who saw the glitter in her eyes and noticed as well how they rested so frequently upon Roxanne, who paid her no mind at all.

THE FAMILY HAD ALREADY RETIRED when Roxanne discovered the letter in the bodice of her dress. She hesitated, then redid her buttons and left the room where her sisters were undressing.

Vilas was stretched on his pallet in the corner of the kitchen, fully dressed and still awake.

"I forgot this, in the furor over Nels choking. Spiker brought it this afternoon. It's from England," she added, handing it down to him.

"From home?" Vilas sat up, reaching for the folded paper and tilting it to catch the firelight. "Ah, my mother's handwriting! Let's see what news from Cornwall."

Roxanne waited, unaware that Christina stood in the doorway behind her, listening from the darkened summer room.

"Is she in good health?"

"Very good, except for the rhumatism in her knees." Vilas's words were absent, and then he exclaimed sharply. "Well! Here's a bit of news that will interest you. Lady Jacobina is dead, and in the same way as Master Thomas; she was thrown from a horse while riding with Lord Windom not long after their wedding. Her neck was broken." His tone turned dry. "Her new husband is said to be prostrated with grief."

"It won't stop him from joining her estate to his," Roxanne surmised, "and enjoying the results immensely. Well, there would have been more justice if she'd been poisoned like Himself, but a broken neck is not totally unjust." She stared into the fire. "We could go back to Cornwall, now, though no doubt it's too late to claim any share of the earl's estates, so we'd be penniless."

Vilas leaned against the wall, the letter resting beside him. "A letter from home does stir memories," he admitted. "Would you really be wanting to go back, though?"

Roxanne snorted. "I have no love for this place!"

"'Tis a fair country, and from what I've heard the settlers in Rhode Island and Virginia are far less rigid in their attitudes toward life. I confess to a lack of love for Puritan edicts," Vilas admitted. "Yet the opportunities in the New World far surpass anything I could have expected in Cornwall." He sighed. "This inactivity is driving me mad. I don't get enough exercise to enable me to sleep at night."

"I'm not sleepy tonight, either. Let me draw two tankards of rum, and we'll talk for a bit."

Christina, watching, withdrew into their sleeping room and eased the door shut, wrapped in misery. Whatever they did out there together, she didn't want to know about it. She wouldn't put it past Roxanne to crawl into bed with him, and not to ease his chills, either.

She told herself that it was really none of her affair. If Vilas had cared for *her*, he would have said so.

There was a low murmur of voices for a time from the adjoining room, and then she heard nothing, though Roxanne did not come to bed. Christina fell asleep at last, tormented by her imagination, which carried over into her dreams.

PATIENCE STOOD THAT NIGHT, holding high the crusie lamp, to look down on her sleeping son.

He was flushed and healthy, his pale hair tousled, a thumb trailing from his parted lips.

He had come very close to dying this afternoon. She knew that only too well, and that she had been helpless to do anything to save him. Yet he had already forgotten the entire episode.

Patience would never forget it. And Roxanne's words were branded into her mind. "The devil take you, come out of there!"

The slut betrayed herself by her own words. Well, Patience refused to further endanger herself or her family by allowing the girl to remain in the house.

She had tried to convey her apprehensions to Father Adam, and to Wesley, with a total lack of understanding from either of them. She wouldn't make that mistake again. Roxanne clearly had bewitched them.

However, if the family would not listen, there were others who would. Patience had sat through many a lengthy sermon and watched the faces of others in the congregation as they reacted, positively or negatively, to what was said.

She knew which of the women would listen to her. Which ones would whisper to their neighbors, until the stories Patience could tell were well disseminated throughout the village.

The local clergy and their pleas for tolerance be damned, she thought. She lowered the crusie to the chest and put on her nightcap. Frightened yet determined, Patience got into bed, carefully so as not to waken her sleeping husband.

Mistress Roxanne would be taken care of, she thought as she blew out the lamp, the same as those other witches in Salem.

Chapter 53

MEGAN HAD GROWN QUIETER by the day, though at first no one other than Cordelia noticed it.

Fitz continued to make her his center of attention, aware of no one else whenever they were both in the same room, moving quickly to assist her when there was something heavy to lift or a door to be opened when she had her hands full. Yet to a keen observer, he was troubled, and Megan no longer smiled. Indeed, tears were seen to well up in her eyes at odd times, when Cordelia could see no cause for them.

A lovers' quarrel, she guessed, and, having no knowledge of the true state of affairs, assumed the breach would eventually be mended.

It had been a fantasy, like one of the stories Roxanne made up about princesses and pirates, Megan thought. They had been right, those who had urged that she keep the birthmark a secret for all those years. She wished dismally that Christina had not rescued that long-ago infant to be nursed by a serving woman; if she had been allowed to die, then she would have been spared the anguish since, and especially what she felt now.

She resolved to talk to Christina, when the opportunity arose, about the possibility of leaving this place that now seemed unbearable. When their indentures were up they would be free to go, though where they would find a better life was uncertain. Perhaps Rhode Island, where it was said others had settled after failing to adjust to life among the Puritans.

Of course it was already too late to find happiness, there or anywhere else. She had already met and fallen in love with Fitz, and she was convinced she would love him until the day she died.

She did not blame Fitz for his inability to accept her as she was. Even at home in Cornwall her father had taken it for granted that there would be dire consequences if anyone knew she was blemished at birth. It was even worse here in the Bay Colony, with any such imperfection commonly accepted as a mark of the devil.

Fitz would put himself at risk to take on such a wife, and how could she fault him for not wanting to do so?

Megan avoided his direct gaze and went about her duties in a silent, dreary way. It was a good thing her hands worked automatically, for she gave little thought to what she did.

From Megan, Cordelia turned her attention to Christina. As the oldest of the sisters, it was reasonable that she would be the one to take the most responsibility, and she did. She was as sensible as she was beautiful, with that spectacular hair and those green eyes, even tempered and hardworking. As a rule she was a problem to no one.

The past few days, however—strangely enough, after young de Clement began to get better, which was surely something the girl had intensely desired—Christina seemed distracted and unhappy. Her primary attention remained focused on de Clement, and as far as the old woman could tell, he talked to her freely and frequently, mostly about his voyage on that privateer ship.

But whereas before Christina had been quietly efficient, she was suddenly inept. She let the beans scorch. She forgot to put wood on the fire. She carelessly went to remove the great iron spider from the hearth without using anything to protect her hand and burned herself.

And she watched her next-younger sister with an oddly wooden expression that occasionally revealed a twinge of anger or resentment, unless Cordelia missed her guess.

Roxanne, of course, had always been Cordelia's favorite performer upon this stage of life. Roxanne had been fascinating from the beginning. She seemed oblivious of the attention directed her way, for the most part, unless it was from one or the other of the men. Roxanne responded to masculine interest as a wildflower responds to sun and rain.

Even old Adam, who had long since lost any desire for further entanglement with females, could be seen to enjoy looking at a pretty young woman. And pretty was an understatement where Roxanne was concerned. The only thing that detracted from that was Roxanne's own awareness of it; she used her beauty, even flaunted it, and clearly enjoyed being the center of things.

Wesley continued to watch her—as Ezra watched Christina—and Cordelia wondered with dry humor if each of them thought himself undetected. How transparent men were, poor souls.

Though Roxanne was not exactly transparent, Cordelia was mildly puzzled for a time. Now she thought she had figured it out. The girl pined for the dashing privateer, who was not coming to heel as readily as Roxanne would have liked, and the silly thing thought to provoke him to jealousy by feigning designs on de Clement.

It was academic to Cordelia, who did not care one way or the other how it came out. The diversion was the main thing, to an old woman no longer of any use to herself or anyone else. If de Clement realized what Roxanne was doing or how Christina suffered over it, the man gave no such indication. Men, Cordelia had decided many years ago, were the most dense of living creatures.

As women were the most devious. Not all of them, necessarily, but certainly the word applied to Cordelia's granddaughter. Patience was up to something, though no one else appeared to take any notice of her. Patience was biding her time, and Cordelia wondered uneasily to what end.

The only thing Cordelia was sure of was that it boded ill for the rest of the household, both servants and family.

PATIENCE'S OPPORTUNITY came more quickly than even she could have anticipated.

The executions of convicted witches went on, and the fury of accusations and arrests continued, unabated. It seemed to those who retained more rational heads that the entire colony had gone mad with bloodlust. Whether genuinely convinced of the guilt of these people or merely taking advantage of the opportunity to rid themselves of old enemies, a majority of the populace took up the chant "Kill the witches"!

A plea went out from John Procter, one of those imprisoned, to the clergy in Boston: many of the confessions had been obtained by torture, he swore, and he begged that the leaders call for removal of the trials from Salem, that new judges be appointed in the interest of fairness, that the jury be chosen from among citizens of Boston rather than in the village where they were presently centered. If the clergymen were to observe in person, they would see that the trials were biased and unfair.

A petition was passed about in Ipswich testifying to the good character of Procter and his wife; it had no effect on the outcome of his trial. Along with several others, the Procters were sentenced to hang. Elizabeth Procter, however, was with child and could not be executed until the innocent babe was born.

Patience saw opportunity rising before her eyes the evening that Shea O'Neal came to the house to plead with her menfolk to remain in Ipswich, to finish the repairs on the *Revenge*, before setting off again to try to bring some order out of this chaos.

"It has already taken longer than you calculated, and my men are restless." It was O'Neal who paced the kitchen, however, his swarthy face glowering. "You decry the way the witch-hunting fever takes the citizens away from their ordinary responsibilities, yet you speak of slowing down the final work on my ship even further by dashing off on some harebrained mission when you've only a day or two left to accomplish the tasks I pay you for!"

Adam regarded him judiciously. "Your argument is well put, Captain. Yet our own responsibilities are heavy and go beyond the needs of any one person or group of persons. The Reverend Cotton Mather himself, who has considerable influence, had urged that unless guilt is proven beyond all doubt, the accused might be exiled rather than executed. And now he, whom we had thought to maintain a voice of sanity in the midst of madness, has assured us that George Burroughs, whom we know well, was not a properly ordained minister and that he was guilty as charged. Our friend has been hanged with the others, and if someone doesn't do something to prevent further atrocities, our entire future as a colony is in jeopardy."

O'Neal was unappeased, his voice as angry as his face. "Damn it, man, the reason I came to you instead of to someone in Boston was that you promised me expert repairs, rapidly done! At this rate the summer will be over before we can sail again, and the ice will be closing in on the St. Lawrence before we reach it! You contracted to perform services, Master Hull, and I insist that you honor that agreement!''

The listeners stood transfixed, for until now there had been naught but goodwill and respect between the two men.

Old Adam straightened his lean frame, his bushy white eyebrows drawing together over the beaky nose. "Two of my sons will continue to work on your ship, sir. Ezra and I must go where cooler heads are imperative if this colony is not be destroyed.''

The cords in O'Neal's neck bulged as he struggled with his fury. "I consider you to have breached our agreement, Master Hull, and be assured I will consider that when payment is made.''

Adam did not flinch before the hot dark gaze. "Do not threaten me, Captain. It will avail you nothing.''

For a moment it seemed that O'Neal would suffer an apoplectic fit. Then he drew in a deep breath and in a voice ragged with suppressed emotion spoke to Vilas. "Three more days. We sail then whether the repairs have been completed or not. I suggest you be on board if you intend to go with us.''

There was a moment of silence after he had stalked from the house. Christina, despair in her heart, hoped she would not cry in front of everyone. If Vilas sailed with the *Revenge* in three days' time, she might never see him again.

Roxanne, too, battled roiling emotions. There had been no sign that O'Neal had even noticed her attentions to Vilas. The devil take him, then, let him go to that distant land with all those foreigners and never return! She'd be better off without him, damn his eyes!

Her own eyes burned, and her throat ached so badly she prayed no one would address her so that she had to try to speak.

Adam sighed and spoke to his eldest son. "We leave at dawn, Ezra. There is merit in what the man says. However, it does not override the need to do what we are called upon to do. The future of the colony is more important than the needs of one ship's captain, no matter how legitimate his claim upon our services.'' He addressed the younger sons. "Give the man the best that you can. If there were anyone else available, I would say to hire him, but there is no one."

Vilas cleared his throat. "I'm no expert, but under supervision I could do something to help, perhaps. I'll be glad to try, sir. I'm in your debt for the care I've received in this house, for I'd likely have died without it."

Adam nodded. "Wesley and Fitz will direct you. Patience, we will have need of provisions for our journey."

"Of course, Father Adam." Of the entire assembled group, only Patience was feeling satisfaction, which she attempted to conceal. She lowered her gaze and held back the smile that would have formed on her lips.

Father Adam and Ezra would be gone for days. With any luck, they might not return for weeks.

She could manage Wesley, as she'd done for years, and Fitz wasn't worth worrying about.

This was the chance she had been waiting for, and she intended to make the most of it.

Chapter 54

PATIENCE MOVED SWIFTLY and with precise planning.

As soon as Adam and Ezra had gone, she put on her best cap and apron, bade Cordelia keep an eye on the children and set out for the house of an old woman well-known for her gossiping tongue.

There, while being plied with tea and small cakes, she related her trials and tribulations since Father Adam had brought home the latest indentured servants.

Goody Wolfe could no longer see well enough to read, so Patience remedied that lack by reading to her from the papers Roxanne had written. She told, with a brazenly fascinating lack of discretion, how the sinful creature had bewitched Patience's own husband, so that his mind was closed to any criticism of the slut herself. In addition to that, Wesley had been turned into a ravening beast in bed, scarcely giving Patience a moment's respite from his demands.

The old woman chortled and pushed the plate of cakes closer to her guest. No matter that it was to have been her own week's supply. It was small payment for the juiciest tale she had heard in years, and nearer at hand than the trials in distant Salem Village.

"If your husband will not listen, then others must," she stated, leaning forward so as not to miss a single word.

"And then," Patience went on, encouraged by this display of attention, "to prove her powers of darkness, she caused my small son to choke on a walnut."

Goody Wolfe drew up in a gratifying display of shock, a gnarled hand on her withered breast. "No!"

"She did," Patience confirmed, by this time fully convinced of her own interpretation of the matter. "And then, when I cried out to God in agony at having another of my children taken from me, she relented, or perhaps the power of the

Lord overcame that of her master. She called upon the devil—her exact words were 'The devil take you, come out of there,' and at once the walnut fell out of his throat, and he began to breath again. They all heard her, everyone, and can testify to it."

"A witch, a true witch, and in our own village," Goody Wolfe marveled. "What are you going to do about it, mistress?"

"What can I do?" Patience made no attempt to conceal her bitterness. "My husband and my father-in-law will not listen. 'Tis the business of the local magistrate to protect us from such as she, but without public protest he is not likely to listen to one poor woman's pleas."

"True, true," Goody Wolfe breathed. "Ah, you poor soul, indeed!"

She could hardly wait until Patience had gone before she reached for her shawl—she was nearly eighty, and her bones were cold even in summer—and set out to relay this delicious tidbit to her nearest neighbor.

Patience would have liked to plant only a seed or two and wait for it to take root. She dared not. Father Adam and Ezra could be counted upon to remain away from home no more than a fortnight at best and could conceivably return within four or five days. Allowing nature to take its course took time. She would have to plant many seeds and water and cultivate them assiduously.

Her way took her, therefore, on into the village. She did not bother with those she knew to be staunchly behind the local clergy and her father-in-law in the matter of witch-hunting. Let them discover the truth when her seeds had sprouted and grew sturdily, beyond the ability of the disbelievers to talk them away.

She was feeling sick with so many cakes and so much tea, as well as very tired, when she finally headed for home. The exertion had nearly done her in, she reflected. Yet it had been necessary. She needed help in putting an end to an intolerable situation.

Within hours, unless she missed her guess, the entire village, with the possible exception of the clergy and the magistrates, would know the sort of serpent Adam had brought into their household.

SHE HATED THIS PLACE, and she'd had her fill of it. Roxanne moved in a reddish haze of rage, against the Puritans in general, the Hulls in particular, and especially Captain Shea O'Neal. She even had a little resentment to spare for Vilas, who had treated her with amused detachment when she had attempted to create a spark of jealousy in O'Neal. She had given Vilas every opportunity to take advantage of her, and he'd acted as if she were his sister.

While O'Neal doubtless considered her no better than one of the harlots he was surely accustomed to.

"What are you doing?"

Roxanne, on her knees on her pallet in the summer room, twisted around to stare up at Christina, who stood in the doorway. "What does it look like I'm doing?" she asked disagreeably.

Christina considered, moistening her lips. She glanced backward into the kitchen before she replied and then kept her voice low. "It looks as if you're packing your belongings, including that jade gown you wouldn't let me dye."

"You're brighter than I'd thought." Roxanne tied the bundle together with a vicious twisting movement.

"Why? What do you think you're going to do?"

Roxanne rocked back on her heels, her smile curiously unpleasant. "I'm going to leave this wretched place and find somewhere I've a chance of making a future that doesn't include Mistress Patience nor anyone like her."

Shock made Christina's jaw go slack. "But you can't! We're indentured for more than another two years! Master Adam paid our passage here in the expectation that—"

Roxanne's rude noise made clear what she cared for Adam's expectations. "He's no pauper; he can consider it a charitable contribution. If Mistress Prudence would get out of bed of a morning and make even a small effort, they wouldn't need three servants, anyway."

She got to her feet and kicked the bundle aside, throwing a quilt over it. She would have left the room and closed the door behind her, except that Christina blocked her way.

"Roxanne, you can't. You are legally bound to work out that passage money—"

"Damn the passage money! I've done enough already to have repaid that debt, and what good was it? We should never have come here! These people are even more narrow-minded and stupid than the villagers at home, and I'm not going to spend the rest of my days among them...."

"No one says you have to spend the rest of your days. You're only sixteen now, you have plenty of time left..."

"These are the best years I'll ever have, and what am I doing with them? I've talked to one of the fishermen, and he's going to Gloucester day after tomorrow. He's agreed to take me with him."

"To Gloucester? Whatever for? There are Puritans there, too."

"I couldn't find anyone going as far as Boston, that's why Gloucester. There'll be other boats there, going farther, and I'll eventually get clear of this miserable colony to some place they've never heard of Puritans."

"What do you intend to use to pay for passage this time? More promises you won't keep?"

Roxanne gave her a look of pure contempt as they faced each other like a pair of fighting cocks. "Are you suggesting I'll have to whore for it? Well, if I do, it's none of your worry. Get out of the way."

Christina held her ground, even to putting out a hand to the doorjamb on either side. "Roxanne, for the love of God, think! If they catch up with you, you'll be publicly whipped! It's a long way to go before you could be free of Massachusetts laws!"

Roxanne set her jaw. "Get out of the way, Christina."

"I won't, not until you agree to at least discuss it with Megan and me. If you run away, don't you realize the bulk of the displeasure will fall on *us*? Wait a bit, and perhaps we can work out something that will enable you to go without disrupting our lives, too..."

"Such as what? By some miracle is someone going to pay off the balance of our debt? You two can stay here and suffer if you like, but I won't. I'm going, and nothing you can say will stop me."

She put a hand on Christina's shoulder and shoved, and the other girl was forced to give way. "At least give me a chance to talk to Vilas."

"Vilas!" Roxanne spat the name back at her. "He'll do nothing! Nothing! He washed his hands of us when he put us aboard the *Edwin J. Beaker*. Open your eyes, Chris! See him for what he is, a cousin who doesn't give a damn for any of us!"

Christina was very pale. "Perhaps so, though I think even a cousin might care enough to help us work out something that will not worsen the situation for any of us. If you care for anyone but yourself, at least wait . . ."

"I'm here," Roxanne told her hotly, "because I listened to you. I came to this cursed place, and I've hated every minute of it, because *you* thought it was the only solution to our problems. I should have stayed in Cornwall and taken my chances with Lady Jacobina, or run away to London where she'd never have found me. At least the place isn't full of bloody religious fanatics!"

Christina's face would have wrung sympathy from anyone less impassioned on her own behalf. Roxanne didn't even notice it as she pushed past her.

"If you had any sense and the courage of a bowl of mush, you'd make plans of your own," Roxanne said flatly. "I'm going to take a walk."

Christina stared after her, biting her lower lip. Day after tomorrow, she thought. What could she possibly offer as a convincing alternative before that?

To make matters worse, when she noticed that the sleeping pallet had been removed from the corner of the kitchen and asked Megan about it, the reply was dismaying.

"Didn't you know? Vilas has gone back to the *Revenge*."

"He's gone?" Distress sent her voice soaring before she could control it.

"Oh, he said he'd be back to say goodbye, before they sail," Megan assured her.

A public farewell, in front of all the others, Christina wondered? No special word for her? It seemed there had been no special words for Roxanne, either, though there was little comfort in that knowledge. She wanted to fling herself down, weeping, but there was a meal to prepare, and the baby needed changing, from the smell of him.

Christina drew herself together as best she could. "See to Emory, will you, Megan? I must get the vegetables in the stew before it's too late to have them cooked in time."

Cordelia nodded in her chair, for once unaware of the drama around her. No one noticed the tears that escaped down Christina's cheeks, to be quickly rubbed away as she began to scrub the vegetables.

PATIENCE WAS RIGHT about the females she had approached with her tale of woe. They wasted no time in sharing the scandalous news. The following morning, a delegation of women appeared to confront the supposed witch and learn for themselves the truth of what they had heard.

Chapter 55

CHRISTINA SLEPT BADLY. She had begged Roxanne to give her time to consult with Vilas, to consider alternatives to so rash an action as running away from Ipswich, to weigh the probable consequences of an ill-conceived plan, anything to make this incorrigible half sister *think* before she acted.

There had been no such cooperation, naturally. Roxanne totally ignored her for the rest of the day. And Vilas had gone back to his ship, beyond her reach. She'd spent weeks of nursing him through fevers and chills and pain, and then a slow convalescence, only to hear him thank *Roxanne* for the care, and she to allow him to think what he would.

Tossing restlessly, she cursed them both for the fools they were. And then, as the tears would no longer be held back, she cursed herself for a fool, as well. She'd said nothing to disabuse Vilas of his notion about who had nursed him so faithfully through those many days and nights—or shared his bed on that momentous occasion when he was finally coming out of the worst of things.

How much difference would it have made, if he'd known she had been the one he made love to?

She could not be certain she had guessed correctly about that matter, but unless he had mistaken his willing partner, how else explain the way he had treated her afterward? With the casual affection he had bestowed on a young cousin for as long as she could remember.

Her disgust grew, with Vilas and Roxanne and most of all with herself. Why did she not have the courage to tell him how she felt, and what she thought? Why allow him to believe that it was Roxanne who had probably saved his life? She loathed herself for being such a coward.

Both of them, Roxanne and Vilas, would be sailing soon. Out of her life, leaving her with nothing. Nothing but more years in this household where, except for Patience, she might have managed, but doubted her ability to do so with Patience to contend with.

For a few moments she was moderately distracted by her mistress. Something was afoot there, she thought uneasily. Patience had been oddly but perceptibly different during the remainder of the day after she'd come home from an unprecedented round of visiting in the village.

Patience had been uncharacteristically without criticism of anyone. While speaking little, except to the children, she had managed to convey a sense of satisfaction about something; several times Christina had noticed the hint of a smile lingering about her lips, and Patience smiling was perhaps a force more formidable than her customary state of bad temper.

Master Adam kept a level head and ruled the household with an iron hand. But he was away, for a week or more, and who knew what could happen in his absence?

While they prepared for bed Megan had finally detected the strain between her half sisters. "What is it?" she asked uncertainly. "Is something wrong?"

It was Roxanne's place, surely, to make her announcement about leaving. She said nothing. Lips tightening, Christina put it baldly. "She's going to run away."

"Run . . . ? But . . . where will you go, Roxanne?"

Roxanne's only response was a shrug.

Megan had not asked *why*. There was no need to do that. Had they not been bound to Adam Hull by the contract of indenture, they might all have left this colony, though she was at a loss to know where they could have gone, penniless as they were. There was nothing Christina would have liked better than to leave the Puritan village, except to have gone with Vilas.

And that seemed a vain hope, she thought as she fell at last into a sleep disturbed by bad dreams.

She woke feeling distinctly unwell. She was afraid to know how she looked; Patience kept a small mirror in her bedroom, but under no circumstances would Christina have ventured there to examine her reflection. She knew her eyelids must be reddened and swollen from having cried herself to sleep, and she felt queasy, as well.

She went about her customary early morning tasks, however: dishing up the porridge of cornmeal, seeing that Wesley and Fitz were sent off to work with full bellies. Megan attended the children and took a bowl to old Cordelia, who was often so stiff she had difficulty getting out of bed without assistance. Christina did not know what Roxanne did, for she vanished the moment it was time to clear the table.

Patience did not descend the stairs until the men had gone and the children were having their chins wiped after their morning meal. It was disturbing to see that she still maintained an unnatural calm, and that the half smile lingered around her mouth.

Christina looked at her and then quickly away, for fear that what she felt would show in her face: her dislike of Patience and her own longing to flee as Roxanne planned to do.

What in heaven's name could she do to stop her? And how would Roxanne's running away reflect on the two she left behind? For all that Patience had made it clear she disliked Roxanne intensely, she would no doubt be furious to find her gone.

Her stomach felt so unsettled Christina did not eat with the others, but a cup of tea soothed it somewhat. Vilas, she thought. She would have to seek out Vilas and ask his advice. Perhaps his words would carry some weight with Roxanne even if her own did not.

She spoke slowly and quietly, yet with a determination she hoped Patience would not oppose. "I have to go into the village," she said. "I can take food to the men at midday, and Roxanne can take over here until I return."

Patience seemed indifferent to this, and unusually placid, which increased Christina's nervousness. It was not like Patience to be placid.

She couldn't wait to be out of the house. She met Roxanne returning as she left and paused to ask, "Where have you been?"

"Walking," Roxanne said boldly, with defiance. "Where are you going?"

"To talk to Vilas," Christina admitted. "I've put bread to rise, so watch it and bake it when it's ready, and iron what's left in the basket and see that the soup is ready for the children at noon."

Roxanne was aloof. "Anything else?"

Irritation sparked through her. "There's plenty to be done, and Mistress Patience's wrath will fall on the rest of us if any shirks." She hesitated, then could not help adding, "We're the ones she'll take it out on, if you leave. Does that bother you at all?"

Roxanne shrugged. "You're free agents as much as I am. The woman is impossible, and I've had enough of her. If you don't like it, leave."

"You know we can't do that. Master Adam would be well within his rights to have us pursued and punished, and without funds or help we've little chance of getting away. He's entitled to the work he's paid for."

"So do it, then. Just don't blame me." Roxanne made as if to pass by her, and Christina added one more order.

"Be sure to keep the fire up while the bread's in the oven. Otherwise it doesn't come out right."

Roxanne made no reply, and after a moment Christina went on her way, not sure how much she cared whether Roxanne followed instructions or not.

If only she and Megan had somewhere to go, to start over, she thought drearily. The day was a lovely one, with sunlight glinting through the foliage overhead and a warm breeze stirring her hair. She could like this place, if only there was not so much unhappiness here.

She didn't know if Vilas could, or would, be able to talk sense into Roxanne. If it weren't that she feared such a defection would be strongly detrimental to those she left behind, she would be glad to see the girl go. Roxanne had been troublesome from beginning to end.

Christina trudged on toward the village, hoping the near nausea of nervousness that occasionally lapped over her in waves would subside once she'd conquered her apprehension at approaching Vilas to ask, once again, for his help.

ROXANNE SET THE BREAD to bake when the time came, but she was disinclined to heat the flatirons and set about that task. After exceedingly brief consideration, she decided instead to write down the poem that was forming in her head. She would be gone before anyone raised a fuss about unironed garments.

She could not wait to be free of this place, and if she never saw Captain Shea O'Neal again, either, that was fine. He had used her, had deceived her, and she figuratively spat upon him. If the pain of betrayal yet endured, why, it would no doubt pass in time.

She was a trifle uneasy about making her own way, since she had not a shilling to her name and no way to fill a purse. It was probably risky to attempt finding work within the Bay Colony; she knew it was true that Adam Hull would be within his rights to set the law on her. She was determined not to give him the opportunity to find her.

South, then, she thought. O'Neal had spoken of Jamestown, in the colony called Virginia. The settlers there were as different from the Puritans here as she herself was from Patience. They grew tobacco and lived in gracious houses, and wore the kind of clothes Roxanne had always dreamed of wearing: silks and velvets in vivid colors. They danced and sang and entertained, and one went to church or not, according to preference rather than according to law. Yes, she might try Virginia. There was a shortage of females there as well as everywhere else in the New World, and she was confident that in such a society she could eventually find a suitable husband.

The problem was how to manage until then. For all her impudent words to Christina, she had neither desire nor intention to buy her way to freedom with her body.

Even thinking that made her remember, with considerable distress, how freely she had given herself to O'Neal. Never again, she resolved, only to immediately amend the thought. Not unless there was truly something to be gained, not lost, by doing so.

She would never, Roxanne mused, be able to lie with any man, without remembering what it had been like with Shea O'Neal.

The rap on the door took her unawares.

Perhaps O'Neal . . . ?

But it was not he who stood on the doorstep.

There were six of them. They ranged from middle-aged to old, and they had one thing in common: on every face was written avid curiosity underlaid with a touch of apprehension, while overlaid with firmness of purpose.

Roxanne stepped backward, not yet realizing their arrival had anything to do with *her*. She drew the door wider open, puzzled, because in all the time she had been a member of this household they had had no more than a single visitor at a time from among the village women, except when Abigail had died.

"Yes?" she asked.

"Where are your manners?" Patience demanded. "Invite them in!" There was, however, no real censure in her voice. Rather, Cordelia thought, observing from her chimney corner, there was an undercurrent of excitement that put the old woman immediately on guard.

Roxanne stepped away, and the women entered the house. They filed past her, warily, several of them catching up their skirts to keep them from touching hers.

"Yes," Goody Wolfe said, peering closely into Roxanne's face. "She's the one. I can read it in her eyes."

Several heads nodded. Roxanne, without knowing why, took a step backward. "What are you talking about, old woman?"

"She's the witch, all right," said Goody Wolfe.

Roxanne had believed herself inured to the idiocies of these people, but now shock held her rigid. "You're out of your mind! Are you accusing me of something?"

Megan, spooning porridge into the baby, forgot what she was doing and the mush slid off onto the floor. Betta and Nels had gone off to their lessons at the Dame School in the village; Megan had one coherent moment of being glad they were not there to see what was going to happen.

And then the nightmare began.

Chapter 56

MEGAN HANDED THE BABY to Cordelia without taking her eyes off the old crone who had spoken. The woman looked a witch herself, with a wizened face, a sharp nose and a humped back under the black shawl.

Goody Wolfe. Megan knew who she was, knew from encounters at Meeting that the dreadful creature was one of those who muttered under her breath when the urgings from the pulpit were for moderation and restraint in the matter of searching out the witches.

Instinctively Megan's hand crept to the neck of her dress and stayed there, pressed flat against the base of her throat, where she felt the pulse that hammered there.

Christina, she thought, Christina would be able to talk sense into them. Only Christina was gone, down to the boat works no more than half an hour ago. She might not be back for hours.

Whatever was going to happen here would take place long before Christina could help in any way.

Roxanne had gone very pale. Her green eyes flashed sparks—of indignation? fear?—as she faced the old women, and Patience.

Megan had heard of one's blood running cold. She looked into the face of Patience Hull and knew for the first time what that meant. If only Master Adam—but he, too, was far away.

If Megan ran to the village, would anyone come to her assistance? It would take time to find the right persons, the magistrate or a clergyman, someone with sufficient authority to intimidate these women, and more time yet to convince them of the urgency of the situation.

No, she couldn't run and leave Roxanne here to face her accusers alone.

"Such evil, right here in our own village," said Goody Allen. She was a person who would normally never have been welcome in Patience's kitchen: dim-witted, sly and slovenly, the woman was constantly being admonished for not coming to Meeting on time, or at all. Those who were forced to sit next to her deplored her stench, for even in an age when bathing was infrequently done, Goody Allen was the epitome of filthiness.

She stepped forward now to peer into Roxanne's face, her dark eyes glittering with the mania that had infected so much of the colony. "Ain't none o' us safe," she stated, "agin a witch."

"She's a danger to everyone," Patience confirmed. And now Megan saw the meaning of that terrible little smile.

Patience had chosen her time well. The men who would not have allowed this to happen would not be back for days. Even her own husband would have stopped it, but he, too, was at the boat works or perhaps on the *Revenge*.

When Goody Allen took another step forward, Roxanne instinctively fell back. It was probably as much from the stink of her as anything else, yet the women took it as a sign that they had her on the defensive; as a group, they closed in around the girl.

"Get away from me!" Roxanne's voice rose, and they actually stopped momentarily when she reached out for the broom that leaned against the wall and held it poised to strike.

"Watch out! It may be she can fly on that thing!" blurted Mistress Lowell. She of them all, a dried-up little wisp of a widow, ought to have known better than to be here. She had been a respected matron for years, though since her husband's death this past winter she had been a bit odd. Ordinarily she would not have defied the orders of the clergy on matters of behavior.

They hesitated, until Patience's words renewed their confidence. "She's outnumbered at the moment, and she's likely most dangerous during the hours of darkness. Is there any who doubts that she's a witch?"

The women muttered among themselves. If they had not seen the writings, they had heard about them, as they had heard the way the girl had made the walnut come out of the child's throat; by calling upon the devil.

"Let's see if she bears the devil's mark," Goody Wolfe proposed. "'Twouldn't surprise me in the least to find the proof of her guilt somewhere on that milky-white skin."

For an old woman she was amazingly quick and strong. She reached out past the broom poised in defense and grabbed Roxanne's collar, ripping it loose from the drab gown.

The broom swung, as if of its own accord—as several would subsequently relate it, further evidence of the justness of their cause—striking Goody Wolfe's spectacles and sending them skittering into a corner.

"Get away from me! Damn you, you stupid old hags. You've let Mistress Patience set you loose like mad dogs! If you do me any harm, you'll surely be punished by your own magistrates!"

Her protests carried little weight, however. The women had worked themselves up on the way here, had discussed what they must do for the good of the villagers and they were not to be denied the satisfaction nor put off by threats.

Megan watched in horror as the women surged forward, in the same mindlessly vicious way as the women who had stoned their sworn enemy in the streets of Boston. Within seconds Roxanne had been knocked down and her garments were being torn from her to the accompaniment of shrieks and kicks.

"No!" Megan's screech was hardly heard above the others. She glanced wildly at Patience, seeking some speck of sanity there, but though Patience did not join the rolling, noisy mass of humanity on the floor, she would not help.

Megan felt herself propelled forward, grabbing for the nearest bony shoulder to pull one of the attackers away. "Stop! What you do is wicked, dreadful! She's not a witch, leave her alone! You'll be thrown in jail yourselves if you do her harm!"

Something landed a stunning blow on Megan's temple. Staggered, she loosened her hold, only to find that she was now the one under attack. Fingernails dug into her cheek and then a hand fastened on the neck of her dress and tugged.

"Oh, God save us!" The woman fell back, wailing in terror. "This un's another o' 'em!"

Gradually the kitchen fell silent, except for the heavy breathing brought on by all the exertion. Roxanne, dazed and with a trickle of blood dripping from her nose, raised herself on one elbow, as stupified by the sudden cessation of attack as she had been by the attack itself.

"Sweet Jesus!" Goody Wolfe howled. "Look at it! Look at the mark of the devil!"

Patience was no longer smiling. She, too, had gone deadly pale. There was genuine fear in her eyes. Her gaze, like those of the others, was fastened on Megan, who sought unsuccessfully to hold the torn bodice so that it would cover the blemish.

For her entire life Megan had thought about the time when her secret would be revealed. Yet nothing could have prepared her for this moment.

As if mesmerized, the women stared, stricken.

Patience was the first to break the silence. "'Tis true, they're both witches! Dear God, have mercy on us!"

Megan heard her own sobbing breath, the blood thundering in her ears, the tick of the clock and the baby's whimper. The horror was complete when Cordelia drew a deep breath and repeated her granddaughter's plea. "God, have mercy!"

Megan closed her eyes and waited, wondering why God had seen fit to punish her in this way, too frightened even to think of a prayer of her own.

ONLY THE HELPER, Worthington, was at the boat works. He was a younger man, pleasant enough though slow of both movement and thought. He turned when Christina addressed him.

"Oh, Mistress Christina, good morning." He put down the plank that was to be incorporated into the deck of the current boat under construction. "You've brought the beans?" He grinned, sniffing appreciatively. "No doubt they'll smell 'em and be in directly to eat." He squinted upward at the sun. "Must be near about time for it."

Christina rested the heavy pot on a sawhorse to ease her aching arms. "Is there any way I can get out to the *Revenge*? I need to talk to my cousin.'

"Master de Clement? I don't think he's out there; he came in on the longboat earlier. He was sent to fetch something, I don't know what."

She glanced around. There was no sign of Vilas. "Where? From here?"

"No'm, in the village, I reckon. Course, he might o' come back without me seeing him. I been busy."

"It's important," Christina insisted. "I didn't pass him on the way. Do you have any signals, between shore and the *Revenge*?"

Worthington scratched his head. "None as I know of. They'll be along soon, though. Their stomachs will send 'em in."

There was nothing to do but wait, and she'd better do it far enough away so that Worthington wouldn't feel compelled to talk to her. Even in her agitated state, she observed that he was admiring and eager for conversation.

"I'll walk back toward the village," she decided. "If I don't meet Vilas, I'll be back. Tell Master Wesley that I may need a ride out when the boat goes back to the ship, please."

Disappointment dimmed his smile. "Yer welcome to sit there, mistress, and wait."

"No, thank you. I need to find him as quickly as I can and return home," Christina told him.

She had not gone a dozen paces along the path into the trees when she saw Vilas coming. His limp was worse today; the leg must be paining him. But the impending crisis was more important.

"Ho, Chris!" he greeted her, and immediately sank onto a fallen tree trunk and stretched out the offending limb to rub at it ruefully. "I needed an excuse to rest this damned leg. Delivering food, are you?" There was a hopeful note in his voice. "Our regular cook was one of those we lost in that last engagement, and the new one's a rank amateur. I swear he can't water down the rum without ruining it."

"By all means, eat with Master Wesley and Master Fitz," she said impatiently. "There's plenty to go around. Vilas, I need to talk to you."

He winced at the pressure he'd put on his thigh. "What about?"

"Roxanne." She glanced around to make sure there was no one else within hearing distance. "She's planning to run away."

Startled, he forgot his aching leg. "Run away? To where, for God's sake?"

"Some boatman is taking her to Gloucester, to begin with. Heaven knows what she'll do from then on."

Vilas whistled. "Old Adam Hull may well set the law on her."

"I've told her that! She's seen people put into the stocks for the slightest offenses; what can she expect if she runs off and is brought back? I'm hoping you can talk some sense into her. I've tried, and *I* couldn't."

His curse was blasphemous. "And what makes you think I have any influence with the silly chit?"

He didn't seem to notice her suddenly heightened color. "The way she's been making over you of late, I thought perhaps she'd an interest in that direction."

His laughter was derisive. "She's an eye for anything in breeches, more like. And though no one's told me a thing, I suspect she seeks to arouse jealousy in Captain O'Neal. A waste of time, perhaps, but when have women ever been sensible about such things?"

A part of her rejoiced in what he said, but she returned to her purpose. "It's not only Roxanne I'm concerned about. I fear what will happen if she carries out this ill-considered plan to run away, if she's caught out at it. And I fear for Megan and myself, as well. Will we not be held at least partly to blame? Especially since we have foreknowledge of it?"

Vilas sighed. "You have a point. They'll want to know why you didn't stop her or, failing that, report to someone who could do so. When is this boatman setting sail?"

"Tomorrow morning, at dawn. I suppose she intends to sneak out of the house when the family's asleep, tonight."

Vilas swore again. "How did I come to be in the position of holding responsibility for her? I have no authority over her, Chris. She's never bowed to anyone, and seldom even bent— the earl carried her bodily away from that hovel she grew up in, after her mother died, and she kicked and screamed the entire way, so they say. Why should she listen to me now, if she's made up her mind to go?"

"I don't know." There was desperation in Christina's tone. "I only know that it will mean serious trouble, for us as well as for her, if she attempts it. I'm not happy here, either, but . . ."

"Aren't you, Chris?" He looked at her, truly looked at her, then, his scrutiny intense, and his hand came down on hers as it lay on the log between them. "I'm sorry to hear it. I'd hoped all was well with you. The Hulls seem decent folk, as these Puritans go...."

His touch sent heat radiating through her; her entire body tingled with it. Her breath came more quickly. "They are, no doubt, except for Patience. There is something about her that makes me strangely uneasy, and she despises Roxanne. If Roxanne is caught and brought back here for punishment, Patience will see that the punishment is severe. It wouldn't surprise me if—" she hesitated, then plunged on "—if Patience accuses her of witchcraft."

"Witchcraft! God's blood, the girl's half-gypsy and acts it, but she's no witch!"

"Of course not. Roxanne *is* headstrong, though, and she speaks and acts without thinking, or caring, what the consequences will be. She's written some poems and stories, and Mistress Patience found them. She was enraged, called them filthy, though I think they were simply imaginative—Roxanne's idea of romantic tales—and it seems she thinks Roxanne's drawing too much of her husband's attention...."

Vilas laughed, as if in spite of himself. "Perhaps because Master Wesley can't keep his eyes off her. As far as that goes, Master Wesley has an eye for *any* pretty female, though I've no reason to think he's done any more than look at them."

There was no humor in Christina at the moment. "There is something unnerving about the way Mistress Patience has been acting the past few days. She's up to something, quite apart from what *we* know Roxanne is planning, and with Master Adam gone she might well be plotting on her own, knowing he won't step in to stop her. I'm frightened, Vilas, and I don't know where else to turn except to you." She hesitated, then added before she lost her courage, "I wish you weren't sailing so soon. I feel so alone when you're gone."

He lifted his hand and grazed her chin with his knuckles in a gesture almost playful. "You're a strong person, Chris. There's a lot of the old earl in you, whether you know it or not."

Her eyes filled with tears. "Yet I'm not a man, and I have no authority. A female's voice counts for little in this world."

"Except to that certain man, when she finds him," Vilas comforted her. He rose abruptly, pulling her with him, then gave her a brotherly hug that did nothing to ease the turmoil within her. "When that time comes, you'll forget about the things that disturb you now. They'll fade into insignificance. Do you walk me to the boat I see coming with the Hulls for their midday meal, or were you on your way home?"

She couldn't speak further in front of Wesley and Fitz. "I'd best be getting back," she said thickly. "You...you will speak to Roxanne, won't you?"

"I'll try, but don't count on my changing her mind with anything less than an ax blow to the head. I've never seen a more stubborn wench."

Did he hear the tears in her voice, the tears she struggled not to shed? "I'll see you again before you sail, won't I?"

"Of course. Would Mistress Patience be generous enough to invite me to supper if I show up this evening when the others go home, do you think?"

"Yes, of course. I mean, she's little generosity, but I can't imagine her turning away any who came to the table. Thank you, Vilas."

She stood for a moment, watching him limp toward the shore, then turned back to the path. She hoped Roxanne would have done the chores she'd been assigned and that Mistress Patience would have gone to bed with another of her headaches by the time she reached home.

And she prayed that Vilas would be able to talk some sense into her aggravating half sister.

That hope lasted until she opened the door and stepped into the Hull kitchen half an hour later.

Chapter 57

SHAME, SCALDING AND HOT, washed over Megan as she stood naked before the encircling women. Having her clothes torn off was bad enough; the examination that followed left her humiliated and bruised in spirit as well as in fact.

Roxanne had fought, so that it took all six of her tormenters—Patience stood aside, taking no physical part in the assault—to subdue her. Megan had no heart for fighting a losing battle; she cowered, arms crossed over her breasts, shivering, resigned to whatever these dreadful women would do to her. It had come, what she had feared since childhood, and now there would be an end to it, once and for all.

Roxanne was anything but resigned. She gave as good as she got, landing blows, kicks, scratches and gouges. She could not hold out against six women, however, even though most of them were elderly. They had discovered a witch, and they were determined that she should not escape them.

Roxanne had been subjected to the same intimate examination of her body, and though she felt violated, she experienced no sense of shame. Rather, she was filled with overwhelming rage; she got in one solid blow with the handle of the broom before it was wrested from her grasp, leaving Patience gasping and with a red brand across her face.

"Damn you all to hell!" Roxanne shouted, and the circle of harpies shrank back from her slightly, though still offering her no escape.

"You see?" Patience asked through set teeth. "She calls upon her master to punish you, as God, through us, will surely punish *her* for her transgressions!"

"There be no devil's marks on this one," Goody Weaver said uncertainly.

"It doesn't matter. We've evidence enough against her," Patience stated.

"What we going to do with 'em, then?" Goody Wolfe speculated. "Turn 'em over to the magistrate?"

Patience licked her lips, unwilling to surrender their prisoners to one who would assuredly insist upon all the legalities of a trial, and that would mean carrying the matter over so that before any action was taken Adam and Ezra would have returned.

Before she came up with a satisfactory response, Goody Allen offered a solution. "In the Bible, didn't they stone witches to death?"

In the ensuing moments of silence, Megan heard her own ragged, sobbing breath and Roxanne's, harsh and rasping. Stoning. Dear God, and for what? Was this how the others had felt, when unjustly accused? How many of those thrown into prison or hanged had also been innocent?

"It would take a lot of stones," Patience said thoughtfully. "More than are to be readily found in the dooryard."

"We could gather some and return," Goody Wolfe suggested. "Only how do we keep them under control until then?"

"We can lock them in the shed," Patience said. "There's a bar on the inner door from this room, and we can nail the outer door shut."

There was a murmur of assent, and Patience stepped forward. "Guard them. I'll secure the outer door of the lean-to."

She turned and hesitated, startled to see the expression on her grandmother's face. Cordelia was white and shaking, having forgotten the child on her lap. Her dark eyes blazed, and she spoke in a hoarse croak. "'Tis a wicked thing you do, Patience. Take care lest God strike you dead."

For a matter of seconds Patience faltered. And then her resolve firmed. She had originally intended no harm to befall Megan, but she would rid herself of Roxanne one way or another, and no possible consequences could compare to the results if Roxanne were allowed to remain. "See to your own soul, old woman," she told Cordelia, "and I'll take my chances with mine."

They remained frozen in place, silent except for Megan's dreary crying, as Patience hammered a board into place against the lean-to door. "Now," she said, returning, "into the shed with you two."

Megan went without protest. Even so, one of the women shoved her as she stepped down at the threshold of the room where they kept firewood and, in winter, hanging fresh meat; she went sprawling and got up scarcely noting the abrasions on knees and forearms. They did not hurt as badly as she hurt inside, in her heart. She had a fleeting thought for Fitz—would he let them do this, if he knew?—and then she knelt in a corner, covering herself as best she could, surrendering to misery and defeat.

Roxanne fought every step of the way. She hurled invective and blasphemous curses at them as furiously as she kicked and bit and struck with her fists.

The old women by themselves could not have accomplished their purpose. Patience was forced to step in or see all that she'd gained suddenly lost. She grabbed for the nearest weapon and came up with the long-handled warming pan; she swung it with all her strength and took Roxanne alongside the head in a ringing blow.

Roxanne staggered and went to her knees, momentarily stunned.

It was at that moment that Christina opened the door.

SHE COULD NOT CREDIT HER SENSES. The room was in a shambles, with benches overturned, a broken cup on the floor, Cordelia clutching at a whimpering Emory and evidence that Patience had just knocked a naked Roxanne nearly senseless with the iron warming pan.

"God in heaven, what's happening?"

"Is this another o' 'em?" Goody Allen asked, panting. She was not used to such exertion, and somehow she had been injured; she felt as if her foot had been broken when the bench had fallen on it.

Roxanne drew in a gulp of air and found her tongue again. "These fools think we're witches! They plan to stone us to death!" She rocked forward, clutching her head, near to fainting from the pain of it.

Christina's horrified gaze went beyond Roxanne and found Megan also pathetically naked, crouching in the lean-to, her hands unable to fully cover the blemish she had always kept hidden.

"You're mad! Who does this thing, and why?"

"It's clear enough *that* one's marked by the devil," Patience said firmly. "And we've no doubts about this one, either. She's called down the devil to take us all, but you see that God's power is greater, for no thunderbolt strikes us. Are you one of them, too, Christina? If not, you will join us in seeing that we are rid of the witches."

Horror made her faint. "You cannot mean this. You are mistaken, terribly mistaken."

"There is no mistake," Patience said. She was so cold she might have been sculpted from ice. Quite unexpectedly, she put out a shod foot and planted it against Roxanne's backside, sending her forward on hands and knees into the shed, then slammed the door on Roxanne's screamed imprecations. She slid the bolt and faced Christina, bosom heaving with exertion and emotion.

"I will rid my household of this evil influence," she said, head held high. "Go," she directed the others, "and get your stones. We will not wait for the magistrates to go through their lengthy procedures. We will handle this ourselves."

Christina struggled to think, to find words to refute the woman. "It's a mistake; they are not witches! You cannot do this dreadful thing; you will be thrown in jail yourselves for taking the law into your own hands."

"I think not. We are respectable citizens. There is clearly the mark of the devil on one of them, and the other has left her devil's mark on *me*." Patience extended her arm, sleeve pushed up to reveal a set of bite marks just above her wrist. "Think you that any will condemn me when they see this? Look well, all of you, that you will remember and describe this!"

Christina stared at what was without question the mark of teeth in the pale skin, which had been bitten hard enough to draw a few drops of blood and would leave bruises to mark the place.

A murmur of fear ran through the encircling woman. "'Tis true! Just the way those girls in Salem described the way the witches bit them!"

After a moment Christina's mind began to function again. She stared more closely at the arm Patience still extended. "My sister could not have inflicted that wound," she said, and wished desperately that the bile that rose in her throat would subside.

Patience allowed her eyebrows to rise. "No? Why not, pray?"

Christina swallowed, fighting to control. "Because if she had, the marks would be on the other side of your arm."

Her antagonist's mouth flattened into an ugly line. "You speak nonsense. Everyone can see the marks, clearly made by teeth."

"Aye, but you made them yourself," Christina accused recklessly. "Look," she appealed to the others, "see this? If I bite myself," and she demonstrated, scarcely feeling the impression she made in her own flesh because she was so angry and so frightened. "You see? If *you* were to bite me—" and here she thrust her marked arm toward the nearest of the old women "—the marks would be on the outer part of my arm, not on the inside. There is no way another could bite in such a way as to leave bruises like the ones on Mistress Patience."

Goody Weaver leaned closer, squinting. "Aye, it does look that way...."

"Don't be a fool!" Patience snapped. "Are you so easily deceived by females already proven to be witches? Go, get your stones, so this business may be concluded before anyone else comes along!"

Muttering agreement, the women departed, leaving Christina feeling limp and sick and helpless. Would they stop her if she tried to run through the village for help? Vilas would not let this happen, nor would Wesley or Fitz, nor the authorities to be found among magistrates and clergy. She took a step toward the door, but Patience reached again for the warming pan, holding it as if it were an ax, ready to chop.

"Oh, no, you don't. You're one of them; no doubt you've known all along your sisters were witches. Unbar the door, and you can join them. Go on, do it!"

Christina cast a beseeching glance at Cordelia, who seemed paralyzed in her chair. "You know we aren't witches, mistress!"

Before Cordelia could reply Patience swung around, narrowly missing the old woman's head with the heavy metal box of the warming pan. "Keep still, or you'll find yourself among them! I will be rid of this evil; I won't have my children contaminated by it, nor my husband!"

The nausea was increasing, and her legs trembled. Christina feared she would collapse at any moment; how could she run so far for help?

Patience moved around her, maintaining a safe distance, and threw back the latch and then the door. "Go in there," she said, and prodded Christina with the pan.

Sick at heart as well as near to fainting, Christina joined her sisters and heard the bar slide into place behind her.

Chapter 58

FROM BEYOND THE DOOR that led to the kitchen, they heard Cordelia's protesting voice. "You cannot do this, girl! 'Tis a wicked thing, and you know it, or you'd not have done it when Master Adam is from home, and Master Ezra! They'd not allow it!"

Patience spoke coldly. "I am protecting my family and my home in the only way I know how. No one would listen or help, and so I must take measures of my own."

"That girl did not bite you," Cordelia said, voice quavering with emotion. "How can you feel that committing evil of your own will bring about justice?"

"I do what I must. I cannot live with witches in my house."

"Then turn them over to the magistrates for trial! There is no call for stoning them to death and having that terrible sin upon your soul!"

Patience had made up her mind long before the final act in the drama was to be played out on stage. "I do but protect my own, and I tell you, old woman, I will do it. Look to your own safety if you try to interfere in any way."

Cordelia sounded strangled. "I will not bear false witness against them, when Master Adam asks of me how this came about."

"What need is there of false witness? The witch convicts herself out of her own mouth, calling upon her devil master to take us all, as she commanded the walnut to come out of my son's throat, and it came!"

"She saved his life, and 'twas but words spoken in the stress of the moment!"

"And the mark, on the other one? You've heard the words often enough, spoken from the pulpit: 'Suffer not a witch to live.' Mind, old woman, if you do not wish to meet a similar fate, do nothing to free them or help them."

After those ominous words the kitchen fell silent except for the whimpering of the baby; within a few moments that, too, died away into silence.

Christina, fighting nausea and horror, finally drew herself together. There was only one small window in the lean-to, which admitted little in the way of light. A row of firewood was stacked along the outside wall, and in the dimness she could make out Megan seated on the ground, her arms around her naked drawn-up knees, her head bowed upon them.

After a moment Christina became aware that Roxanne was speaking, softly at first, then louder until the words were flung toward the kitchen door in a shout. "I curse you, Patience Hull, and call upon the powers of darkness to strike you blind and dumb! May you suffer the plagues of hell before you die, and may you die soon, and in agony! May your children die, as well...."

Megan, drawn out of her benumbed state, lifted her head in dismay. "No! For the love of God, don't curse the children, they're blameless—"

"So are we!" Roxanne snarled. She picked up a chunk of wood and hurled it at the locked door, followed by further blasphemous oaths.

"Don't," Christina begged. "It's bad enough already, don't make it worse! If they make us swear in court as to what you've said, don't make it impossible for us to speak the truth without convicting you!"

"Are you really...a witch? Like your mother?" Megan asked tremulously.

"I don't know." Roxanne sounded merely annoyed now that she spoke in a normal voice. "Some of the curses my mother cast came to pass, didn't they? So maybe she was a witch as well as a gypsy. Maybe I am, too. At any rate, Mistress Patience will have something to think about."

"She's thinking right now," Christina pointed out tiredly. "Of getting rid of us before someone with a grain of sense comes along to stop her. And you've made it worse because now even Mistress Cordelia will be forced to admit you threatened her. Vilas said he'd come home with the men, only that won't be for hours yet. Vilas wouldn't let them harm us."

Roxanne snorted. "What good is that to us? Those old harpies are out there picking up stones to throw at us, and you can be sure they'll return before the men do. We'll have to save ourselves."

"How?" Christina asked.

Megan's voice was a whimper in the dimness, her face a blurred, pale oval. "Do you think they'll give us back our clothes, before ... ?"

"We'll have to fight," Roxanne said, as if she hadn't heard. She seemed oblivious of her own nudity. "When they open the door to release us, we'll have to fight as if we were men, protecting our lives. Except for that bitch of a Patience, they're old women, and they're afraid of us. We'll have no more mercy on them than they intend to have with us."

"But where can we go? What can we do?" There was quiet desperation in Christina's question. "You two don't even have any clothes, and there's nowhere to run to! No one in this colony will give us shelter or protection from them, once they've had a chance to tell their tale! And you added to it, Roxanne, by your threats and curses! We wouldn't have a chance in court now if they bring us to trial! I told you that what you did would reflect on us, as well, and see how that prophecy has come true. They'd never have attacked Megan if it hadn't been for you...."

"Be still, and let me think," Roxanne told her, without apparent malice. She turned to put her mouth close to the door. "Mistress Cordelia, can you hear me?"

For a moment there was no sound, and then they heard shuffling footsteps and a wavering voice. "Aye, I hear you."

"Let us out," Roxanne commanded. "Mistress Patience will pay for this, but there's no need for you to suffer, also."

There was a hesitation, then she replied, "I cannot, Mistress Roxanne. It's worth my own life to interfere."

"It may be worth your own life if you don't," Roxanne countered.

Megan stirred. "If only she would get us some clothes!"

"Yes," Christina agreed, and put her own mouth near to the door. "Mistress Cordelia, you cannot allow my sisters to be sent out into the open without covering. At least gather up some garments for them to put on!"

Cordelia's distress was evident, as was her fear of her granddaughter. "I dare not open the door, mistress! Do not ask me!"

Christina looked up at the window above the stacked wood. "Then fetch something and put it through the window. It's too small to permit us to leave, but you could hand in clothes. Please, Mistress Cordelia! No decent human being would leave females in this present state! I'll break out the window, if it cannot be opened, and you can hand in garments and shoes!"

"If Patience intercepts me..."

"Be damned to Patience," Roxanne said, and Christina gritted her teeth, wanting to strike her.

"Please, Mistress Cordelia! Gowns, petticoats and shoes," Christina pleaded. "You know you will eventually have to face Master Adam, and he would not want them to be seen naked...."

When Roxanne would have spoken again, Christina pinched her, hard, on one hip. "For the love of God, be still, for once," she hissed, and miraculously, Roxanne obeyed.

Megan did not rise from her cowering position until the welcome garments were actually thrust past the shards of broken glass after Christina had hammered them out with a length of firewood.

Patience, of course, would have heard the glass breaking. Would she come to investigate, or would she stay upstairs with her baby until her coconspirators returned?

"She's a coward," Roxanne guessed. "She won't try to get near us alone."

"I hope she doesn't harm Mistress Cordelia." Megan shivered, hurrying into petticoats, stockings and shoes, then tugging the dress over her head. It was one of Christina's, and too big for her, but she was grateful for whatever old Cordelia had been able to find in her agitation.

Though nothing had changed, they felt better fully clothed. Roxanne began to test the doors, and even tried to see if she could escape through the window, which was clearly impossible. No one bigger than Nels could have passed through that opening.

Christina sat down on the lower level of the woodpile, wishing her own brain would send her some wondrous idea. All she felt was weariness and fear. Gradually she became aware of an odor, and at last leaped to her feet. "The bread! It's burning!"

"Let it burn," Roxanne said indifferently. "Let the entire house burn." Then she stopped pacing. "If only we could start a fire here!"

"And end up roasting ourselves?" Christina asked caustically. "Mistress Cordelia! Rescue the bread before it starts a fire!"

They heard a muffled exclamation, and then Patience, perhaps calling from the stairs. "What is that smell?"

"The bread," Cordelia told her. "I think it will have to be thrown out, 'tis charred so I doubt the birds will eat it."

From the ensuing sounds, they guessed that Patience came to help carry out the ruined bread. And then, through the broken-out window, they heard Patience say sharply, "Whatever are you doing home this time of day?"

The young voice was subdued. "Mistress Bellamy sent me. She said my coughing disrupted the recitations. I couldn't help it, Mother. I tried not to cough, really I did."

"Well, go and see to Emory. He's screaming again with his teething, and I must have time to go to the privy."

Immediately the sisters trapped in the lean-to moved as one to the locked door. It was Megan who spoke, quietly, so that she would not be heard by the woman outside. "Betta? Betta, can you hear me?"

"Mistress Megan? Where are you?" the child asked.

"In the shed. The bar must have fallen accidentally, locking me in. Slide it back, child, and let me out."

To their immense relief, Betta obeyed, and a moment later they emerged into the kitchen, which was hazy with smoke. "What . . . how did you get locked out there?" Betta wondered innocently.

Old Cordelia staggered toward them, waving aside the smoke. "Oh, dear, she'll blame me."

"No, she won't," Christina said. "Come, we'll put you both in there and lock the door, and no one can say you're to blame for anything."

She gave the old woman no chance to argue; neither was there time for more than minimal sympathy when the poor soul nearly fell going into the shed as Roxanne hurried her along.

Bewildered, Betta demanded as the door was closed in her face, "What is the matter? Why must we stay in here?"

No one wasted breath in explanations. "What are we going to do?" Megan asked.

Roxanne and Christina locked gazes, and for the first time in months they were in agreement. "Run," they said in unison.

Chapter 59

IN THE DISTANCE the baby's fretful wailing went on. Nearer at hand, the smoke from the burned bread eddied in the breeze from the open back door.

Roxanne took a step toward the room where their belongings were kept, but Christina stopped her with a sharp exclamation. "No, there's no time to gather anything, and we'll move faster if we have nothing to carry!"

"Where are we going?" Megan asked fearfully, darting a glance over her shoulder toward the lean-to, where Betta was plaintively begging for an explanation.

"She can't do anything against three of us," Roxanne pointed out. "I've some papers I want to take."

"More writings? Didn't you learn anything from the first ones she found?" Christina asked with asperity, moving to peer out the door. "Dear God, I think those horrible old women are coming back! Forget the papers, Roxanne, there's no time for *anything*!"

"You're right." Roxanne capitulated at once. "I think I heard the privy door slam, too. Let's go!"

She chose the opposite door from the one Patience would use, but what had always seemed dense woods beyond the house now appeared to have opened up, with plenty of visibility between the trunks of the trees. "Where . . . ?"

They ran, away from the road, where the witch-hunters and their stones presented the immediate danger. They heard Patience scream in rage inside the house behind them and plunged toward a stand of evergreens that offered more concealment than the elms or birches.

Megan, less used to regular exercise, was gasping by the time they reached a gulley that allowed them to drop down out of sight of the house. They followed along it, Roxanne leading, until abruptly she stopped.

They paused to listen. The only sounds were the rustle of leaves overhead and their own rapid breathing.

"Where are we going?" Megan asked again. "How can we hope to escape them?"

"We can outrun a bunch of old women," Roxanne said scornfully. She sucked at a long scratch on the back of one hand from a blackberry thorn. "If we can get down to the shore we may find a fisherman who'll get us away from here."

"Three of us?" Megan demanded, remembering the sizes of the boats used for fishing.

"Without telling anyone where he's taken us, once he learns why we've fled?" Christina added. "We'll be lucky if anyone even speaks to us, let alone helps us, if they know the circumstances. It's like dropping a hot coal into a straw stack to mention witches in this place. We can't rely on village fishermen to save us."

Roxanne frowned. "Who can we rely on, then?"

"Vilas and Captain O'Neal. They're neither of them Puritans, and they've no sympathy with the zealots. If we can reach them, we've at least a chance."

Roxanne's frown deepened to a scowl. Shea O'Neal was the last person she wanted to see; she put down the quickening of her pulses to the exertion of the past few minutes. Yet probably Christina was right; there was no reason to think either O'Neal or Vilas would surrender them to the authorities, should it come to that, which she sincerely hoped it wouldn't.

Patience was a craven sneak, and while she'd stop at nothing underhanded, she wouldn't want to call in the magistrates, knowing their stand on such matters. Or would she? Maybe she felt she had witnesses aplenty to back up her charges; maybe she would feel compelled to carry through, now, to protect herself. If charges were brought against three fleeing servants, and the situation was already in the hands of the authorities, not even Adam Hull would necessarily be able to intervene with any hope of success.

"All right," she said. "Only how do we get there? We can't use the road, nor the beach, without being seen."

"We'll have to stick to the woods as best we can and maybe wait until dark," Christina decided. "Or until we can intercept Vilas on his way home with Fitz and Wesley."

The important thing, they agreed, was to keep out of sight until they could reach Vilas or the *Revenge*. More slowly now, and very cautiously, they began to circle around and head for the shore.

THEY HAD TO CROSS THE ROAD at some point. When they emerged from the trees, the track stretched emptily in both directions. "Come on," Christina urged, and the other two moved quickly to follow her.

They had not yet lost themselves in the forest on the other side, however, when there was a shout behind them.

"There they are! Stop them, stop the witches!"

Christina glanced back and saw that the original group had evidently gathered new recruits. The two women pursuing them were younger and better able to run. Unfortunately the trees here were widely spaced, and there was no hiding place.

Roxanne, evaluating the precariousness of the situation, suddenly came to a stop. Facing them, while their opponents were outnumbered, might be wiser than continuing to run until the yells brought others to join them.

The young women stopped, too. One was an ignorant, slatternly servant called Mary Durning. Her companion, not yet twenty, was of dubious repute as well as homely, yet there was grim determination in Alice Fletcher's face.

"Ye can't get away," she stated, and threw the first stone.

It struck Megan squarely in the forehead. She cried out and stumbled backward, pressing both hands to the blood that poured out of the wound.

Mary Durning, drawing courage from her fellow attacker, hurled a second stone. It caught Christina on the shoulder and felt far larger than it was; she had a moment to contemplate what it would be like to be hit by hundreds of stones, until she died of her injuries, and then she was aware of Roxanne beside her, holding up her hands to stop their advance.

"Enough! The next of you to throw a stone will die, and that I promise you!" Roxanne said grimly. "You think us witches? Well, if you're right and we invoke the powers of the devil, where will that leave you? Think on it, very carefully, before you use another stone."

Mary Durning's mouth dropped open, and her companion swallowed convulsively, the stone in her upraised hand unthrown.

Deliberately and slowly, Roxanne took a step toward them.

The girls hesitated, and then Alice Fletcher, eyes nearly bugging out of her head, panicked and fled. Mary Durning was not far behind her, neither of them looking back.

Christina, rubbing the place where the stone had struck, breathing heavily, watched with mixed feelings. "Now you've as good as admitted you're a witch! If they catch us after this, we haven't a hope!"

"Did we have one before?" Roxanne demanded. "All the fun's been taking place in Salem Village, and there are some who want to share in it, here. They want blood, and blood they'll have. Megan, are you all right?"

Megan, her face and hands smeared crimson, had begun to laugh hysterically. "Oh, their faces! They believed we were witches, all right! Oh, dear God, what are we going to do?"

Christina snatched off her apron and began to try to clean off the blood. "Don't, Megan. Here, take this, and press it to the wound. I don't think it will bleed much more, it's already slowing." She looked around. "Where are we going to go? Those two will be back with a mob before long, and they mustn't find us here."

"As close to the shore as we can get," Roxanne said decisively. "Over that way."

Megan brought her hysteria under control, though she continued to tremble. "There is really no chance we'll escape, is there?"

Christina's eyes met Roxanne's, and they spoke simultaneously.

"We're certainly going to try."

"If we can reach the *Revenge* they'll save us."

Christina knew that Vilas would protect them if he could, and probably Captain O'Neal would do the same, but it might not be possible to stand against the powers of the entire Massachusetts Bay Colony authorities. Not only did the trio stand accused of being witches, they were runaway indentured servants. They owed Adam Hull more than two remaining years of service.

When they broke out of the woods on the shore, they were both relieved and increasingly cautious. It would not take genius mentality to figure out where they had been headed, even if those two girls had not seen them cross the road. The only avenues of escape were the trails that led overland toward Boston or Salem, and the boats that offered withdrawal by sea.

They kept within the fringe of trees, moving more slowly now, keeping a sharp eye out in every direction. They had been driven off a direct course by their pursuers, and they walked for twenty minutes before they rounded a slight projection of the coastline and saw the masts of the *Revenge*.

Christina's breast swelled with relief, for possible rescue was within grasp. Within seconds, however, her elation died.

On the beach between them and the longboat that waited to carry crew members back to the ship was a milling crowd of people. Their costumes were so similar, they looked like a dozen brown wrens flitting about, and it was difficult to see individuals from this distance. Her heart sank when she heard Roxanne say sharply, just above a whisper, "That one going down the bank is Goody Wolfe. They knew where we would come, and they got here before us."

The trio dropped flat, still concealed in the fringe of trees, to watch the activity below, and wondered how to proceed next.

IT WAS QUITE OBVIOUS that they could not approach the longboat nor any crew member in daylight. The witch-hunters might even set a guard come nightfall, and their numbers had increased since the original group had gathered in the Hull kitchen this morning.

This morning? Had it been only hours ago, rather than days? Christina wriggled into a more comfortable position and tried to ignore the rumbling of her empty stomach.

Apparently the sounds were audible to the others, as well, for Roxanne suddenly grinned at her. "I'd eat one of those burned loaves at the moment," she said. "We should have delayed long enough to find food to carry with us. Theft would be a small charge on top of what they already believe we're guilty of."

"There's Fitz," Megan said, gaze fixed on the men gathered at the longboat. There was such longing in her face that Christina's heart constricted in pity for her. If they could safely reach the *Revenge* and sail away from this place, Megan would never see Fitz again.

While she—Christina's heart thudded in her chest—would still be with Vilas, for a little while. As long as they were not at opposite ends of the world, there was at least a slight possibility that Vilas would awaken to what Christina had known for years.

"We're going to have to stay here until dark," Roxanne stated. "Then maybe we'll have a chance. By this time Vilas and Captain O'Neal know what's happened. They may be keeping a lookout for us."

It was, perhaps, a forlorn hope, but it was the best they had.

Chapter 60

INCREDIBLY, CHRISTINA DOZED. She woke to find the air gone chill, for the sun had descended in the western sky below the tops of the trees. Beside her, Megan also slept, head resting upon an outthrust arm. There had been no opportunity to wash, and there was caked blood between her slender fingers.

Blood.

Christina sat up, memory flooding through her. They were fugitives, and she had not eaten since morning. Her shoulder ached where she had been struck by the stone.

She turned her head and encountered Roxanne's level gaze, the green eyes so like her own, yet so different in the dark face.

Roxanne sat leaning against the trunk of a hickory tree, chewing on a long tough blade of coarse grass. "I wondered how much longer you could sleep in that position," she said, returning her attention to the beach.

"Are they still there?" Christina raised herself on an elbow, winced at a new bruise there, then rolled over and rose onto her knees to crouch beside her sister. "Oh, good heavens! There are more of them than before!"

"Gathering more of them all the time." Roxanne spoke dryly. "And," she added unnecessarily, "they've built a fire. My guess is that means they'll stay the night, to make sure we don't make it to the ship."

Despair eroded Christina's courage as if it were eaten away with acid. "What are we going to do?"

"Hope our faith in Vilas and Captain O'Neal isn't misplaced, I suppose. Now that you're awake, perhaps I'll try to sleep. I thought it best to keep guard, so no one crept up on us. We'll need to be rested when the time comes to act."

Christina smothered a pang of guilt, that she had left the guard duty to Roxanne instead of sharing it. She had simply never dreamed that, terrified as she was, she would be able to sleep. "I wish there was a way to get something to eat."

"If we get on board the *Revenge* tonight, we'll be fed." Roxanne's reply was philosophical as she stretched out flat, looking upward through the leaves. "If we don't, if that mob down there finds us, well, being hungry will be the least of our problems."

She closed her eyes, and Christina crawled forward to the place she had vacated, to stare bleakly down over the embankment.

There was indeed a fire, and the figures about it were more numerous than before. If she had hoped that the situation would have been quieted by the authorities, she might as well give up the notion, she thought bitterly. After Roxanne had as good as put a witch's curse on those two girls, everyone in the village undoubtedly considered the accusations against them to be valid.

Of course the clinching evidence had been Megan's birthmark, and Roxanne wasn't responsible for that. Christina sighed and tried to relax for what promised to be a considerable vigil.

She did not hear the intruder's approach until seconds before he appeared in the twilight, when a twig snapped under his foot.

She spun, rising, heart in her mouth, to face Fitzhugh Hull. So much for keeping watch.

Terror held the breath in her chest, until it became so painful she had to exhale. Behind her Roxanne and Megan slept; she saw his gaze drift to them, and perhaps he flinched when he saw Megan and the bloody gouge in her forehead, though she could not be certain of that.

"We are not witches," Christina said, with a mouth so dry it was a wonder he understood her. "We have done nothing wrong."

Roxanne sat bolt upright at the words, then sprang to her feet, awkward, still groggy from sleep, stumbling so that she put out a hand to the nearest tree trunk for balance. Megan, too, stirred, rolled over and stared up at Fitz with dismay.

"I thought I caught a glimpse of a white cap up here," Fitz said. "Hours ago. And then it disappeared. I had to wait until now to invesitgate. You'd be less visible if you removed the caps."

In unison the girls pulled off the caps that Cordelia had brought with the rest of their clothes. Christina began to hope. "Are you going to help us?"

Fitz's steady gaze lingered on Megan before returning to her. "I'll try. That mob is determined to rid the village of witches. They'll kill you if they can."

Roxanne's words cut in with the sharpness of a well-honed razor. "They've already tried, on several occasions, under the direction of your precious sister-in-law."

Fitz nodded. "The sanest heads, like my father, are away. We've already tried reason, and you can see how well we've succeeded. So we've worked out a plan."

"We?"

"Master de Clement and Captain O'Neal and my brother. Yes, even Wesley. He has guessed at his wife's part in this, and I assure you he has no wish to see anything happen to any of you. Wesley, Vilas and Worthington are busy with a project, assembling several 'bunks' to be taken aboard the *Revenge*. They've let it be known, subtly, we trust, that they intend to finish them and take them on the longboat on its last trip for the day. They've also arranged for additional supplies from the village to be delivered in the morning . . . to further the impression that the *Revenge* will still be here."

Christina's heart hammered now so that she pressed a hand over it as if to keep it from breaking through her chest wall. "What are we to do, then?"

"Remain here, for the time being." He handed over a bundle she had not previously noticed. "We thought you might be hungry. We didn't have much on hand, and I didn't dare fetch anything beyond what was left from our midday meal," he apologized.

Christina clutched the parcel, cheered by the very mention of Vilas and Captain O'Neal. "Thank you. We are hungry."

"We'll keep working, or appearing to work, on the so-called bunks to be fitted into the ship, until it is full dark. With any luck the fog will come in by then, too, to further obscure our activity. If it's miserable enough, perhaps most of those fools on the beach will go home, but there are bound to be at least a few who remain. They are determined you shall not escape.''

Megan, whose gaze had never left his face, slowly got to her feet. Her voice was so low that they could scarcely hear it over the distant sounds of the surf. ''Do we have any chance?''

''We think so. Captain O'Neal is willing to come in after the three of you with swords and muskets, if necessary, but that might mean killing people and being forever unable to return to the Massachusetts Bay Colony. It's been decided it will be better to do whatever can be done secretly. Therefore they sent me to tell you to remain hidden here until you see our signal. It will consist of an armload of brush dropped into the fire; it will send up a shower of sparks for just a few moments. When you see it,'' Fitz instructed, ''you'll have to circle around that way.''

He waved an arm, indicating the route they were to take. ''Be careful crossing the path, that there's no one about. You'll have to proceed slowly, for there is no smooth way from here. Approach the boat works from the other side. One of us will meet you, and you'll be loosely sealed inside the framed bunks—and one coffin we're taking aboard—and we'll attempt to get you into the longboat that way. It may be necessary to handle you rather roughly, stand you on end and so on; it won't do to make it look as if we have anything other than our usual woodworking projects on our minds.''

Roxanne fixed him with a hard stare. ''And if those harpies down there are suspicious? If they demand to inspect your coffin and bunks?''

Fitz shrugged. ''Then we'll change plans, obviously. De Clement will be armed, here on shore, and Captain O'Shea will be using the glass from the *Revenge*. He'll come in with muskets if he must.''

He started to turn away. ''Keep watch and start down when you see me carry the brush to the fire. Good luck.''

He was gone, melting into the trees in the twilight. Roxanne gazed after him with an uncertain expression. ''Can we trust him? Or is this some sort of trap?''

''Of course we can trust him.'' Megan was pale. She began to smile. ''If he were not sincere, he would simply have led some of them up here, after us. We're outnumbered and unarmed; we'd be an easy matter to capture if they surrounded us.

Chris, what has he brought us to eat? I'm so empty my stomach aches."

They ate the bread and cold beans with relish, and while there was not enough to fill them up, the food took the edge off their hunger. They settled in then to watch the dark figures moving about the fire below them, shivering as the cool fog began to drift in off the sea.

THEY COULD HEAR THE VOICES of those around the fire, but they encountered no one on the path as they crossed over it and into the woods on the far side. Moving cautiously was a necessity; they could not see where they stepped, and Megan turned an ankle before they'd gone a dozen yards.

"Can you walk on it?" Christina asked softly.

"Yes. I only hope I'm not called upon to run, though," Megan murmured.

Roxanne led the way, pausing frequently. It was easy to keep their general bearings because of the fire that glimmered between the tree trunks. There were still at least a dozen people standing watch there. All of them were women.

They were not reassured by that fact. These female Puritans had already demonstrated that they were more dangerous than the males and capable of considerable violence.

The trio came to the edge of the trees behind the boat works and halted. Christina heard the others breathing on either side of her, as if they had been running. Someone was wielding a hammer or some other noisy tool, intermittently pounding and shifting planks about on the sawhorses silhouetted against the second fire they had built to illuminate their work.

The woman's voice came unexpectedly, so nearby that they froze for an instant until they realized it was not they who were being addressed.

"You labor most industriously and past the hour when most would have returned home to supper."

"Aye," Wesley said, grumbling, "and it's hard to know whether I'm more weary or hungry. Captain O'Neal has always been a good customer, but to tell the truth, I care not if he contracts again for repairs with us. I did not expect to spend half my nights here, as well as my days, in order to satisfy him. Fitz, do you see where I put down the axe?"

Fitz's reply was too loud, Christina thought, to have been intended only for the woman who had wandered over from the fire. Was she suspicious or only bored at her vigil?

"I'll get it. You left it beside the sawbuck, over there, I think."

"O'Neal is only a privateer. What need does a Puritan have to cater to his demands?" the woman asked. They saw her now, and when she turned so that her profile was etched against the leaping flames, Christina recognized her with a sinking heart.

Mistress Cunningham was a respected matron, one who might have been expected to resist the hysteria generated by Patience Hull and old Goody Wolfe. She was probably smarter than they were, too, which suggested that she had not wandered over to the working men to make idle conversation.

"A man takes his coin where he can get it," Wesley told her, "and O'Neal pays promptly. Stand back, mistress, so that you're not struck by the chips as they fly."

The woman moved, though not far. "What is this you make, Master Hull?"

Rustling sounds nearer at hand brought the watchers to renewed attention, and Fitz's whisper issued from the deeper shadows. "We'll try to get rid of her. If we can't, there's no way we can seal you into the boxes. We may have to try a diversion of some sort. Be alert for it, and if it comes, run for the longboat. The crewmen there are ready to push off at a moment's notice."

He gave them no time to reply, and a moment later they saw him emerge into the firelight adjusting his breeches as if he'd been off in the darkness to relieve himself.

Megan's whisper was nearly inaudible. "If there's an alternative to being carried to the boat in a coffin, I'd prefer it," she said.

For an interminable period then, they waited in silence for the opportunity to act. Christina's heart leaped every time she caught a glimpse of Vilas, working out in the open between the two fires. He seemed to be mostly fetching and carrying for those who did the actual construction, and he never once glanced in the direction of the place where the girls stood in the deep shadows.

The fog thickened, bringing with it an unwelcome drop in the temperature. A few of the women gave up and went home; several were dragged off, protesting, by angry husbands. Yet enough remained, wrapping their shawls more tightly around themselves, to prevent open action unless the men were prepared to pit themselves in a physical struggle against the women.

Christina thought it was surely going to come to that. Her attention wavered, contemplating the next few hours. She would not feel safe until the *Revenge* had lifted anchor. She was taken off guard when the shouting started.

"Come, and hurry!" The command came without warning that anyone had crept so close to them. Her nerve ends screamed, but she was moving with the other two, following the figure who must, from its height, be Vilas.

Behind them, they heard Wesley's bellow of concern. "Good God, man, did you cut if off entirely? Quickly, something to bind it up before he bleeds to death! Mistress Cunningham, we've grave need of a petticoat, anything, to tie over it!"

Under cover of the confusion, they ran toward the longboat. Christina cast one glance toward the scene as she went over the side to life flat on the bottom. It would forever remain imprinted in her mind, though she did not know the full significance of it until she heard the story later.

As a diversion, it was a success. Fitz had brought a hewing hatchet down on his left thumb with a resulting fountain of blood that covered him and everyone else who got close to him.

The women ran to observe, if not to help. It was mostly left to Wesley to staunch the bleeding, which he did with much in the way of shouted expletives and demands upon the bystanders to produce strips of petticoats or whatever else they might provide.

Megan came over the side of the boat, falling atop her, quickly followed by Roxanne.

"Get down, stay flat," Vilas said tensely, and then they felt the longboat scraping the strand as it was hauled into the surf.

Suddenly they were afloat, and the only sound near at hand was the creak of the oarlocks and their own blood, pounding in their ears.

Chapter 61

MANY YEARS LATER, Megan would recall that night in detail. Standing at the rail of the *Revenge*, hearing the shouts that carried across the water, knowing that Fitz was injured, perhaps seriously.

"Bleedin' like a stuck pig, he is," one of the oarsmen had said with satisfaction as they pulled away from the shore. "Nothin' like blood to get 'em churned up, forget whatever else is going on."

Megan had started to lift her head to see over the side of the longboat, only to be pushed roughly downward by a large hand. "Keep down! They may not all be drawn to Fitz's blood, and the fog's not thick enough to ensure our safety yet!"

"How badly is he hurt? Did he do it on purpose?"

Vilas's response was terse. "It seemed the best way to draw their attention, to create a genuine emergency. Hopefully he didn't chop off his entire hand."

Numbed with horror, Megan had closed her eyes and prayed. Not for herself, but for Fitz.

WHEN AT LAST THEY WERE ALLOWED to sit up, the fires were no more than a ruddy pink glow through the swirling mists. They climbed the side of the privateer ship and were helped aboard. Shea O'Neal's swarthy, scarred face loomed over them, grinning broadly.

"I was beginning to think I'd have to come after you myself. Did you bring the rest of my repair sections as well as these unfortunate witches?"

"We had to leave those. If we're still here tomorrow, we can get the rest," Vilas told him, vaulting the rail behind Roxanne. "The temper ashore is high, however. My own recommendation would be to lift anchor with the tide and be away from this place. If they figure out where their victims have gone, I've no doubt they'll have the authorities after us.''

"Well, I suppose enough of the repairs have been effected so we won't come to disaster over what's left undone. I've not paid the Hulls for the work they've done, though. I don't suppose Wesley sent along his bill?''

Christina, stupefied with fatigue and the aftermath of fear, felt disconnected from the jesting between the men around them. It would have been fine with her if they'd set sail immediately.

Megan's voice was thin. "Is there any way of finding out how Master Fitz is?''

O'Neal rested a hand on her shoulder. "We'll have to make contact at least once before the wind fills our sails. I'd not leave Master Hull holding an empty purse on my account, not unless those voracious females come after us with their husbands' muskets. Ah, well, you've had a difficult day, and none too much to eat or drink, I'll wager. My men have turned the salon into quarters for you, and de Clement can take you there and see that you're fed.''

He walked off then, and Vilas took them in hand to direct them to the salon. It seemed eons since they had been there before, when they had been rescued after being stranded on the island off Boston Harbor.

Roxanne stared after O'Neal, her lips compressed in a flat line. He had given her no special words of welcome; indeed, from the way he acted he might never have seen her before. Damn his eyes, she thought, and followed Vilas to the salon.

MEGAN WOKE FEELING SUFFOCATED, panicky. The ship rose and fell gently, and she threw off the quilt that had entangled her, gasping.

Where was she? Why did she feel this overwhelming fear? And then she remembered. The perspiration drying on her skin chilled her, though the evening was not cold. She sat up, hearing subdued voices and the sound of the longboat bumping against the hull of the ship.

Had someone been to the shore? Would they have news of Fitz?

She groped for her dress and hastily pulled it on over the undergarments in which she slept. There was no light; she had to feel her way between the sleeping pallets toward the door onto the deck.

The voices were clearer now, and the men were coming over the side. Someone swore, and others laughed. There were other sounds, and after a moment Megan decided they were lifting the longboat. That meant there would be no more shore excursions before they weighed anchor.

Anguish, deep and bittersweet, swept through her with almost physical pain. Wherever they went now, they would surely never return here. She would never see Fitz again. But at least these men should know how serious an injury he had deliberately inflicted upon himself to allow her and her sisters to escape.

"You can bunk next to me," Vilas's voice said, only yards away. "Harris's hammock is still vacant."

And then, so stunning that she felt dizzy, Megan heard another voice that sent a thrill of hope and relief through her.

"I'm much obliged. I don't suppose you've a tot of rum at hand, to dull the throbbing of this cursed thumb?"

Vilas chuckled. "You did a bloody good job of it, I take it."

"If producing a flood of blood was what it took, yes," Fitz muttered. "I thought it might all run out upon the shore before we got it stopped. I hadn't thought to cut it quite so convincingly."

Megan spoke without thinking. "Fitz? Is that you?"

There was a heartbeat's worth of silence, and then his dark bulk materialized beside her, more sensed than seen. "Megan?"

"I'll get the rum and come back," Vilas offered with rare diplomacy, though they had already forgotten him. They stood close together in the damp, foggy darkness for long seconds as the sounds of his footfalls diminished along the deck.

"Are you all right?" Megan's voice was tight with strain.

"It hurts like the very devil at the moment," Fitz admitted. "I didn't take the thumb entirely off, only enough to keep me from working for a bit. How are you?"

She swallowed hard. "We're safe, I think, though I've no idea what's going to happen to us. Where we're going to go. We owe you great thanks for coming to our rescue." It seemed inadequate after what he had done on their behalf.

She suddenly made the connection between his presence and the fact that the longboat was even now being hoisted on its davits into the place where it would be carried during the voyage.

"You...how are you getting back to shore?" Her heart was racing, even before he reached out and took her hand in his good one.

"I'm not," Fitz said, and drew her toward him. "I'm going with you, wherever that turns out to be."

Megan stood stiffly, unable to respond to the pressure of his arms as they came around her. "But you know about me, know that anyone who sees the mark will think as Mistress Patience does, that I am a witch...."

His words were ragged with emotion. "Patience is a fool, though no bigger a one than I've been. I never for a moment thought you were a witch, but I was idiot enough to consider what others might think if they knew your secret. I saw your suffering and shared it, yet I could not quite take the necessary steps to ease it. Not until I knew that you were a fugitive from those horrible women— Megan, you haven't stopped loving me, have you? It isn't too late for us?"

The joy that flooded through her wiped out everything else. She did not even hear Vilas when he returned, nor the men, who had operated the davits, as they passed by on their way to their hammocks for what was left of the night.

She clung to Fitz, melded her body with his, fused warm lips to warm lips, and even, finally and after a considerable time, thought to thank God for His blessings.

CHRISTINA OPENED HER EYES and gazed upward at an unfamiliar ceiling. The motion of the deck on which she slept was such that she would have known they were no longer at anchor even if she hadn't heard the creak of rigging and sail.

They were safe away from Massachusetts Bay Colony, and she was on board the *Revenge*, with Vilas not far distant on the same vessel. She lay quietly, letting happiness seep through her, and vowed that if Vilas did not speak up to her before this voyage ended, she would somehow find the courage to speak out to him. And then, as she came more widely awake, an uneasiness formed in her midsection and crept upward.

She was never seasick, she thought distractedly. Not since those first stormy days when they were just out of England.

Yet sick she was, and she'd best find a basin or slop jar, and quickly. She crawled past Roxanne's sleeping figure, saw Megan curled on her side as she had done in childhood, a smile on her face, and staggered around her, barely making it to the rail in time.

"GOOD MORNING, Mistress Roxanne! A night's sleep seems to have restored your beauty!"

Roxanne swiveled to face Shea O'Neal, willing herself to remain coolly distant, to ignore the inner tumult his presence excited. "We owe you thanks, Captain, for providing us refuge."

He was grinning, impudent, mocking, the same man who had both strongly attracted and repelled her for months now. "I would have rescued any females under such circumstances, fair or not."

There was a strong breeze, which caught her dark hair and set it billowing about her face. Her green eyes were sober. "Where do we sail?"

O'Neal shrugged. "North. I trust you have no specific destination in mind that must be reached."

Roxanne turned away, leaning against the rail to look at the shore that seemed to be moving slowly beside them, seeing no signs of habitation, only rocky outcroppings and thick forests. "Anywhere away from the witch-hunters will suit. Except that I know not what will happen to us when we finally go ashore."

His grin softened, fading. "Since we will not put you ashore until it is safe to do so, I urge you not to worry unduly until then. Of course, if we encounter and engage enemy ships, there may be some danger. At any such sign, you will go below decks and stay there until any hazard is past, of course. Do you speak any French?"

"French? No. Christina does, and Megan." She snorted. "They would have included me in the lessons, but that was one area where I successfully resisted Himself's efforts to make a lady of me. It was bad enough to have to suffer through the rest of the lessons, reading and improving my speech. French is a strange and difficult tongue.''

''Aye, yet oddly melodious, and very handy to know if you get into French territory.''

''And is that where we go? Into French territory?'' Uneasiness rippled through her. It was unnerving to think of being landed in a place where she could not understand what the natives said, nor they her.

O'Neal waved a hand, and the small gesture, insignificant though it was, sent a stabbing memory through her: his hands caressing her naked flesh, his mouth seeking hers in the darkness. Roxanne looked down into the water that rushed past the bow, unwilling to have him read in her face what she felt.

''There are a few English settlements above this point, but beyond are mostly those of the French. Some of them are repeatedly taken back and forth between them, like some child's toy in dispute.''

''Why?'' Inadvertently she had glanced around at him again, and felt her stomach muscles tighten. Why couldn't the scars have made him ugly? Why did she remember so much she'd be better off forgetting? How long would it persist, this maddening desire to be swept into his arms and kissed senseless?

His black eyebrows rose. ''Why? Why what?''

''Why are the settlements in dispute? This New World is so huge it would swallow up England or France a thousand times, a million times. Surely there is land enough for all.''

''Ah, true. But some of it is so choice that everyone wants it. The fishing off Nova Scotia and Cape Breton is said to be fantastic, perhaps the richest in the entire world. It is very valuable, that fish. They dry it and ship it back to Europe, exchanging it for everything else they need, and the Englsih would like a share of it even if they have to fight for it. And there are the furs, in demand everywhere. Men are greedy. They want whatever is to be had, and many are willing to take what is not freely given to them.''

''Including you,'' Roxanne observed, maintaining at least an aloof exterior. She could do little about the cauldron that boiled within.

He threw back his head in a laugh that made her gut twist ever tighter. "Ah, you are right! Even me! I want my share, and perhaps a bit more! Of all the good things in life. A ship's deck under my feet, the wind in my sails and the companionship of good men to share my tankard of rum. What more could a man ask? Except..."

"Except?" Roxanne echoed, and then could have bitten her tongue for playing into his hands.

His smile was lazy, intimate. "Except for a good woman," he completed his list.

It was all she could do to feign indifference. "Ah, yes. Well, *good* women are hard to find, are they not? Excuse me, Captain, if that steward is bearing hot water for morning tea, I'm more than ready for it."

His hand shot out to grasp her wrist before she could move away. "The tea will surely wait. We have something to settle between us, mistress."

Could he detect the rapidity of her pulse under his fingers? He would not use her again, she thought angrily. He stood here, balancing so easily with the motion of the ship, confident, in control. But he did not own *her*, and she would not yield to him again unless the yielding was on her own terms.

"I cannot imagine what settling you speak of," she told him, and flushed when he laughed again.

"Oh, you can imagine," he contradicted. "Your imagination is excellent, or so I've been told. You wrote some poems, or some such, which contributed to your being thought a witch. I am only sorry that I did not have the opportunity to read them."

She stared directly into his eyes then, her own challenging him. "Am I to take it that you extract a price, Captain, for rescuing us from the witch-hunters? Let us be blunt, then, if that is what you wish. Anyone may be seduced once, misled, betrayed. Only a fool allows it to happen repeatedly."

He seemed genuinely astonished. "Seduced? Misled and betrayed? By God's blood, woman, it appeared to me that the attraction between us was mutual, that you came to me willingly enough! I pride myself on being a considerate lover, and your response was everything that a man could ask for."

She jerked free, surprised that he let her go without resistance. "I was innocent, ignorant and a fool. I'm a little wiser now, I think." The staccato pulses belied that claim. "And while I hold not to Puritan standards of behavior, I find that I do have standards of my own. I'll be no pirate's mistress, to be discarded when it pleases him. Excuse me, sir, I really do want that tea."

She spun, and he did not stop her. She walked briskly away from him toward the salon, her spine straight and stiff.

Not until she was inside, out of range of his perceptive eye, did she allow the scalding tears to slip down her cheeks, oblivious of everything but the ache in her heart.

Chapter 62

THE REVENGE SAILED NORTH AND EAST, along the coastline of Nova Scotia, driven by strong winds under mostly fair skies.

Captain O'Neal and his crew were exuberant now that their days of inactivity and boredom on shore were ended; they looked forward with eagerness to whatever the next adventure would be, around the next point of land or wherever it overtook them.

Megan floated in an euphoric haze. Fitz's hand healed, and he had no duties to perform, except for finishing up as many of the remaining repairs that could be done with the materials it had been possible to bring on board the ship.

He was a tender and considerate suitor. Shame over his own earlier cowardice might have continued to burn within him, but Megan freely forgave him everything. She had only to look at the scar where he had nearly severed a thumb to be convinced of his sincerity now and to wonder if she would have had the courage to bring down that ax upon her own flesh had their position been reversed.

"We'll be married," Fitz promised, "as soon as we find one of those Frenchie priests with the authority to do it."

In the meantime they spent nearly every waking hour together, walking the deck arm in arm or huddled out of the wind in sunny nooks, where they never seemed to run out of things to say to each other.

For her sisters it was both a joy and a torture to watch Megan with Fitz.

A joy because they genuinely wished her well and approved of Fitz. A torture because their hearts were heavy regarding their own futures.

Roxanne was determined that O'Neal would not use, then abandon, her again. There was no denying the surge of emotion when she encountered him on deck or watched him climb the rigging or even sat across from him at mealtime. She had memorized his features and saw them when she closed her eyes: the saturnine face that could be either fierce or gentle, sardonic or gleeful, and the strong, lithe body that moved so confidently either on deck or aloft.

When he was engrossed in matters pertaining to the ship, he scarcely seemed aware of Roxanne's presence. At other times, however, he treated her with gallant consideration. Of course he behaved in much the same way toward Megan and Christina, which was a source of little satisfaction to Roxanne.

There were subtle differences, of course. He would look up and find her glance upon him and flash that grin that had the power to turn her insides to jelly. And there were moments when his words, spoken in private, were not subtle in the slightest.

As when he said to her, their third day out from Ipswich, "If you tire of your improvised quarters with your sisters, milady, I'll be happy to share mine with you."

Roxanne looked him straight in the eye and said flatly, "Go to hell, Captain." But when he walked away laughing, she had to grip the rail to steady herself as the hot, sweet longing swept over her, intermingled with a rage that did not quite overcome the anguish.

She had been introduced to the delights of love; even knowing that all the love had been on her side, with only lust on his, did not change that. She needed a man, Roxanne admitted, and if it couldn't be Shea O'Neal, then eventually it would have to be someone else.

Deliberately she took stock of the men available among the crew.

Vilas was far and away the most attractive of the lot. He was the cleanest and best educated of them. He was also, of course, the focus of Christina's longings, though as far as Roxanne could see, he was unaware of it.

Oh, he talked to Chris all the time, about things like the ship and how the sails were rigged and what he knew about the New World, either from observation or hearsay. In Roxanne's mind Vilas was fair game. So was any other man aboard, except Fitz Hull.

Once, when she'd been carrying on a meaningless flirtation with the crewman called Spiker, she intercepted O'Neal's amused glance. Damn the man anyway. Far from making him jealous, she only caused him to laugh at her.

Well, she thought angrily, when they dropped anchor along some distant stretch of coast where those foreigners lived, she'd look for a real man there. From what Vilas related of them, the Frenchmen were strong and independent and passionate. No doubt there would be one who would make her forget Shea O'Neal, and there was a shortage of women in this part of the world. In the meantime she would practice on Vilas, since Christina seemed simpleminded in that regard.

She did not talk to Christina, of course, and Christina therefore had no idea that the flirtation was, in fact, innocent. She saw only that Vilas often stopped to talk to Roxanne, that they laughed together and that Roxanne took advantage of every opportunity to touch him.

If Vilas did not make overtures in return, he certainly made no effort to avoid Roxanne. He seemed amused by her, and was perhaps flattered.

He undoubtedly believed, Christina reflected darkly, that it was Roxanne who had nursed him through his struggle with infection and loss of blood. And while she wanted, with something approaching desperation, to set him straight on that score, she could not do it.

It did not ease Christina's unhappiness to any appreciable degree that Vilas talked to her as well as to Roxanne. He was busy much of the time, since he was now O'Neal's second in command. When the days were uneventful, though, he had a reasonable amount of free time. When he encountered Christina standing in the bow, red-gold hair streaming in the wind, he would pause beside her.

Once she shivered, looking at the land they passed. "It's beautiful, but so desolate. There are no people."

"There are settlements on the lee side of the peninsula," Vilas informed her. "There's Port Royal, on the Bay of Fundy. Now *that* is a sight worth seeing, where 'tis said the tides are highest of anywhere in the world. At the mouth of Chignecto Bay they can rise over fifty feet and drop that much when the tide goes out. I'd like to see it again one day, but it's in the heart of French territory, and they're not hospitable to English ships.''

Christina, gaze still fixed on the evergreens that lined the shore, shivered. "It frightens me, all those miles of emptiness. If we were to be shipwrecked, we might never see another human being until the day we died."

Vilas shrugged. "True. But there's plenty of game, and these are some of the richest fishing waters ever known, and there's an endless supply of timber for building houses and boats. There are worse places a man might be marooned."

She lifted her eyes to meet his. "It wouldn't bother you, to be shipwrecked here?"

"I'd prefer not being shipwrecked anywhere, but the idea isn't one that frightens me, no. I was a green boy when I left England a year ago. I've learned a great deal since. About life and living, and about myself. I'm man enough now, I think, to take life as it comes and twist it to my own advantage."

How she wished she could say the same, Christina thought with a trace of bitterness. She had dreamed so hopefully of being reunited with Vilas in the New World, of having him fall in love with her, and it hadn't happened. She had little reason to believe it would ever happen.

The seasickness continued to plague her from time to time, though mostly it was no more than queasiness. She was glad it hadn't sent her to the railing again; she could imagine the ridicule *that* would subject her to, among the crew and her sisters.

She watched Roxanne and wished, even while deploring the other girl's tactics, that she had Roxanne's brazen courage.

The air grew perceptibly colder as they reached Cape Breton Island and changed course to a more northerly one and then rounded the cape and sailed northeast toward the Gaspé.

Off the Iles de la Madeleine they encountered a French merchant ship, floundering sluggishly in gray seas. The *Revenge* heaved to, and O'Neal shouted across the water in French. Though Christina knew only the textbook version of the language, taught by a tutor who had traveled upon the continent, she understood the gist of what was said.

O'Neal asked the name of the captain—St. Cyr—his cargo—dried cod—and his destination—France.

"Except, captain, that we seem unlikely to get there. We've damaged our hull on a reef, and we're taking on water at an alarming rate."

The ships were very close, so that it was possible for Christina to see the French captain's face, pale above his dark beard.

Vilas stood beside O'Neal. "Will we take her cargo, Captain?"

"We'd have to return to Massachusetts to transfer it to an English ship," O'Neal mused. "On the other hand, we might be able to sell it on the Gaspé, to another Frenchie." He raised his voice to carry across the expanse of open water. "In the name of William and Mary, sir, we claim your cargo!"

St. Cyr shrugged, spreading his hands in a gesture of submission. "It is of no use to us, Captain, if our ship carries it to the bottom. Would you consider taking my crew aboard and setting them ashore at some safe place where they can fend for themselves?"

"Why not?" O'Neal shouted over his shoulder to his own men. "Prepare to aid the French crew in transferring their cargo to the *Revenge*!"

It was a tedious task, taking the remainder of the day to accomplish, and even then there remained casks of dried cod in the hold of the French vessel. O'Neal elected not to remain after darkness had fallen to complete the removal. The other ship had continued to take on water, and lay dangerously low in the sea; the risks of further work were greater than the potential rewards.

With the French crew aboard, the *Revenge* was overcrowded. It was no longer possible to give over the salon to the use of three females; they were shifted into O'Neal's cabin, so that the larger number of men could be accommodated in the salon, and they sailed on toward the mouth of the great St. Lawrence.

"Wait until you see it," Vilas told Christina, enthused. "It's like no river in England. Not muddy, but clean and cold, and so wide where it enters the gulf that you cannot see across it."

She couldn't help noticing the light in his eyes as he spoke. "You've only seen this land once, and yet you sound as if it's your homeland."

"Do I?" Vilas considered for a moment, then nodded. "You're right. There's something about it that draws me, as to a homecoming. It is, no doubt, bleak and lonely to some eyes. Yet it has a beauty of its own, like none other I've ever seen. And the people who have settled here are hardy and courageous; Frenchies or not, they're a people I admire."

Christina's gaze drifted beyond him, to where Roxanne was the center of an enchanted circle of the French sailors. Even with the handicap of speaking different languages, there was communication between them, in their gestures, their laughter, the spate of clearly admiring words.

Why, then, she wondered, was it so impossible for her to reach Vilas? To make him understand how much she cared for him? To inspire him to return her love? Especially when she knew there was no one else?

It was midafternoon when a shout from the crow's nest brought everyone on deck in anticipation.

The weather had turned colder, as the wind blew down from the north carrying the hint of snow. The sky and the sea alike were a sullen gray, and O'Neal had for several hours kept a close eye on the weather, ordering the sail adjusted as the winds grew stronger.

"Percé Rock ahead, off the port bow!" the sailor sang out, and all attention turned in that direction.

The rock Vilas had told her about was clearly visible without a glass a short time later. Christina stood with her sisters and Fitz at the bow, straining to make out details of this monolithic monument that signaled their approach to the place known as the Gaspé.

The rock loomed darkly over the pewter sea, and she shivered, for it seemed to her ominous and forbidding. It might from a distance have been taken for a gigantic ship, rising at the "prow" nearest the mainland to three hundred feet above the water, and was nearly a third of a mile in length.

And then an amazing thing happened. Through some gap in the clouds overhead an opening appeared, and the sunlight broke through, falling directly upon the great rock.

As if a drab and heavy curtain had suddenly fallen away, the rock was revealed in the brilliant orangey-gold of the sunlight, and Christina drew in her breath in wonder.

The rock was not drab at all, but a rusty red, with green and soft gray, the whole of it lighted as it it were an incredibly huge jewel. As the *Revenge* drew nearer she saw that the rock supported life: thousands and thousands of seabirds dipped and soared and screamed in raucous voices above and around it.

Quite suddenly, Christina felt her fears fall away. She had not understood the attraction this land held for Vilas. Now she was captured by the wild beauty of the rock and guessed that what lay beyond might also draw her, as Boston Town had done before the horror of the witch-hunters had spoiled it for her.

"Didn't I tell you?" Vilas materialized beside her, grinning, and rested a hand on her shoulder. "We'll be putting in at the Baie de Gaspé to unload these Frenchies and see if we can make a deal on the fish they've so generously provided us, and you'll see the rock from the other side. It's different from each direction, but impressive from all. I'm glad you're here to see it, Chris. I imagined showing it to you, when I first saw it."

She swallowed, acutely aware of the weight of his hand, the warmth that emanated from the muscular body so close to her own. Someone pushed forward in order to see better, and he was thrown against her and put an arm around her waist to keep her from losing her balance at the impact.

Her mouth was dry. "Did you think of me, a little, while you were far away, then?"

He was gazing at the rock, growing so near now that she could make out the hole worn through it by the seawater and the birds nesting on its ledges and in its crevices. "I thought of you when I saw things like this, places I thought you'd enjoy, too. Remember how you squealed with delight when you were about eight and I brought you the baby rabbit I'd found on the moor? I've never seen a baby rabbit since then that I haven't remembered your face that day and how you cried when it died because we couldn't find a way to feed it properly. You always had such a tender heart; it was easy to break it."

She stood frozen, pressed against him, wanting to scream out words that refused to be said. If he knew she had a tender heart, why didn't he understand how important *he* was to her? Why did *he* keep breaking her heart?

He dropped his arm and moved away. "I'd better get moving. There'll be work to do."

Long after he had gone, when the ship had left the great Percé Rock behind, she stood at the rail, watching it. The setting sun, now peeking below the clouds that grew even darker overhead, gilded the rock-ship in first gold, then orange and finally a rosy red, until finally it was lost in the mist that crept over it.

It was only when gusting winds carrying the first spattering of rain struck her face that she realized everyone else had gone, that she was alone. She hoped that when she joined the others, they would take the moisture on her cheeks for rain.

Chapter 63

THE STORM STRUCK in all its fury just before dusk. Sea and sky turned to slate, and the downpour was such that it seemed to scour the skin from any face exposed to it. The mountains and the shoreline disappeared from view, and the world shrank to encompass only the *Revenge*, bobbing as aimlessly as a cork on the threatening sea.

The ship's cook gave up trying to prepare a hot meal in his galley after the pitching of the ship sent boiling soup over the edge of the kettle. Cursing and favoring his burned hand, he cut bread and cold meat to put out for those who had time to eat.

The crew took in sail and kept a sharp watch for dangerous reefs. Darkness soon overtook them, and they could then only trust to Providence that they would not be driven onto the rocky shores.

The girls ate in Captain O'Neal's cabin, sitting on the floor to avoid being thrown there. A lantern, swinging from a hook over their heads, threw shadows first one way, then another, and several times when the ship heeled over they suspended their chewing until the *Revenge* was able to right herself.

Roxanne, who was more troubled at being quartered here than she would have allowed anyone to know, was the first to finish eating and stand up, only to grab at once for the end of the bunk to keep from being sent sprawling.

"I, for one, will be glad to make land, even if it's only amongst the Frenchies and the savages who don't know a word of English between them," she said crossly. And then she went on, "Damnation! Of all the miserable times to need clean rags, when I've none at hand!"

"What's the matter?" Christina asked absently, her mind on that wind that howled over and around them, dreading the cracking sound of a splitting mast.

"My monthly show has begun, and I've nothing to staunch it with," Roxanne said crossly. She opened the trunk secured to the deck at one side of the cabin and began to paw through its contents. "Ah, I wonder how the captain would like to donate one of his shirts to the cause! If you ask me, I'd say it's a worse curse than anything we could have cast as witches."

Christina, who had started to rise, felt a sickness begin within her that caused her to break out in a cold sweat.

How long had it been since her own monthly show of blood?

Too long, she thought. Much too long.

Not seasickness.

Pregnancy.

A wave of nausea swept over her now, so that she swallowed hard. She reached out for something solid to enable her to get to her feet. Megan was helping Roxanne tear the shirt into suitable strips to be useful, neither of them paying any attention to Christina.

She felt blind and dumb and terrified.

It had never occurred to her that a few brief moments of love, the first she'd ever experienced, could entrap her this way. Now she had no doubts. Only her own stupidity and her absorption in the events that had driven them out of Ipswich could have kept her from realizing the truth earlier.

She was carrying Vilas's child, and if she'd guessed correctly he didn't even know it was she he'd made love to.

The irony of it, the bitter, terrible irony!

She jerked open the door of the cabin, and before either of her sisters could voice a protest, she had burst out onto the deck.

She had momentarily forgotten the storm. She welcomed its frenzy as the icy wind whipped her hair about her face and nearly tore the garments from her body. She was soaked to the skin almost at once, and she could not tell if the icy spray came from the sea or the sky.

"Chris! What the hell are you doing out in this?" Vilas caught her in a violent parody of embrace, drawing her away from the rail before she could be blown overboard. He could only have identified her in the moments the door was opened into the lighted cabin, for it was black as pitch on deck.

"I'm sick," she said, and tried to draw away from him.

"Then use the slop jar, you shouldn't be out here! You can't keep your footing in this sea, and the wind alone is enough to scalp you!" He drew her backward through the nearest door, the one that opened into the salon. The French sailors were there, bracing themselves against the bulkheads or trying to sleep in their rocking hammocks. They looked at the intruders, not speaking. They had no English whatever among the lot of them.

"I hadn't thought you susceptible to seasickness," Vilas said, drawing the door closed to shut them inside, "but I'll admit I've seldom seen a worse storm than this."

"I'm not seasick," Christina said, feeling half-frozen yet as if she were running a fever all at the same time. The words came of their own volition. "I'm with child."

For a moment Vilas stood frozen, still gripping her shoulder with one powerful hand. He moistened his lips then, and something shifted in his eyes, something she was too ashamed to face.

"Let me go," she said, looking away.

He was having none of that, however. His hold tightened. "You don't think to throw yourself overboard, do you?"

She had not in fact thought of anything except the humiliation ahead and the impossibility of providing for an infant when she could not even provide for herself. She could not return to Massachusetts, nor to England, and it was highly probable that the French would not welcome her, either. Yet she fastened on the suggestion with at least a surface show of acceptance.

"It would solve a lot of problems," she said scathingly.

He took her seriously, his fingers biting painfully into her flesh through the wet fabric of her gown. "Chris, don't be a fool. There are other solutions...."

"Oh?" She looked at him then, and her words were caustic. "And what might they be, pray?"

"You could marry me," Vilas said, "and no one would ever know the child was not yours and mine."

The shock sent her reeling, or perhaps the ship rolled; she never knew which, only that she would have fallen had he not held her up, pinned against the bulkhead.

"Marry you?" She echoed the words and felt her mind splintering and hysteria rising in her throat. For years, ever since she was a child, she had dreamed of this moment, or rather of a romantic moment when Vilas would ask her to be his wife. And now he had, and under such circumstances that she could not accept!

Not without love, she thought in a searing moment of grief. To marry Vilas, when he did not love her and she loved him so desperately, would be worse than losing him altogether, for in the end how could he not come to hate her?

"I don't know who took advantage of you," Vilas said in a low, angry tone, "and I'd run him through if the opportunity arose. But we've been friends since childhood, and I won't abandon you in this kind of trouble any more than I would have left you to the mercies of those witch-hunting females in Ipswich! I'll confess to being somewhat put out that you didn't tell me instead of contemplating doing something stupid."

Christina was speechless.

The anguish that had consumed her moments earlier was dissolving, overcome by wrath so intense that she saw spots before her eyes.

The cry that issued from her throat sounded more like a wounded animal than a human female. "I wish you would run the culprit through, and with a dull sword!" she managed at last, pulling free of his grasp. "You-swine, *the child is yours*, and I wouldn't marry such an insensitive clod if I were otherwise to be given over to be hanged with the witches!"

Choking, the nausea again rising in an inexorable tide there would be no stopping, she plunged past him, jerked open the door, and half-fell onto the deck.

She had a brief glimpse of his face, jaw gone slack in disbelief, before she ran into darkness.

"Chris!" She heard the footsteps behind her, pounding even over the crashing of the storm, and did not pause. "Chris, for the love of God, stop!"

Perhaps he thought she was about to fling herself over the rail, instead of merely lose her last meal. She clung tightly to the rail, bracing herself as best she could, and let it come up, then sank to her knees in exhaustion, outrage and tears.

"Chris! Where are you? Damn it, answer me!"

She had no intention of replying—what was there to say?—
and even wondered, just before the impact came, how she could
have had the misfortune to have fallen in love with such an imbecile as Vilas.

There was no warning before the *Revenge* hit the rocks.

The jolt sent a terrible shudder through the vessel. The ship
screamed like a woman in labor as its hull was rendered into
kindling. The deck tilted beneath her, the rail was torn from her
hands and Christina was thrown, screaming, into the black sea.

She felt the icy water close over her head and struggled upward, gasping, crying out wordlessly. When she came to the
surface, something struck her a numbing blow on the shoulder, and only instinct made her grasp hold of whatever came to
hand, to hold herself afloat.

She could not swim, nor could most of the crew. In a land
where swimming for the fun of it was a forbidden activity, most
were drowned under such circumstances.

Christina knew, suddenly and without question, that she did
not want to drown. She was being dragged down by her ham-
pering skirts, heavy and wet, and there was debris all around
her. She clutched out, cut her hand on some unseen object and
then experienced the miracle.

Her feet touched something solid.

"Chris! Where are you, Chris?" It was Vilas—alive, she
registered that through shock and cold—his words carried away
on the wind. She had no breath to reply.

Was she on solid land or only on a sandbar or a rock? She
battled her way through the darkness, deciding that she was
close to shore. Of course, now she could hear and feel the surf
all around her, strong enough so that if she'd had to move
against the wind, in the opposite direction, she could not have
done it.

Behind and around her there were cries and more sounds of
splintering wood, loud enough to be heard clearly above the
wind and the surf.

The *Revenge* was dying, disintegrating as the waves forced
the shattered bow onto the rocky shore.

Christina staggered onward and encountered solid flesh.
"Help me," Megan said, and Chris felt for her hand and pulled
her along.

"Are you hurt?"

"I don't think so. Where's Fitz? Dear God—and Roxanne. She was right beside me..."

Lanterns appeared on the shore, bobbing through the drenching downpour and voices called out in French. And then one, miraculously, spoke in English.

"Here's a survivor, got his head caved in, but he ain't dead yet. Give me a hand, drag him ashore."

Head caved in? Christina stumbled, went to her knees, and discovered that her chin barely touched the water until a wave caught her from behind and knocked her flat. She lost Megan's hand momentarily and then the younger girl found her, dragging her to her feet.

Where was Vilas? He had been on deck when the ship struck; he must have been thrown into the sea, too. "Vilas?"

There was a loud grown. "Over here. Something's pinning my bad leg. I can't get free."

"Here, mate, we'll get you out, don't you worry." One of the lanterns was lifted to show both Vilas, with a heavy timber pinning him in the surf, and the face of the man who spoke English.

He was of middle years, well fed, darkly bearded, and there were gaps in his teeth. He handed the lantern to Christina with a grin. "Females, yet! Imagine that! Hold this, dearie, so we can see what we're doing! Here ye go, blokes, one, two, three, *heave*!"

Vilas swore and groaned again when the timber was lifted off him; someone else cursed when a new wave of water shifted the timber and knocked down its second victim.

The Englishman seemed to be in charge, at least he issued orders right and left, though since no one replied in anything but French it was unclear how much each understood of the other's language.

The lantern was taken from Christina's hand, and someone jabbering French urged her toward the bank. She was too stunned to take it all in. Vilas and Megan survived, and where were the others?

She tried to resist being steered toward the stationary lights that were visible through the curtain of water, for there were others to be rescued. Her own rescuer was insistent. He would see that she was taken inside where it was warm and safe, and then he would return, he told her. "Do not worry. We will save all we can," he said.

The house was high above the sea, reached by a narrow and treacherous path; without a lantern they'd have broken their necks, she thought, looking back to where men scurried about like ants crawling over an apple core.

Their destination was a welcoming one. The cabin was sturdily built of logs, with a roaring fire in a stone fireplace and colorful rag rugs on the floors. The woman who met them was young and eager to help, and there were two shy little boys who peeked around at them from behind her skirts. The woman spoke English in a heavy French accent.

"Come to the fire, and I will bring you dry garments to put on," she offered. "Are there many more of you?"

"God only knows," Christina muttered. There was a purple welt across one of her hands. "Was it your husband who brought us up here? We're very grateful."

"My husband is the one who speaks English," the young woman affirmed, smiling. "Do you have families, on your wrecked ship?"

"My betrothed and two sisters," Megan told her. "There was our own crew and that of a French ship that was sinking when we came upon her. Many men. I pray none were lost."

Their hostess made clucking sounds, gesturing for them to sit before the hearth and peel off their clothes to be exchanged for some of her own that she had brought out the moment she realized there were females among the shipwrecked. "The storms are bad this time of year. There are many wrecks, though most of them take place in Chaleur Bay, to the south. There are those who take it for the mouth of the St. Lawrence, only to find that it is not the river at all, and they are blown ashore there in less wind than this storm tonight. Please, take off your wet gown, *mademoiselle*, before you catch the death," she addressed Megan, who was hesitating.

One of the children loosed a string of incomprehensible French, and his mother smiled apologetically. "Excuse me, if I leave you to your own devices. I will be back shortly, *mademoiselles*."

She vanished into the other room of the cabin, and Christina hurriedly assisted Megan to make the change, anxious lest the woman return too soon and catch sight of the birthmark. They did not know how these people looked upon such things.

It seemed hours before they learned what was happening on the beach below the house. They had been fed hot soup by that time and had learned that they were in a small village, in the home of the Englishman, Amos Beardsley, who had also arrived in these parts by way of a shipwreck some years before.

"I found him on the shore," his wife said cheerfully, "more dead than alive. I brought my brothers to carry him to our cabin, and there I nursed him back to health. After that," she paused, her teeth flashing in her dark face, "he had little choice but to marry me, no?"

The word struck Christina's heart with the force of a hammer on an anvil. Marry. Vilas, thinking she carried some other man's child, had offered to rescue her from a lifetime of shame by offering to marry her.

"The men, they come!" Mistress Beardsley exclaimed, and ran to open the door to them.

The crewmen of both ships had obviously been taken elsewhere. With Amos Beardsley, a giant of a man, were only Vilas and Fitz, and Captain O'Neal, carrying Roxanne.

Christina and Megan sprang up, newly alarmed, but when O'Neal lowered Roxanne onto the rug before the fire, she stirred, moaning.

"Get her warmed up, Antoinette, and something hot into her. She was in the water too long, clinging to a broken spar, and she was unable to walk. Nothing seems to be broken, so it's most likely the cold that's done her in. First, my new friends," their host addressed the other men, "a bit of cognac to warm your innards, and if they like the ladies can sip at real English tea while my wife prepares a meal."

There were no protests to that idea. Megan held up a quilt to shield Roxanne from view, while the other two women stripped her and rubbed her skin to a rosy glow with a coarse towel and helped her into simple garments before she was wrapped in the quilt to sit close to the fire, teeth still chattering.

"For that one, I think, cognac rather than tea," Beardsley decreed. His wife held the glass and exclaimed encouragingly when Roxanne choked on it.

"I've seen my share of shipwrecks in these parts," Beardsley stated with satisfaction, pouring more cognac the moment his own glass was empty. "But never ladies washed ashore! 'Tis a true pleasure, I assure you!" He looked at them speculatively, raising his glass as if in a toast. "There is only one thing more to be desired by a man than a virtuous lady and that is a lady without virtue, no?" He laughed uproariously at his own joke, while his wife cast him a reproving glance.

Fitz, his hair plastered to his skull and dripping onto Mistress Beardsley's rug, seemed oblivious of anyone other than Megan. They began to murmur softly together, until their hostess protested their embrace.

"You are so wet, monsieur! And I have no more dry gowns for your—how do you say?—betrothed. My husband's garments will be ill-fitting, but perhaps dry breeches and a shirt?"

For a few minutes the room was full of talk and movement, as each of them was given the opportunity to retire to the adjoining room to change clothes, to the accompaniment of much hilarity from the little boys upon seeing the other men in their father's garments.

Christina pretended to be busy adjusting the quilt around Roxanne's shoulders when they emerged into the main room. She could not meet Vilas's eyes; she felt scalded, simply knowing he was looking at her.

He wasn't satisfied with that, however. His hand closed around her wrist with a purposefulness that convinced her he would not settle for less than he sought, and at once. "She's all right, leave her alone. She just needs to soak up the heat, and have some soup. Come over here in the corner and talk to me, Chris."

There was no escaping him. None of the others would rescue her from him. She allowed herself to be led aside and put into a chair at one end of the table, while Vilas chose one close enough by to prevent her rising. Even before he spoke, low and with intensity, she felt the heat rising into her face.

"Now, what do you mean, the child is mine? To the best of my knowledge, I've never touched you."

She gulped, furious both with him and with herself. "You were having chills, and you begged for more covers. There weren't any."

In the silence their host laughed at another of his own jokes, and the others joined in less robustly. Vilas spoke very softly.

"And you...came into bed with me? To get me warm?"

"That's all I came for!" Christina snapped. "But I fell asleep, and when I woke..." She strangled, unable to say the words. She prayed the others could not see, in this darkened corner, that her face looked as if she'd been out in a blistering sun.

"And I," he said, as if the memory only now was fully returning, "took advantage of you, not realizing."

"You said," the words came with an effort, "that you had...been wanting...it...for a long time."

"I had been on a long voyage, had touched no woman in months."

"I thought you meant...me," she said, and was unable to conceal her tears. "And then you said...you didn't think I'd still be a...a virgin, and I realized, finally, that you didn't even know that *I* was the one you'd made love to."

Her final words were so low that if he hadn't leaned toward her, he would never have made them out.

"I wasn't sure, at first, that it hadn't been a dream," Vilas told her. "I...had such dreams. And when Roxanne was there in the morning, well, it was the kind of thing I could picture *her* doing. You never said anything, gave me no sign."

She suddenly looked into his face, her own twisted with the effort of controlling the emotion rushing through her. "How could I? What could I say? It meant so much to me, and you didn't even...remember!"

She had said too much, blurted out more than she'd intended. She wanted to crawl under the table, wished she'd drowned in that black night sea, wished she'd never ever heard of Vilas de Clement.

Vilas lifted a hand as if to touch her, then withdrew it. "You have a...mole, or something."

It was impossible to become any more embarrassed or miserable. The mere lack of denial confirmed what he had said. She huddled in the chair, wondering how much more she'd have to endure before this was over. And then she remembered the new life inside her and knew that it would never be over.

"I should have known," Vilas murmured. "That it was you, and not Roxanne. I'm sorry I didn't. I meant what I said earlier, Chris. I'll marry you."

The resentment that had subsided rose once more in a suffocating wave; she blinked back the threatening tears and spat the words at him with venomous emphasis. "I don't want to marry you!"

Would it have made a difference if she'd been able to voice the rest of her thoughts? If she'd added, *The only reason I want you to marry me is because you love me*?

She could not reveal what was in her heart; the words stuck painfully in her throat and Vilas did not speak, either, the phrase that would have made all things possible.

Chapter 64

ROXANNE'S MEMORIES of that fateful night were always to be confused. The beautiful ship had shuddered along its entire length when it hit the rocks, the lantern had swung so violently that it flew off the hook and the cabin was plunged into darkness.

The *Revenge* rolled, and this time there would be no righting her; Roxanne slid onto a bulkhead that had been transformed into a deck, striking her head so that for an undetermined period of time she was unaware of her surroundings.

She would dimly recall hearing Megan's voice calling her name, and then Fitz's; there were cries for help and shouted orders and then . . . nothing.

She had no memory of how she came to be in the water. She was there, freezing, clinging to a broken length of mast, entangled in what was left of the rigging, choking on the water that washed over her.

She heard a sailor cry, "Here she is, Captain! Mistress Roxanne!" and then her cramped fingers were pried off the floating spar. Strong arms carried her ashore through surf that knocked her rescuer down several times. She heard Shea O'Neal's voice and recognized that the muscular arms were his.

She was so cold and exhausted that she had no strength to help herself when she was carried into the cabin on the hill. She sat passively while other people rubbed her down and wrapped her warmly, taking whatever they held to her mouth, grateful for the warmth that issued from the huge stone fireplace.

Gradually she came out of the near-stupor as the chill seeped out of her. Christina was there, and Megan, and Vilas. She turned her head and saw Fitz, and the large man called Amos Beardsley.

And, of course, Shea O'Neal.

Safe, she thought, as if she viewed them from a great distance. All of them safe. That was not true of the crew, she knew, for that was another of the misty memories. Tomorrow she would weep for their losses; tonight she wanted only to sleep.

Her head folded forward on her knees, and she let the blackness envelop her once more.

THEY HAD BEDDED DOWN on the cabin floor, wherever there was space. Roxanne woke slowly, feeling bruised and sore, aware of voices around the table on the far side of the room.

"I remembered, after I'd gone to bed last night," Shea O'Neal was saying, "why your name seemed familiar. Amos Beardsley. Black Amos, of the frigate *Prudence*. A curious name for a pirate vessel, sir."

Their host had a laugh that rattled windows. "Ah, my reputation survives, after these many years! Well, 'tis true, I was known as Black Amos in those days. The *Prudence* was a bonny ship, that she was. Went down the same as yours and almost in the same place, in a storm much like the one last night. Most of my crew was lost; the ones that were saved had no desire to return to Boston to face the law, after having helped ourselves to some English ships as well as Dutch, French and Spanish ones. They settled here, married and are raising families. And I, well, without a ship, I'd no desire to leave, either. Not after I met my Antoinette."

He cast an affectionate gaze on his wife, who was carrying a heaped platter to the table. "She saved my life and insisted I owed it to her to marry her." Mirth bubbled out of his massive body. "I managed to float a chest ashore with me, with some of the profits of the past years. Don't matter to these Frenchies if the coin is Spanish or English; it spends the same. I hope you won't mind, Captain. I have my men scouring the beaches this morning for what can be salvaged from your ship. Spoils of the sea, you know. Finders, keepers."

"The *Revenge* was a fine ship," O'Neal said, sighing. "And, unfortunately, I didn't have a shilling in my pockets, let alone manage to rescue a treasure chest. I suppose it's a forlorn hope that we might discover it amidst the wreckage. How long would it take you, Master Fitz, to build me another ship?"

"I'm a builder of boats, not ships," Fitz replied, helping himself from the mound of fried fish and thick slabs of bread. "And without experienced help, having to train someone as I went along, it would take some doing. Eventually, I suppose, I could build a ship. I went over the *Revenge* pretty thoroughly while we made the repairs, admiring the workmanship that went into her."

"The first thing we'll have to do, seems to me," Vilas put in, following Fitz's example, "is to build some cabins, before winter sets in in earnest."

Black Amos waved a plump hand. "Take your choice of sites, and there's timber for the cutting. Rock for the chimney. Will you be marrying your young ladies, when Father Paquet returns in a week or two? My wife is hoping for a wedding celebration or two, and the villagers always enjoy an excuse for drinking and feasting."

In her rolled-up blanket Roxanne tensed. The question had fallen into a small silence. Then Fitz said, "Yes, Megan and I wish to be wed as soon as possible. It will be awkward until then, since obviously we can't impose on your hospitality for long. . . ."

Neither Vilas nor O'Neal said anything, and after a moment Black Amos laughed. "Ah, we have no resident priest, you understand. Sometimes it's a month or two between his visits, and in winter perhaps longer than that. Winter on the Gaspé is no time, my friends, to be without a woman to warm your bed! The good fathers are realistic men. They understand these things. No one will censure those who share a bed a month or two before the actual wedding. God is a reasonable being, no?"

Was He? Roxanne wondered, closing her eyes and wishing they would eat and get out, so that she could get up. Clearly they were stranded in this godforsaken place; luckily there was one man and his wife who spoke a language she could understand. How did you go about learning enough about a foreigner to know if you wanted to marry him, when you couldn't understand what he said?

THE DAY AFTER THE STORM was bright and clear, almost warm, though the changing colors of the leaves gave promise of winter soon to come.

The men who were left—half the crew of the *Revenge* and nearly that many of the French crew had perished, and their bodies would continue to wash ashore for days—wasted no time in self-pity or dreaming of returning to what some considered civilization. There would be no leaving this place before spring, if ever, and shelter must be provided before the arctic winds and the snows made building more difficult.

Fortunately game was plentiful, and fish, and the local people provided muskets and shot. There would be trading aplenty once the newcomers were established, and there seemed no hesitancy to accept them in spite of their being English and the crew of a privateer. Inhabitants were needed in this New World, and pirates, privateers and ordinary colonists were all valuable.

Putting up a cabin was quickly done with many hands joining in the work, even when those hands were inexperienced. The first dwelling was very small, intended for the three sisters, and the girls were put to work scavenging on the beaches.

"The *Revenge* was right on the shore when she broke up," O'Neal pointed out. "That should mean there are pots and utensils, bedding and supplies. Black Amos's men are going to be hauling in casks and crates, but they won't get it all. The surf is down today, so wade out in it and pick up anything that sank close to shore, so you'll have something to set up housekeeping with. And for the love of God, keep your eyes open for my sea chest."

The wind was cold, and the water was colder. They grew accustomed to numbed feet and legs as they retrieved various odds and ends that would be useful. They also recovered several of the drowned sailors, who would be buried on the hillside, and each time were reminded of how near they themselves had come to a similar fate.

There was little time for brooding. Megan, of course, was ecstatically happy. Soon the priest would come, and she and Fitz would be married. It mattered to them not in the slightest that they would begin their lives together with nothing. There was no boat builder in the village; Fitz was welcomed, and goods were provided in expectation of his future services.

Roxanne and Christina were eager to see their cabin completed, bare though it might be. Even Roxanne turned her hand toward sewing, for they were without garments. Vilas and O'Neal helped with the heavy work, then departed for the woods after meat and furs, and there was also firewood to be cut and hauled to see them through the coming season.

Though Antoinette was a gracious hostess, it was a relief to be able to move into the sweet-smelling cabin, where they had privacy and felt they were ready to begin their new lives.

The problem was, in what direction would those lives go?

Christina vacilated between a longing to seek Vilas out and tell him she would marry him and an aversion to tying him to a lifelong commitment that he must eventually come to resent. The thought of having him hate her, especially if he found someone among the French women whom he came to love, was intolerable.

Vilas brought fresh meat every day or two. Boys from the village brought fish, and Antoinette showed them how to prepare skins so that they could be made into moccasins and warm garments.

Vilas worked as hard as anyone and took a major share of the responsibility for their provisioning. He did not linger, however, though it seemed to Christina that when he was present he watched her in a different way than he had before, as if he were both puzzled and sobered by her attitude. He would have been even more baffled if he'd been aware of how often she cried herself to sleep.

Roxanne had, at least on the surface, regained her good humor. She would make the best of this life, which in many ways appealed to her more than life among the Puritans. These Catholics were always crossing themselves and calling upon God for the simplest things, from catching fish to deliverance from a shrewish wife, but they were realistic about their pleasures. They played cards, they danced, they sang. And when, as they freely admitted happened, they sinned, they had only to confess to a priest to be forgiven.

There were no stocks, no compulsory church attendance—though apparently everyone went to services when the priest was there to officiate—and no restrictions as to clothes, according to their status in society; the women dressed as finely as their husbands could provide for, except for the widows, who invariably wore black.

To be a widow, one must become a wife. And life on the Gaspé was going to be difficult, Roxanne foresaw, without a husband. She therefore set her mind to finding one.

There were plenty of men eager to oblige her. They would have obliged Christina, too, if she hadn't been so withdrawn. Females were at a premium in this land where they were so outnumbered, and beautiful females were in even shorter supply.

It mattered little to the local men that Roxanne did not speak their language. "It is easy," they told her in the English words they had sought out from a cooperative Antoinette. "Me," thumping a broad chest, "Jean-Baptiste Denys. Trapper." Or "Basil Duperre, the fisherman." At first she had trouble keeping track of them, there were so many.

There were also the crewmen from both the French ship and the *Revenge*. Any one of them would have been happy to take a wife, and the English crew were especially appreciative of a woman who spoke their own language, though it was not a major factor.

"What takes place between a man and a woman in bed," as Black Amos cheerfully pointed out, "has no need of spoken language."

Regardless of that, Roxanne began to pick up a few words. From Antoinette, from the men. Especially when she discovered that the Beardsleys were the owners of several books, some in English but mostly in French, she was motivated to learn to read the language she had always held in contempt.

She reveled in her new freedom. Though there was plenty of work to do, there was free time, too, to write poetry. She composed it in her head as she went about her tasks, then painstakingly wrote it out on the sheets of birchbark that provided the closest thing there was to paper.

Christina, watching, felt both disgust and envy. Roxanne was blatantly flirtatious in a way that Christina had no desire to be, for Roxanne seemed not to care on whom she bestowed her smiles and coquettish words. Yet there was envy because this came so easily to Roxanne. The men flocked around her like bears drawn to a bee tree.

Christina was too conscious of the growing child within her to feel flirtatious, and she could not in good conscience marry anyone without telling him of her condition. How long would it be before it became evident to everyone, whether she told or not? And what would she say when that time came?

The morning sickness had passed. She felt fine, except for the inner hurt that would not go away. The ache was there constantly, and she wondered if it would ever go away, for as long as she lived.

Chapter 65

IT WAS DECIDED that having raised the last of the cabins, so that no one was without shelter for the coming winter—a few tiny white flakes had already given warning of it—was excuse enough for a celebration.

"Music and dancing and plenty of good French cognac flowing," Black Amos said genially, "and no doubt there'll be more than the three couples already lined up to be wed when the good father returns." He winked broadly. "Nothing like the heat of the moment, after a night of frivolity and a head filled with the fumes of brandy, to remind a man that he's going home to a cold bed, eh? The hardest cases tend to soften under those circumstances."

Roxanne, overhearing, thought wryly that there were some hard cases, all right. So far she hadn't decided that any of those who were willing suited her purpose. Any man was eager to pinch a pretty bottom or carry a willing female into a haystack for a rough-and-tumble. Only marriage ought to consist of more than that, she thought. Perhaps she could enjoy sleeping with any one of several suitors, but what about the hours not spent making love? If she didn't care passionately about the man himself, for how long would she be willing to cook his meals, scrub his clothes and endure his conversation about fishing and hunting?

She went to the dance with no expectations except to have a good time. Music, lively, stirring the blood like good wine, made her giddy. Why the Puritans should have banned it she couldn't imagine.

She had a dozen partners in the first hour. She was led onto the rough wooden floor—the Beardsleys' house, the largest in the village, had been cleared for dancing—by Black Amos himself and then went whirling from one man to another. They grew progressively louder and wilder as the cognac flowed.

The attention was not limited to the new females in their midst; the young women among the villagers were intrigued by the unattached Englishmen, also. Vilas, tall, blond and handsome in a different way from their own men, drew many a feminine eye, though they were puzzled by the way he spent so much time providing for the English miss with the red-gold hair, when she seemed indifferent to him.

Shea O'Neal was another who drew many sidelong glances. He danced with a few of them, setting their hearts to fluttering and their mothers to murmuring hopefully. For the most part, however, he stood on the sidelines, never without a glass in his hand, watching everyone else.

He was, Roxanne suddenly realized toward the end of the evening, watching her rather more than anyone else.

The knowledge lent her recklessness. When her current partner, whose name she could not recall, proposed for the second time in the past half hour, she laughed gaily and made a great pretense of having a marvelous time, even as she told him it was much too soon to know how she felt about him.

"But what is there to know, *mademoiselle*, except what a woman feels for a man? There is no time to waste. The priest comes soon, and then the ice and snow, and there may be no priest again for months!"

Conscious of O'Neal's scrutiny from across the room, she became ever more animated. "So be it, then, monsieur! I am not yet ready to marry!"

She did not see the privateer captain leave his post against the wall, was startled when he stepped in to swing her away from the Frenchman in a way that suggested a protest would be hazardous as well as useless.

He didn't dance more than a few steps, however, before he maneuvered her through the doorway into the darkened bedroom. There was a murmuring of French words beyond them as some other couple took advantage of the comparative privacy; O'Neal ignored them.

"'Tis a dangerous game you play," he said, his words harsh.

"Game? What game? It's a dance, isn't it? A celebration. We're gathered to have fun."

"Take care the fun doesn't turn about and destroy you. This is a small community, and they expect you to take a husband, to conform to their ways. Don't alienate them by inappropriate behavior."

Indignant, Roxanne pulled back from him. "When I need your advice, Captain, I'll ask for it. What I do is my own affair, and if I choose to take a husband, I will. If not, I won't."

"And how will you live, a female alone? Right now de Clement is providing for Christina, and therefore for you, as well, but what happens when they marry?"

"Marry? Chris and Vilas? I've not heard that that's in the wind. Besides, the Widow Lizotte lives alone, I'm told, and she's little older than I. I'm sure she'd be willing to advise me, so that I shan't need a man to do it."

She did not at first understand the cold amusement she saw in his face.

"The Widow Lizotte? Oh, aye, she lives in her own house, but she's scarcely alone, at least not at night. She exchanges her favors for things that send half the village to the good Father Paquet for lengthy confessions whenever he appears. I doubt that her advice would enable you to plan a future any decent woman would contemplate."

When understanding finally broke through, she blushed hotly at her own naïveté. She did not doubt that what he said was true; in fact she was instantly convinced that he knew whereof he spoke from personal experience, and she was furious at her own reaction to the revelation.

"Oh. Well, I will not marry a man who does not appeal to me, whether it pleases the Frenchies or not. And I fail to see how it is any business of yours!"

"I'm making it my business. This is no country for a man to live alone, and these French women are all much tied to their church. I've no desire to dwell with a female who's forever crossing herself and going to confession to reveal my shortcomings as well as her own." His words slowed, becoming a drawl. "I've in mind to have me a countrywoman, whose passions will match mine and who's bright enough to talk to a man of more than cooking and babes."

The hot retort that had been forming died on her lips. Roxanne stared at him, the beginning of strange sensations creeping out from her stomach to her extremities.

Was he proposing?

"My cabin is large enough for two, to begin with," he said, and from the humor now crinkling at the corners of his eyes, she knew he had read her face correctly. "And you heard what Black Amos said, about living together before the priest can say the words over us that make it legal. There's nothing to keep us waiting until he shows up."

He *was* proposing. Roxanne drew in a tremulous breath. "I've no intention of moving in with you before it's legal," she said inadequately.

O'Neal threw back his head, laughing so immoderately that the couple on the Beardsley's bed ceased their murmurings.

"All right. Just come over and see it then and tell me what else you have need of, before the priest arrives."

She would have liked to remain aloof. She would have liked to tell him she would have none of him, but that would have been for spite only, not the truth. The truth was, her blood was racing and she couldn't wait to be alone with him. She retained enough sanity, however, to resist a little longer.

"It seems to me that something remains to be said between us before we talk of marriage," she told him, and waited.

For a matter of seconds his eyes were blank where the lamp-light struck them through the open doorway. Now it was he who moistened his lips, and for the first time ever she saw him display uncertainty.

"You speak of love, milady? A declaration of love?"

"It's not unusual, when a couple become betrothed." Did he hear her heart? Could he see the pulsing at the base of her throat?

"I swore once, some years ago, that I would never use those words again, with any other woman," O'Neal told her, and though she could smell the brandy, she knew beyond doubt that he was as cold sober as he'd been the night he waded out of the icy surf onto the Gaspé shore.

"She's dead?" Roxanne remembered Vilas's story.

"Aye, she's dead these four years past. But I swore."

Tied forever, to a man who was honor bound not to say he loved her? Roxanne searched his face, and all at once he was more than a romantic figure, a handsome privateer and adventurer, a seducer of innocence. He was a man who had suffered, who was lonely, who needed her, and not only to warm his bed on the cold northern nights.

"There are other words for love," Roxanne told him. "I wrote a poem the other day, about adoration."

"Adoration?" For a moment he frowned, and then the lines eased from his face and his mouth softened. "Adore. Yes, that might do, might it not? Or maybe, as the French say it, *je t'aime*."

Roxanne began to laugh. "Maybe I'll learn their damned language after all!"

His mouth stopped her words, and she forgot whatever else she might have intended to say.

CHRISTINA HAD NOT GONE to the dance. Though common sense told her that if she would not marry Vilas, she should get acquainted with the other men, she could not bring herself to join the festivities. As scarce as women were, there might be a man who would want her in spite of the fact that she carried another man's child, but she was repelled by the idea of marrying for security only.

She had obtained cloth from Antoinette, who had asked no questions about the use to which it would be put, only giving her such a perceptive look that Christina wondered if her secret was no longer her own. Now, while Megan and Roxanne were gone, she was cutting out the small garments she would need in the spring.

She jumped at the knock on the door. Thinking it must be Antoinette come to urge her to reconsider dancing, she called out, "Come in," and shoved the revealing scraps out of sight

It was not Antoinette, however.

She went rigid when Vilas stepped over the threshold, ducking his head to keep from knocking it against the doorframe.

The pounding of blood in her ears was almost painful "What do you want?" She could hardly have sounded less hospitable as Vilas advanced toward the fire and threw another log on it before turning to face her.

"I want to talk to you."

She waited, giving him no encouragement, not even when he handed over the bundle he carried.

"It's a cloak, lined with beaver skins. It will keep you warm through the winter."

He thrust it into her arms, and she took it numbly, aware that it was indeed a luxurious cloak, finer than anything she'd ever owned. Her fingers curled into the fur, soft and warm, and she felt the tears forming, though she was not sure why.

"You could thank me," Vilas suggested after the silence had stretched on too long.

Her throat ached. "Thank you," she said, sounding wooden.

"It would be nice if you meant it."

She blinked and turned to lay the cloak across the end of the bed. "I do mean it."

"You sound as prickly as a hedgehog."

It was a relief to feel anger rather than anguish. "It's not uncommon among women in my condition, I believe, to feel short-tempered."

"It's a wonder someone doesn't throttle them."

The stinging tears were back. "It's not entirely our own faults," she pointed out.

"What are you going to do, Chris?"

The question was put so quietly, in such a concerned tone, that she prayed she wouldn't start blubbering all over the place.

"I'm going to have the babe when the time comes. What else is there to do?"

"And how will you manage, when your belly makes it impossible to chop your own wood and keep the pot filled with meat and provide for yourself?"

Was he telling her he'd done it so far and now it was time to stop depending on him to look after her? Again anger engendered a few sparks.

"No doubt I'll manage, one way or another," she said indifferently, though in truth the question had given her sleepless nights ever since she'd landed in this place.

"Sooner or later," Vilas told her, "you're going to have to marry. A woman can't live alone here, especially not with an infant."

She had no response to that and wished he would go.

"The priest will be here shortly, so everyone says. He will probably only stay a week or two, to christen the babies and

marry everyone who requires it. When he leaves, if the winter
is severe, it may be months before he returns.''

Why was he telling her this? Everyone in the village knew
about it. What did it have to do with her?

''It would be better to wed before the child is born, Chris.''

She had not been meeting his eyes. Now she glared at him,
poised like a wild cat ready to spring. ''Wed? Wed who, for the
love of God?''

''Wed me. Chris, it's the only sensible solution to the problem. The child is mine. I did not intentionally seduce you, I
swear it by God's blood, but the responsibility is mine! We've
always been like brother and sister, good friends—''

Her control snapped and she shrieked at him. ''I've *never*
been your sister, nor felt like it!''

''I cannot be your enemy, Chris. I want to marry you, and I
want to do it when the priest comes, in the next few days. I want
to take care of you. I know that at the moment you can't bear
the sight of me, but surely that will pass. We can be friends
again....''

''I don't want to be your friend!'' She fairly howled the
words, and there was no stopping the tears now as her face
contorted in misery. ''Marriage isn't for *friends*!''

''Who is it for, then? There's no one I'd rather take to wife
than the girl who's always been my good friend....''

She choked, struggling to regain control. She knew her face
was a mess, and she wiped it carelessly with the backs of both
hands. ''Get out! Leave me alone!''

''Stop it, Chris, you'll harm the babe or yourself.'' He
reached for her, then, gripping her shoulders and shaking her
so that her head wobbled. ''Listen, you have to do something
and soon! I can't wait until the priest comes again in the spring
nor can you! You have to be sensible! I don't understand
it; you've always been sensible before, but these past few
weeks...''

''Sensible! What does *sensible* have to do with getting married? Vilas, you idiot, people get married because they fall in
love!''

His hands slackened their viselike hold, though he did not let
her go. ''Love?''

"Yes, love! What a man and a woman feel for each other that makes them want to *make* love, to go to bed together and whisper loving words! You—you," she spluttered, "are about as romantic as a . . . a turnip!"

His face altered in the candlelight. "Romantic? Good God, is that what this is all about? You want *romance*?"

Before alarm took over he drew her firmly into an embrace. Wordlessly he bent his head and claimed her lips.

For a matter of seconds she fought him.

And then, as the kiss deepened, as he crushed the wind out of her, she felt the resistance drain away, to be replaced by sensations she had felt only once before, in the arms of this same man.

She didn't know when repudiation changed to acceptance, when the anger was submerged in ecstasy. Her mouth was bruised, her ribs possibly cracked, when he finally allowed her to surface for breath.

"Now, will you shut up long enough to let me say what I'd have said days ago, if you'd given me any chance to do it? You've kept me at arm's length and avoided me and screamed at me like a fishwife."

"I have not!" Christina yelped. "You acted as if I were a burden that you must, as an honorable man, be responsible for, but I don't want you that way—"

"I told you to shut up," Vilas said firmly. "What I'm trying to say is that I love you. Not as a cousin, but the way a man loves a woman he wants to marry."

She opened her mouth to speak, and he clamped a hand over it.

"It seems," he said, "there's only one way to keep you quiet."

His mouth was no longer tender but hard and demanding, and by the time he finally released her she had forgotten what she'd intended to say.

"This is a beginning, at least," he told her earnestly then. "Isn't it? Enough to build on, so that eventually you may come to care about me, too."

"I've loved you since I was a child," Christina said, her voice breaking.

And when the tears again formed in her green eyes, Vilas kissed them away.

She slid her arms around his neck, reaching up to him, and that was how Roxanne found them when she came home.

"Well," she said, "I hope that priest comes soon."

Christina leaned against Vilas, smiling blurrily into his shoulder.

"So do I," she said.

A page-turning combination of romance,
suspense and international intrigue!

TELL ME NO LIES

Lindsay Danner is the only one
who can lead the search for the
invaluable Chinese bronzes.
Jacob Catlin is the only one who
can protect her. They hadn't
planned on falling in love....

ELIZABETH LOWELL

Available in DECEMBER at your favorite retail outlet, or send your name,
address and zip or postal code along with a check or money order for $4.70
(includes 75¢ for postage and handling) payable to Worldwide Library to:

In the U.S.
Worldwide Library
901 Fuhrmann Blvd.
Box 1325
Buffalo, NY 14269-1325

In Canada
Worldwide Libary
P.O. Box 609
Fort Erie, Ontario
L2A 9Z9

Please specify book with your order.

WORLDWIDE LIBRARY   LIE-H-1

Could she find love as a mail-order bride?

MARIANNE WILLMAN

PIECES OF SKY

In the Arizona of 1873, Nora O'Shea is caught between life with a contemptuous, arrogant husband and her desperate love for Roger LeBeau, half-breed Comanche Indian scout and secret freedom fighter.

———————————•———————————

Available now at your favorite retail outlet, or order your copy by sending your name, address and zip or postal code along with a check or money order for $5.25 (includes 75¢ for postage and handling) payable to Worldwide Library Reader Service to:

In the U.S.	In Canada
Worldwide Library	Worldwide Library
901 Fuhrmann Blvd.	P.O. Box 2800, 5170 Yonge St.
Box 1325	Postal Station A
Buffalo, New York	Willowdale, Ontario
14269-1325	M2N 6J3

Please specify book title with your order.

(()) **WORLDWIDE LIBRARY**

SKY-H-1R

Anne Mather's

➤ NEWEST BEST-SELLER ◆

The Longest Pleasure

Author of more than one hundred books, including
Wild Concerto, a *New York Times* **Best Seller, Anne Mather**
captures the hearts of romance readers everywhere with
The Longest Pleasure, **her most gripping story yet.**

Available in JANUARY at your favorite retail outlet or reserve
your copy for December shipping by sending your name, address
and zip or postal code along with a check for $4.25 (includes 75¢
for postage and handling) payable to Worldwide Library to:

In the U.S.	In Canada
Worldwide Library	Worldwide Library
901 Fuhrmann Blvd.	P.O. Box 609
Box 1325	Fort Erie, Ontario
Buffalo, New York	L2A 9Z9
14269-1325	

Please specify book title with your order.

**WORLDWIDE
LIBRARY**

PLE-H-1

WORLDWIDE LIBRARY IS YOUR TICKET TO ROMANCE, ADVENTURE AND EXCITEMENT

Experience it all in these big, bold Bestsellers— Yours exclusively from WORLDWIDE LIBRARY WHILE QUANTITIES LAST

To receive these Bestsellers, complete the order form, detach and send together with your check or money order (include 75¢ postage and handling), payable to WORLDWIDE LIBRARY to:

In the U.S.
WORLDWIDE LIBRARY
901 Fuhrmann Blvd.
Box 1325
Buffalo, NY 14269-1325

In Canada
WORLDWIDE LIBRARY
P.O. Box 609
Fort Erie, Ontario
L2A 9Z9

Quant.	Title	Price
_____	**WILD CONCERTO,** Anne Mather	$2.95
_____	**FINGER PRINTS,** Barbara Delinsky	$3.50
_____	**DREAMWEAVER,** Felicia Gallant/Rebecca Flanders	$3.50
_____	**EYE OF THE STORM,** Maura Seger	$3.50
_____	**HIDDEN IN THE FLAME,** Anne Mather	$3.50
_____	**ECHO OF THUNDER,** Maura Seger	$3.95
_____	**DREAM OF DARKNESS,** Jocelyn Haley	$3.95
_____	**EDGE OF DAWN,** Maura Seger	$3.95
_____	**WITHIN REACH,** Barbara Delinsky	$3.95
_____	**TWIST OF FATE,** Jayne Ann Krentz	$3.95
_____	**TRIAD OF KNIVES,** Tom Cooper	$3.50
	YOUR ORDER TOTAL	$____
	New York residents add appropriate sales tax	$____
	Postage and Handling	$ .7
	I enclose	$____

NAME _____

ADDRESS _____ APT.# _____

CITY _____

STATE/PROV. _____ ZIP/POSTAL CODE _____

WWL-A-I

WORLDWIDE LIBRARY®

WWL-L-1